I0763395

"McIntosh's sparks flying writing style propels Little Yellow Stickies as quickly as the intrigue itself, which could only be told by a defense industry insider. Working Girl has met The Net, but the issues are too real-world to ignore."
- James Perloff, author of
The Shadows of Power* and *Truth Is a Lonely Warrior

"A dark, sharp, laugh-out-loud at times depiction of the US defense industry in the late Nineties, and laden with the Generation X symbols of that era. Rachael L. McIntosh is one to watch!"
- Charlie Flowers, author of the *Riz* series

AMAZON REVIEWS

Five Stars Isn't Enough
I could not put this book down! Every chapter boils over into the next with dynamic anticipation that only a skilled author can forge. As I turned page after page, I kept telling myself, there's no way this is a first-time author.

Witty And Quite Entertaining
Stickies as a story is brilliant. With its factual based structure, eye for detail and accuracy it is sometimes difficult to tell where the fact leaves off and the fiction picks up the trail again.

Shades of Beige in Techicolor!
Little Yellow Stickies offers fantastic insight into politics, money and war from the inside of a military contractor. We begin to learn the truly absurd machinations of keeping the nation safe.

I loved this story because it's real
A real person's life in the military industrial complex lane. Most novels in this space are horsepucky, full of wily heroes and heroines. I loved this story the most because this is how it really is. Grey rooms and accidental people. This should be a best-seller. I laughed reading this book more than I have at any book in 20 years.

Currently listed #2 on GOODREADS BEST DEBUT SERIES 2014!

Security Through Absurdity

BOOK ONE

LITTLE YELLOW STICKIES

Rachael L. McIntosh

EntropyPress

Security Through Absurdity
Little Yellow Stickies

EntropyPress books may be ordered through booksellers or by contacting:

www.entropypress.com
EntropyPress
PO Box 2254
East Greenwich, RI 02818
USA

ISBN - 13 : 978-0-692-48918-5
ISBN - 10 : 0692489185

NOTE FROM THE AUTHOR

ALMOST TWO DECADES AGO, I worked for a defense contractor during the day and made paintings at night. Half of me wanted to go back to Boston, where I had been illegally living in an old tuxedo factory making music (or more correctly noise), installation art, zines, and huge abstract oil paintings. The other half wanted to adapt and fit in with my new environment, to have money and live like those ordinary Americans you see on TV.

Connecticut was supposed to be my shot at adulthood. And because it seemed like it might be a decent mix, I ended up becoming the Urban Artists Initiative coordinator for the cities of New London and Norwich. I would attend artists' meetings after work or on the weekends, teeter-tottering back and forth between the cool artist I had been when I lived in Boston and whatever the equivalent might be as a defense contractor. As much as I tried, I was never able to fully reconcile these two realities. Oil and water. At some point, I guess I took the easy way out and just accepted the defense-contractor thing as a theatrical role in order to get my head around it.

Now as I see the stuff that I was living through making the news and people becoming alarmed by it, I realize that what I experienced during my six-year stint may be an important document in some way. It was a time of technical transition and national transformation. Living through this with one foot in a paint-splattered combat boot and the other in a sensible heel is what compelled me to write this book.

Of course, everything in this book has been fictionalized, meaning names have been changed and locations skewed. But some of what you will read is true and informs the next books in this series, which were developed in exactly the same way. *Security Through Absurdity* contains a string of moments saved in such a way that people might enjoy consuming this information while feeling safe to share it.

CHAPTER ONE

AS JOCELYN LEFT THE PARKING lot and headed toward home, she began to ruminate. Not about the beige florescent flicker hell she had just left. No. She was focused on how her car was handling and she was pissed. With her significant jump in pay, her husband took it upon himself to wholly embrace his irresponsible side to offset Jocelyn's new found responsible one. It hadn't taken long for Yin to take Yang's two-week-old, factory-new C-class Mercedes out for a ride with his friends, decide to "whip a shitty" (otherwise known as an extremely high speed U-turn) compromise the automobile's axle, bend the rims, blow out a tire and, after punching the steering wheel in disgust, deploy the airbag.

It had meant thousands of dollars in repairs and Jocelyn having to take her husband's car — a beat up salvaged junker of a Porsche with a big sticker that inexplicably said "PORN STAR" under the driver-side window — back and forth to work. Needless to say, she was happy to have her car back.

But naturally, she was still fuming as the Mercedes slid through the remains of a city crippled by the departure of the Navy and the arrival of a casino. The product of two urban-renewal grants that she had found and applied for loomed large on the hill, and her car, as if on autopilot, pulled into the driveway.

Her husband, Bobby, was lounging on the couch gearing up for the Red Sox game when she came in. Somehow, during the two-year-long, painstaking renovation process, it hadn't seemed unnatural to find him drinking while they were swinging sledge hammers into horse hair plaster or applying the dark Jacobean Minwax stain to the floors. But now that the renovations were done, it all seemed out of place and vulgar.

"Getting an early start, eh?" she said as she grabbed a couple of his empties and took them to the unsightly pile of bottle returns where all the mementos of her late night calls to Al-Anon lived.

Bobby glanced up and said, "Gonna watch the game with me?" Then, looking at his watch he giggled, "in two hours."

"No," she answered drily as she made her way through the cinnabar-and-stainless kitchen. The exposed original bricks behind the stove somehow led naturally into the deep purple of the ceiling and wainscoting of the dinning room. An aggressive floral- print wallpaper held the color schemes of the two rooms together. "Some of us don't have the luxury of doing swaps."

"Don't hate the player, hate the game!" she heard him call out as she grabbed hold of the mahogany banister and headed up the twisted olive stairway to their bedroom, the unexpected crown jewel of the house.

During the demolition, Bobby had mistakenly smashed through a ceiling joist. And after much hemin' and hawin' and many beers, he noticed a circle window in the attic which was centered perfectly above a regular window. It was Jocelyn who had realized that they didn't really need the confines of a flat ceiling after all.

The cathedral ceiling and walls were mocha latte accented with ebony woodwork. Voluminous red drapery spilled onto a huge crimson oriental carpet which served to accentuate the presence of a wrought iron sleigh bed placed dramatically in the center of the room.

Jocelyn slipped out of her simple grey sheath dress and pulled on her well worn, ripped jeans and paint splattered combat boots. Now she was home. It was no wonder the beige of work literally made her brain hurt. But that might have been due to the Multiple Sclerosis she had been afflicted with since before marrying Bobby. She was very good at hiding it, but some days were harder than others.

Anyhow, she was an artist who, through a bizarre twist of fate otherwise known as home ownership, ended up working at the local Defense Contracting office. As an artist, she was used to getting things done on a shoestring-and-a-piece-of-caramel budget. She was used to writing grant proposals. She was used to riding the buzz of no sleep to get a project done.

"Hey! I'm running out to get a twelve-pack! You need anything?" Bobby called up the twisty stairway.

She cringed.

"No," she called down. "I'm good."

"Oh. OK."

She heard the back door slam and the PORN STAR rev it's engine. For as much as she had looked forward to getting home, she was now counting the hours until she could get back to work. She glanced at the clock. Hopefully the Red Sox would win.

CHAPTER TWO

"SOME GAME LAST NIGHT!"

"I believe you owe me ten bucks, Jerry. The Yankees won fair and square."

"Bullshit! Did you see that call?"

"How could I have missed it? The playback has been studied and debated more than the Zapruda film at this point. That ball was clearly out. Now give me my ten dollars."

Jocelyn forced a smile and silently finished pouring her coffee. She left the break room with its intense critique of televised playback technology. She had lost more than a mere ten dollars the night before. She had told Bobby it was over. Again. Of course, it hadn't been as simple as that. There had been chairs flying and there was screaming and crying and Bobby was laughing. But this time she meant it.

"Jocelyn! Hey, Jocelyn McLaren! Hold up!" Adam Polska's personal assistant, Sharon, called out as she dashed over to meet the youngest employee in the Office Complex. "I've got something for you," she panted.

Jocelyn stopped in her tracks and, although tired, smiled. She was impressed with Sharon's Dress Barn outfit. It was very fashionable for five, six ... who was she kidding, fifteen years ago. But it got the job done, especially considering that almost everyone else on the payroll was seemingly stuck in the company's glory days of "the Big'80s," back when alpha- and papa- class nuclear-submarine-reactor melt-downs were keeping the Marketing Department here in Groton, Connecticut fueled. But that was before Jocelyn's time.

Sharon's hands were covered with yellow Post-It

Notes, which everyone from Accounting to the warehouse knew was the preferred method of communication from Adam, the President and CEO.

If Adam's messenger, Sharon, was stuck in the '80s, then Adam, although he dressed like a normal person, was still floating around somewhere in the mid-1970s. Jocelyn had correctly surmised that the company founder's wardrobe was attributable to his girlfriend, who was even younger than Jocelyn and certifiably forty years his junior. Despite the odd fashion timeline confusion, there was no denying that it was 1998. Everyone, almost as if through osmosis, was absorbing and processing the suggestion of partying like it was 1999. Or that they should maybe start freaking out about Y2K.

Sharon plucked a Post-It off her ring finger and, without smiling, hastily stuck it to the black, three ring binder Jocelyn was holding. Then, as quickly as she had appeared, Sharon rushed off to distribute the other messages stuck to her fingers.

Jocelyn followed Sharon's bouncing shoulder pads for about fifty yards down one of the most nondescript beige hallways in the world. The industrial carpet, the walls with their redundant rectangles ... everything was beige. It even smelled beige. The twitching of the florescent ceiling lights and the cut of Sharon's dress, for some reason, made Jocelyn think of an old fashioned animation of a horse galloping.

But, before Jocelyn could get too lost in thought about the magic of animation, people began emerging from their offices. The hallway between the engineering department and accounting took on the appearance of a kennel. A dozen long-in-the-tooth employees, who at first glance seemed amazingly irritated, hopped out of their crates. Little yellow sticky notes where being shaken like Polaroids as the now almost daily ritual of an impromptu "What-the-heck-does-Adam-want-now?" emergency meeting convened.

"Oh, for shit's sake! What's that guy's name in the AutoCad office again? I've got to get Adam's new specs over to him," griped Martin Mays, who everyone knew had quit and begrudgingly returned to Adam's company not once, not twice, but three times during his illustrious hydrodynamics career. Martin already had his hand tucked down the V neck of his well worn brown sweater and was grabbing a pack of Newports. He was anticipating the moment when the whole thing would inevitably move outside for an extended smoking break.

A female voice from Accounting wailed, "Why does Adam want me to do this over? It's perfect ..."

This month's edition of a program manager, obviously not in possession of anything remotely yellow, rifled through his file but had no clue how to answer the accountant.

The Director of Engineering, Theo Cullian, a balding guy who recently had a bunch of skin cancer burnt off his pink scalp, was sucking the inside of his cheek and shaking his head as he listened to the comments now flying around and bouncing off the beige. He smirked at Jocelyn, and that's when a theory she had been working on for the past year finally crystallized. It just jelled.

Her hypothesis: These people weren't really upset.

Sure they were stressed to the gills and probably ready to blow some sort of critical internal gasket, but they stayed. They had, over many decades, weathered plenty of storms on Adam's ship, and these Post-It notes had become merit badges. They proved to everyone else, as they got waved around like team flags at a rally, that you were important. That Adam needed you. That the guy who was basically abusing you, loved you. And that the lucky recipients were all one big dysfunctional family.

Jocelyn concluded that this wasn't so much a hallway gripe fest but a bonding session in which everyone was congratulating themselves for being an integral cog in Adam's machine. And although she was now finally aware of the weird psychological dynamic, Jocelyn was not immune to getting caught up in the fervor. At least not today.

This was her first time receiving her very own merit badge from Adam. And she was kind of proud to be included on the distribution list. Especially now since Adam's company had been acquired by the Conglomerate. With the retired Generals moving in, her sticky pretty much confirmed that she had a place reserved on the new org chart. Of course, she wouldn't know exactly what her new title would be until word came down from corporate headquarters, but it was fairly obvious that she would remain with those who were at least somewhat cognizant of current fashion: the marketing department.

"You got one too, eh, Joss?" Theo said while using his sun-bleached eyebrows like an index finger to point at the yellow square on Jocelyn's binder.

Jocelyn was surprised that she didn't know how to respond to Theo. Should she join in on the boisterous lamentations? It seemed like the thing to do but it was contrary to her typically sunny disposition. She peeled her sticky off the binder and stared at the nearly illegible scribbles. Jocelyn was confused. Her first direct call to action from Adam made no sense.

"Well, what's he got you doing?" Theo asked not so much for conversational purposes but to glean a valuable clue about what was going on. Jocelyn frowned. Now she really was unsure how to respond.

"Um ... I don't know."

"Yeah, only Sharon knows how to decipher his chicken scratch," Theo Assured her. And he walked away to gather more clues.

But Jocelyn had read it just fine.

SHRED ALL DOCUMENTS. TAKE TO KINKOS TONIGHT. NOT TO BE PRODUCED HERE.

Convinced that Sharon had given her the wrong Post-It note and not hearing any sort of rational connection to the other conversations happening in the hallway, she made her exit. The conversation was winding down anyway, and most everyone was heading out for the eagerly awaited smoking part of the emergency meeting.

Deliberately walking slower than necessary, she looked at her note again as she toyed with the idea of asking her direct superior, Robert King, director of sales and marketing, what Adam meant. But she quickly changed her mind. She could already see the jagged path of confusion that would create. Getting Robert involved in deciphering Adam's intentions would be like a random lightning strike taking out half the marketing department for the rest of the day. And she really wanted to spare everyone, herself included, that unnecessary calamity.

Especially since her department was already in a shell-shocked state from the recent introduction of yet another of Adam's conceptually brilliant but functionally flawed brainstorms, an emergency management software package called Catastrophe!. The unfortunate name, which Adam would not consider changing despite repeated criticism from the marketing department, was devised over drinks while aboard his sixty-six-foot Formosa schooner with his good friend Stan. And Stan wasn't just any good friend. He was a good friend who happened to be a Senior Congressman. The name was staying.

The sales team joked that Catastrophe! was a self-fulfilling prophecy, considering it's less than useful tag line: "It's a toolkit of modules."

Anyway, Jocelyn was closer to Adam's office than Robert's. Why not go straight to the source? She turned on her Nine West sensible heel and made her way through the beige labyrinth. The men, all of whom had been in the navy back in the day, took the time to watch as she cruised by. The appearance of a young, smiling, five-foot-nine-inch, size six, strawberry-blond female at work was akin to the sighting of a seagull during the final days of a long deployment. It was very much appreciated. Creeping smiles were all that she left in her wake.

Jocelyn's plan was to give this Post It back to Sharon and get on with the government proposals, website content, trade shows, advertising and PR ... basically just about anything that did not fall under the heading of direct sales work that she had neatly organized and waiting for her in the utility closet—the utility closet which had recently been converted into a tight, desk sized office just for her as per Robert's latest, not so subtle, power play maneuver.

CHAPTER THREE

LOCATED AT THE FAR END of one of the longest branches of the single-story, sprawling office complex, Adam's office was otherwise known as the Inner Sanctum. It was the antithesis of Jocelyn's closet/office. The door to its antechamber was propped open, revealing a cozy wood-paneled reception area complete with a collection of fishing magazines, houseplants, and warm incandescent lighting. The window allowed for a much-cherished glimpse of the wooded landscape outside. The only thing missing was some sort of generic piped-in music.

Jocelyn entered, plopped down in one of the comfortable up- holstered accent chairs, and waited for Sharon. Unlike Jocelyn's desk, Sharon's was riddled with little reminders of her family. Her daughters' prom and graduation pictures were taped to her computer monitor. A coffee cup full of random pens and pencils, some topped off with crazy bobblehead erasers with pink fluffy hair, seemed out of place in this otherwise convincing piece of theatrical stage design. (No, it really was. Every time the press was called in, this room was used as a backdrop for the interview.) Jocelyn knew that if a guest was scheduled to appear, all the personal stuff would be stashed away. That was the policy.

Looking at the pink fluffy-headed bobble thing sitting right out in the open, Jocelyn surmised that Adam was neither in with nor expecting any important visitors today. She sat in silence waiting. At least the lights in here didn't flicker—but she did notice, over by the ficus tree, one of those white-noise machines, like the one in her counselor's office waiting room. Watching the brass pendulum swing on the wall clock opposite her, she wondered if Sharon was in with Adam. She didn't hear them, but then again, with that white-noise machine in full effect ...

She just wanted to get to the bottom of this Post-it. Feeling al- most like a small child, although she didn't quite know why, Jocelyn quietly and carefully made her way toward Adam's door, which was slightly ajar. She knocked deliberately and slowly opened it. Adam, a fit, good-looking senior with a silver-lined bald head, was leaning back in his burgundy wingback executive chair. He was almost in full recline while talking on the phone. With one hand behind his head, the other holding the receiver, he motioned for her to come in and take a seat.

If Sharon's reception area had a staged cozy and gracious air about it, Adam's office was all that but for real and five times as large. It was a tastefully arranged hodgepodge of souvenirs from his well-traveled and exciting past coupled with the requisite scale model of his sailboat and casual but extremely expensive furnishings. Framed photos of him with various international dignitaries and random entertainers were on display by the fully stocked built-in bar. A Japanese painting older than the United States of America was prominently featured behind the teak desk that he had bought for himself upon starting this business thirty-five years ago.

Clearly he was speaking with a lawyer, so Jocelyn found a comfortable spot on the couch near the expanse of picture windows and attempted to look as if she couldn't care less about what he was talking about.

Eventually he concluded with, "Okay, I'll see your one case of Dom and up you a dozen Cubans ... Great! I'll see you then. Thanks. I owe you one." He chuckled as he hung up the phone, held up his finger to signify "hold on," and wrote something hastily on a legal pad.

"Yes, Jocelyn. What brings you here?"

He reminded Jocelyn of her father, but not so much in

the way he looked or spoke. Jocelyn really wasn't sure why she thought that. She knew Adam possessed the unique talent of making a person feel very special but yet completely useless at the same time. She had seen it in action during the growing pains otherwise known as "getting ready for acquisition," when Adam was hammering the upper management who were eager to unseat him. She had watched him with curiosity and was amazed by his ability to convincingly speak out of both sides of his mouth. Her father had been a successful businessman, but she had barely known him. He died a couple of years ago in a plane crash, so maybe she was just imagining Adam was like her father.

"Oh, Sharon gave me this note, and I think it belongs to some-one else. I came here to return it and," she added, because she was thinking of that new org chart, "to find out if there was something that you needed me for." She produced the "Shred all documents" Post-it and handed it to him.

"Oh yes. Yup. That's for you."

"I don't understand."

"Indonesia. You've got to get that thing done tonight, but not here. Sharon just told me about the new copy machines that came in two days ago and how they store all the text in memory. We can't have that. Corporate espionage. Our competition will be here sooner than flies on shit. I'm leaving tonight and will pick up the proposals myself in Jakarta ..."

"Seriously?"

Indonesia had been the bane of everyone's existence since before Jocelyn had started working here. It was an enormously lengthy document outlining the specifics of Adam's multiyear sales dream- quest to outfit six training schools with everything from simulators and curriculum to rope for the knot-tying demonstrations for the Indonesian Maritime Academy. The problem was—or more correctly, *one* of the problems was—that Adam was trying to insert his new Catastrophe! product into all six of the schools. The academy didn't want any part of it. And quite frankly, they didn't need it. But Adam was hell-bent on not only getting his software installed some- where so that he could reference the installation in future marketing, but more importantly, on winning the long-fought contract battle. Meanwhile, Adam's nemesis, the Japanese and German defense companies, were hell-bent on snatching the contract away. And when they would come in and offer something more for less, the whole next quarter would be spent redoing the proposal to one-up whatever it was that had been offered. That's how length of rope got included and how it turned into six schools when originally it had been one.

"Which version of the proposal are you talking about? I have RevG15.45 on my desk right now, but that's days away from complete."

"No. Go back into the archive. This one." He held up a tired looking photocopy of the proposal cover he was referencing, which Jocelyn instantly recognized as preacquisition vintage by the format- ting and font used.

"I'm confused, Adam. That's got to be at least three years old. None of the specifications will be the same now. And I'll have to reformat the thing so that it looks like it came from corporate. That doesn't look right at all. I'm going to get fired if I just make a copy of a three-year-old proposal and send it out."

"Jocelyn, who do you work for? Who is going to fire you? *I'm* telling you, right now, this has to get done and shipped out tonight. I don't give a rat's ass who is going to get a hair across their crack about some fancy lettering."

Adam stood up and hastily threw his legal pad and a soft-cover copy of *Debt of Honor* by Tom Clancy in his leather briefcase and snapped the lid down.

"But Adam," she objected, "that isn't even our logo now! The division and specifically I am going to be in deep trouble if I don't redo that entire thing. Do you know how many times I have heard from corporate's lawyers in the past two months about branding standards? That's kind of going to be my official job now, according to them. Branding. I know that the specs for the computers must have changed by now, not to mention the shipping costs, so I'll have to ..."

"I don't really care, Jocelyn. I've got my bags packed, and Sharon is taking me to JFK in less than an hour. I'm glad that you stopped by to see me. I'll have my satellite phone, and I'll call you when I get there. It should be about two days from now. After dealing with the folks in Jakarta, I'll be at the Singapore office if you need me."

This is where Adam's longtime employees would have stopped. But this whole thing made no sense to Jocelyn, and she wanted to live up to her valuable employee-merit-badge status. She still believed that no question was a stupid question. *How did shredding documents fit in with getting the proposal of the decade done in one night?*

"Adam, that proposal fills three four-inch binders with its drawings and spreadsheets, and the one you are holding is outdated. And I don't know how—"

"Look, honey, if it's that big a deal, then just make a new cover for it. I need fifteen copies in the mail tonight. Sharon will give you the address. I think the nearest Kinko's is just over the state line. Stay with it until it gets packaged. Do not leave it unattended. Do you understand?" She nodded feebly. "Do not let that thing out of your sight!"

Proposal work was part of Jocelyn's job, and she, unfortunately, excelled at it. But she was still confused.

"What am I supposed to be shredding? The Post-it said 'Shred all documents.'"

"Oh, that. Get rid of the e-mails."

"What e-mails?" she asked, honestly confused.

"All of them."

"Adam, what the heck are you talking about? Since I started working here, this proposal has been discussed via e-mail by almost everyone in this building."

"So shred the e-mails."

Okay, now Jocelyn understood why he had picked her for this specific Post-it note. She had originally been hired as a temp to print out, make several copies of, and distribute said e-mails to everyone three times a day. Some sort of weird, antiquated navy process that made sense to these people. Jocelyn had known while she was marching around doing it that it was ridiculous and took it upon herself to convince the company, which meant climbing up some ladders and convincing Adam that forwarding e-mails could be made ISO compliant.

Obviously, ease of communication was not the most compelling point during her presentation. It was only after Adam understood the cost savings in terms of paper, not to mention ink and toner, that he was thrilled but also highly irritated that it had taken a young female temp to challenge him and insist that the company join the information age. Jocelyn was hired immediately. The funny thing was, she hadn't even known what ISO meant at the time.

"Adam ..." She took a deep breath through her nose. "*Eeeee*-mail. As in, electronic. As in, there is no paper. All this communication lives on a server here in-house and, I would imagine, simultaneously gets forwarded to the corporate server. Ultimately, it gets archived again. We only print the e-mails out on paper and put them in a filing cabinet because it's a way for people to find stuff in a pinch." She continued on while studying him, hoping to find a glint of understanding. "Pretty soon, when we are officially connected, our e-mails will come directly through the corporate server."

That made sense to Jocelyn as she said it, but it did not seem to make any impression whatsoever on Adam. He looked at her with a "this affects me how?" blank expression.

"I'm telling you, Adam, I can stay up all night at a Kinko's to chaperone binders of outdated proposals at the risk of corporate tossing me and/or you, or even this whole division out. But I can- not—like literally, seriously cannot, I don't have the skills or the know-how to—kill over four years' worth of e-mails on the topic of the Indonesia proposal on a password-protected server."

Jocelyn took a breath, and they stared at each other for a bit. Jocelyn was not backing down on the e-mail shredding, simply because she couldn't do it. The fact that this request was highly suspect in terms of compliance with just about every corporate standard she was aware of was secondary only because it was obvious that Adam was not receptive to that part of Jocelyn's problem.

"Okay, look, I've got to get out of here. You go make the new cover up as pretty as you want and head out to Kinko's." Adam reached into his back pocket and out came his wallet. "Here. Take this credit card to pay for it. Stay with the document. Do not leave it unattended. I'll see you in a few weeks. Thank you, Jocelyn." He paused and scribbled something on a Post-it Note and handed it to her. "Oh, and give this to the guys in shipping. Now go."

She glanced at the Post-it, which read:

ALL CHARGES INDO

CHAPTER FOUR

LEAVING THE INNER SANCTUM IN a bit of a daze, she retraced her steps through the banality and headed over to shipping, where she gave a guy devouring a Snickers bar the Post-it from Adam. Then she headed over to the proposal archive, which housed every single page of every single proposal that had ever left the building over the past thirty-five years. The archive was sometimes locked and sometimes not. It really depended if Nancy, manager of all things related to copies, had left the door open.

The door was locked today, so Jocelyn headed over to find Nancy, who turned out to be sitting at her desk sporting one of her usual looks that Jocelyn had only recently recognized as nicotine withdrawal. It made for habitually unpleasant interactions with the woman.

"What do you want?" Nancy snapped.

"Oh, the archive is locked, and I need ..."

"Of course it's locked. King Adam decrees it."

Jocelyn couldn't help but smile. "Yeah. Well. I need to get in there because Adam needs me to work on an old Indonesia proposal."

"Let Adam know that we'll have RevG15.45 ready in a couple a days."

"No. He's made it clear that he wants an old proposal."

"No. Tell him no. That's not how it works. He always, *always* does this, and it screws everything up."

Jocelyn found herself nodding her head in agreement with the outrageously suntanned woman who unknowingly, by the end of the day, sported a fury of black hair not unlike the pink of the bobblehead she had seen on Sharon's desk. Jocelyn was starting to more fully understand why Adam had picked her to do this. Adam and Nancy had worked together at General Dynamics back before Adam decided to break away and start his own contracting company, taking Nancy, Martin Mays, and a bunch of others with him. Adam wouldn't be able to break Nancy of over thirty years of government-contracting work experience. *But this isn't the US government. This is Indonesia ... right?*

"Nancy, I know. I know. Adam is just very set in his ways. He's a salesman and doesn't see beyond what he has to do to make the sale. You know how he is better than I. But I'm in a pinch. He is expecting me to get this done tonight ..."

"What? Tonight?" Nancy flew off into a spiel about nobody knowing what she goes through, which eventually culminated in a literal panic attack. Nancy's face, despite the tanning booth, had grown colorless. She was hyperventilating, and her hands were shaking.

"Okay. It's going to be okay," Jocelyn said, trying to calm her. "He just wants me to make copies of it. I'm taking it to Kinko's so that it won't disturb what you've got going on in the copy room. Here. Let's go outside and get some fresh air."

Fresh air is the term Jocelyn had noticed the smokers used for a cigarette break.

Once outside, Nancy—who was perpetually trying to quit smoking—produced a package of Newport Lights from her purse and inhaled three cigarettes in rapid succession. This seemed to calm her down to the point of at least being able to talk coherently.

"Are we still going to bother working on G15.45?" Nancy finally uttered.

"I guess so. But it's just not as important as that old proposal is now."

Nancy took another drag off the cigarette. "Okay, so what are we calling the old proposal that's going out?"

"Hmm ... wouldn't that be what it's always been called?"

"No. I mean, what is the proposal number going to be for the proposal log?"

Nancy, "master of all things copies," not only kept the key to the archive but also kept the all-important proposal log that documented the proposal number, the date submitted, the customer, the product being pitched, and by which salesman. If there was going to be a different cover on the proposal, then even just for internal purposes, there needed to be a different proposal number because it wasn't the same document.

"Oh, I hadn't really thought of that. You're right." Jocelyn thought for a minute as Nancy continued to smoke while staring off at nothing. "What if we use the same proposal number and put a dash at the end followed by this year's date?" Jocelyn suggested.

"That's kinda gonna screw up my system," Nancy said. "My logbook isn't formatted with enough spaces for that. I'll have to redo the entire thirty-year-old logbook with a new format."

"Whoa ... wait a minute, Nance. That seems over-the-top. I know that you've been keeping that thing pristine forever, but can't we just pencil it in for this one occasion?"

Nancy took another drag off her cigarette and thought about it.

"Yeah, why the hell not? Since we got acquired, things aren't even close to being correct around here." Nancy dropped and squished the cigarette under her taupe faux-leather Easy Spirit. "What does it matter? This place is going to be gobbled up by one of the larger divisions eventually. Let them deal with it." And she let out what Jocelyn perceived as a mournful sigh.

They walked slowly back into the building. Nancy got her keys, and they walked through the copy room where three people were gathered around a copy machine that was emitting a painfully sharp beeping noise.

"Oh, brother. These new machines. Hold on! I'll be there in a minute!" Nancy unlocked the door and allowed Jocelyn entry to the archive. Then she grabbed the new copy machine's manual and expertly set to work on the piece of equipment, leaving Jocelyn to find the old proposal by herself.

The archive, a long, skinny space adjacent to the copy room, was full of filing cabinets and bookshelves. The flickering of the florescent light was, amazingly, even more pronounced in here. On the bookshelves were the dusty old binders that contained the very first proposals submitted to the US Navy by Adam's company. Their pages—typed out with electric typewriters—now yellow and fragile with age, emanated the glow of pride with which these documents had been created decades ago. The nation had been at war, and the technology offered inside these binders was critical to the eventual outcome. In some strange way, Jocelyn felt that a quiet reverence was appropriate in this setting.

She walked through the rows of filing cabinets scanning for the letter "I." *Found it.* She opened the metal cabinet's drawer and located the file that said *Indonesia.* Inside the file was a reference to a numbered bookshelf. She put the file back and made her way to the shelf. There were two full bookcases filled with binders regarding Indonesia. All Jocelyn had to go on was the memory of the image of Adam's old photocopy that he had waved around in his office.

Damn, why didn't I take down the publication number? She saw for the first time the true necessity of the process of numbering and logging each proposal. Luckily for Jocelyn, she had a near-photographic memory for images—not so great with numbers, but images, for some strange reason, were not a problem.

She decided to look for the first proposal on the shelves that included the new branding and then work her way back from there. She found Adam's proposal almost immediately. *That's a relief!* But then she realized that the image on the cover and the title had been used not just on the version she was holding, but on three others as well. *Great ...*

She collected up the first binder of all four of the possible versions and told Nancy, who appeared to be genuflecting next to the photo- copy machine, to check out the versions for her, and she would return them ASAP. She just wanted to check the covers against Adam's.

"Those things aren't supposed to leave here!" Nancy shouted. "Well, I would make a copy, but it appears that the copy machine isn't working properly. Adam told me not to make copies of them here anyway. I'll bring them back, Nance. I promise. Like I need another proposal jammin' up my tiny office."

Jocelyn headed out into the hallway holding a precarious stack of binders and swung by Adam's office. *Empty.* She headed to the building's main reception area and asked Mimi if Adam and Sharon had already left.

"Oh sweetie, you just missed them. They left five minutes ago."

"Does Adam's satellite phone work if he's only five minutes away? Or does he have to be in Nigeria or something for him to take a call?"

"I guess it would work. But I think it would be very expensive. Wait! Wait! Sharon has a cell phone, let's call her. She's always got the thing on. I have her number right here."

Mimi, a petite, dark-haired, amply endowed divorcée who had been turning fifty-nine for the past two years, sat at the epicenter of "all things interpersonal communication," otherwise known as the company's reception desk. Mimi started to quickly finger through her Rolodex. Within milliseconds, she produced a little tabbed index card containing not only Sharon's home and cell-phone numbers but also Sharon and her children's birthdays, husband's name and current military rank, wedding anniversary, emergency contacts, and allergies.

Not that gathering any of this information was required. Quite the contrary. Mimi was the epitome of a "people person." Taking pride in looking well-groomed and professionally answering phone calls for her coworkers, she always took time to engage in a brief but probing personal conversation before she patched in the incoming call. If she had acquired a pertinent piece of information about the employee, she took it upon herself to document it in her special front-desk Rolodex in case it might later prove somehow helpful.

"Okay, here! I'll dial it. Use that phone right there." Mimi pointed her salon-perfect fingernail at a beige phone on a glass-and-chrome end table next to one of the brown Bauhaus-design chairs in the reception area.

The call connected. Sharon answered.

"Hi. It's Jocelyn. I need to speak with Adam."

"Yes ..."

"Adam, do you have the publication number for that proposal you wanted me to copy tonight? I have four different versions with the cover you showed me."

"Not at the moment. Just use the latest version, but use the specifications from the second version and the pricing from the third. Use a copy of the legal agreement from corporate in the latest G15."

"Wait a minute, Adam, this isn't just about making copies all night long. You want me to produce a brand new proposal. Is that correct?"

"Not really. Just copy the parts and stick them together. There is nothing new about this."

Jocelyn took a deep breath.

"This is really going to freak Nancy out."

"I told you to go to Kinko's, Jocelyn. Remember?"

"How could I forget, Adam? It's just that I spent about half an hour calming Nancy down because she didn't want ... oh, it doesn't matter ..."

Adam cut her off. “You told Nancy?”

“Told her what?” asked Jocelyn, confused by the question. “That’s what I’d like to know. What did you tell Nancy?”

Jocelyn’s automatic response based upon his accusatory tone would have been.

“Nothing!” if she wasn’t so concerned with seeming professional at this obviously critical moment for Adam. She thought through her interaction with Nancy and tried to carefully recall it for him.

“I just told her not to worry. That what I was working on wouldn’t disturb her because you had told me not to use the copy machines here in house and to take everything to Kinko’s. And that I’d have everything back to the archive as soon as possible.”

“I see,” said Adam. And he was very quiet.

Cutting through the silence, Jocelyn asked, “This still has to get out tonight?”

“Yes.”

“If you insist,” she said in a forced joking tone, but she was irritated beyond words. Adam really didn’t understand what he had just asked her to do. And unfortunately for her, Jocelyn did not fully understand what she had just gotten herself involved with either.

CHAPTER FIVE

AFTER GETTING CONFIRMATION FROM ADAM that yes, it did have to go out that night, Jocelyn went directly to her utility closet/office and made up a crackerjack version of the latest corporate-approved cover. Then she took all four complete versions of the proposal and the latest legal section out to her car. She was going back to her house to change. It was going to be a long night, but in a weird way, she was very much looking forward to it. There was no way she was going to be able to sit at home and pretend everything was okay with Bobby.

She snapped on her radio, getting herself into the mindset for Adam's mission. By the time she landed in her driveway, track eleven of her Foo Fighters CD was cranking. Thankfully, the beat-up PORN STAR wasn't in the driveway, and she rushed in to quickly change into her comfortable painting duds and, more presentable than paint-splattered combat boots, red Chuck Taylors. She threw some makeup and an outfit for work the next day into a duffle bag. Jocelyn wanted to avoid Bobby at all costs. However, she didn't have to rush on his account. On her way back out to the car, she noticed the smashed chair from the night before and a note stuck to the TV.

I'm out of here. Take it. It's yours. It looks like a drag queen on acid decorated this place. I always thought you were a dyke anyway. Fuck you and have a nice day. - Bobby

Not sure whether to laugh, cry, or jump for joy, she left the note dangling where it was and headed out. She had serious business to attend to and didn't really care if he meant the TV, the busted chair, or the house, so long as she didn't have to deal with him. She much preferred the drama of work at this point.

And nothing said "work" like coffee. So Jocelyn pulled into the nearest Dunkin' Donuts to grab a cup for the interstate ride to Kinko's. As she stood at the luminescent pink and orange plastic counter deliberating the merits of Boston cream or blueberry cake, deep within her purse, her cell phone rang.

Anxiously, she tried to retrieve the well-buried phone before the ringing ended. *What if it's Adam? Or worse, Bobby?* Unable to locate it, she quickly dumped the contents of the purse on the doughnut shop's counter and answered the call as the acne-spotted kid, still holding a piece of waxed paper and waiting for her to make her selection, looked on unfazed. A lone quarter continued to spin and finally fell off the counter onto the floor as she answered.

"This is Jocelyn."

"I forgot to tell you, make sure you personally bring it to the UPS distribution hub, the one about twenty-five miles from the office. Sharon has already done up the shipping paperwork with them and they are expecting you. Got it?"

"Okay, why not? Got it."

SURE SHE WAS FRUSTRATED BY time she got to Kinko's and started the project, but around two forty-five in the morning she was not only tired, she was mad. Why on earth would Adam just assume that she would put herself through this? And worse yet, why had she done it? The whole thing was just wrong on so many levels. She was more upset with herself than with any of the corporate rules, or Adam's complete disregard of them, or his total inability to perceive that he was asking her to compromise her own job, not to mention her morals, while she slaved away on his proposal.

There is no way they are asking for a three-year-old

computer system. Adam's trying to pull a fast one ...

And it must have been right about the time Martin Mays was starting up the coffee at the office, around five thirty in the morning, when she and the lone Kinko's employee—whose life story she was forced to endure, the highlight of which was that he and his truck- driver lady friend were the king and queen of the national medieval-faire circuit—finished the job. Jocelyn paid for it with the credit card Adam had given her, and she and his royal medieval highness loaded up the Mercedes. The trunk, the backseat, the passenger seat, and of course the floors—no area was without a proposal for the ride to the UPS distribution hub back over the state line.

It was 7:18 a.m. the morning after Adam had issued his near-aerobic publishing instructions when Jocelyn, still sporting her red Chuck Taylors, triumphantly returned to the office to confirm that the Indonesia proposal, all fifteen sets, or depending on how you wanted to stack them, a fifteen foot tall monolith of binders, had been shipped out. And that she had personally been there with the proposals through the whole process and had never left them unattended. Not once.

She was so tired that she didn't think it odd that Marty Mays and Darlene Fossbinder, the default chief financial officer, were both there loading up on coffee and looking equally as tired as she.

It wasn't until Jocelyn got back to her tiny office that she was truly pissed with herself. What the heck was wrong with her? Why had she submitted to Adam's insane request and not just said, "I can't do that"? She didn't know if was lack of sleep, the Bobby thing, or just some sort of suppressed Gen-X punk in her coming to the surface, but she wanted to scream. And holding that scream back almost hurt.

Naturally, she didn't make a peep, but somehow, somewhere along the way, she began to envision the whole episode as a poignant piece of site-specific performance art. And she didn't care if she was the only one who got it.

So as she was changing into her business attire to start her next work day, which officially began at 8:30 a.m., she felt compelled to take the black eyeliner pencil she had packed and start drawing a large Helvetica Bold capital letter *L* on her forehead.

Loser.

The process of applying the makeup seemed to calm her whole body. It was kind of funny, and it made perfect sense. At least to her.

Emerging from the ladies' room fully looking the corporate part in her black pencil skirt and white non-wrinkle blouse with the letter *L* expertly rendered on her forehead, she walked proudly over to the break room next to her utility closet/office. *I'll just nonchalantly grab some of that hot brown water and see if anyone notices.* It was then that she locked eyes with Jay Clarke.

Jay was a computer programmer just a little older than Jocelyn, young by company standards. He was originally from Texas and only ended up here when his wife got offered a job at the nearby nuclear power plant. He was extremely easygoing and, because he was closer to Jocelyn's age, abundantly more interesting to chat with than most of the characters at work—that is, if Jay decided to emerge from his office. He didn't come out but to go to the men's room. He had everything he needed right there in his office: an ergonomically correct chair, state-of-the-art sound system with killer headphones, and most importantly for the Starbucks generation, his own espresso machine.

"Whoa," Jay said in his mild-mannered Texas way. "What happened?"

"Oh, I got the Indonesia proposal submitted early this morning."

"That's cool. What's with the thing on your face?"

"Oh, you mean the *L*?" she said, pointing to her forehead. "Yeah. That stands for *loser*! I'm a complete loser for running around like some masochistic fraternity pledge all night so that Adam can make some crazy-ass commission on some outdated hardware!"

"I see," said Jay, whose eyes sparkled with amusement as if he knew something she did not. However, he maintained a completely nonplussed tone of voice. "Want a coffee? A real one from my office?"

CHAPTER SIX

JOCELYN NODDED, AND THEY WALKED together to his deluxe programmer's lair. She was glad that Jay had been the first person she happened upon when she saw the early-arriving workers staring at her from inside the break room as she entered his office.

"So you've been up all night working on that proposal?"

"Yup. Adam put me on the task yesterday afternoon." Attempting to figure out exactly how many hours had elapsed, she looked at his "Pop Quiz Wall Clock for Geeks," which looked like a round black- board with complex math problems chalked in where the numbers would normally be. "What the heck time does that say? Almost 8:00 a.m.?"

"Yup."

"Why are *you* here so early?" Jocelyn asked.

"Apparently, some big changes have to be made to that Catastrophe! program. I guess there's been some interest in it. Cullian mentioned your Princeton report?"

Jocelyn looked blankly at him, not really knowing how her report could possibly impact Catastrophe! "I honestly think I was at the wrong conference, Jay. That was all about the stock market and, for some reason, online pedophilia. It was really weird."

"Yeah, well, anyhow, it looks as if Catastrophe! is going to be rejiggered and marketed to a new industry instead of just municipal fire departments and police stations."

Jay handed her a dainty little red-and-black cup filled with a triple shot of espresso.

"Wait. I thought Adam was trying to sell that thing to

FEMA for federal emergency management situations. How on earth could that possibly be used in a different industry?" She thought about that as Jay fussed with the espresso machine. Then she added, "More importantly, isn't the whole problem because of the different departments' radio frequencies? The police can't even talk to the firemen. That's where the money should be spent. Streamlining the first responders' communications. Not on our software, for goodness' sake."

"I don't know. I just have my list of stuff to complete. I check the items off as I go along, and I don't really try to figure it out. Not my job. That is, until my part of the code doesn't work with someone else's part, you know?"

The espresso machine gurgled and made its steamy hissing noise. Jay downed his triple shot and started preparing another.

"Oh no," Jocelyn said, "I don't think I should. I didn't realize this was going to be a triple shot of *good* espresso!"

"Who said it was for you?" replied Jay without looking at her. "I need two cups of this stuff first thing before I even turn that box on. That coffee they have over in the kitchen is subpar, if you know what I mean. Like it might be good if you were trapped in a submarine for a month or something, but I've got a lot to do today."

She smirked, understanding what he meant. "Well, thank you for the espresso. I'll let you get to work. Believe me, I understand," Jocelyn said as she emphatically pointed to the greasy black *L* on her head.

Jay laughed. "Are you really going to keep that there all day?"

"I feel like I want to, but you're probably right. I'll go take it off right now. Thanks for being the audience for my impromptu rant. I'm actually really glad I got that off my chest and that it was you who saw me first. Thanks again for the espresso."

Leaving Jay to his checklist of fixes and redos, Jocelyn

headed back to the ladies' room. By this time, people were filtering in to their windowless workstations to start their busy day of making or promoting some type of military-grade something or other. It was easy money, some of the longtimers had a habit of saying as they shuffled through the colorless hallways on their way to complete some random, perpetually over-budget project.

Preparing to erase the *L* from her forehead, Jocelyn pulled her hair back into a tight bun. She turned on the hot water and attempted to pump some pink liquid soap onto her hands from the wall dispenser. *Empty*. She tried to gently wash off the eyeliner from her forehead with just water. The removal was not working quite as planned. She yanked some scratchy brown paper towels from the dispenser, folded them down, and added a more deliberate scrubbing motion to the process.

Okay, this isn't working. What's going on? Jocelyn was starting to recognize the espresso buzz, which seemed to heighten her annoyance at the failed attempt to remove the *L*. She stared at herself in the mirror. *Damn*. She looked old. And weird with a smeary black spot stuck in the center of her forehead. Her flesh was now pink and irritated from all the scrubbing. She riffled through her purse and retrieved the *waterproof* eyeliner.

"Wow. What a great product this is," Jocelyn sarcastically mumbled.

The only person she could think of to help her was mom-like Mimi. She'd know what to do. And if she wasn't there yet, which was unlikely, maybe there would be some hand cream tucked away in one of her unlocked desk drawers. But before Jocelyn could reach Mimi's telecommunications command center, the vice president of operations, Janice Malkfert, was upon her.

Janice, a mousy woman with long scraggly dark hair that must have looked gorgeous in the 1970s, had worked for Adam since she was nineteen years old. She had never gone to college. She got her start as a typist and soon became Adam's personal assistant. She had literally been the equivalent of Adam's right arm while he was creating this company. Being that she was such a loyal and hardworking employee over the past thirty-five years, she had eventually been promoted to the position of vice president. Her title was conferred not so much for her managerial style, knowledge of the industry, or even her organizational ability, but mostly due to the fact that so many professionals Adam had hired for the position had simply walked off the job.

"Hello, Jocelyn," Janice said, looking smart in a mauve blazer. "I heard you got the Indonesia proposal submitted early this morning. Very good."

"Thanks for mentioning it."

"What's that on your forehead?"

"Um ... oh, it's an *L* ... for loser. I stayed up all night working on that proposal, and I feel like a total loser."

"I see. You do know that the *L* is backward."

Jocelyn's right hand flew up to touch her head. In her fit of self-absorbed resentment, she had carefully rendered the block letter *L* while looking in the mirror. Of course, it looked perfect *in the mirror*.

Jocelyn could feel not only her heart sinking but her stomach as well. She was now all jacked up on caffeine, and the realization that she really *was* a loser—and not just a somehow meaningful (at least in her mind) theatrical representation of such—made her want to throw up. Or was that all the caffeine on an empty stomach? Either way, Jocelyn did not feel well, and it showed. She tried to reply with as witty a comeback as she could muster: "Form following function, I guess."

"Go home, Jocelyn, and get some rest."

And that is what Jocelyn did. She silently nodded at Janice, grabbed her bags from the ladies' room, did the walk of shame past her coworkers (when she should have been doing a victory lap), and headed out to the parking lot. She got in her silver Mercedes and drove home. Once home, she couldn't sleep because of the triple espresso Jay Clarke had given her. She spent the whole caffeine buzz crying until she finally crashed and slept for fifteen hours.

When she woke up, she felt empty. Rested, but broken. She was actually surprised that she didn't have a headache. What was that emptiness she was feeling? She didn't know. All she knew was that she had snapped, and she wasn't sure how to feel about that.

CHAPTER SEVEN

STILL IN HER PAJAMAS, JOCELYN figured that it was time to start her day and lazily went up the tiny non-code-compliant stairs to the tower. The little tower had been a sea captain's lonely wife's widow's watch. Now the little space with its double arched windows was her painting studio. As in her bedroom, the ceiling had been removed, so all that was left was angled, gallery-white drywall.

Jocelyn let her gaze slide across some of the artwork she had been lugging around since forever. These were things that she or someone she knew, or at least used to know, had made. She looked at her oil paints and brushes and at the mediums she had lovingly concocted like some sort of mad scientist or clever chef. The honey-colored liquid was packaged up in jars, sitting and waiting for her like a long-lost friend.

She opened one of the jars. The smell of turpentine and Damar varnish slowly steeped into the room, and she took in a controlled breath. The smell brought back all the old feelings of purposeful action. Even though she hadn't touched these things for a long time, just being near them made her feel somehow more connected to something inside of her, something that used to be so joyful and easy to access. She was happy before. Now she wasn't.

She and her husband were done. That much was clear. The Victorian house they had both worked so hard on restoring was, although impressive, lonely. It had been that way for a long time. For Jocelyn, the entire house had been built around this studio, a space in which she had imagined herself creating some sort of masterpiece that would change the world.

Art could change the world! She had strongly believed this at one point in her life, but she didn't feel that way now. Now that she and Bobby had experienced firsthand the reality of owning stuff—or more correctly, owning stuff via proxy, otherwise known as a bank mortgage (or two), some car payments, phone bills, and a couple of credit cards, not to mention heating and electric bills, water and sewer, grocery bills, and, naturally, taxes. They were lucky compared to some of their friends who had college loans to pay down on top of all this other stuff.

They had gotten a fixed rate on a distressed legal two-family that, once fixed up, would provide income to help pay the mortgage. Jocelyn had gotten scholarships to go to college, so she was free and clear of educational loans, and Bobby had been in the military. No loans there. They were conscientious and paid their bills and did not extend themselves too much. That was because Jocelyn paid all the bills. All of them. This was while her husband was allowed the luxury of cashing his check on payday and spending it on whatever he wanted, which was typically cases of beer or some drunken nights out. Why? One word: control.

Once the happy couple got the house rehabbed, the alcoholism that was so rampant in her husband's family started to make itself more and more apparent. That in turn made Jocelyn want to control some part of this spiraling emotional roller coaster. Nights sitting in the bathroom on the telephone with Al-Anon and going to Al-Anon meetings didn't seem to help her, other than to illustrate how crappy life could be living with an alcoholic.

What is wrong with these people?

Which led her to, *What is wrong with me?*

This naturally progressed to her working ten-hour days to escape the issue. And seeing as she was making more money than her husband, this led to her pulling the purse strings, first to "manage" the problem of his alcohol consumption but later to make things “just perfect” in her world while he flailed around, apparently happily oblivious, in his. It wasn’t fair that he was happy and oblivious and she was slaving in some beige hamster wheel, all to be left with this house and the taxes. Not fair at all!

Now fairly oblivious herself and not knowing what day it was, Jocelyn went outside and looked around. The flower bed she had so lovingly crafted needed weeding. Clearly that wasn’t the only thing in her life she had not been tending to lately. Resolving to take care of the flowers, she sighed and decided to take the next day off too. Why not?

On the third day, she rose again and decided that it was okay to go back to work. She was rested, the flower beds were weeded, she had done some sketching, and she had read something other than a government request for proposal before bed each night. Things were okay, she reasoned. *The people I work with are dealing with war, and here I am all upset because I couldn’t get a good night’s rest. Suck it up, Joss!* She couldn’t leave those other proposals hanging and impose on Nancy, Cathy, and Gail with her absence.

CHAPTER EIGHT

WHEN SHE GOT TO HER office, the very first thing Jocelyn did, even before she took off her coat, was tape a piece of red paper to her wall. During her time off at home, she had theorized that maybe the colorlessness of the office was causing her to freak out. Of course, the lack of color paled in comparison with the fact that she was now forced to deal with mercenaries.

The defense conglomerate that owned Jocelyn's division had bought (retired) Four-Star Army General Claude Vaughn's company and morphed its functions and personnel into her diminutive division, thereby growing her workload severalfold over the past few months.

General Vaughn was a highly respected figure in the United States Army, and when he retired, he started one of the first specialty government-contracting companies. The business grew and now offered not only the functions of commissary, outfitting, and shelter to the US Army, but also included specially trained former army personnel who could be shopped around to any government or concerned interest on the planet to help with waging a war, inciting a revolution, rebuilding an infrastructure after the war that they had so handily helped win, and setting up a fledgling democracy.

Jocelyn was first introduced to General Vaughn's business via a Netscape Navigator Web search that landed her at *www.thiscompanysucks.com*. The site was filled with Vaughn's disgruntled employees' comments about pay and benefits—the usual stuff. But it was the links to the legalities of the situation in Serbia with the underage kids that some of the employees had taken to getting their jollies off with that made Jocelyn go to Adam and ask him if it was a smart move to get involved with these people.

"This could be a PR nightmare," she warned.

"Oh, I'm sure the boys can take care of themselves," Adam had responded in his typical off-the-cuff way. He didn't seem too bothered by the whole matter.

The thing that struck Jocelyn was that the parents of these girls and boys, some as young as nine, were not so much outraged that a US military-type person would have his way with their child, but that they had not been offered fair market value for their kid.

She remembered the conversation she had heard in the break room.

"Sisters?"

"Oh, it was like *heaven*," one former Special Ops guy quietly gushed to a small crew gathered conspiratorially. The grown-out buzz cuts, even though officially done with their "time in the suck" and now working for one of the tendrils of the Conglomerate, still wore the colors of the army. They didn't even seem to notice Jocelyn as they passed around the photos. "It was just weird having their mother make breakfast for me the next morning."

That's how war-torn and poor the places Vaughn's company involved itself in were. And the employees of General Vaughn's mercenary branch knew this and exploited it. The employees who had been there long enough knew there would be no consequences. This was not to say that everyone who worked for Vaughn was involved in some sort of seedy scandal. Many were military guys who honestly did not know what they might possibly do outside the scope of their military training and enjoyed the fact that they could find a good-paying job with their credentials. Of course, some were just flat-out adrenaline junkies.

Despite all the recruiting techniques playing upon emotional triggers like patriotism and proud service within the US Armed Forces, employees were merely contractors playing the centuries-old part of mercenary. They could go home to their wives puffed up with their own bravery, sense of purpose, and tax-free compensation at the end of their 365-day OCONUS (Outside Continental United States) contract. As far as Jocelyn could ascertain, it was just like an adventure getaway in which employees got paid many times more than what they had been paid while in the service.

And Adam had been right. The situation with *thiscompanysucks. com* never did present itself as the pimple on their complexion that Jocelyn had feared. Resolution came simply in the form of cash pay- outs to the affected children's families and then, at a much higher cost, purchasing the domain name *thiscompanysucks* so that it would never see the illuminating glow of the Internet again.

Jocelyn knew that her coworkers were not officially in the military but in that grayish, muddy, beige area outside the reach of any international rules of engagement or US military standard of conduct. This area, otherwise known as "anything goes," was where the phrase "war is hell" took on yet another layer of interpretation for Jocelyn, as the employees would intermittently send her clips of them gunning down "ragheads," hoping to impress her or, in their own confused way, thinking that it might somehow be helpful in the media outreach effort.

These e-mails, with the attached videos, had caused Jocelyn to complain. She didn't want to see that. It wasn't cool watching some poor guy running for his life across a pixilated black-and-white street and having his head instantly explode like a watermelon accidentally dropped off a kitchen counter. Unfortunately for her, when she went to submit her official request that she not be on the recipient list for these e-mails, the person she was handing her paperwork to was so distracted as he visually devoured the latest "must watch" clip of a beheading that was currently being passed around the office that he just told her to put it in his inbox on his desk. "Okay, Joss, I'll take care of it. But remember, war is hell, baby."

Recognizing "war is hell" as a standard response to just about anything, she became desensitized to it and just stopped asking if a war had actually been declared in *any* of these "hot spots" she was monitoring. And it was around this time something funny started to happen. As there was no point of reference in terms of right or wrong in her daily environment, Jocelyn started to literally see things in terms of the beige area. She would walk into work and feel almost numb at the colorlessness of the place. It was just so incredibly beige. The walls, the rug, the desks. Beige. It made her almost want to cry—but of course, she never did.

So today, she had decided that she was going to do something to fix that. She stood back to appreciate the red, six-by-eight-inch, torn and wrinkled strip of wrapping paper in front of her. At once it took on some sort of minimalist/dada quality. As she continued to study it, she took off her coat. The little arbitrary punctuation mark of red looked good floating on a sea of Navaho Bone. She liked it! It was staying.

CHAPTER NINE

FEELING AS IF SHE HAD accomplished something with that red scrap, Jocelyn began organizing her office so that Indonesia would be as far away from her as possible. She gathered up random notes and pages and filed them appropriately. Then she headed back to the archive to make sure that all the versions of the proposal were returned properly and in the right spot. As she passed by Nancy's office to say hello and catch up on the status of the proposal work, Jocelyn was surprised to find Nancy dry heaving into a trash can.

"Oh Nancy," she blurted, "are you okay?" But before she could get any closer, Nancy waved Jocelyn away. *Oh man ... I better not catch what she has.* Jocelyn nodded and retreated. On her way back to the utility closet, she decided to swing through accounting and see why Darlene Fossbinder had been at work the night she was hauling proposals all over the place.

Jocelyn poked her head into Darlene's office and saw that the woman acting as CFO since the last one dropped dead of a heart attack was not at her desk. And oddly enough, the room was not in its typical state of ankle-deep spreadsheet drafts. In fact, Darlene's office was very tidy and clean. *Weird. Maybe they moved her office.*

As Jocelyn turned to leave, Susan Ritter, the sometimes friendly accounts-payable clerk who should have been an elementary-school teacher, as she was always festooned in some sort of celebratory seasonal gear, gave Jocelyn a big smile and said over her cube partition, "I heard what happened with Indonesia. Good for you!"

"Oh ... thanks," said Jocelyn, thinking that Susan was talking about her getting the proposal out on time.

"Everyone has been talking about it," the clerk added. "We loved it! Loved it!"

"Loved what?" Jocelyn asked, walking over to her.

"That you not only got the job done but you told someone off! That was great!"

Jocelyn slumped down onto the chair next to Susan's desk and said, "So everyone's heard about it?"

Susan nodded vigorously.

"I didn't tell anyone off, Susan. I just was yelling, and Jay Clarke happened to be standing there. I guess I was just super tired and stressed. Sorry about that. I shouldn't have made such a scene."

"Oh no! They deserve it! They can't keep treating employees like this." Susan's eyes sparkled as she spoke. "You missed it. Darlene had been up working on something for Adam, and she didn't complete it on time. Janice told her that you were able to do five times the amount of work in the same night. Apparently that made Darlene lose it, and she quit on the spot. Right there. Walked out."

Jocelyn felt her jaw drop ever so slightly. "No way. She's worked here for, like, fifteen years. She'll be back ... right?"

Susan leaned in close and whispered, "I don't think so. She'd been kind of hinting that the ledgers were impossible lately. All of Adam's businesses keep getting swapped around. Like that darn Argentinean vineyard he got for his girlfriend and the import/export business that goes with it. Darlene complained a lot since that thing came on the scene." Susan shook her head. "I don't think she'll be back. People were afraid that you wouldn't be back either." But then she smiled and finished it all off with, "I'm really glad you're here!"

This exchange made Jocelyn feel a little better. But she wasn't sure who was better off, Darlene for quitting or herself for staying. As Jocelyn stood up to get back to work, a wave of panicky mumbles rippled past her. She turned to look just as a rescue crew burst through the nearby lobby door, pushing a stretcher toward the publications area.

"Oh dear. That's gotta be for Nancy." Susan sighed. "She's been telling everyone that she thinks someone is poisoning her."

Jocelyn's eyes darted back to Susan. "She has?" she asked with alarm.

"Oh, you know how Nancy is—kind of a hypochondriac. She's probably got that virus that's going around."

As Jocelyn headed back to her nauseatingly small Silly Putty–colored office, she spotted a ream of copy paper sitting next to a copy machine. She looked at it and blinked. *Red.* The copy paper's wrapper was red. Jocelyn walked over to it and tore a bit of it off. *Perfect.* This was going on her wall too.

CHAPTER TEN

THE NEXT MORNING, JOCELYN FIGURED she'd swing by the publications office to see how Nancy was doing after she got all the spec sheets from engineering together. Yeah, it was strange that an ambulance had to come and get Nancy the day before, but then again, the woman was always complaining about something. Jocelyn collected the papers and embarked on her customary early-morning trek to the break room. Someone there would undoubtedly have the scoop on Nancy's status. Once there, she grabbed a coffee cup and listened in on the small talk, which was centered not around Nancy but the Conglomerate's new stock-price display, located on the corkboard near the coffee machine:

SEPTEMBER 4, 1998
GOLD: US$285
OIL: $14.89
NYSE: GLOM $15.656 vol: 696.20

"Wow. Look at the price of gold!" Vince, the perpetually ready- to-retire maintenance man, said and let out a low whistle.

"I think they should make this thing more colorful if I have to look at it each time I get a coffee. I mean, the stock is called GLOM, for goodness' sake," said Gary, the shipping/receiving guy from the warehouse, shaking his head. "They should use a color to make it look more interesting."

"They can't just use any old color," Christy from accounting authoritatively pointed out. "Green means that the stock price is going up, and red means that it's going down."

"Well, would GLOM be green or red right now?" Gary wanted to know.

"Green."

"Oh. Good!"

After adding copious amounts of Cremora and sugar and hearing lots of speculation about what "vol: 696.20" meant while not catching any mention of Nancy, Jocelyn headed to the publications area. She rounded the corner fully expecting to be greeted with something on par with, "I could really give a rat's ass about you, but here's a rundown of the tests they did on me yesterday." Instead, she was confronted with a stranger telling her, "Nancy is dead."

"What?" Jocelyn blurted, not believing the neatly dressed thirty- something sitting in Nancy's blue ergonomically correct high-backed chair. "What do you mean she's dead?"

"Oh, I'm so sorry. I thought everyone knew. That's what they told me, that I'm here to cover for someone who died," the woman said somewhat apologetically as she straightened her horn-rimmed glasses.

Jocelyn was silent as she realized that not only did she not know the name of the person delivering this news, but she also hadn't heard this from Mimi yet. And Mimi would obviously be the authority about Nancy's health. "I'm ... I'm sorry too. What did you say your name was?"

"Oh, Shelly Johnson. I'll be covering this position. I'm a really good typist."

"Well, that's a plus ..." Jocelyn chewed her lip as she studied Shelly. "Who told you Nancy was dead?"

"The woman at the temp agency."

"Uh-huh. Okay, hold on. I'll be right back."

Jocelyn turned around and trotted directly to the front desk, where Mimi was carefully hanging up the phone. Mimi looked up and blinked. A tear rolled down her cheek, and that's when Jocelyn knew it was true. But she had to ask anyway. "Did Nancy die?"

Mimi nodded and more tears came. Despite not particularly caring for Nancy, Jocelyn was quite disturbed by the woman's death, and it made her uncomfortable.

She wasn't entirely sure why she was so bothered by it at all. Nancy had been complaining about not feeling well since the day Jocelyn first met her. Thus, Jocelyn had concluded pretty early on that Nancy was one of those people who took a perverse pride in being perpetually miserable and enjoyed being the point of departure for a personal conversation revolving solely around her.

First it was carpal tunnel syndrome. Then it was the drawn-out and mysterious fibromyalgia, which was quickly followed by the Epstein-Barr episode. And of course, one would be remiss if a mention of the sleep apnea debacle was not made. *But this poisoning thing ...* That's what bothered Jocelyn, even though she knew Nancy didn't eat very well and certainly didn't exercise. She was constantly stressed out, was a closet smoker, and, and ...

People were starting to exit the building in an almost spooky mass migration. At first it was just one or two, like little drops of rain before the deluge. Then it appeared that the whole place was evacuating en masse to join the haze outside the glass front doors. No one seemed very concerned about being ten feet away from the entrance, and more and more nicotine-laced smoke breezed in as each successive person filed out to get some fresh air.

"Honey, will you cover the phone for me?" Mimi asked between sniffles. "I need to get out there with everyone."

"But you don't smo ... Oh, okay, Mimi. Sure." And Jocelyn sat down in Mimi's chair behind the big circular front desk. Naturally, she had no clue how to operate the phone system, and at least twenty calls must have been lost while she was sitting there watching people hug and console each other outside.

Many of these people had worked with Nancy for

decades. The news of the coworker they had met as a young woman, with whom they had toiled and partied and traveled with when they had all embarked on Adam's company-wide Caribbean Booze Cruise, now dead at fifty-six, was beyond unbelievable. Nancy was younger than most of the occupants of the cube warren Jocelyn now found herself working in. The unexpected realization of the length of their own mortal coils was hitting the smoking crew pretty hard as Jocelyn watched them eventually filter back inside.

"No ... I don't know. No. I guess that's why she's getting cremated."

That comment about cremation caught Jocelyn's ear, and she asked the women now passing by the front desk, "Nancy's getting cremated? What religion is she? Sorry, *was* she?"

"I'm not sure. But Mimi says that Nancy is being cremated," the cube worker said.

"Wow, um, well, is there going to be a service or something?"

"I don't think so. Nancy didn't want a wake or anything like that. She was such a fun-loving person ..."

Although Jocelyn had clearly experienced another Nancy, she nodded, and the two women headed back to the accounting area.

Martin Mays, who had been outside for the past twenty minutes, rolled up to the desk. His blue windbreaker smelled strongly of smoke, and he stood directly in front of Jocelyn as the phone rang. "You gonna get that?" he said, pointing to the enormous monitor with a telephone receiver hanging off of it.

"Uh ... No. I gave up. I don't know how this thing works."

"Smart," Martin said. "They'll call back. They just want to talk with Mimi anyway."

Just then, Mimi rushed in, leaned over the counter, and grabbed the phone, giving Jocelyn an obviously feigned look of disgust be- cause she was just sitting there with the phone ringing off the hook.

Jocelyn sort of shrugged, got up, and made her way to the front of the desk. She asked Martin, "So, are you okay? You know, with Nancy being dead and all? The two of you have known each other for a long time. It seems so, I don't know, so quick, whatever it was that killed her."

"Oh. Well. Yeah. Of course. I'm fine," Martin stumbled, but then quickly composed his thoughts and continued as if he were practicing a eulogy while the two of them walked back outside. "She was a good woman and a hard worker. Attention to proper protocol when dealing with the military and the government was her best attribute when the rest of us were flying around being complete jackasses." He held the door for Jocelyn. The moment they hit the pavement, Martin lit up, sucked some nicotine into his lungs, and picked up right where he had left off. "She helped to do up the original ISO procedures back in the day. And she did a lot to keep Adam in line in those early years; you know, before we grew. We had almost three hundred employees here at one point. You'd never know it now." He paused and took yet another drag off the cigarette. "Well, that was when she was part of my VAX team. Before she was relegated to the final stages of proposal work in the copy room. I don't think this company would have been the same without her."

This last statement must have made him realize that the company, which had been gobbled up by the Conglomerate, was now without her and that it was, in fact, no longer the same company that he and Nancy had helped start up. Nancy and their company were officially dead. Martin was clearly appreciating the current circumstances in a way that Jocelyn would never be capable of.

"It's been a heck of a ride." He paused and inhaled.

Jocelyn was silent. There wasn't much she felt she could offer in condolence that didn't sound corny or clichéd. He finished his cigarette.

"Take the money and run, Joss," Martin said. And as

effortlessly as he had lit it, he pinched and flicked the remnant of his cigarette toward an overgrown bramble of unmanageable shrubs and weeds that flanked a soon-to-be-naked deciduous forest. He watched the cigarette butt intensely as if it were sailing in slow motion to its final resting place among the browning residue of late season Queen Anne's lace, poison ivy, and soon-to-be-in-full-glory bittersweet.

"I'm getting out of here," he said as if in conclusion. "You should too." He winked at her as he patted his hip. Jocelyn looked at him, confused by his arbitrary hip pat. "I've had my life insurance policy right here for the past fifteen years," he said by way of explanation. When it was clear Jocelyn still had no clue what Martin was talking about, he flashed her a glimpse of a pistol in a holster. "Just take the money and run, Jocelyn. Keep your head down, and take the money and run. They're all assholes."

CHAPTER ELEVEN

Four Years Later
September 2002

JOCELYN OPENED THE DOOR TO her tiny office and smiled. She loved it! Years and years' worth of red paper scraps greeted her. When she had asked Adam if she could paint her wall red after the Indonesia debacle, he said, "Sure, honey. Whatever it takes to keep you happy and productive."

And when Jocelyn came in the following Saturday sporting her paint-splattered combat boots, a gallon of Sherwin Williams Cherry Tomato, and a paint roller, Janice, who was seemingly always at work, had stopped her at the front door and told her, "No paint."

This is what had prompted Jocelyn to start the red-wall collage in earnest. It didn't take long before Jerry Apario, the IT guy, and Jay Clarke were offering her their red scraps to add to her collection. Almost every area of wall space on every side of her was covered at this point with chunks of random red, from warning tags to snack-sized Doritos bags. The guys called it the REDRUM project, making reference to the movie *The Shining*. But Jocelyn preferred to think of it as if she was surrounded by a field of poppies as she hung her olive drab Calvin Klein trench coat on the hook behind her door.

Things had changed since the meager beginnings of the REDRUM collage. Firstly, the Bobby issue was settled. She got the house but had to pay him $20,000 in the divorce. It hadn't been pleasant, and during that time Jocelyn had come to appreciate her tiny office as a sanctuary. With the door closed, she could cry, nap, or whatever. That was the benefit of being tucked away in a utility closet—no one noticed what she was up to so long as she got her work done. All she had to do was emerge looking the part of "Corporate Important Person." And it didn't take long for Jocelyn to nail the role. With each successive raise, she could spend more money on more expensive brand-name items to reinforce the idea that she actually gave a hoot about what she was doing each day.

Secondly, Adam was no longer in the Inner Sanctum. General Walton was. Adam's office was relegated to another building down the street in the same office park. Adam's company, after being assimilated into the Conglomerate, was sold to another of the Conglomerate's divisions and promptly transformed itself into a subdivision. So they were still running with the Conglomerate's logo and branding, only somehow the place was, on paper anyway, technically different.

Adam still worked for the company, but only to make sure that the Indonesia proposal bore fruit. The deal was, incredibly to every- one but the marketing department, still in the works. With Adam's business being passed around like a trading card, Jocelyn was stuck working on revisions and reiterations of the proposal, which had become more like a multiyear sales lead, for over four years. Adam had bought a condo in Singapore so that he could stay on top of the negotiations, and Jocelyn had to admire his tenacity. He was like a pit bull and wasn't letting go. Apparently, neither were the Japanese. The Germans had dropped out of the contest almost three years ago.

And thirdly, she finally got a real title! She was officially a marketing communications specialist, and she had the business cards to prove it. Of course, no one could say what her title meant, not even the HR director, Elaine Gibson. Regardless, it was a great icebreaker when she had to go network or man a trade-show booth:

"Hi, I'm Jocelyn McLaren." (Passes business card to

unsuspecting cocktail-party attendee.)

"Uh ... hi." (Guy flips card around.) "What's a 'marketing communications specialist'?"

"Well, sometimes I have to wear latex gloves ..." And the conversation took off from there.

Jocelyn was doing okay. The MS had kicked up a bit during the divorce, but other than that, she was fine. The product lines she was dealing with had completely shifted away from the navy and were more centered around simulation systems in general. Cars, trucks, ships, tanks, cranes, helicopters, handguns, unmanned aerial vehicles (UAV), you name it. It was like she was working for a pumped-up- on-steroids arcade-game wholesaler.

The mercenaries were still rolling around fighting bad guys and spreading the joys of democracy. Which meant that the service of government training was a hot proposal lately. And of course, Adam's Catastrophe! was still alive and kicking. In fact, the Conglomerate had spent a lot of money to relocate some really high-powered sales guys specifically for this product. But then again, those guys would sell anything. Jocelyn had secretly code-named them *drosophila melanogaster*, the Latin name for fruit fly she had learned in high school, because they would always swarm around her office door just as the request for proposal (RFP) and request for quote (RFQ) lists were being released. These jokers had absolutely no problem marching into the gaping maw of Hades to make a sale. They also had absolutely no problem flaunting their commission checks when they did.

"Nice weather we've got today," Robert said as he attempted to casually mosey in and awkwardly shut the door, closing out the *drosophila melanogaster* who were orbiting around outside. Jocelyn looked up at him and blinked, amused that he even thought he'd be able to shut the door with both of them in there.

Robert was easily the most expensively outfitted person in the building. He was a Coast Guard man, which made him an outsider in this ex-navy-dominated shop. But his ex-wife had been a state senator, and she knew Adam's friend, Stan the congressman, and that seemed to help balance the scales for a while. Of course, with the Conglomerate buying Adam out and then swapping the company over to one of its divisions, and all the ex-army generals filing in, the place had taken on the atmosphere of a football rivalry, only more fierce because it was fueled by the winning combination of the self-imbued importance of corporate life *and* national security.

Robert, despite his title—which vacillated between vice president and director—was clearly the water boy in the game. His only hope was to wow headquarters and get transferred to the corporate office in New York City. And he made no secret of his intention to do just that.

Everything about Robert was perfect, almost plastic, from his graying temples—which he had just recently started dying a conspicuous shade of youthful dark brown—to his whitening-strip-bleached teeth. He looked good, but at the same time oddly freakish, with smooth manicured hands that were always accented by some sort of expensive watch and overly important cuff links.

Jocelyn feared that Robert's crisp white Brooks Brothers dress shirt was going to be soiled as he squeezed past the outline on her whiteboard. And she sincerely hoped that he would finally recognize how ridiculous the dimensions of her office were. It was the exact width of her desk that was pushed against the red patchwork wall opposite the door. Her computer's hulk of a monitor and her phone took up most of said desk. The wall-mounted file holders did help. However, the place really was barely workable, and she doubted that it had passed any sort of building code. But she managed it and had made it a room of her own.

Robert finally wedged himself past the little filing cabinet and shut the door with a seemingly coordinated flap of hundreds of little red paper butterfly wings.

"Well, it looks like we need you in DC for a conference, Jocelyn. It's a corporate thing jointly hosted by the Pentagon. All the marketing communications directors will be there. You have to go and ..."

"Oh, I'm a 'director' now?" she asked excitedly.

"Um, no. I didn't say that," said the *director* of sales and marketing. "But you do have to go to it. The Pentagon is going to be outlining its plans for the next few years, and you might as well go and take some notes—you've always been very good at that—and enjoy yourself."

They looked at each other and shared a pause that was either dramatic or comedic, Jocelyn couldn't tell which. The last time he'd sent her off to a conference with no real direction, she thought he was going to have an aneurysm when she came back and submitted her massive report—a report he hadn't been expecting. Her account of the conference was chock-full of information about the New York Stock Exchange, Wall Street cybercrime, online pedophilia, and Drumthwacket, a.k.a. the New Jersey governor's mansion.

Luckily, out of the two conferences being held that day, she had fallen in with the group Adam had been expecting a full report about. Robert had only received a yellow sticky that said "*Princeton Tomorrow Conference*" and sent her in his place. He had been out of his mind when she returned. He'd thought she was going to be shmoozing with firemen and trying to pitch Catastrophe!.

Currently, whatever the look Robert was giving her meant, it was clearly meaningful. "It's at a nice hotel, I've stayed there myself a few times. Adam says you deserve it."

Adam? Adam is telling me to go to the director's conference? But it didn't matter.

"I'll have Mimi do up your travel paperwork for you. Don't worry about anything." As he opened the door to let himself out, he noticed the smear on the whiteboard.

CHAPTER TWELVE

IT WAS JOCELYN'S FAVORITE TIME of year. Autumn. The day was classic back-to-school weather. The air was not quite as humid, and the atmosphere had a different type of light bouncing off of everything. Jocelyn found the effect genuinely more pleasing than the direct, harsh-lit days of summer. The leaves would be changing colors soon, but not yet. It was very much the type of day she remembered as a kid when she would wear the sweater and corduroys that her mother had bought during the annual back-to-school sales and then almost faint from heat exhaustion by morning recess.

Succumbing to the Indian-summer September heat was not her concern today. She was neatly tucked into a hermetically sealed, air-conditioned, pine-tree-scented taxicab that was creeping laboriously through traffic on the beltway around Washington, DC.

Jocelyn looked out of her window as she thought about the Malaysia proposal sitting on her desk back in Connecticut. She still didn't have that special document that Robert had indicated she needed. As she figured there wasn't much to be done while stuck in a cab at eight thirty in the morning, she instead pondered why they always sent her to Baltimore Washington International Airport and not to Reagan.

Why did she have to get up at some ungodly hour and get on that early flight only to be greeted with an additional land journey nearly as long as the flight? It would be so much easier if she could just get them to understand that the extra money spent on a ticket to Ronald Reagan Washington National Airport would be money well spent. She'd be there on time and not have to spend so much money on taxi fare. She was perpetually mystified as to why they would rather pay her to drive around in a cab—or worse yet, to sit in traffic in a cab—than spend the money on a ticket to the airport closest to her destination so that she could actually get work done.

She would always feel anxious as the interval between looking at her watch and looking at the cab's meter got shorter and shorter. Inevitably, she would end up trying to calculate if she would be at her meeting on time and/or have enough cash to see her through the entire trip. Sure the company would eventually give her the money back when she returned to the office and took the time to do up the much-dreaded travel reimbursement form, but the thought of eventual payback did not alleviate her present displeasure with the company's choice of BWI.

Eventually she got to her destination, which was in fact nice, as Robert had promised. Sheraton. Corporate always used Sheraton, and Jocelyn always paid for it with her company-issued American Express card. If she had landed at Reagan, she would have been checked in already. A Reagan arrival would have given her time for a leisurely change into a new outfit, a coffee, and possibly mingling with the directors who were now assembling.

But because of the company's travel contracts being crafted for the benefit of some interwoven web of business interests far out- side the scope of Jocelyn's immediate worldview, she was instead high-tailing it through the lobby and down a long hallway while half-rolling, half-dragging her wheeled carry-on luggage, which was prone to tipping over once she hit cruising speed.

"Clearly not built for a corporate road warrior," Jocelyn huffed as she picked up the baggage and carried it like a child to her room. She would deal with the malfunctioning retractable handle that was stuck in the upright position later.

When she got to her room, she quickly changed into a new blouse, looked at herself in the mirror, and decided that there wasn't enough time to do anything to make her appear any more presentable. She set out to find Ballroom B and, noticing the doors were closed, tried to quickly and quietly sneak in unnoticed.

The decor in Ballroom B was technically called "gold," but it was still basically beige. The carpet-covered walls had been collapsed to make room for a dozen skirted banquet "crescent rounds." Each half-moon table conveniently seated six in such a way that no one was forced to have his or her back to the speaker at the podium or the enormous PowerPoint projection that was obviously the main attraction for the marketing communications directors in attendance. There were sixty-five divisions within the Conglomerate, and just about all of them seemed to be represented at the meeting.

This was the first time Jocelyn had actually been to a meeting of this scope. Usually she just e-mailed the concerned parties, such as the company's communications vice president or the corporate-approved graphic designer, both of whom she had never met. They would often vaguely promise to meet someday in person as they signed off. Or, less frequently, when she would speak with them on the phone.

Phone calls from corporate were typically a bad sign, and she didn't get many. The few phone calls she had received were from the lawyers who were presenting as she walked in. It appeared that one of the divisions in California was having a really hard time with a tariff/customs issue, and the lawyer recommended that everyone take a five-minute break while California and he "talk off-line." He'd be back to wrap up his presentation with important information regarding government procurement and mandatory domestic-product content.

This was just fine with Jocelyn, because coming in

late, she'd had to position herself at the table farthest from the podium and closest to the skirted row of eight-foot banquet tables that were piled high with the typical contents of a hotel's version of a continental breakfast: muffins, doughnuts, bagels, Danish, coffee, and juice. Jocelyn tried not to look as if she was desperate for sustenance as she claimed her cheese Danish with the provided tongs.

Cheese Danish always go first was her rationale as she eagerly grabbed her own. She then proceeded to prepare her coffee. She took a napkin and headed back to her table. It was at this point that she noticed everyone was conspicuously sporting a name tag.

As she sat down with her continental breakfast, Jocelyn introduced herself to the man sitting at her table and asked where she might get a name tag.

"Didn't they send one to you?"

"Um ... No. Robert King told me I was supposed to come to this a few days ago. I didn't know I should have been expecting a name tag. Who should I be talking to about that?" Jocelyn asked as she scanned the room for a likely name-tag-issuing suspect.

As if on cue, a woman who had been eyeing Jocelyn approached. She was carrying a black leather legal-pad portfolio smartly embossed with the defense company's logo.

"Can I help you?" the woman asked.

"Yes, actually." Jocelyn stood up. "I'm Jocelyn McLaren, and I was told to come here today and take notes. Robert King sent me."

"Oh. Is Robert here too?" the woman asked as her eyes darted around the ballroom.

"No. He sent me in his place." Jocelyn was starting to wonder if Robert had actually given her a name tag. But then she knew he hadn't.

"I see. He didn't alert me to your being here today. Would you mind if I call him and verify that you are who you say you are?"

"Sure. Of course not. By all means ..."

Jocelyn took this as an indication that she was supposed to sit down and make friendly with the gentleman who was looking at her now somewhat suspiciously. She took a sip of her coffee and asked him which division he was from. Acknowledging his response, she took a bite of her cheese Danish a bit more conscientiously than she would have if she hadn't felt as if she would soon be getting interrogated. She smiled and feigned extreme interest in gyroscopes and then listened with only half an ear as the man talked about the impending layoffs that he had heard rumors of.

Moments later, the woman with the leather legal-pad portfolio reappeared and introduced herself to Jocelyn while apologizing for having made her wait.

"Oh my goodness!" Jocelyn popped up from her seat and shook the woman's hand heartily. "You're Donna ... Hello. It is a pleasure to meet you!"

Donna Bolton, a.k.a. "the little firecracker," was the Conglomerate's executive vice president in charge of communications. After a few big-smile niceties, Donna presented Jocelyn with an embossed leather portfolio.

"Don't take shit from these generals. You are in charge of communications at your division, and you answer to me. These military guys have a hard time with this concept. Don't ever let them intimidate you. Your mistakes are my mistakes. So don't screw up. Got it?"

Assuring Donna that she would do her best, Jocelyn took the leather portfolio and proceeded to document everything as precisely as she could. It was only a bit later in the day, shortly before the lunch break, that Jocelyn experienced the vague sensation that she may have accidentally entered Bizarro World, as a fully uniformed general from the Pentagon presented his overly wordy PowerPoint presentation outlining the countries that would most likely be areas of military engagement within the next decade: Liberia, Somalia, Sudan, Afghanistan, Pakistan, Iraq,

Iran, Yemen, Syria, Libya, Lebanon, and Haiti.

Scribbling it all down, Jocelyn looked around the room expecting to see people visibly freaked out by this frank and direct overview of the Pentagon's plans. None of this seemed to make any sense to her. *Haiti? Syria? What the heck does that have to do with us?* However, much to her astonishment, the other communications directors were simply munching on their cheese Danish and looking bored.

The general paused for dramatic effect. "With the wild card, of course, being Central and South America. That has always been an ongoing situation down there. Our job as military professionals, with the direction of our Congress and commander and chief, is to decide which is more important: the spread of democracy or plain old police work?"

Police work? Jocelyn thought that was weird, but she hung with it because the PowerPoint was so wordy and she just wanted to make sure she got everything down.

The general continued, "Which is going to bring a sustainable and equitable end to the conflicted region's present situation? Either way, the Pentagon is making a transformation in this new information age. And we need your help."

Jocelyn circled the word *transformation* in her notebook, as the general had specifically used his laser pointer to underline it and circle it, making sure the audience recognized the significance of that word and absorbed it.

Apparently, the Pentagon was all about utilizing as much in- formation-age technology as it could get its hands on. The general presenting seemed very proud of the fact that soldiers would now be wired. He spoke of things like the need for remote cameras on helmets and bounced the term *interoperability* around like a ping-pong ball in an old bricks-and-mortar warehouse.

The room was getting antsy. It was closing in on lunchtime. As soon as the general seemed to be finished with his presentation, people started getting up from their seats to stretch, and the low hum of polite conversation filled the space. Donna stood up at the podium to thank the general and offer lunch options, but before she could utter her first word, the hotel's fire alarm started blaring and would not stop. The lights shut off in Ballroom B and the emergency lights snapped on.

It took a moment for the signal of the fire alarm to be processed by the startled collective. Donna grabbed the general's arm and appeared to be shouting at him as her posture became very stern and demanding. Jocelyn couldn't help but notice this exchange. *People don't normally treat generals like that.*

But she didn't have time to think. She hurriedly grabbed her purse and leather legal-pad portfolio, which was full of notes from the presentation. She was already exiting the room when she heard

Donna announced to the group over the noise, "Do not take the elevators! Take the stairs!" and "Meet a little ways down the street from the main entrance so that people are able to exit safely. Don't create a traffic jam!"

The hotel alarms were still blaring like some sort of apocalyptic metronome. Jocelyn went as quickly as she could down the lobby stairway and out the front door. It was only upon hitting the sidewalk that she noticed that all the other hotels on the street were blasting their fire alarms too. In the long view, it appeared that people were being systematically vomited out onto the sidewalk all the way down Jefferson Davis Highway. This is when she noticed that she was trembling.

As she gripped her leather portfolio tightly to her chest, her gaze was forced upon the most prominent feature of the landscape: the Pentagon. With her commitment to make the red-eye flight and get to the director's meeting on time, Jocelyn had somehow conveniently forgotten that today was the first official recognition of Patriot Day, the first anniversary of September 11.

CHAPTER THIRTEEN

LIKE EVERYONE ELSE NOW ASSEMBLING on the street, Jocelyn had no idea what caused the fire alarms to go off in all the hotels at the same time.

Is this another terrorist attack?

Quite uncontrollably, she was suddenly reliving vivid recollections of September 11 from the year before. Adam, Robert, and Stan had been heading out to a meeting in New York City that morning, and naturally, they had wanted her to do up some sort of impromptu marketing presentation as they left the building. She had agreed and told them that she would place it on the company's FTP server for Robert to pick up once they arrived in NYC. They were going to be flying out in Adam's personal airplane. He was a pilot and simply preferred to fly himself, when at all possible, to avoid the hassle of absolutely everything associated with the commercial airlines.

It had been while she was speed-editing a PowerPoint to fit the latest pitch that her phone rang. Surprisingly, it was Bobby reporting that a plane had hit one of the World Trade Center buildings. She hadn't heard from him in a while. "Oh," she had remarked, figuring that it must have been a small plane. "That's too bad. Listen, I'm re- ally busy. Can I call you back in like an hour or so?" She knew that her dad had flown her around the World Trade Center in his plane when she was a kid. She assumed it must be something like a Piper Cherokee or similar little private craft. Barely giving it a thought, she changed one of the bullet points to more correctly articulate the benefits of their product.

"Hey! Did you hear that a plane just hit the World Trade Center?" Jerry Apario shouted into her office as he hurried off toward the main conference room. "I've gotta get CNN patched into that big-screen projector!"

"I'll be there in a minute. Almost done," she answered back.

It was right about then that she noticed everyone exiting their offices and heading toward the big conference room. *Must be a slow day here for these folks.* She deftly grabbed a newer JPG file of a photo of one of their newer simulators and pasted it into the now complete PowerPoint. Jocelyn uploaded it along with a short seven- ty-eight-page proposal with appropriate annexes to the FTP server.

Only when she was convinced that all her files had landed safely at their intended destination did she call Robert on his cell phone to tell him that the presentation files were available for pickup. He didn't answer. She called again. No answer. Not even his voice mail. A bit puzzled but knowing that she could try him again later, she made her way to the conference room.

When she entered, CNN was being projected onto the big screen with the audio issuing from the surround-sound system. It was standing room only, everyone watching as smoke billowed out of one of the towers. "Wait. A plane did that?" Jocelyn asked, pointing to the screen.

And as the crowd mumbled that they had heard the same thing and marveled that it was actually a commercial airline jet, one of the women from accounting said, "Oh, thank God. I thought it might have been Adam's plane."

Jocelyn decided to call Bobby back and apologize for making light of what he was trying to tell her. Just as she was about to leave the room to make that call, a WESCAM military-grade camera system belonging to L3 Communications, installed on an unidentified and prepositioned helicopter, filmed the only available "live" footage of another jet righting itself with military precision to squarely hit the other World Trade Center tower—footage originating from ABC7 that within eleven seconds would be simultaneously synched to CNN, FOX, and NBC.

Everyone in the room let out a collective gasp. It was apparent that this was no longer a fluke accident. This was intentional. As Jocelyn stared at the screen, her first split-second, unfiltered emotional reaction was one of empathy. But it was not for the passengers or the inhabitants of the building, or even their families. Rather, this bizarre momentary twinge of empathy was for the pilots.

Within that brief sliver of a millisecond, she could physically sense how divinely euphoric they must have felt being able to pull off such an operation. They had made a worldwide exclamation, the echo of which would resonate across the entire planet for a very long time. She had to admit, she was impressed.

"That's fucked up!" someone yelled.

The reality of the situation instantly snapped into proper position and bore down upon Jocelyn like a lead fog. She heaved the now heavy, toxic atmosphere into her with one short, quick breath. The US was officially at war. Her body tightened, and she braced herself for instructions as the conversation in the room started to intensify.

"What do we do now?"

"No. Like, really? Do we need to be doing something?"

"Does the office have emergency protocol in cases like this?"

Many of the people in the conference room had been employed by the military in their previous incarnations working for the government, so they knew to man their stations and had already started to head back to their work spaces. Everyone else was looking for Janice, VP of operations. Maybe she would know the right thing to do.

CNN was scrolling text announcing that all aircraft had been ordered down and that another commercial jet had defied orders to land and was circling back toward the White House. Soon it was reported that the Pentagon had been hit. This caused many in the room to utter "no way" in disbelief.

Months later, it would be disclosed by CBS and PBS that the area Jocelyn and her coworkers were currently viewing at the Pentagon, via CNN, was undergoing renovation and not many people were in the impact zone. The area housed the Pentagon's accounting department. The only people present at the time of the attack were the civilian accountants who were already working in crisis-management mode. They had been tasked to figure out and help prepare testimony as to where US$2.3 trillion had gone. US Secretary of Defense Donald Rumsfeld had stated under oath only the day before that he had no idea where it might be and that the Pentagon couldn't account for it.

Cathy the clerk started to scream and cry hysterically. Jocelyn felt compelled to console her, but honestly, she didn't know what to say. So she just held Cathy's hand. Sharon, Adam's personal assistant, took a different tack. She slapped Cathy across the face. This caught Cathy completely off guard and silenced her. Jocelyn had always suspected that Sharon really didn't like Cathy, but this slap thing pretty much confirmed her hunch.

It was at precisely this moment that Adam, Robert, and Stan sauntered in. "Jeez, I'm gone for a couple hours and already I have the women fighting," Adam said, reverting to his "Mr. I'll Buy Everyone Here a Drink" good ol' boy persona.

"What happened? Did you see it?" The questions were being lobbed toward Adam as Robert and Stan turned to watch the proceedings on the big screen. Obviously, they had not seen any of this. Adam relayed his account of how he had received an all-points-bulletin alert from the tower that he had never gotten before: to immediately land at the nearest airfield. Seeing as they had just taken flight, Adam opted to turn around, land, and come back to the office.

After assuaging everyone's concerns about personal safety in the building and assigning Janice to chair a committee to draft emergency protocol, Adam told everyone that they should stay and continue to get more work done. "There's plenty to do here at the office, and we have running water. It's probably the safest place to be."

"Yeah, but what about the bridge?" panicky Jerry Apario questioned. All heads turned toward him. "They could blow that up and the subs would be stuck. And ..." He was referring to the Route 95 bridge spanning the Thames River and the nuclear sub base just down the street.

"That bridge is probably one of the most secure in the world, Jerry. The subs have already been sent out. They're not going to start bombing us." Adam was sure that word would come down if anything was needed of their division.

Needless to say, the coffee machine was brewing at full bore that day as people aimlessly mulled around the office complex in a daze. Someone actually went out and bought several dozen boxes of doughnuts for communal consumption as if it was a holiday or something. People just didn't know how to act. However, Mimi the receptionist did.

Mimi was operating at peak performance levels. She was taking calls from all over the world and relaying to the division's international clients who had called in concerned and offering condolences the in-depth emotional reactions of the staff coupled with a play-by-play of Adam's downed flight. More importantly, of course, that she and her family were fine.

CNN stayed on all day in the big conference room. Footage of the impact into the iconic twin towers was replayed again, and again, and yet again. The personal histories of the heroic passengers on another jet who attempted to overtake the terrorists before the plane ended up crashing in Pennsylvania became an instant hot topic.

Jocelyn and her coworkers would venture back to the conference room between trips to the break room to see if any new information or instructions had been issued as they nursed their coffees.

It was getting later in the day. People were heading home, but Jocelyn didn't feel like leaving. She might as well use this time to do something productive. Maybe organize the marketing filing cabinets? She didn't know. She swung back to the conference room to look at the big screen again with its hypnotic scrolling text. And it was then that she and several other people witnessed another building falling to the ground.

"Oh! That's the building we were supposed to install our Catastrophe! command and control center in!"

"Dodged that bullet, eh?" Martin Mays said, taking a gulp of coffee with eyes still locked to the screen.

"Yeah ... remember that company PlanGrafix brought in the blueprints of that building?" one of the more irritating sales guys said.

Jocelyn clearly remembered that the sales team from PlanGrafix, Stan the congressman, and someone, Jocelyn had assumed, from the New York City mayor's office had brought the blueprints of World Trade Center Building Seven into their division's mock-up of an emergency control center.

It had been a fascinating meeting. PlanGrafix demonstrated how it could render a virtual building complete with where all the utilities were—electric, gas, water, and sewage. Perfect information for first responders who needed to know this sort of stuff when they were preparing to enter a burning building and might need to tear down a wall. The only problem was that first responders really didn't have the hardware available to use the PlanGrafix software.

Jocelyn was trying to convince Adam to buy the tiny company and maybe somehow make the visualizations Web-based. The technique of creating three-dimensional computer-graphic models of a building based upon the blueprints was among the best available, and Jocelyn had discovered, after giving one of the guys her business card, that they were eager to sell. They were over their heads in debt, as they had banked on all of NYC getting rendered for emergency purposes two years before, and were now looking for a buyer.

If she remembered correctly, the man from the mayor's office had wanted to install an emergency-response command center in a sub-basement of the building they had just seen collapse on CNN. It was going to be a big deal. The plans called for not only every single technological piece of hardware and software wizardry the company had to offer but also space for long-term water, food, and air reserves. Basically, the plans called for a structure that could withstand a nuclear attack. A really big deal. Meaning a really big contract. Meaning a really big welcome and lots of special attention paid to this visit.

Unfortunately, they didn't get the contract. Someone else did, and the command and control center got built upstairs on one of the office levels. Jocelyn guessed it was because their software really wasn't up to speed. Sure they could get all the fancy hardware, no problem. But honestly, so could anyone with a credit card.

"Weren't there a lot of banks in that building?" someone asked.

Someone from accounting chirped, "The IRS was in there. I know that."

"The Securities and Exchange Commission was in there too," a female voice added from the back of the room. "I don't know why I remember that. I guess with all the stuff on TV about Enron lately ..."

"Yeah, I saw that thing about Enron," the annoying sales guy said, trying to reclaim some sort of anchor to reality by focusing on something less traumatic. "They were a mess. Trying to do stock trades or something ... derivatives, I think that's what it's called, based on weather. Weather, of all things! A seriously out-of-touch bunch. Anyhow, the show I saw mentioned that all the evidence from their trial was being stored there in that building."

Everyone was sipping coffee, transfixed by the big

screen and the scrolling text as the free-form conversation swirled around everyone's stunned heads.

"Maybe it was a real intelligence/security target. The CIA and Secret Service were in there too."

"Sheesh—good thing the mayor wasn't in there today, he'd have been crushed like a grape."

"Wasn't that why they wanted to build that thing in the first place—emergency response? Weird he wasn't even in there."

"Nah. They had to take it down. You know national security— protect our secrets. Like when a jet fighter crashes, they just blow it up so the enemy can't reverse-engineer it. That sort of thing."

"Standard operating procedure."

"Yeah. SOP."

Everyone in the big conference room seemed pretty secure with the SOP assessment of the situation, and in Jocelyn's humble, non- military opinion, demolishing the building seemed like the prudent thing to do. She grabbed her coffee cup and headed back to her office sadly shaking her head. On her way out, she heard someone say, "Fire? No fucking way ..." But she didn't hang around to chat.

THE NEXT DAY, EVERYONE SHOWED up for work a bit frazzled. The world, swaddled in Chinese-made American flags, seemed different. Waking up in a war was a new experience for most of America, and it felt odd and uncomfortable; not the best fit, seeing as no one really knew who the enemy was. Sure, they had mentioned it almost immediately on TV—al-Qaeda—but who the heck was that? And why was there no *U* after the *Q*?

The only folks who seemed to be totally in their element were the retired generals marching around the building. These dominant type-A men worked as upper management but clearly had some sort of symbiotic relationship with the division's CEO, Adam. The generals accepted Adam because he obviously could sell this stuff, and Adam accepted the generals because they allowed him entry to new avenues within the Pentagon. Other than that, the generals reverted to their military hierarchal structure for chain of command, and Adam ... well, he was a loose cannon. So long as he was making a sale, he could stay. But if he wasn't, the generals and the Conglomerate had no use for him, despite his longtime personal friendship with some of the world's most influential naval officers.

It was the son of one of Adam's naval officer friends who was of concern the morning after September 11.

CHAPTER FOURTEEN

AHMED WAS HIS NAME, AND he was the eldest son of the third in command of the Egyptian navy. Ahmed's mother was the first of the commander's three wives. This position within his family made Ahmed a bit full of himself. Jocelyn had attempted to be friendly with him during lunch breaks throughout his summer internship, which had been arranged by Adam as a favor to his commander father.

Naturally, and this all went without saying, it was clear that Ahmed's presence in the largest office in the building (almost as large as Adam's), with one of the nicest real-wood desks and most luxurious of executive leather chairs, was arranged in hopes of working some sort of upgrade and maintenance contract deal with the Egyptian navy.

Ahmed was perpetually bored and, quite frankly, pissy as he sat in his expansive office alone looking at his computer. No one was quite sure what he did in there, and quite frankly, no one cared. Ahmed was clearly childish and spoiled, outfitted like an English prep-school wannabe in his khaki Burberry trousers. One day, he felt compelled to exert his Egyptian manliness by telling Jocelyn that if he was home, he would beat his girlfriend for not obeying his command to see a dentist. But seeing as he was here in this poor excuse of an office, there wasn't much he could do, and he was frustrated.

Not liking what she heard, Jocelyn shot back at him, "Ahmed, if you did that here in the United States, you would end up in jail. And besides, doesn't she have parents she should be answering to? You aren't her husband. Don't go smacking a girl around if you aren't man enough to at least marry her." As strange as that seemed to be while she was saying it, she knew it would shut him up for a while.

Ahmed showed up later and asked Jocelyn if he could borrow her credit card; he wanted to rent a car. Of course Jocelyn said no, but when Ahmed asked Jerry Apario, Jerry said yes. Jerry had formerly worked at Hertz Rent-a-Car, setting up the company's national network, and he knew some folks there who could extend a discount. On his corporate AmEx card, Jerry secured a midsize car for Ahmed's weekend getaway.

"Man, that's really nice of you, Jerry," Jocelyn said.

"Yeah, well, he doesn't have anyone around here, and he wants to visit some friends in New Jersey. I figured he's leaving in like another week, so what's the big deal? I'll help him out, and next time they send me over to Egypt to deal with his dad's contract, he'll hook me up while I'm there. I'm planning ahead!" Jerry said with a grin.

ON MONDAY, AHMED WAS BACK from his New Jersey weekend, and he was clearly agitated. He came into Jocelyn's office and asked— actually more like demanded—that she book him a flight to Cairo immediately.

"Nope. Not my department. Sorry, Ahmed." But he persisted. "Honestly, Ahmed," she told him, "if I put it in for you, you'll probably end up at BWI. They never send me where I want to actually go. Ask Mimi. She's got a knack with the travel group."

Jocelyn then escorted Ahmed out of her office and to the front desk, because he just wasn't leaving on his own, and presented him to Mimi. As she turned to leave, she heard Mimi say, "Oh Ahmed, I've booked a bea-u-tiful first-class ticket for you. Not this Thursday— next Thursday. I know you want to see your girlfriend, but you'll be there quick as a bunny, honey! You just enjoy yourself while you're still here with us."

Apparently this was not an acceptable answer for

Ahmed, and he proceeded to ask every female he could find during the next two days to book him a flight. It got so bad that Mimi had to tell him very publicly to stop bothering everyone about travel, because they had other work to do. Travel was not their expertise, it was hers, and she had him all set up. He didn't have to worry about anything. Thursday, Ahmed did not show up to work, and no one really noticed.

Friday, Ahmed did not show up to work, and Mimi—being the mom-like figure that she was—started calling over to the company condo, where he had been camped out for the past two months, to see if he was feeling all right.

Monday, September 10, Ahmed still had not reported to work, and Mimi asked Vince, the perpetually ready-for-retirement maintenance man, to swing over to the condo and see if the guy was okay. Vince came back and reported that the place seemed empty, but that he hadn't actually gone in.

Tuesday, September 11, all hell broke loose.

Wednesday, as American flags were draped literally everywhere, it dawned on the accounting department that Ahmed had conveniently gone missing at a very inauspicious time.

Mimi bemoaned to all who would listen that it was disappointing and somewhat strange that out of all the international clients who had called her, she had not yet taken any calls from one of their longest-standing customers: Egypt.

It also dawned on Jerry Apario that maybe he should start freaking out about being the sole purchaser on record of a rented car transporting a high-ranking Egyptian military man's kid to New Jersey about a week before the twin towers imploded. Would someone start sniffing around and want to question his involvement?

Acting out of self-preservation, Jerry, because he could as the IT guy, went into Ahmed's office and started to look though the files stored on Ahmed's computer. It wasn't long before his stomach did a somersault. He decided that he was too repulsed to immediately tell anyone other than Jocelyn what he had discovered. He burst into Jocelyn's office holding up Ahmed's computer's hard drive.

"You know what Ahmed has on here?" Jerry dramatically whispered, shaking the hard drive for emphasis.

"No," Jocelyn responded flatly.

"Boy-on-boy porn!"

That got Jocelyn's attention. She looked up from her monitor. "What the hell? Seriously? That's what he has been doing in that office for the past two months?"

"Yup."

"No! Wait ... you said 'boy.' Like, little boys? Or gay adult porn?"

"Both!"

"Eewww!"

Jocelyn stood up and snatched the hard drive from Jerry. She marched directly into Robert's office without knocking, the IT guy trailing behind.

"Robert, do you know what Jerry just found on Ahmed's computer?" she blurted out as Robert lazily looked up from his paperwork. "I'll just tell you. Gay porn, and some of it is pedophile stuff. What do you advise?"

Robert looked wearily at Jocelyn and Jerry. "Look, guys. This isn't a big deal. They have very different views about women in Egypt, and somehow it gets twisted around so that it's okay for guys to be holding hands with other guys as they walk down the street. Women, because of the religion, are perceived to be much too unclean to even be associated with. Women are pretty much on the level of cattle over there. Just forget about it."

Jerry and Jocelyn looked at each other in disbelief. *Just forget about it?* Both of them had been in parts of the world where women obviously did not have the same standing as men, but this "just forget about it" comment didn't make sense to them. A chunk of Manhattan just got blown up, and this hard drive might be a clue. Why couldn't Robert see that?

"But the kiddie-porn stuff, Robert ..." Jocelyn was

looking for some hint, an expression or body language indicating that he had at least heard her and processed the news. She got nothing from him. In fact, he appeared to be almost sleeping with his eyes wide open, if she didn't know better.

"Okay, let's forget about the porn stuff for a minute. Ahmed was in New Jersey last week, and as soon as he got back he was practically in tears because he needed to get home. What the heck? Don't you think that's odd?"

"Jocelyn. Jocelyn. Please. I know. But seriously, this is the last thing we need to be getting ourselves involved with right now. Just forget about it, okay?" And he turned his attention again to his paperwork, a clear signal that he was done with the conversation.

Jerry and Jocelyn shared a look of confused frustration and left Robert's office with the hard drive. They decided to go out to the parking lot so that they could talk more freely. Once there, they both jumped into Jerry's car, a souped-up black 1989 Dodge Omni that sported a "Ham Radio Operators Do It Better" bumper sticker and another proudly proclaiming how much he appreciated the Buffalo wings at Hooters.

"Dude, Carol in accounting told me that I shouldn't call the FBI. But Joss, I think Ahmed knew something was up. Why else was he freaking out when he got back from New Jersey?" He paused, searching her face. "I want to call them."

"I know. I heard the same thing from Adam directly this morning. He made an announcement basically saying that he knows the FBI is asking for tips, and that we should all disregard that." Jocelyn's brow was tightly furrowed. "He said that the FBI was already so inundated with phone calls that our calls would just jam up their phone lines when real important info might be coming in."

"Adam said that?"

"Yup. I thought that was weird."

"Screw it. I'm calling and telling them that I have this guy's hard drive. It could be a big clue. I mean, Ahmed was in New Jersey last week, Joss! All this porn stuff might be a code or something." Jocelyn thought about it as Jerry continued. "I mean, it's so repulsive to the average person, like who the heck wants to look at that? It would be a perfect cover for some sort of messaging system. All they'd have to do is utilize one little pixel out of the entire picture to relay a message."

So, sitting in the front seat of the Dodge Omni, they both decided to get out their cell phones and call the FBI to report what they knew about Ahmed. Later that day, they heard from about a dozen other people who, despite Adam's request not to do so, had called the FBI and reported Ahmed's bizarre panic about needing to get back to Egypt the week before.

Of course the FBI was, in fact, swamped with calls, and this was just one more tip to be presumably entered into a vast database of clues. Or at least that's what everyone who called in that day imagined was happening with their information about Ahmed. It wasn't until ten months later, when Sharon Parente, Adam's assistant, noticed that an acceptance letter from Egypt for a renewed contract was signed by Ahmed's father, that they had cause to wonder.

Sharon noticed that the man's title had changed. He was no longer third in command of the Egyptian fleet. Ahmed's father had been promoted and was fully in command of the entire Egyptian navy. And now, two months later, on a packed sidewalk in Virginia with a mile of hotel fire alarms screaming, Jocelyn found herself thinking things she did not want to think.

CHAPTER FIFTEEN

"FUNNY THIS SHOULD HAPPEN TODAY, on the one-year anniversary, don't ya think?"

Hearing that familiar light Texas twang broke Jocelyn out of her rumination regarding the events of the year before.

"Ken Palmer! What the heck are you doing here?" Jocelyn turned to shake his hand—but then, when Ken offered a hug, she took it. It was nice to see a friendly face in the middle of the blaring confusion of this avenue-long fire drill.

"Oh, I walked over from that hotel, about three buildings down," he said while pointing to the building. "I was in a meeting with the Southern Bell folks when the alarms went off. Looks like the whole street got the same treatment. Nice view of the Pentagon, though."

"I guess. You still working that ACCESS lead?" Jocelyn asked, knowing full well that he was because she was pretty much at the center of the division's marketing communications.

She had recently accompanied Ken to a couple of meetings regarding the ACCESS centers, and quite frankly, she didn't understand why Ken was so fixated on this project. In her nontechnical estimation, it was clearly an ill-defined project, seeing as it was marketed to both schools and the military. *What would public schools and the military have in common?* she would always be left wondering. And she still had no concept as to why Southern Bell, which had recently become BellSouth, would have to be involved—*something to do with renting space somewhere? How big a space? And exactly where? It could be the size of a closet for all I know ...* It all seemed so ill-defined. But there they were at every meeting, as she had noticed in Ken's reports.

Ken is really on a wild-goose chase with this one. Death of a Salesman– *type stuff.*

"Sure am," Ken said with a wide grin as he responded to her ACCESS center question. "I'm close to ropin' that pony."

The fire alarms had started to systematically shut off, which rendered the crowd on the sidewalk seemingly paralyzed. No one knew if they should go back into the buildings or remain outside as the late arriving military-style fire trucks began to converge en masse.

"My God. Better late than never," said a fully uniformed two-star army general who had wandered up to Jocelyn and Ken.

"General Briggs! Good to see you sir!" Ken shook the man's hand and introduced Jocelyn. The threesome stood by and made idle chitchat as they watched the firemen hustling about.

"Let's get out of here," the general said. "Nothing is going to get accomplished at these afternoon meetings. Care to join me?"

Ken gratefully accepted the invitation, but Jocelyn was worried about the meeting she had just left.

"Let me just check with Donna," Jocelyn said, pointing to the petite woman who looked as if she was about to morph into the Incredible Hulk.

Somewhat frightened by what she was approaching, Jocelyn held her logo-embossed legal-pad portfolio like a shield across her chest and asked, "Are you okay?"

"These goddamn shitheads!" And then, seemingly pulling herself together, Donna added, "Yeah. I'm okay. But the rest of the program isn't. Take an extended lunch break. The speakers I had lined up just went back across the street." She tossed a smirk to the Pentagon.

Jocelyn nodded and made her way back to Ken and General Briggs, who where both laughing a polite, fake kind of laugh.

"Yup. I can go," she interrupted.

"Great. A car will pick us up shortly, and there will be food when we get there," the general said.

It was a matter of minutes before a white utility van signaled the general, and they all got in. They were not alone. There were five other people already sitting on the benches inside the dark van.

Everyone exchanged business cards from their respective defense-related companies and "nice to meet yous." The fire-alarm topic could only go so far, seeing as there were no windows to look out of and everyone was forced to make eye contact. Ken, possessing a salesman's personality, kicked up the conversation when it got uncomfortably silent.

They were in the van for about twenty minutes, and as far as Jocelyn could tell, they were going in circles. But she couldn't be sure. Finally, the van pulled into a parking garage in the basement of a newer brick office building. General Briggs apparently was the master of ceremonies and assisted everyone out of the van. He led them to an elevator that didn't work, and everyone ended up following him up the stairs to an office suite on the third floor.

The wayward travelers were greeted by a young woman who thanked them for coming and asked that people help themselves to the wrap sandwiches and cans of Coke arranged on a table in the reception area. A moment of insincere reluctance ensued, followed by a full on feeding frenzy. Once the lunch had been effectively devoured, the group headed into a small, dimly lit conference room. An oblong table with no chairs took up most of the room. Everyone filed in and, unsure of where to go, stood against the wall or leaned/ half-sat against the conference table.

The presenter introduced himself and the company,

and Jocelyn immediately concluded that this man was not a sales professional—he was a bandit. A Beltway bandit. A programmer who had gotten a tax number in Delaware because of an RFP that he had seen floating around the DC area. He certainly was not military, and he was not associated with any of the "big six" defense contractors. But he would gladly subcontract or sell his company to any of them.

Two young men who were obviously uncomfortable in their suits were introduced, and the lights were completely dimmed as a poorly designed (in Jocelyn's opinion) logo appeared on the large pull-down screen at the end of the room. Music that Jocelyn recognized as stock production music, most likely titled something like "The Heroic Struggle," started up as a video of various natural and manmade disasters began looping faster and faster. When the disaster montage reached epileptic-seizure-inducing levels, various currency symbols started whipping around. Finally the cinematic ambrosia resolved itself by revealing the original poorly designed logo centered atop the Times New Roman bold text: **Project LISA**.

With the overly dramatic music having ceased, leaving a vast expanse of silence in its place, the standing audience busied itself by looking at their shoes, plucking lint off their jackets, or sipping on their Diet Cokes while the men adjusted the computer connection. The hostess took this opportunity to roll in chairs for everyone and distribute nondisclosure agreements that, once signed (though that part was unspoken), allowed an attendee to receive a chair at the table.

Eventually, the desktop of the computer the men were fussing with appeared on the projection screen. This was everyone's first look at the user interface for this curious Project LISA. It was unclear to Jocelyn what LISA actually did. She also wondered if LISA was a military acronym or if it was just the name of the woman who was acting as hostess who coincidently or not was also named Lisa.

The major thrust of Project LISA, as far as Jocelyn

could surmise, was to monitor bank transactions. The presenter explained that organizations, much like people, do the same things the same way every day.

"You get up with your alarm, eat breakfast, take a shower, get dressed. You put your socks on, right foot then left, the same way every day. Money moves like that too. The same sequence of events happens every day at the same time as money literally moves around the world. When a bank's transaction cycles are even a minute off the regular schedule, LISA sees it and backtracks to see what other accounts could have affected the holdup."

The presenter took a sip of his Diet Coke and glanced at the logo on the screen before he continued. "This time anomaly becomes a specific point of reference for LISA, and all communications of all shareholders around this vector are assessed. Less than even a minute with access to several million dollars and the power of a well-placed Wall Street trade can be a long time for a terrorist."

That's kind of interesting.

Not really understanding how she even ended up at this meeting (she thought she was just going out to lunch), Jocelyn straightened her embossed leather legal pad from the pre-fire-alarm meeting. Again it was acting as some sort of shield. The logo signified that she belonged here. Her company was vastly larger than the presenter's. And Jocelyn realized that if she had been a man, this metaphor would have taken on more a personal attribute.

While Jocelyn inwardly grinned about her revelation regarding the power of corporate logos, the presenter explained that the military had documented response plans in place for countless numbers of natural and manmade disasters. Each of these plans had a major accounting aspect to it. Jocelyn knew this part quite well, as this was what Catastrophe! was essentially all about.

However, she must have missed the leap from the "terrorist Wall Street trade" to this military accounting function while she was getting out her logo shield and a Pilot Precise V5 pen. Although she knew both concerns this guy was talking about were legitimate responses to government RFPs, she didn't see how they were related or could be included in the same product. But she figured she might as well take notes and enjoy the show. She was standing in for Robert after all, and Ken wanted her to come to this so it was probably important.

At this point, the screen was populated with roughly twenty square icons representing everything from tornadoes to military tanks to biohazards to mushroom clouds to ...

"What's that one all about?" Jocelyn asked with hand raised.

"I'm sorry, which one?" the presenter responded.

"This one," Jocelyn said as she walked up to the screen to point it out. "It looks like a UFO." Jocelyn's smile quickly faded as she noticed that everyone in the tight conference room was looking at her as if she didn't belong there.

"It is a UFO."

"Oh."

If she thought she had entered Bizarro World earlier at the Sheraton, this just kicked it up a couple of notches. She suddenly felt embarrassed for asking the question. *Oh, okay. So like now, I'm the freak. Sure, why not?* she mentally grumbled as she headed back to her seat while attempting to look as professional as possible.

General Briggs stepped in to clarify the issue. "The Pentagon has to have plans in place for things that, even if highly unlikely, might affect the population. We have teams of people whose sole purpose is to cook up and work through the most exotic of disasters so that we might prepare an effective response. For instance, it is highly unlikely that a nuclear bomb would ever be dropped on US soil. But in the off chance word came in that something like this was about to happen, the Pentagon has preapproved sets of plans at the ready that can be unsealed and followed for an optimal outcome."

"Of course. Makes sense," Jocelyn commented.

Ken's Texas twang piped up and broke the tension, "I for one am glad that I don't have to worry about UFOs. They do!"

A round of polite snickers followed, and the presentation continued without so much as a peep let alone another question. That is, until the very conclusion when someone asked about the legal issues surrounding the tracking of financial transactions and the assessment of the related telephone and e-mail communications.

In Jocelyn's opinion, the answer was complete fluff. She couldn't see how Project LISA would be able to get around what she perceived as warrantless wiretapping and Constitutional rights violations. But the rest of the group seemed to accept what the presenter was saying and eagerly shook his hand as they exited the office suite.

CHAPTER SIXTEEN

WHEN JOCELYN RETURNED TO THE office, she carried with her a renewed sense of patriotism and purpose. The fire alarm had successfully picked away at some deep-seated scab, revealing raw determination for personal and national survival. That morning, as she entered the reception area, she felt a real sense of pride to be working for the Conglomerate. Of course, Mimi was there to welcome her, and Jocelyn wasn't really surprised that Mimi had already heard about the fire alarm.

"Oh, honey!" Mimi ran out from behind her circular reception desk and hugged her. "Ken called in and told me all about it! How scary!" She paused and dramatically held Jocelyn by the shoulders with both hands. "So he found you, and the two of you were together while all this was going on?"

Jocelyn nodded and politely wiggled out of Mimi's concerned clutches. Mimi then went on for at least the next five minutes re- calling her memories from the previous year's disaster. As Mimi was spiraling back toward her chair, Jocelyn thought to ask, "Hey Mimi, remember that kid Ahmed from Egypt? Did we ever find out what happened to him?"

"You know, honey, it's the strangest thing," Mimi said, smoothing her silky lavender blouse and adjusting her floral scarf as she perched herself behind the reception desk. "It's like he just disappeared. No one seems to know how to find him. I sent him a card for his birthday ..."

"You did?"

"Well, sure," Mimi answered as if she was surprised

that Jocelyn was surprised. "Adam has been friends with his father for a long time now, and Egypt is one of our best customers ..." She pushed the Rolodex just a smidge. "But the card got sent back to me with no forwarding address."

The phone rang, and Mimi placed her meticulously maintained manicured hand on the receiver while looking at Jocelyn. "Oh, honey, that reminds me. Stan will be here today, and he wants to see you."

Jocelyn gave the thumbs-up and heard the rote greeting being recited behind her as she made her way back to her utility-closet-cum-poppy-field, prepared to bury herself in the paperwork associated with government contracting. She was ready for it.

But not so ready for Stan. Jocelyn braced herself for the eventual arrival of her congressman. She really did not care to see him and only dealt with him when absolutely necessary. The busy proposal season was just about to smack her in the head. And if it hadn't been for the fact that Stan was responsible for most of the leads that came rolling in lately, she probably would have slapped him across the face a long time ago.

The majority of her government-contacting-proposal work these days corresponded to the funding promised by the United States Agency for International Development, otherwise known as USAID. The popularized condensed name was still easily confused by Jocelyn with some sort of benevolent, feel-good charity like FarmAid.

USAID and International Monetary Fund (IMF) monies were very intertwined in the proposals she was crafting. She knew that she just had to grin and bear the seasonal workload. Money was falling from the sky at this time of year, and all the government contractors scrambled to catch it.

It was in Jocelyn's best interest to get to know this international funding cycle as well as the domestic funding cycle. She had taken it upon herself to monitor the request for proposals (RFP) and request for quote (RFQ) lists being issued. She had also recognized with mild interest while scouring the award histories that there seemed to be some sort of relation to the US election cycle. But she wasn't concerned about that. The sheer volume of paperwork was more concerning.

"Jaaaaaaaaaahh-cel-lyn! Are you home?" Stan Garfunkel, the congressman, hollered before he knocked on her open office door. This five-foot-eight, mustached suit was Adam's long time drinking buddy, a lecherous career politician who routinely swung by the facility and made it a point to sit down unannounced in Jocelyn's crammed office, mispronounce her name, and shamelessly flirt with her. Naturally, Jocelyn was not encouraging this behavior, but what the heck could she do but laugh and say things like, "Oh, Stan! What would your wife say?" He might have been a real lady-killer somewhere during the era of Sharon's Dress Barn outfits, but right now he seemed like he was just trying too hard. And Jocelyn found it almost funny. Almost.

The money is what kept Stan relevant for Jocelyn. He was an important (as in critical) part of having an "in" to federal funding. If there was an opportunity for some federal contracting money to show up in his state, Stan would make sure Adam and his company were on the short list. Stan would always take time to personally let Jocelyn know that Congress was "in talks" and that perhaps it might be time to introduce one of the division's products to his colleagues.

And naturally, Stan was always available for the photo op, helping Adam and some lackey who had no clue as to why he had been pulled from the floor of the warehouse hold up the king-sized, sweepstakes-style check made out to the company for the amount of the winning contract. So, like the busy proposal season, dealing with Stan was one of those grin-and-bear it things.

"Why yes, Stan. Yes, I'm home," she said from her wheeled office chair, her back facing the door. "Did you bring me that document for the Malaysia proposal?" She swiveled around to greet him and crossed her legs. "I have the proposal done, but I guess I'm missing something."

"Oh, you're not missing a thing, sweetheart," he said, obviously ogling her "nude" legs poking out from under her standard office uniform of an Anne Taylor gray skirt. Stan was proudly smoothing his well-maintained dark mustache with his thumb and forefinger as he appreciated the full range of her feminine attributes.

What a creep.

Stan was one of those men who would die with a head full of dark hair. He was not fat but not very fit either. His suit and shoes, although moderately expensive, looked almost shabby on his sixty-seven-year-old frame.

"Oh, Stan. Please. Seriously. Please stop," she nearly begged. "I need to know about this piece of paper. Robert sent me an e-mail about it and said to ask you. It has to do with the Malaysian navy. He said that it has the president or prime minister's signature on it. But don't they have a king there?" She slid the RFP toward her and arbitrarily flipped through the pages so she wouldn't have to make eye contact with him. "I'm pretty sure I saw a king referenced in the RFP. Anyhow, I need to know where this paper is."

"Ah, yes. Malaysia. Didn't I give that to you already? Oh wait. Maybe I didn't ..."

"No, Stan. You didn't give me anything the last time I saw you, except for a kiss on the hand."

"Which I shall never forget."

Jocelyn rolled her eyes.

"Well, since you've asked so nicely, and I love it when you pout ..."

Jocelyn would have bitten back an expletive had she not been fully aware of how Felliniesque the whole scene was—her congressman appearing amongst the trash-scrap REDRUM collage, slinging inappropriate innuendoes.

Jocelyn held up the finished proposal and calmly said,

"Malaysia, Stan. We're talking about Malaysia."

Stan grinned and, glancing at the bits of red paper curling off the wall, said, "You know, red is the color of sex."

"You've told me that before, Stan. It's also the color of power and vitality. Plus I like it. Now what's the deal with Malaysia?"

Stan seemed to appreciate her response. He chuckled a little.

"Well, Malaysia has a prime minister. And they have nine sultans who elect a supreme king for a five-year term. The supreme king of Malaysia usually trumps everyone because he can constitutionally disband Parliament if he wants."

"Wow. I've never heard of anything like that," Jocelyn said, enjoying the fact that she was learning something new and had diverted Stan's harassment. "Interesting. But what about this prime minister, Stan?" Jocelyn asked, trying to redirect him to the matter at hand.

Stan, meanwhile, made himself comfortable by uncomfortably seating himself on the corner of her little filing cabinet.

"Oh, the prime minister. Yes. I have, or at least had, the document that the prime minister signed. That's the document you originally needed."

"Great! Can you—" Jocelyn interjected, but Stan quickly cut her off.

"Now hold on there." Stan stood up. Apparently sitting with half a butt cheek on the edge of a filing cabinet wasn't as comfortable as he thought it would be. He positioned himself, arms crossed, against the doorjamb. "Recently it has gotten very, oh how shall we say it, *political* with Malaysia trading with foreign countries, specifically Israel. Obviously, we are American, so this technically shouldn't be an issue for your proposal. But what has to happen is that the king has to have his signature on a statement very similar to the one that the prime minister signed. And I've called over there and gotten them to FedEx a document to you."

"Oh, that's great. Thanks," Jocelyn said, not really thinking about how her congressman would have had access to the phone number of a foreign king. It was par for the course with Stan. It wasn't unusual for him to ask her to put together a marketing pack of brochures regarding the Conglomerate's latest products and include them in a letter from him on his personal stationery to someone like her majesty Queen Noor of Jordan.

Stan would explain to Jocelyn that the package was "just a favor", nothing that needed to get documented, and it might help the queen's son out. Jocelyn would have no idea what Stan was talking about, but so long as he kept feeding her the leads from Congress and she didn't have to rearrange her schedule too much, what did she care? Stuff like that happened every so often with Stan, so Jocelyn wasn't really fazed.

"Stan, let's go talk to Robert about these letters. I'm not getting very far with this, and it's due in less than a week. Which means it needs to be in the mail like tomorrow if I'm going to be able to ship this thing without taking out an equity line of credit to pay for it getting there on time."

"Fantastic idea."

Jocelyn grabbed her yellow legal pad and, armed with the file about Malaysia, headed with Stan to Robert's office.

CHAPTER SEVENTEEN

"DID YOU GLEAN ANYTHING FROM Project LISA?" Stan asked as they strode purposefully down the hall to Robert's office.

"Jeez, Stan! How do *you* know about that?"

"Well, you went to it, didn't you?" He glanced over at her. "I let General Briggs know that you were there. His nephew is supposed to be a real computer whiz."

His nephew? Is that who we were meeting with?

"Um, yeah. Ken was with me too, otherwise I would have never crawled into an unmarked utility van like it was cool." Jocelyn's mind was chugging out a bunch of questions for Stan, unsure which one she should ask first, when Stan started in.

"Adam and I have been batting around your Princeton report from a few years ago, and I knew that Briggs was working that LISA thing ..."

"Princeton?" she blurted. "Oh, okay. The New York Stock Exchange thing I ended up at a while ago. Yeah ..." She could see the connection to LISA now.

With the both of them still walking and smiling past the hallway office windows, Stan said, "Right. And Adam wanted to know how Catastrophe! compared with LISA, and he figured you'd be the best face for the job."

Fantastic. It would have been nice to know this before I headed down to DC. Does Robert get this information and not give it to me?

Picking a random starting point, she said, "Well, we don't have a UFO icon."

"Oh, that's probably a good thing to have," Stan said, nodding, as they rounded the corner.

"And unlike us, they are into tracking banking and financial movements. They claim that they can backtrack financial transactions that appear anomalous and use that financial event to start tracking other banks that might be connected. Ultimately, they track related communications, such as e-mails and phone calls."

Stan stopped so Jocelyn stopped. "Ah, Southern Bell," he inexplicably said.

Resisting the urge to correct him and say, "BellSouth," she faced him and continued, "They seemingly have all the same accounting features as Catastrophe!, but we give more attention to streamlining emergency public relations during the event. They don't have any of that. They do have a better user interface, though. Much better."

"Jocelyn, if it wasn't for these office windows, I would kiss you on the lips. That's my girl!" He patted her shoulder heartily, flashed a smile at the occupant of the nearest office, and started walking again.

"But why, Stan? I didn't do anything. They are marketing vaporware. I don't think they can really deliver on what they were talking about, technically or legally."

"That doesn't matter, Jocelyn! Come on, girl, you should know that by now." Jocelyn thought about what Stan had just said and concluded that he was right.

When they arrived at Robert's empty office, Jocelyn walked in, picked up the phone, and called Mimi. She would know if Robert was still in the building, if he was in a meeting, or if he had left to go get a colonoscopy. Mimi somehow knew everyone's whereabouts and was, of course, more than happy to share the information.

"Oh, he's just passing by the front desk. I'll send him back."

Jocelyn and Stan made themselves comfortable, knowing that Robert would be there momentarily. Not wanting to get too comfortable, though, Jocelyn stood by the door and studied Robert's modest collection of books featured behind his Staples-quality desk in a matching bookcase. The books were mostly general pop management how-tos and college statistics and marketing textbooks interspersed with a smattering of travel guides. Also sandwiched in, so seemingly haphazardly that she noticed them, were a tiny book entitled *Numismatics for Beginners*, a leather-bound edition of *The Aeneid* by Virgil, and a Robert Mapplethorpe coffee-table book.

"Oh, he should display that photography book so people can see it," Jocelyn said, attempting to break the awkwardness of hanging out in her boss's office with her congressman.

"What's that?" Stan said, swiveling around in Robert's supple, saddle-brown executive desk chair to see what she was looking at. It took a moment for it to register. "Oh. Mapplethorpe?" Then seeming genuinely surprised, he said, "You know about Robert and all that?" She quietly nodded. She was now really regretting bringing his attention to an artist like Mapplethorpe, because some of his photographs were explicit to the point of pornographic. She braced herself for his comments, but Stan uncharacteristically sighed and shook his head as if saying, *Such a shame*.

At first she was surprised that Stan even knew who Robert Mapplethorpe was. But then she remembered the national debate about censorship and funding of the arts because of a Mapplethorpe exhibit back when she was in art school. *Of course Stan would have had a sound bite ready for that.*

She smiled and quickly let her line of vision skate away from Stan across the twelve-by-fifteen-foot otherwise non-noteworthy beige office to the window that was framed by an out-of-place credenza and a fake plant. Sure, Robert's office was larger than hers, but whose wasn't? It was all about the window anyway.

Jocelyn had concluded a while ago that windows were status symbols dangling like carrots on a string at this place. If you had one, that meant you were higher on the totem pole than someone who didn't. But if you had an office, even if it didn't have a window, you were higher up than someone in a cube. Windows were there to remind you that all you had to do was work harder and maybe, someday, you'd be afforded the luxury of seeing the outside world.

Gee. I wonder how utility closets fit into this grand scheme?

Robert returned to his office to find Jocelyn leaning against the doorjamb staring at nothing in particular and Stan sitting at his desk.

"Hello, Stan. You look mighty important sitting there," Robert said as he shook the congressman's hand.

"I always look important, Robert. Listen, the lovely Jocelyn tells me that she still hasn't gotten the document from the Malaysian Royal Office and that the proposal has to be in the mail tomorrow to hit the deadline. Did the letter end up in your office?"

"I have this one with the king's signature on it," Robert said as he riffled through the bulging inbox on his desk. "I have no idea what it says, though."

"Robert! Why didn't you give it to me?" Jocelyn almost whined.

"Because, Jocelyn, it has nothing to do with this proposal. It's from years ago when we proposed a different type of simulator. Look at the date."

Sure enough, the letter was a relic from a previous attempt to conduct business with Malaysia. She instinctively flipped open the Malaysia file she was holding and said, "Whoa! Robert, is this the letter that you told me I needed? How'd this get in here?"

The two men craned their necks to look at the letter from the prime minister that she was holding. She put the file on Robert's desk so that they could both see it.

"Yeah, well, uh, you were gone, and I just put it where it belonged to save you the trouble."

Oddly, she felt a bit violated by Robert's helpful assistance. He must have gone and looked through the files on her desk while she was out dealing with fire drills and sales pitches. Not that any of that really mattered—she had nothing to hide. They were all work files. But still, she didn't go rummaging through the stuff on his desk. Plus, why was he acting like this? He seemed like he was lying. But she couldn't imagine why. She was starting to suspect that he was somehow messing with her. *Is he fooling with me? Trying to trip me up?* But she reminded herself that it made no sense. He was probably the one who was going to get the commission on this. He wouldn't jam her up. Not with personal income on the line.

"Ah! Yes!" Stan helpfully interjected. "We basically need this letter from the prime minister but signed by the king." Robert nodded like he knew it all along, and Jocelyn resigned herself to that whole "just let it go" thing that she had been talking through with her counselor.

"I'll call and harass them again to fax something," Stan said.

"This has been going on for about four years. I cannot have this just drop like this," lamented Robert. "This is part of the acquisition agreement."

Stan turned his back on Robert as he left, saying, "Good luck, guys. I know Jocelyn will think of something creative." He punctuated the comment with an even creepier-than-usual depraved smile and a disturbing wink.

Jocelyn just let it roll off her. *Typical Stan.* Robert looked at her somewhat suspiciously as she leaned over his desk and began flipping through the notes in her Malaysia file.

As soon as Stan was down the hall, Robert shot behind his desk, snapped on his computer's monitor, grabbed the mouse, and started clicking around. "What did you see?" he asked, not looking at her.

"Huh?" Jocelyn responded, not sure why her boss appeared to be breaking into a sweat. "You mean LISA?"

Robert blinked at her. And then without warning, he lunged, grabbed her by the arms, and angrily shook her as he literally spat, "What!? Where did you ... who gave you that name? Stan?"

Although adrenaline began pumping, her mind hadn't caught up. Robert was clutching her uncomfortably, and she didn't know what the hell was going on.

"LISA," she blurted, too stunned to try to wiggle away or do any of that womanly self-defense stuff that she had seen on TV. "LISA. That's the name of the computer program Ken Palmer and I saw demo-ed yesterday." He released his grip and flopped into his executive chair looking as if he was going to faint or vomit. Her heart was pounding so ridiculously fast that it was hard to catch her breath.

"What the hell, Robert?" she nearly screamed. When he made no answer, she rubbed her neck and asked, just because she knew he wasn't, "Are you okay?"

He blinked himself back to the here and now, wiped his brow, and said, "Yeah. I'm okay. I'm just ... I'm just exhausted."

Or really frickin' high, asshole!

She wanted to run out of there. She had suspected that Robert was maybe stoned enough times to have this little episode settle it for her. She eased herself over to the doorway as he reached over and slid the file that Jocelyn had been looking at across the desk. She watched as an amazing transformation occurred right before her eyes. He was now completely composed.

"Jocelyn," he said, his voice sickeningly saccharine as he flipped the page, "do you think you could sign like the king? Put it right there next to the prime minister's signature?" He pointed to the spot on the document, his gold Rolex winking at her in the fluorescent light. "I honestly don't have an artistic bone in my body, and you seem like you're pretty good at drawing." Robert produced a notebook out of his top desk drawer. Apparently he had already been practicing.

Recovering her breath and her wits, she replied, "What? You're kidding, right?" She was taken aback by the suggestion. "I don't think that's really the best use of my artistic talents." She nudged a little closer to the exit.

Sensing that they both definitely needed some alone time after that forgery request, she turned abruptly to leave. It was easier to just pretend that all of this never happened. A little trick she had picked up, she wasn't even sure when. *This never happened* rolled around and around, under and over, in her head, and it caused the adrenaline that had been coursing through her veins to level out and reset her to default settings. "I'll do up a report about the director's conference and Project LISA for you." Calling back over her shoulder, she added, "Remember, we have that division-wide meeting later today. I'll put Malaysia on hold until that new letter comes in."

He nodded but watched her closely as she headed into the hall- way. "Will you shut my door on your way out, please?"

She spun back around and grabbed the knob. "Sure thing, Robert," she said, shutting the door.

As soon as she hit the hallway, the beige carpet turned into a moving sidewalk. She became somehow acutely aware that she didn't feel her legs or feet anymore, and her head moved slowly, almost as if floating, back to her red immersion chamber, the utility closet. She wondered as she coasted along if she should report Robert to anyone. Human resources? *Yeah, right! Like she's gonna do anything.* He hadn't really hurt her, just freaked her out. *Whatever. Dude's a jackass. He's addicted to something.*

The redundant rectangles scrolled past, and she mentally ran through a bunch of stuff that she had gleaned from her Al-Anon experiences. She decided to just make a note of what Robert had done, as if that might make all the difference in the world if he did it again and she had to take him to court or something.

Her attention was diverted and the conveyer belt stopped when she noticed the fruit flies buzzing around her closed office door. Luckily, Jocelyn could hear her phone ringing from the hallway, and she quickly wedged herself into her office to pick it up, narrowly avoiding having to engage with one of the *drosophila melanogaster* salesmen.

"Jocelyn," Mimi's familiar voice reverberated, "it's your lucky day! You have two calls. Your husband, oh sorry, ex-husband, and Adam. Want me to put the ex into voice mail? Adam's calling from Singapore."

"Oh ... okay." She wasn't really prepared to deal with the irony of Bobby calling her right now and was thankful for the escape hatch of voice mail. "That sounds like a good plan. Send Adam through. Thanks, Mimi."

"Oh, and by the way," said Mimi, who as per usual felt the need to extend this *while I've got you on the line* moment, "I asked Robert before I sent him back to his office about our Egyptian friend, Ahmed. He said he didn't know anything."

"That's great, Mimi. Thanks. I'll take Adam now."

CHAPTER EIGHTEEN

JOCELYN COULD TELL THE CALL was coming in from Adam's satellite phone. It had a distinct type of background noise that she recognized.

"Good work, Jocelyn. The latest round of negotiation paperwork got to Indonesia on time, and everyone has copies. They look great. Thank you for putting that together for me on such short notice."

"No problem," was all she could think to say. *No problem? Where did that come from?* She wished she had said something a bit more snappy or witty in reply. This Indonesia thing would be practically a running joke at this point if it wasn't so frustrating.

Sure, things had gotten a lot easier now that she wasn't cutting and pasting and reformatting Lotus Notes and trying to merge it with the product of three other word-processing programs, one of which was some sort of custom typing tool developed by the engineering department a million years ago, which of course they were the only ones who had felt the need to use it. This was one good thing about being part of the Conglomerate now. No more fighting with random software. The whole place had to switch to Microsoft Word and Excel. And it did make a huge difference.

Adam continued, "You're batting a thousand here, Jocelyn."

"Oh, thanks." She sat down and glanced at her Daily Planner wall calendar with its days marked off like prison time. "That's good to know," she said. She grabbed a pen and sliced through the past few days on the calendar. This brought her up to date.

"Did you get to see LISA?"

"Yup. I did. I just told Stan all about it, and I'm writing up a report for Robert. I'll send it over to you too."

"Oh, don't busy yourself with that. Low priority. How's Malaysia working out?" he asked.

"Funny you should ask. I have everything done. But apparently I need the supreme king's signature on some document that Stan is calling around for. It doesn't look like it will be here in time."

"Really? Okay, we have dealt with Malaysia in the past. Is there something that says just about the same thing in the marketing files that you can use?"

Jocelyn immediately knew where this was going, and obviously she didn't like it.

"Yeah. Robert just showed me something from a few years ago ..."

"Perfect! Use that. Honestly, they don't read anything. They are much more impressed by volume. They like lots of paper. That's why Indo is so great!" Adam gave a little cough and continued before Jocelyn could say anything about her growing concerns about the Indonesia proposal—namely, that what they were currently proposing was now a seven-year-old computer system. "I was thinking, Jocelyn, you really need a bigger office. I can't believe that Robert still has you in that coat closet. I'm sure it's only temporary. Especially with the layoffs that corporate has coming up. Look, I've got to get going. This is getting expensive. Keep up the good work!" And with that, Adam hung up.

Layoffs? Jocelyn huffed as she smashed down the receiver. This, of course, caught the attention of not one but two of the *drosophila melanogaster* who were buzzing around outside her office door. She glared at the two of them and then shot a glance at the flashing red light of her voice mail that was now poking her in the eye and decided to ignore it. At least for now. She was really starting to have a deeper understanding as to why Nancy in the publications office had been so sick and miserable all the time before her unexpected demise.

Jocelyn thought it might be helpful if Robert and Adam were both on the same page about Malaysia. So she wrote up an e-mail to Robert and cc'd Adam, even though she knew Adam didn't actually read e-mail. Sharon still read his e-mails and printed them out for him. Seeing as Adam was in Singapore, he probably would never even see the e-mail. But Jocelyn thought that it added a nice bit of legitimacy to the whole thing.

Robert—Adam just called from Sing to tell me that it was OK to use your letter from the King. Haha that rhymes!—J.

Just as she pressed send, Jocelyn thought maybe she should let Stan the congressman know too. He seemed pretty heavily invested in this project for some reason. So she forwarded the e-mail to him.

Sweet. Just a photocopy. Malaysia is off my list. Feeling as if she had just taken the reins back from a runaway pony, she checked off one of the hand-drawn boxes on her yellow legal pad.

Within moments, Robert bumbled into her office, jacket off and necktie loosened. Sweat rings were becoming apparent under his arms.

"No. We can't use that letter. It's about something else. I just told you that!"

The hairs on the back of her neck bristled. "I thought you'd be relieved. Didn't you just tell Stan that you didn't know what the letter said?" She honestly felt like she was dealing with Bobby, sans the boozy smell.

"I can't read that letter, Jocelyn," he whined, gesturing emphatically toward his office. "But I do know that we had proposed a different type of simulation system, a truck simulator, five years ago, and I know that we would look like complete assholes if we used it."

"Oh." She sighed, looking down at the check box she had just checked. "Well, Adam thinks I'm going to be making a copy of that letter and including it in the proposal. If the proposal is going to compete, it has to get out of here very soon, Robert."

"Look, the king's signature has to be on that letter from the prime minister," he said almost frantically. "I don't know how else to tell you that. Why do you keep listening to Adam? Who do you work for, Jocelyn?"

She threw her pen down on the desk and crossed her arms across her chest. "Jeez, Robert, Adam asked me that exact same question once. Between corporate and Adam and all the other salesmen at all of the new subdivisions, and these darn generals marching around all over the place, I guess I'm unsure. Who do I work for, Robert?"

In some sort of body-language-mirror death match, Robert crossed his arms across his chest too. "You won't be working for *anyone*, Jocelyn, if we don't get that Malaysia deal. Delivering on that Malaysia job is part of Adam's purchase and sales agreement with the Conglomerate. So is Indonesia. That's why Adam is there right now, in person, working his magic to get that thing done."

She was appreciative of this background information but was still confused. "But didn't the Conglomerate sell us? I mean, of course to one of their own divisions, but ..."

"It's complicated, Jocelyn!"

"I see. So what happens if we don't get those jobs?"

"I don't even want to think about that," he said, arms still crossed.

"No really. What happens?" probed Jocelyn. She wasn't going to be the first to put her arms down.

"Well ..." Robert was silent for a long moment. "If neither of them goes through, the Conglomerate drops us because we didn't hit the milestones we had made as part of the original purchase and sale agreement. Our operation here in Connecticut would officially be insolvent. No one would get their retirement, because Adam opted to use the old pension-fund money to sweeten his deal and had that money invested in Conglomerate stock options. So if they drop us because we didn't perform on our promised deliveries, almost four decades of everyone's life will have pretty much been flushed down the toilet."

They both stared at each other for a while as Jocelyn tried to figure out if what he had just said was even legal. Finally, Robert ran his hand through his hair and found his pockets. Jocelyn asked, "So ... uhhh ... you're saying it all comes down to this king's signature?"

"Pretty much. I don't know what Stan has been up to over there, but I believe him when he says that they want our product. That king's signature is the only thing standing in the way of getting our proposal looked at. Just looked at, Jocelyn. We can't be left out of the bidding process. Not now, for fuck's sake."

"Wow. This sucks," she said, scratching her chin.

"Yup. It does."

More silence.

"Let's get some coffee," Robert suggested.

Typically, Jocelyn would have said okay even though she had already been in the break room exceeding recommended daily allowances for caffeine and sugar. But seeing as Robert had officially creeped her out and had just thrown a giant backpack full of lugubrious redirected culpability for everyone losing their nest eggs upon her shoulders, she didn't quite feel like it.

"C'mon. Let's at least get something before the meeting." Robert said.

So Jocelyn grabbed her yellow legal pad, and the two of them headed solemnly to the break room. That backpack on her shoulders was going to get heavier.

CHAPTER NINETEEN

"THE MEETING IS STARTING IN the big conference room," Martin Mays announced as he topped off his coffee for the upcoming event.

Jocelyn, Robert, and a few others drearily followed Martin to the conference room, which was awash with concerned-looking faces and a hushed troubled murmur. The near-powerless director of human resources, Elaine Gibson, was accompanied by Janice, the vice president of operations. It was clearly an important meeting, but seeing as everyone in the room appreciated that Janice was VP by default and that Elaine was simply someone who relayed messages from corporate, everyone knew that what they were about to hear was coming from on high and not from Adam, which would have normally been the case preacquisition.

The HR director, considered "a real looker" back in the decades before she was dealing with her decrepit mother's ongoing end- of-life issues, was about to take the podium and start the meeting. Jocelyn tried to imagine Elaine as forty pounds lighter with long black "don't hate me because I'm beautiful" hair, but she just didn't see it. Elaine looked miserably around the room, cleared her throat, and apparently being too choked up, decided to acquiesce her position of speaker to Janice.

The room collectively became more anxious as Janice took over and, as carefully and gently as her emotional-intelligence quotient was capable of, let the employees in attendance know that the company that had been in existence for about forty years—longer than Jocelyn had been alive—

would be dismantled over the next eighteen months.

The room sat in silence. Eventually Martin Mays, who had never held Janice in very high esteem, spoke up. "I've noticed that historically, when corporate decides to do this, they take the useful employees and place them on a related project at another division. Is that going to be the case for us?"

"I have no information at this time."

"Okay," Martin continued, "so am I to understand that this meeting today is just basically a warning? Or should we all go and start looking for another job this week?" he asked, clearly agitated.

"Well, that might not be the best course of action, but of course now that you know, you can make your own decisions."

"Well," Martin shot back, mocking Janice's tone, "what would be more helpful in making my decision would be to know what the deal is going to be with our stock." Martin could regularly be found reading the *Wall Street Journal* as he sat in proximity to the corkboard in the break room that boldly announced the ticker symbol and stock price of the Conglomerate. Stocks were commonly offered instead of pay increases, and most, if not all, of Jocelyn's division was heavily invested in the Conglomerate.

"Your stock should still be your stock."

"Oh, 'should,' that's comforting. No. I mean, now that the corporate board has approved a new series of stock that apparently only the principals of the company are allowed to invest in."

The room couldn't look more like the audience at Wimbledon as Martin lobbed question after question regarding his well-researched concerns about his, and his longtime associates', financial security.

Attempting to insert something of value, Elaine began handing out professionally printed booklets about applying for state unemployment and COBRA health insurance.

Jocelyn estimated that the booklets must have cost at least eight dollars each for everyone in attendance, with all the color photos of the concerned and smiling people pointing to computers at the unemployment office. But the Conglomerate had probably printed the booklet in mass quantities, making it more affordable.

It was, of course, the Conglomerate, and that's what it did. It gobbled up little productive companies started up by that rare breed of entrepreneur who hired locally and powered the local community's economy. And then the Conglomerate transferred that creativity, potential energy, and profit or loss onto ledger sheets that affected the Conglomerate's ultimate concern: its stock price. When that was achieved, the Conglomerate was on to another willing victim while the government took care of the fallout. So it made sense that they had boxes of these unemployment booklets printed up and sitting at the ready.

The Conglomerate didn't build anything other than an IRS-approved accounting framework for a ticker symbol. The Conglomerate didn't produce anything; the divisions did. That's why corporate headquarters was so small. Headquarters didn't do much but stay on top of the IRS's ever-evolving corporate tax shelters and deal with the cosmetic imagery necessary to keep its creation relevant in the media and thereby on the trading-room floor. It corralled little productive companies into something that could loosely be called, for the unwashed, uneducated worker, a communal profit-sharing scheme. The principals of the Conglomerate enjoyed the benefits that only a living, breathing person who was intimately familiar with the particulars and peculiarities of Wall Street stock splits and corporate income-tax laws would be able to appreciate.

At least, that's how Jocelyn had understood what Martin explained to her back when it was apparent they were going through with the acquisition. Not that he explained it in those terms. Or that she even understood it. That's just how she imagined it. And she figured Adam wouldn't have sold the company unless it seemed like a decent deal.

"What the hell is this?!" Martin exploded, waving his *Understanding Unemployment* booklet. "Why are we getting this now? So we *are* officially all laid off. Is that what this means?"

Janice tried to maintain an aura of authority, but no one was listening to her. Robert took the opportunity to step in and assert his tenuous, and by most counts debatable, leadership position. He straightened his necktie, but the sweat rings under his arms were clearly visible and were completely distracting, considering his choice of diamond-studded cuff links.

"Listen. Everyone. Please," Robert began. "We all knew when Adam sold the company that things would be changing around here. It was just a matter of time. You should all know that we have produced and supplied our end of the bargain, and we will be rewarded accordingly. We should all be very, very proud of what this company has achieved and what we will continue to do in the future. We have eighteen months of work to finish. The contracts that have been signed have to be executed, and those will most likely be handed off to another division. The other division will probably want someone familiar with the client and product to stay on the project. We have so much going on here that I am sure there is going to be a place for just about everyone once the hard work of placing products"—he nodded at Janice, who nodded back at him—"and personnel"—an extended open hand toward the HR director—"is done. I encourage everyone to display the very best that they have to offer at this time to ensure a future position within the corporation."

People sat with their corporate-issued *Understanding Unemployment* primer on their laps, looking bewildered. Jocelyn scanned the room trying to ascertain what everyone else was thinking. She figured if all and sundry would have had the ability to divine what their coworkers were thinking, the resounding tonal hum of "bullshit" would have reached such a tremulous pitch that the resulting harmonic would have been enough to shatter a wine glass in all of their heads. Everyone knew that they were effectively out of work, but when? Assuming that the meeting had achieved its objective, the crowd spontaneously dispersed, leaving Robert, Janice, and the now completely powerless HR director to shut off the conference-room lights.

So much for that renewed sense of purpose I had this morning.

Jocelyn stepped back into her office. There on her desk was the Malaysia proposal file. The letter from the king and both Robert's and Adam's requests were, of course, on her mind.

This thought alternated with the unsavory math of trying to calculate how long she might be able to maintain her house and bills without a job while she looked for a new one. She didn't want to deal with looking for a job. Going through the temp agency to get this gem of a job four years ago had adequately informed her of what the industries were in her area. The casino and a toilet-paper distribution company. *Shit.*

She didn't even like this job, but what was out there was decidedly worse. Now she'd have to put her resume together and make this reoccurring nightmare appear to be the highlight of her life. She knew that a bachelor of fine arts degree was not going to sustain her current lifestyle. She'd have to downsize, especially with Bobby officially gone. What was the point of keeping the house? *Maybe I should try to work something out with him. We could just be roommates. Maybe he'll get into rehab or something ...* She quickly dismissed that fleeting pipe dream, knowing that she'd "been there, done that" and it never worked. It was officially over anyway. *Well, at least there's unemployment.*

Jocelyn really didn't want to think about it. She was freaking herself out about stuff that was just too unknown.

Meanwhile, the little flashing red light of Bobby's voice mail taunted her. She grabbed the phone, punched in her code, and listened to Bobby's drunken account of getting a new tattoo. The fact that Mimi must have noticed his inebriated state before she connected him to her voice mail made Jocelyn wince. *Great. Just great.*

She picked up the bound document on her desk and flipped through the entire Malaysia proposal. It was well done. It looked good, really good. She did have a flare for it, for what that was worth.

Damn ... Nobody's even going to look at it if we don't get that letter signed ... Robert wants me to sign this thing ... He's crazy.

But what if she did? *I can't sign it. That's even crazier.*

Then what? If she didn't sign it, would all of her near-retirement coworkers face destitution because she didn't get that proposal just looked at? What would Adam do if she didn't just photocopy Robert's two-year-old letter? Fire her? Well then, of course, she wouldn't be eligible for unemployment. What would Robert do if she did what Adam told her to do? Move her to an even smaller office? Not likely, because there really wasn't anywhere smaller than her office.

"This place is crazy. It's making me crazy, for goodness' sake," Jocelyn grumbled to herself. Luckily, she had yoga that evening after work, and she imagined that after a series of downward dogs and deep breathing, she would gain some clarity as to how to effectively deal with Malaysia.

CHAPTER TWENTY

JOCELYN'S MOMENT OF ZEN, COSMIC convergence, divine intervention, or whatever you want to call it arrived the next morning. At first, she had thought it was an unruly cable in the tangle of computer wires under her desk and didn't pay it much attention as she settled in for the day.

As she swiveled around in her chair and considered the possibilities for extending the red-wall collage up onto the ceiling, she noticed Robert lumbering down the hall. And for whatever reason, probably closely linked to the fact that she really wasn't doing anything productive, she looked under her desk at her computer and succumbed to some sort of random obsessive/compulsive urge to straighten the cables before Robert got to her. She reached down and attempted to tuck the unsightly mass behind the computer.

And it was then that she and the snake became acquainted. The snake, a nearly two-foot-long *Coluber constrictor*, was so far outside of her predefined expectation of what she might find under her desk that she didn't think twice about grabbing it up. It took a moment for Jocelyn's brain to register that what she was touching had not been purchased at an office-supply warehouse. She held it for at least a second, long enough for Robert to walk in and witness Jocelyn's moving and personal revelation that she was, in fact, holding twenty inches of writhing, shiny black snake.

"Aaaaaaahhhhhhhhhhhhhh!" she shrieked as she threw the snake to the ground. The snake and Jocelyn both decided to quickly exit the scene. Jocelyn pushed her way past Robert and cut a path out into the hallway. And the snake immediately slithered between the wall and the filing cabinet in the corner of her office.

"Could this place be more like hell?!" Jocelyn shouted at no one in particular.

Robert laughed and said he would go find someone to take care of it for her.

Someone to take care of it for me? Like he can't? Some man he is!

People were looking curiously out their office doors, wondering what all the yelling was about as Jocelyn paced the hall.

Yeah ... he can't even do it himself. He has to go find someone else ... Someone else to take care of it ... Someone else ... That's it! Jocelyn had just figured out what to do with Malaysia. She'd help someone else get that signature where it needed to be.

Jocelyn summoned up all of her courage and quietly tiptoed into her office so as not to disturb the snake. She grabbed the Malaysia proposal and its associated file folder. As soon as she had her hands on the documents, she leapt through the door—out of the snake-infested, red-paper-poppy field formerly called a utility closet—and back to the safety of the hallway. At that point, Vince was coming down the hall with what looked like a long hook.

"You actually have a tool for this?" Jocelyn asked incredulously.

"Oh, we get them in here every so often at this time of year. They come in and eat the mice," he said while looking around the office and adjusting his grasp on the hook. "Now, where did you see it last?"

"Wait. Wait a second. We have mice running around here too?" Jocelyn asked in wide-eyed disbelief.

"Oh, we have a contract with an exterminator. But some years are worse than others. I don't see it, Jocelyn. You say it went over here? By the filing cabinet?"

"Yeah."

"Well, she's not there now," Vince said as he made a

cursory check behind the cabinet.

"Check by my computer, please. Maybe it went back under the desk to get warm again."

Jocelyn kept Vince in her office searching everywhere, inside the filing cabinet and desk drawers, for the next thirty minutes. When Vince would have no more of it and had explained that the snake was harmless at least a hundred times, Jocelyn finally decided to pull herself together and get back to work. Of course, she would have to accept not only the specter of the snake but also the mice that were cohabiting with her. Hoping to delay the getting-back-to-work moment, Jocelyn asked Vince if he anticipated getting laid off too.

"Me? No," Vince said, leaning against the snake hook like a cane. "Adam owns the building under a different company name, and the building pays me my salary."

"Oh. I didn't realize that."

"Yeah, the cleaning crew," he thumbed over his shoulder, "a bunch of people in the warehouse ... even Mimi used to get paid by the building. But when the acquisition was about to take place, Adam offered her a paid position with the same company that employs you, so that she could get stock."

"Fascinating. Just when I think I know the place I've been working at every day," Jocelyn said.

"Yeah. Adam's always been good at shimmying around companies for his benefit. He actually had the building listed as his personal residence at one point." Vince shook his head and made a sort of custom snort/chuckle sound. "Ever wonder why he has a full master bath hanging off his office?"

Jocelyn hadn't really thought about it, but now that Vince mentioned it, it did seem kind of odd that Adam had his own marble-floored bathroom with double sinks, shower, Jacuzzi, toilet, and bidet attached to his office. She bit her lip and looked at Vince quizzically, which was more than enough to encourage him to go on.

"Yup. I helped build that! That was some summer,"

Vince said as he shifted his weight from the snake hook and repositioned himself on the edge of her desk. "His ex-wife was livid. Adam had gotten all that stuff for their summer house on the island. But wifey didn't like it, and Adam couldn't return it. Lord knows how he got all that stuff in the first place; he had it all shipped over here and made it into his own personal bathroom." He paused for a moment. "That kid from Egypt probably used it more than Adam. He was in there like three times a day."

"You mean he got to use Adam's personal restroom?"

"Sharon told me it was okay because Muslims have to clean up before prayers or something. Us guys in maintenance and the warehouse figured it was either that or the poor kid had a case of the runs."

Jocelyn could tell Vince was clearly enjoying the experience of relaying this piece of company folklore. She listened with raised eyebrows as she continued to not so nonchalantly survey her office for rogue wildlife.

"Adam already had a little bathroom with a cheap Home Depot shower stall. And he had been claiming the building as one of his residences on his taxes for a few years already because of that shower stall. So once the grout was dry in the nice bathroom, he decided to move in." Vince leaned in closer to Jocelyn and lowered his voice. "Between you and me, I think the scene with his wife not liking those marble tiles helped that along." He smirked and continued, "He lived here until the town's tax assessors came to check the place out, which tipped off the zoning office ..."

Vince let out a laugh as he reminisced. "It's probably why they ended up getting divorced. The ex owns half of the building, and that's why you see her every so often coming around with that little yapping dog of hers talking with Mimi." He chuckled again and wiped under his nose. "Oh, yeah. Mimi is happy to update her about Adam's latest girlfriend. Anyway, the ex is usually here on the third of the month making sure she gets her rent check from Janice for the space your division occupies."

Jocelyn listened with curious interest. Vince was on a roll. "Anyway, I honestly think Adam thought he was going to be able to take corporate for some sort of ride, but I'm pretty sure they figured him out."

She stopped searching for snakes and looked directly at him. "What do you mean, Vince?"

"Oh, he's pretty used to getting his way. I mean, he sued the US Navy and won. Of course, it took him almost twenty years in court to do it—but he did it. That never happens, Jocelyn. Never. Adam is relentless. He just sticks to his guns and gets what he wants. No matter what."

Jocelyn nodded and thanked Vince for trying to find the snake. Once he had cleared out, she began to execute her inspired solution to the conundrum otherwise known as Malaysia. *I'm gonna get this thing off my desk once and for all.*

Looking under her desk every few minutes, Jocelyn clicked the button on her computer's desktop for the MKT scanner. This was a fairly new piece of equipment, and all of the marketing department shared it. The digital scanner wasn't used all that often, and by Jocelyn's estimation, no one knew how to use it. Heck, *she* didn't know how to use it. She fussed around with it for a while from her desk and then directly at the scanner in the common area. In frustration, Jocelyn ended up calling the help desk at Hewlett-Packard, and when that failed, she called Betty Lambert, PhD in psychology from Brown University.

No one really knew why Dr. Lambert was still with the company. The doctor really didn't do much but appear in proposal appendices for work that she had done over twenty years ago—some study about how humans interacted with simulated environments. Jocelyn's best guess was that Adam kept her around to keep her away from the competition. For whatever reason, Betty Lambert was now basically the company's network administrator. And with her skittish, overly chatty personality and reliance on manuals and help lines, she was ill- suited for the job. That's why, Jocelyn figured, they ended up hiring Jerry Apario. Jocelyn would have called him, because he seemed to have more of a clue about this sort of stuff, but Jerry was in Algeria for an install.

Dr. Lambert hustled her short, running-shoe-wearin', sweat-suit-sportin' plumpness into Jocelyn's office. She was holding little scraps of paper, a chewed-up pencil, and a bag of trail mix. Seemingly oblivious to her environment while holding three conversations at once with herself, she hastily sat down at Jocelyn's desk, put the HP help line on speakerphone, and began jotting down everything that HP told her on one of her handy scraps as she compulsively munched on trail mix.

Jocelyn, meanwhile, busied herself looking over the RFP list like it was a newspaper's classified section. Within the hour, the scanner functioned as it was designed to, and Betty left Jocelyn's office, taking her empty trail mix bag and a nervous, rambling conversation with her.

Checking under her desk once more just to make sure that the snake wasn't stalking her, Jocelyn now focused on what she thought was a brilliant idea. She began by scanning the letter from the Malaysian prime minister and saving it as a JPG file. Then she opened Photoshop. She was lucky. Jocelyn's was one of the only computers in the building to have Photoshop. Although she was not necessarily a pro at it, she did have a decent understanding of how to use it.

She plopped the JPG of the prime minister's letter into Photoshop and worked the whole thing over so that it looked like an unsigned letter. She printed it out with her personal printer. This was also a luxury not afforded to everyone at her division. Because she had to deal with changes on the fly before marketing presentations, Adam had approved a printer for her. Robert didn't even have one.

The doctored page stuttered laboriously as it deposited itself onto the paper tray of the bubble-jet printer. Jocelyn grabbed it and eyed the document critically as she compared it to the original.

"This looks like crap," she said out loud. Disappointed with the results, she took another tack. *Forget Photoshop. Let's do this old school.* Taking the two important letters with her, she went down to the older model photocopy machine tucked in the corner of the engineering department. But before she left her office, she grabbed some white-out, a number-two pencil, her Pilot Precise V5, an X-Acto blade, and a glue stick.

Needless to say, Jocelyn's longtime familiarity with Kinko's in her past life as a struggling artist played into the picture. She enlarged, shrunk, trimmed, clipped, glued, touched up, and then copied again and again and yet again the king's signature and the prime minister's signature. When all the copying was complete, not only did she have some pretty decent-looking signatures, she also now had two pristine unsigned, undated copies of both the king's letter from four years ago and the prime minister's recent letter.

Feeling very satisfied with her handiwork, Jocelyn headed back to the marketing area. She scanned her creations and saved them as JPGs. Then, just to make sure that her efforts were not in vain, Jocelyn e-mailed Robert:

Robert—I cannot do what you asked me to do. However, I will send everything necessary to SING. Consider Malaysia done. —J.

Once again, just as he did earlier, Robert appeared almost instantly at her door. "Jocelyn, what are you up to?" he asked.

"I have it figured out." She showed Robert all the pieces of her puzzle: the unsigned, undated letters and the cleaned-up signatures of both the king and the prime minister.

It took a moment for the lightbulb to go on over Robert's head without Jocelyn explicitly laying it out for him, but when illumination finally occurred, he asked, "So how are you getting these to Singapore? You can't e-mail this from our corporate e-mail."

Thinking fast, because she hadn't really considered this, she simply said, "I'll open some Yahoo e-mail accounts and let Singapore know to look for communication from them. I'll put the proposal on the FTP server for them to pick up and print out."

That seemed to satisfy Robert.

"So I've got your okay on this?" she asked.

He nodded his approval gravely, but Jocelyn saw his shoulders slowly, almost imperceptibly, relaxing. She knew that he was greatly relieved, and she felt fairly proud of her accomplishment.

Once she had set up the Yahoo e-mail accounts, she called the Singapore office to let them know about the impending incoming communications. She told the tiny Singapore office manager, Rachel, what to expect and what to do. *Just paste that JPG into the second document and print it out.* Impressed, as per usual, that Rachel would be so chipper and friendly at three in the morning Singapore time, Jocelyn was thrilled to hear that all four copies of the complete proposal could be sent via FedEx from the Singapore office by eleven thirty in the morning local time.

As soon as she hung up the phone, Jocelyn got busy pressing "send." She sent the king's signature via one of the Yahoo accounts and the now unsigned and undated prime minister's letter via another Yahoo account. Then she placed the Malaysia proposal on the FTP server so that Rachel could pick it up, print it out, and mail it to the proper authorities.

But Jocelyn knew how things in Corporate Land worked. Always, as in *always*, cover your ass. With that in mind, and making sure to check for any unwanted visitors before she reached in to pluck it up, Jocelyn took a floppy disk out of her top desk drawer. She made copies of the Yahoo e-mails sent to Singapore and then made sure to include the e-mail she had just sent over to Robert about considering Malaysia done.

Scanning through the e-mails on her disk and thinking it through a moment longer, Jocelyn decided to e-mail Robert and confirm that he had given her the verbal approval to do this. She knew full well that he wasn't going to respond to that, but once the e-mail had a time/date stamp on it, Jocelyn included a copy on her floppy disk as well. Not knowing exactly why, Jocelyn knew that this HD, light brown (otherwise known as one of several variations of beige), IBM-formatted, 3.5 inch, 1.44MB diskette might be a special type of insurance for her in the future.

All this deliberation wasn't so much due to her thinking that "touching up" the king's signature was wrong or that she might get into some sort of legal trouble about it. Although she did experience that familiar childlike sensation of getting away with something and it made her kind of giddy, she fully believed that sending all this stuff to Singapore was the only logical course of action that could be taken at this critical juncture. More than that, it was encouraged and approved. She had it all on the floppy.

Her trepidation came because she could easily see this whole ep- isode morphing into something very office-politic-y as layoffs were imminent and people like Robert would be attempting to make themselves look as vitally important as possible as they simultaneously diminished the importance of the team around them. *If I'm going to go down, I might as well have company.*

CHAPTER TWENTY-ONE

April 2003

THINGS WERE SWIMMING ALONG PERFECTLY for Jocelyn. Proposals flinging out the door on time. Trade shows lined up with booths and bunnies (welcoming-looking females who jammed brochures into people's hands). Scripts written for the marketing videos now in production. Artwork approved. Press releases hitting the wires. Her whole little red world was like a well-oiled machine. She loved that feeling of having everything under control.

That is, until Adam got back from Singapore. He looked tanned and happy, and his girlfriend, Dani, who looked as if she just tumbled out of an Abercrombie and Fitch mail-order catalogue, was flittering in and out of the office proudly sporting the gargantuan emerald ring she had thrown at Adam and mysteriously lost last Christmas. Adam had apparently decided it was time to take the twenty-two-carat oval-cut emerald set in a double band encrusted with tiny round diamonds out of his office safe and present it to her again. Although Dani seemed to be very happy to have the ring back, she told Jocelyn privately, "Oh, he probably just gave it to me because he felt guilty that he was getting his dick sucked by some Asian whore."

"Okay, too much information," Jocelyn said as she ushered the young woman out of her vibrant REDRUM. *What's wrong with kids these days?*

It didn't take the accounting department, or Mimi, long to figure out why that ring showed up when it did. Evidently, Adam's trip to Singapore paid off. Although it was not officially official yet, Adam was sure that the Indonesians were going to buy, via the EX-IM Bank and USAID, his proposed multi-city training school for the Indonesian Maritime Academy.

The schools would house virtually all of Jocelyn's division's simulators and, unlike the other contracts that her division typically won, this time they would be responsible for the construction of the schools. This construction aspect was news to Jocelyn. That was not in the proposals she had been doing up over the past five years. *He must have thrown that in during the sit-down negotiations to sweeten the deal or something.*

Anyhow, it just so happened that Adam's emerald-wearing girl- friend's father was a big-time construction contractor in Texas. His company was listed by *Engineering News-Record* as one of the top twenty construction contractors in the United States. And it coincidentally happened that this construction contractor and his wife, in one of the largest cars Jocelyn had ever seen in real life, arrived at the office parking lot just as Jocelyn was leaving work that day.

"Howdy!" the bleached-blond, middle-aged female passenger of the car called out of the window as she waved. Her husband sat stone-faced behind the wheel.

"Hello!" Jocelyn greeted the woman with a smile as she walked up to meet the newcomers.

"Where should we park, hon? All the parking lots around here are so small!"

"Well, for a chariot like this, I'm sure it would seem that way." Jocelyn looked around, trying to think of where it might be best to send them to park the vehicle. All she could think of was over by the loading dock in back of the building. Thankfully, Vince came out and took over the parking situation as Adam came up and boisterously greeted his girlfriend's father, who looked a quite bit younger than Adam. "Dad" did not appear nearly as excited to see Adam as

Adam seemed to be to see him.

"My daughter tells me she's getting married!" the woman practically shouted as Adam swooped over to give her a hearty hug.

Oh my, thought Jocelyn as she smiled awkwardly watching the whole scene. Just as she was attempting to leave them to enjoy their newfound familial bliss, Adam called out, "Jocelyn! Jocelyn, have you met my soon-to-be in-laws?"

"Not formally."

Adam introduced everyone and proposed that they all go to dinner together.

Despite graciously declining more than once, Jocelyn ended up going out to dinner with the parents of Adam's girlfriend and Adam that night. They settled on one of Adam's favorite places to bring out-of-towners: a cozy, low-beam-ceilinged, colonial-period-pub-only-fancier type place. Its white linen tablecloths, proper silverware, candles, and hundreds of dollars' worth of opulent flower arrangements made a person feel as if she had stumbled upon a secret wedding reception. The restaurant was pretty well known in the area and served up lots of lobster, fish, and steak with an impressive salad bar and wine list. Adam's emerald-wearing girlfriend wasn't there. Apparently she had "issues" at the hairdresser's and couldn't make it to dinner on time.

Adam began to explain what a fantastic job Jocelyn had done on the Indonesia proposal and started chatting her up as if she was quite a bit more important than she really was. Jocelyn smiled and carefully played with the stem of her wineglass, figuring there was a reason why Adam was doing this. She was right.

It wasn't long before Dad finally laid into Adam, and incidentally Jocelyn, and told them flat-out that the budget Adam had sent him to work with to build six schools in Indonesia was a joke. "It's impossible! Whoever came up with that budget clearly has no concept of the construction business! There is no way in *hell* I'm putting my good name on something so underfunded."

"Oh, Rick ... C'mon now. You know there's always wiggle room to cut a project's expenses," Adam parried as he smiled his patented good-ol'-boy salesman smile. He was feeling very comfortable negotiating on his home turf and ordered another Johnny Walker Blue Label on the rocks.

Jocelyn, conversely, was feeling completely out of place. She wasn't sure if she should be playing the supporting role for Adam's negotiations or diverting Mom's attention with conversation about wedding arrangements. Thankfully, Adam's fiancée showed up to fill the table with comments about her hair and the news of the wedding.

Aside from the food, it was a pretty miserable evening for Jocelyn. However, she did garner some fairly important information regarding the particulars of the Indonesia contract. First, and most interesting to Jocelyn, was that the wine import/export business that Adam had purportedly bought for his now fiancée to "keep her busy" while he traveled would be utilized to help get needed supplies for the construction project into Indonesia.

Also, it appeared that Dad and Adam had agreed upon setting up a new company that would specifically hire Dad as a consultant to oversee the management of the building aspect of the Indonesia contract. Jocelyn didn't really understand the logistics, but she had the distinct impression that just having Dad on board as an extremely well-paid middleman was going to make things much easier for her division as it attempted to build the six schools on a shoestring-and-a-piece-of-caramel budget.

CHAPTER TWENTY-TWO

FEELING THAT SHE HAD EVERY reason to show to up to work later than usual the next morning, seeing as she had just donated her time to Adam and his Indonesia project, Jocelyn rolled in at nine fifteen. She decided to cut through the accounting department, as it was a more direct route to her office. Not that finding someone experiencing an emotional meltdown at nine fifteen was completely surprising, especially in accounting, but it did take her off-guard when she found Cathy in tears next to a paper shredder.

"What's wrong, Cathy?" Jocelyn asked.

"Oh, I've been doing this for the past two days, and I can't stand it. The paper shredder broke, and ... and ..." Cathy broke down in tears.

"You've been doing what for the past two days? Something for accounting? Aren't you supposed to be a marketing person?" Jocelyn had been utilizing this free-floating employee for all sorts of filing and basic stuff down in her department. It didn't really bother her that Cathy was over in accounting, but it did concern her, on a humanistic level, that Cathy was crying.

"They told me that there were going to be layoffs in marketing so they were going to move me to accounting so that I could still have a job. I told them I didn't know the first thing about accounting, but they said that's okay, we have lots of work for you," Cathy said between sobs and the obnoxious mechanized grinding sound of the shredder.

"So you're overwhelmed with the accounting work?" Jocelyn asked, still not sure why Cathy was crying.

"No. Yes. No! It's this! I can't take it anymore! I've been doing this," as she pointed to the shredder, "for the past two days. I'll never finish it, and I simply can't take it anymore! I've got paper cuts, and I fell asleep last night to *that* sound. It was stuck in my head!"

Jocelyn looked around the tight labyrinth of workstation cubes in which she and Cathy were standing. Evidenced by the nodding heads popping up like little hedgehogs, she knew that what Cathy was telling her was probably true.

"It can't be that bad, Cath. C'mon." Jocelyn reached down to turn off the shredder, but despite her best efforts at pushing the little power button, the machine would not shut down. So Jocelyn just unplugged it from the wall. "Hmm ... it really is broken. I think they have one in the publications area. How much more do you have to do?" Jocelyn asked.

Cathy didn't even speak. She just pointed to a line of black plastic garbage bags that were bulging and tossed all the way down the hallway, which ran the full expanse of the building.

"You're kidding me!" Jocelyn couldn't believe her eyes. "Someone expects you to shred all that with this little shredder? Who put you on this task?"

"Janice," Cathy whimpered, lip quivering.

The image of the "Shred all documents" Post-it note Sharon had given her years before was clear and sharp in Jocelyn's memory. "Janice. Figures," she said out loud. "Hold on, Cath. Take a break or something. I'll take care of this."

With the workstation hedgehog population clearly captivated, Jocelyn marched through them and made a beeline to Janice's office. Without knocking, she walked into the corner office—which was, as per usual, a complete mess. Papers were stacked all over the place: on the desk, on the floor, on top of filing cabinets with their drawers still open. Janice turned from the computer monitor to face Jocelyn, whose posture declared as loudly as any verbal communication could have that she was on a mission.

"Yes, Jocelyn."

"I just finished talking to Cathy. She's in tears. She's been shred- ding for the past two days, and the shredder is broken. I unplugged it," Jocelyn belted out.

"Oh, that's why it's so quiet. I'll have Vince pick up a new one for her."

"Janice, you want one person to shred all those bags of paper on a little personal paper shredder? I'll go price out how much it would cost to have one of those companies that comes over with a truck-sized shredder come do it. I bet it could be done in half a day," Jocelyn said.

"That won't be necessary, Jocelyn. But thank you." Janice turned her full attention back to her computer.

The hedgehogs looked on with interest as Jocelyn exited Janice's office and headed down the trash-bag-lined hall to the marketing department. Cathy was waiting at the door of the utility closet when Jocelyn arrived. "Do I still have to shred? Can I come work for you over here today?" Cathy asked.

"You might as well until Vince comes back with the new shredder, Cath. I've got to put together some trade-show stuff today and could use your help. Don't worry. I'm going to make some calls to see exactly how much one of those mobile shredding companies would cost."

Cathy looked at Jocelyn gratefully, and they both started their workday. Once Jocelyn had called around to get a few quotes for a truck shredder, she typed up what she had discovered in an Excel spreadsheet. She highlighted, in yellow, the cost savings of having a company come and do it compared to buying a new shredder and paying Cathy at her current rate of shredding to complete the job. She then brought the document down to Janice's office. This time, she knocked on the partially open door, and Janice acknowledged her before she entered.

"Hey, Janice. Look. I called around and found the best deal for us. They can be here tomorrow after lunch and stay until they have the shredding job complete. And ..."

Janice cut her off. "I think I mentioned before, Jocelyn, that it wouldn't be necessary for you to do this. You should get back to whatever it is you're supposed to be doing right now."

"Janice, I don't understand," she said as her smile faded and her shoulders dropped. "I think it would clearly save the company some money to have this outside service come do the shredding for us. Not to mention it would preserve everyone in accounting's ability to think straight."

"Jocelyn, these documents are proprietary. We can't have just anyone drive up with a shredder, give them all of our corporate intelligence, and believe that they would not be piecing it all back together and selling it to someone else."

Holy moley. This is like Adam's photocopier phobia. She distinctly re- called the logic behind her all-nighter at Kinko's with the Indonesia proposal.

Not knowing whether to believe if Adam and Janice were justified or just diabolically paranoid, Jocelyn decided to advocate for Cathy and the rest of the accounting department. "Okay, I see your point. But this is a huge and noisy job for one person to sit through day after day. Maybe we can hire a bunch of temps to come in and just bang it out in a couple of days?"

And that is exactly what Janice did. Not because she had thought it a great idea at the time. Hardly. That afternoon, Janice directed Vince to put the new shredder in a closet (about the size of Jocelyn's office) over by the warehouse so as to give accounting a break from the nonstop shredding noise. Of course, a shredder can't work with- out an operator, and it was less than twenty-four hours later that Cathy submitted her immediate resignation. Jocelyn wasn't there to see it, but evidently Cathy quitting her job was accomplished with lots of tears, random screaming, and internationally known hand gestures that served to enhance ten minutes' worth of what could only be described as a free-association soliloquy outlining her work experience at the Conglomerate and subsequent dependence on anti- depressants and painkillers. Ultimately, Vince the maintenance man had to escort her out of the building.

CHAPTER TWENTY-THREE

JOCELYN RECEIVED A PAPER MEMO in her inbox that said she would be soon moving into a new office. The memo included a floor plan and measurements of her new (hopefully snake-free) workspace. Jocelyn couldn't believe it! On the map, it actually looked like a real office. Nice and spacious. Lots of privacy. It was located over in the longest branch of the office complex. Over by the Inner Sanctum and off the hallway where all the retired generals had their offices, otherwise known as the Gauntlet.

"Looks like you're moving up. Good girl," Mimi congratulated as Jocelyn walked in early on the morning of her move. "Good for you, honey. You show those generals what you're made of!"

Jocelyn hadn't really thought of it in those terms, and the compliment made her blush a little. "I'll do my best, Mimi," was all she could think to say. For the first time, Jocelyn headed down to her new office. How exciting this was! She walked all the way down the hall and took a left where the map on her memo indicated her office was supposed to be.

Hmm? This can't be it ... She was inside a very small and very clean kitchenette (much cleaner than the kitchenette in the other area where her office used to be). Just then, two men dressed all in white with white shower caps and white disposable shoe booties came in from a door opposite Jocelyn.

"Oh, hello!" one of them said. "What are *you* doing here?"

"I'm supposed to be moving into my new office today.

And the map I was given told me that it's supposed to be right here." Jocelyn whipped open Prada's leather version of a courier bag and produced the document.

The two huddled around to look at her map.

"Yup. That looks about where we are. But this is our break room. You're welcome to come and have coffee with us whenever you'd like, though."

Jocelyn looked at them in dismay. "There's nothing in there?" she asked hopefully as she pointed to the door they had entered from. They both shook their heads.

"Nope. Not for you."

"Really?" She just couldn't believe it. She looked at her map again. "Okay, I guess I'll take you up on that coffee then. I'll admit it, I'm lost."

"Nah! You just wanted to try our coffee and see if it was better than yours over in Contractor Land!" one of the white-clothed men joked while pouring her a cup.

Jocelyn gratefully took the coffee and inquired as to what they did. She had never been this far down this hallway and didn't know that there were people down here, let alone people who looked like attendees of an all-white scrub-room theme party.

"Oh, we work on electronic components that would get damaged by static electricity. That's why we dress like this."

"That's cool. I didn't know that there was anything worth seeing after Adam's office."

"It's always Adam, Adam, Adam. That's all I ever hear the girls talk about," the first electronic scrub-room guy joked.

"Maybe if you started buying the ladies some nice jewelry like Adam does ..." the other shower-cap-wearing guy chided back.

"Well, let me know when he—" Jocelyn pointed to the man who had given her the coffee "—starts throwing around the large-caliber gems, and I'll come back and have more coffee with you guys, okay? Right now, I've gotta find an office that's missing something: namely, me!"

The guys grinned, and Jocelyn thanked them for their time and the beverage. She headed back down the long hallway to the main reception area, hoping that Mimi would know where her new office was located.

Smiling, she smacked the map and memo down on the reception desk. "Mimi, where the heck is this office? I can't find it."

"It's supposed to be in that new area that Vince is working on. And it's supposed to be very nice. Wait till you see it!" Mimi said. Just then, off in the direction from whence she had just come, the sound of a very loud saw cutting through drywall could be heard.

"Let me guess," Jocelyn said. "That's coming from my new office."

Mimi's phone rang, and she smiled at Jocelyn as she picked it up and recited for the sixteen billionth time the greeting that she always answered with. Jocelyn returned the smile and headed back down the hall toward the sound of light construction. She arrived just as a piece of drywall fell away and Vince shut off the Sawzall.

"What do you think, Joss?" Vince asked her from inside the newly fashioned aperture. "The door was supposed to be finished yesterday, but when it showed up, it swung open the wrong way. So I had to send it back. Building codes, you know ..."

From the hallway, Jocelyn peered through the opening in the drywall into a very large room. She could smell the new carpet and paint.

"Wow. This whole thing is for me, Vince?" Jocelyn asked in disbelief.

"Ha! Don't bet on it. As soon as the fellas finish this door, they'll put together the workspaces." Two men who had been standing be- hind Vince expertly placed and secured a prehung steel door within the hole that Vince had just created.

"Hey, this is like false advertising, Vince!" She looked

at the map and the memo and shook her head.

"We'll start with your office, Jocelyn. Why don't you come back in a little while?"

Disappointed, Jocelyn headed to the break room. Jerry Apario and a couple of guys from engineering were in there getting their morning coffee. Jerry was making an impassioned case that the US shouldn't be "shock and awe-ing" Iraq while the two older ex-navy engineers argued that because of 9/11, the US couldn't let the terrorists win.

"Can you think of a better way to showcase US military might?" one of the engineers exclaimed.

"Look," Jerry allowed, "I was all for going into Afghanistan, but this Iraq thing doesn't even make sense."

"Sure it does," the other engineer said with a sly smile. "You drive a car, don't you?"

"Yeah. So?"

"Do you put gas in it?"

"Well, yeah."

"Case closed. If you put gas in your car—or, more importantly,

if your car has plastic in it, or if you use plastic in any way, shape, or form, maybe at a hospital or something—then you are pro this war and you should just shut your yap. This is about preserving America as we know it. We have freedoms here and ..."

Jocelyn poured her coffee and glanced at the stock-price display.

April 27, 2003
GOLD: US$327
OIL: $30.10
NYSE: GLOM $39.19 vol: 05.69m

The scene in Iraq certainly didn't seem to be improving her stock portfolio. It was valued less than it was this time last year. She really thought the war would have made the stock price spike by now, seeing as the big "shock and awe" display was last month. And she was sort of disappointed. Owning stock was funny like that. She felt richer and spent money more freely when the stock was doing well. When it wasn't, she found herself thinking about clipping coupons even though the ticker price had absolutely nothing to do with the balance in her checking account.

Her economic situation made her remember the first time she had seen Iraq getting bombed back when she was in art school. Sitting on a stinky and totally uncomfortable black futon, she had cried watch- ing it on the news. It had really shaken her up. "Why is the United States doing this?" she asked her professional layabout boyfriend, who was busy trying to figure out where he could get his hands on the Desert Storm trading cards the newscaster had just showcased.

Then, like an old slide-show presentation, her mind snapped over to her ex-husband, Bobby, who had actually been in Desert Storm. And how he and a couple of his friends claimed to be suffering from Gulf War Syndrome. She was never really sure if he was for real or just making stuff up.

Jocelyn finished her coffee just as one of the gray-haired engineers was explaining to Jerry that it was better that we do it *over there* and not here. She was surprised by how different her reaction to the whole Iraq thing was this time around. She felt nothing. She was neither pro nor con. Nothing. The realization of this sort of startled her. But that quickly passed.

Maybe it was because she was now aware of the fact that the US Congress had, the previous year, passed the Authorization for Use of Military Force Against Iraq Resolution of 2002, which concerned itself with enforcing United Nations Security Council resolutions that were prompted by Kuwaiti and Iraqi relations back in 1990, when Bobby was rolling around with the marines. It was not an official declaration of war, but, then again, the United States hadn't officially declared a war since 1942.

Jocelyn wanted to tell people to just forget about the claims of yellowcake. It was all about the RFPs calling for earthmovers, sanitation systems, and water filtration that had been floating around since before the 2002 resolution was even signed. Marriott Hotels for the past year had already been claiming property in the not-yet shocked-and-awed center of the ancient Islamic empire. Despite (or was it in spite of?) its impressive history, Baghdad was far more Western and open than people were allowed to imagine, seeing as Saddam Hussein had been installed back in the 1980s by the American CIA.

She had no doubt that the mission would be accomplished in record time, but Jocelyn knew that contractors, who were getting paid much more than the US service members, would still be all over the place for quite a while. The contracts said so.

She waved good-bye to the guys in the break room and headed back.

When Jocelyn returned, she saw that the new area, although painted the same Navajo Bone as the rest of the company, featured a new color within the corporate approved palette: battleship gray.

Jocelyn also had to deal with the hard truth that the term *office* used in the memo she had received was a bit of a misnomer, seeing as what she really got was a very tall cube. Albeit more spacious than her converted utility closet, it was still of traditional office-cube construction. What made the "executive cube" supposedly more special than the other cube workstations scattered throughout the facility were the seven-foot-tall walls, which included a privacy door with a real doorknob.

This workspace arrangement, aside from being initially disappointing, actually was doable. The only thing she felt more than a little bummed out about was that her red wall collage hadn't made the move successfully. The tape had pulled the Navajo Bone off the wall, and the scraps were all torn and messed up. Vince was aggravated that he had to pick little chunks of tape off the wall and was going to have to repaint the utility closet/snake habitat. "You know, Jocelyn," he said, "taping stuff to the wall wasn't a very good idea. Why didn't you just paint the place red?"

But other than that, she had no complaints. She had finally accepted the fact that the more money she brought home, the less she was going to be exposed to daylight and color. Her windows to the outside world were officially out of reach so long as Robert was the guy signing off on her progress reports.

CHAPTER TWENTY-FOUR

A FEW WEEKS LATER, MARTIN Mays was displaced in the company-wide office shuffle and directed to relocate in the "new marketing area."

Martin's computer beeping every few seconds as he typed code into the antiquated VAX system really started to piss off some of the cloistered executive-cube workers. People would silently protest the beeping by lobbing crunched-up paper balls over their seven-foot walls into his walled workspace. The paper projectile would usually be answered by Martin angrily yelling out something like, "Hey! Someone around here has to work at making this place some money! Leave me alone!"

Finally, Jocelyn marched out of what would have been a sensory-deprivation chamber had it not been for all the beeping and yelling and asked Martin what the heck all the noise his computer was making was about.

"Why on earth does your computer have to sound off like that, Martin? Can't you turn down the volume?"

Martin pressed *enter* on the keyboard, and it beeped. He was pretending not to notice her as she stood at the entrance of his executive cube. He pressed *enter* again, and it beeped again. She stared at the outdated computer with its tiny built-in keyboard and monitor. She could tell by the yellowish tone of the beige that it was really old. And she wondered why it was wired to something out in the common area about the size of two of the publication office's industrial-strength photocopiers. "What *is* that thing? An old beta version of ColecoVision?"

Again the computer beeped at her. She could hear all

the cube-dwellers moan.

"It might as well be, Jocelyn," Martin said. "It might as well be."

"What the heck? Can't they give you a new computer?" she said, leaning on his executive cube's privacy-doorjamb, arms folded across her chest. She was outfitted in her office uniform of a gray skirt, white blouse, and sensible heels.

"Jocelyn, why do you think Adam keeps me and Dr. Lambert here?"

"I don't know. Your winning personalities?"

"No. Because he's cheap. I wrote this code for our ship simulator twenty-eight years ago on a VAX machine."

"What's a VAX machine?"

"You're looking at one." He paused for what Jocelyn figured was dramatic effect. "Adam claimed that the navy stole the code, and he took them to court. The case went on forever, and the navy just figured he'd run out of steam and give up. No one just sues the navy."

Martin reached up to his chest pocket, fishing for a cigarette that, once found, he tapped on the desk. "Anyhow, in the meantime, Windows came along. And instead of just paying people to rewrite the code for Windows machines because God forbid they should steal the code, he had us running this VAX stuff through a type of translator. Has everything to do with that original VAX code still being a critical part of him doing business. Part of the lawsuit." Now Martin was rolling the cigarette between his thumb and forefinger as he spoke.

"So ... why do we have to hear that beeping?" Jocelyn asked. "Ever hear of a Windows update?"

"Yeah. Who hasn't?"

"Well, every time Windows comes out with an update, which is like every other week, I have to go back into the original code and rewrite parts of the damn thing." He popped the cigarette in his mouth and took out his Zippo lighter.

"Long story short, this noisy old computer is his claim to that money." The cigarette was flopping up and down as he spoke. "It and what's left of the team that helped write that code is not going anywhere until that check for $26 million clears. Adam promised the development team a cut of the settlement. Seven of us worked to develop this thing, and now there's only two of us left—me and Betty Lambert. That means five brilliant people who were associated with this thing"—he took the cigarette out of his mouth and used it to point to the little monitor with the built-in keyboard—"because of this, five of us dropped dead right here in this office complex. I swear the bastard is killing us off." He abruptly stood up. "I've gotta get some fresh air." Jocelyn stood out of his way and let him pass.

This type of free-flowing cube banter and beeping didn't help the sales staff, who were attempting to make cold calls. Consequently, Martin was pretty much forced to move into a real closet (the one that Vince had originally put Cathy's shredder in before she quit), where he was happy to shut the door and beep all he wanted.

ONCE EVERYONE WAS SETTLED INTO the new area, Jocelyn began to receive an influx of visitors from the foreign offices. First the UK office came to visit her. They were a fun bunch who seemed like they might actually be smarter than the US crew but didn't take themselves as seriously. Jocelyn heard Martin Mays and one of the UK engineers get into a near fistfight about hydrodynamic models, but then it all settled as quickly as it had started. Jocelyn chalked it up to the pub culture that these people came out of. It seemed that so long as the day concluded with someone taking them out for a pint, everyone was happy.

Next on the visitor list was the Singapore office. Jocelyn finally got to meet Rachel, the helpful office manager she had dealt with on the phone so many times. She was quite the contrast to the tall, office-attire-sporting Jocelyn. Rachel was short and perky with long, well-styled black hair, and she wore some variation of a silver mini dress and arm warmers (apparently the latest fad in her part of the world) every day of her visit.

The two salesmen from Singapore used the tiniest laptop computers Jocelyn had ever seen. Mimi had organized a potluck dinner for the Singapore office's arrival, and upon hearing Martin Mays's definition of potluck—"Oh, everyone just brings their leftovers from the night before"—Rachel could not be convinced otherwise and would not eat anything at all for the duration of her visit.

Last rolling in was Mikhail. He was their representative working the Russian oil-producing sector in hopes of selling them Adam's Catastrophe! software system. He would pull Jocelyn aside and talk to her in hushed tones with his heavy Russian accent about how "United States is now going same path Soviet Union go. I maybe make arrangement now to get out of country for you, Jocelyn."

Jocelyn was fascinated to learn that Mikhail's wife and daughter lived in Australia and that his daughter was taking Chinese lessons. Jocelyn burned a bunch of disks that included every single PowerPoint she had made in the past year. Mikhail could use these while making presentations. She had told him that she could make him one especially for whomever he was meeting with, and she'd e-mail it to him or put it on the FTP server for him to pick up. But he declined, moved in very close to her, and emphatically whispered, "All communication, e-mail, computer, will be surveillance. My phone, they tap, you know?" and he insisted on a CD to take with him.

Jocelyn reported this last statement to Adam, seeing as he seemed very concerned about corporate espionage. She was surprised by Adam's answer: "Oh, he's just been through that whole Soviet, Communism thing. Don't worry about him. He's a little crazy, but he's a really good salesman. Just give him the PowerPoints he asks for. He's harmless."

Finally, on the day before they all left, Jocelyn found out why all the foreigners were there and making time to meet privately with her. They had all heard, most probably from Mimi, about the meeting where everyone had gotten the *Understanding Unemployment* booklets, and people were curious as to how this would affect them, seeing as they were employees but out of the country. Would they be absorbed into another of the Conglomerate's divisions or just cut loose? Was Adam being moved to another division? How about Robert, and "What about you Jocelyn? Are you going to be moved?"

"I don't know. Why don't you ask the human-resources director?" Jocelyn honestly replied.

"Oh, she's helpless," Marcy from the UK office matter-of-factly stated with what Jocelyn perceived as more of an Irish accent than British. "She's no help a-tall, and I don't believe a word Robert is a-tellin' us."

Ian, the engineer who had almost clobbered Martin Mays, rushed to augment what Marcy had said. "Aye, so it be. I don't trust Robert since he has, three times now, taken information we have sent him and produced proposals with his name on them. He's gotten fantastic commissions on projects that took Charles and I literally years to cultivate and produce. Years!"

Similar accounts came in from the other international offices, and Jocelyn of course saw and understood their extreme distrust of Robert. They had come to report it to her because she was supposed to be in charge of the proposal work flow. Knowing about this made Jocelyn feel fairly inept, because she didn't know how to get Robert to stop doing what he apparently had been doing for years. Jocelyn also knew that Adam wouldn't give a hoot. So long as the division kept moving the units, Adam didn't care who got the commission.

After getting her "must do today" list done, Jocelyn decided to confide in Martin, tell him about what the international staff had told her about Robert, and ask what his opinion was regarding their fate.

"Robert is a dick, Jocelyn. You haven't noticed that yet?" Martin said, leaning back in his chair. "Notice that your office is in another part of the building, far away from him."

"Yeah, but so is yours."

He nodded and motioned for her to sit down on one of the stackable white plastic lawn chairs next to his desk. He had brought them in along with some framed pictures of oil tankers to make his closet more homey.

"Exactly my point. Robert has removed from sight the people who might be construed as effective at turning a profit. He has them—i.e., you and me and a bunch of good salesmen—hidden and tucked away in a warehouse." He folded his hands on his stomach and started slowly tapping his thumbs together. "Meanwhile, Robert has his newly renovated, quadruple-the-square-footage, windowed office with a mahogany conference table and leather couch just in time to be meeting with everyone from corporate. You know, as he schmoozes with them in hopes of getting a position at headquarters."

"Yeah, well, that's a given, Martin." Jocelyn crossed her legs and started making circles with her foot. "Seriously, everyone knew he was going to do that. So what do you think? Are they going to cut the international offices loose or stick them with some other division?"

"They'll probably be cut loose, unless they can make themselves look good on paper. Which, from what you're telling me, Robert has taken credit for all of the sales, and that makes this office look good. Corporate doesn't want to deal with international bullshit like Rachel getting smacked ..."

"Huh?" Jocelyn stopped swirling her foot around. "What does that mean? Rachel getting smacked?"

"Oh, remember when I was in Singapore last year? Adrian, that pompous salesman with the tiny computer ... funny, when I was young, it was all about whose was bigger.

And these Asian guys are all about whose is smaller." Martin shrugged. "Anyway. Adrian didn't like something that Rachel did, and he hit her. Smacked her in the head as I sat right there in the chair by his desk."

"What? Like, he was joking around with her?" Jocelyn suggested, disbelieving that someone would actually hit a coworker, especially a man hitting a little woman like Rachel. "He didn't really maliciously hit her, did he?"

"Yup. She ran out of the room crying."

"What did you do?"

"Nothing. We just picked up our conversation from where we left off."

"You're kidding! Seriously?" Jocelyn's legs came uncrossed as her brows became more furrowed. She leaned forward ready to jump up in objection.

"They have all sorts of different rules, standards, and perceptions in different parts of the world, Jocelyn. What was I gonna do? If that's the way they do business over there, God bless 'em. I talked to Rachel later, and she told me that he does that every so often."

"You're joking, of course," Jocelyn angrily responded. And when she saw he wasn't, "Martin, we are an *American* company. We have laws here against this stuff. Adrian should be reported..."

"The operative word here is *here*, Jocelyn. They are *there*. I'm thinking that they are going to be roaming free-range pretty soon anyway. Corporate doesn't want to deal with them, and they don't have to. Especially since Robert is making it look like he is driving all the sales anyway."

Still smoldering about Rachel getting hit, Jocelyn went to speak with Elaine, the HR director, who, during a mere three-minute conversation, provided yet more proof of the widely held working hypothesis that she was, in fact, completely useless. "Uhhhh ... I'd have to consult corporate. It doesn't say anything about someone hitting a subordinate in this binder they gave me. Rachel looked okay when we saw her though, don't you think?"

Although Jocelyn was not particularly stunned by this short exchange, it still disappointed her greatly that she couldn't help Rachel. Jocelyn left the human-resources office and decided to go check out Robert's new digs that Martin had described. Sure enough, what was the old marketing department had been breathtakingly transformed to make room for a personal secretary for Robert. This special "waiting to speak with Robert area" took up the entire space that used to house the marketing filing cabinets and then some.

Robert's office now filled a space that used to be four offices. From the hallway windows, Jocelyn could see that Vince and his crew had knocked down the dividing walls and transformed Robert's workspace into something that might be showcased as a successful renovation on PBS's *This Old House*. And as with any successful renovation, the office still maintained elements of its meager beginnings and elevated these idiosyncrasies to levels of aesthetic appreciation. Specific to this approach was an unabashed admiration for the color beige. *Keeping it real, I guess.* Jocelyn had to grin as she thought about her own upgrade to battleship gray.

As she approached the entrance to the new office, a suited man she had never seen before scurried out with a Styrofoam coffee cup that he seemed to be spitting into. *Ewww ... a spittoon? Don't see that much around here.* The man headed toward the emergency exit sign at the far end of the hall. Robert and a woman wearing a maroon cashmere cape accented with a somewhat gaudy Louis Vuitton scarf were slowly making their exit when she got closer to his office.

"Robert, your new place looks great," Jocelyn called out, causing the woman and Robert to notice her.

Robert looked up and grinned. It was a fake smile. Jocelyn knew it. He said as she approached, "Oh hello, Jocelyn. Thank you. I think Vince and the team did a great job."

"I like that you have a conference table in there now. That's kind of cool," Jocelyn said while smiling at the woman, who she theorized must have had a facelift.

"Oh, I'm sorry. Miriam, have you met Jocelyn yet? She makes a real nice PowerPoint," Robert said while thrusting his hands in his pockets.

A real nice PowerPoint? What the heck! But after her recent conversation with Martin Mays, it instantly dawned on her what was going on. Not missing a beat and keeping her smile intact, Jocelyn said, "PowerPoint? Oh, that's the least of my talents, Robert! Hi, Miriam, I'm Jocelyn McLaren." Jocelyn greeted the woman while shaking her hand. "I'm in charge of out-of-house communications. Mostly I spend my time on proposals, but I also deal with trade shows, press relations, and art direction of the website, videos, and printed collateral material."

Miriam's eyebrows let on that she understood what Jocelyn's job was all about, but before Miriam could be introduced and the attempt made to redirect her attention onto something more Robert-centric completed, from across the "waiting to speak with Robert area" came the familiar call of, "Jaaaaaaaaaahhhhhcelyn! There you are! Where are they hiding you now?" It was Stan, and for the first time in her career Jocelyn honestly couldn't help but be happy to see him.

"Oh, that's Stan," Jocelyn told the confused-looking Miriam. "He's our congressman. He likes to stop by and look me up every time he's around. He's a real character."

Robert took the opportunity to not-so-discreetly whisper the backstory of the congressman to Miriam as Stan approached. "He's a good friend of mine. He's been in Congress now for over twenty years." That news seemed to make an impression on Miriam. Her posture and facial expression changed.

Stan briskly walked up to Jocelyn, and as she extended

her hand to shake his, he took it and kissed it. "The Malaysians. They are buying it! Good girl, Jocelyn. Another one out of the park!"

This was completely unexpected news for both Robert and Jocelyn.

"Jeez, I forgot about that," Jocelyn blurted out.

"I have been working with the Malaysian navy for the past several years, cultivating a friendship based on mutual trust ..." Robert directed toward Miriam.

"Hello, Robert," Stan said as he extended his hand for a shake, interrupting the description of Robert's multiyear sales quest.

"Why hello, Stan," Robert said as he enthusiastically pumped the congressman's hand. "That is wonderful news. Thank you for personally delivering it. May I introduce you to Miriam Stein. She is a member of the board of directors. Miriam, this is Stan ..."

"Miriam! Of course! I met you at my son's restaurant opening over on K and 19th a while back. It's a pleasure to see you again," Stan said as he warmly shook her hand with both of his.

Man! Stan is a machine! This guy was made to be a congressman. He literally knows everyone ... wow.

CHAPTER TWENTY-FIVE

INTERESTINGLY ENOUGH, BOTH MIRIAM AND Stan were at the office that day to check on the shaky status of Adam's division and its ability to hit the milestones set forth in the acquisition agreement. Stan's initial rationale for his visit was to make sure he got that favor he had done for Adam repaid at some point, sooner rather than later. His reelection was coming up, and he had always been able to rely on Adam to get out the vote.

Before the acquisition, Adam's company had been one of the largest employers in that area of the state. That is why Stan consciously made it a priority to visit Adam regularly at the office and get his face in front of the ever-fickle proletariat. Unbeknownst to Jocelyn, because she just didn't care, was that Stan's longtime popularity had been taking a nosedive ever since the casino opened. Stan had helped get the much-contested casino passed on the referendum with promises of it providing local jobs and improving the economy.

Naturally, the inverse happened.

Jocelyn's property taxes went up to pay for more police because crime went up. Way up. The casino was not hiring local people as advertised but instead was hiring migrant workers from all over the place. People were getting green cards to work there, and because of that, the already stressed public school system had to provide English as a Second Language classes for thirteen different languages. Jocelyn's taxes went up again.

And if that wasn't bad enough, the scene with the

water started to enrage the local residents. The water supply had been considered plentiful for the residents of the towns, but this was not the case for the casino and its associated hotels with their water-starved golf courses and swimming pools. The water bills, which had previously been almost free, were starting to become alarmingly high.

The casino, truth be told, had listened to the complaints of the town residents. To avoid the "speeding drunk" and "someone broke into my house for the third time" complaints, the casino, because it could, rerouted the roads so that all significant traffic led directly onto the casino's property, thus bypassing the town centers that had hoped to renew their local economy with casino traffic. This wasn't good. Longtime residents were leaving, and property values were going down as taxes were going up. Meanwhile, the casino had paid off its loan ahead of schedule to its Malaysian bank.

There really was nothing Adam could offer Stan, the Democratic congressman, this election, especially now that the Conglomerate was actively advocating that their employees vote Republican if they wanted a job. However, after seeing Robert with Miriam, something other than the upcoming election was now in play for Stan.

Miriam's visit to Jocelyn's division was to make sure that she would be ahead of the game if she, as the only woman on the board, had to save face for recommending Adam's business for acquisition. She had recommended it based on the tip she had received from Stan at a restaurant opening in DC. Of course she had researched it. It looked great on paper. But she had not visited the facility until now.

Miriam had worked hard for more than thirty years to get where she was. She had devoted herself to a lifelong study of economics, the stock market, and business. Surviving and outperforming her classmates as the only female in any of her classes at Stanford and Wharton in the 1960s and '70s, she forwent having children or any sort of traditional or lasting relationship with a man. It was rumored, back in her younger days, that she was a lesbian. Regardless of her motivation, Miriam was clearly driven to succeed.

Both Stan and Miriam were now personally invested in Jocelyn's division. They needed this place to stay afloat in order to keep something even more important than Robert's or Jocelyn's measly job intact. They were there hoping to preserve their reputations as go-to movers and shakers.

For some reason, Stan and Miriam's small talk in the waiting area outside of Robert's office began to revolve around Jocelyn and her contributions to the company. "Because of her, this company's communications have been electrified," enthused Stan as he leaned back to admire Jocelyn.

Is he talking about the fact that we use e-mail now?

"She's a one-armed paper hanger. No one will ever forget how she single-handedly got fifteen copies of that Indo proposal out in one night."

Jocelyn was now blushing. "Well, I just made copies of something that took the whole place years to do, but yeah, that was a tough night."

"Oh, don't be so modest! Adam says he wouldn't have been able to pull this off without you."

Jocelyn was of course thrilled and tried to act humble about all the accolades that Stan was throwing her way. Meanwhile, Robert, although sporting a handsome smile, looked as if he was going to break his own jaw. Robert didn't have to live through it very long, though, because both Stan and Miriam were on a tight schedule. They pleasantly made their exits, leaving Robert and Jocelyn to re- turn to their new offices without so much as a glance between them.

When Jocelyn got back to her office, aglow with her accomplishment of one-upping Robert, a little light was flashing on her phone. Someone had left her a voice mail.

CHAPTER TWENTY-SIX

"UHHHH ... I HOPE THIS IS you ..." And the man hung up. Jocelyn didn't recognize his voice.

What the ...? Probably the wrong extension. She immediately set to work on putting together the schedule and budget for the trade shows, print advertising, and press releases for next year. This corporate-issued task was particularly onerous, given that she knew there was a high probability that she wouldn't even be employed by this company next year. But what the heck, she had just blown Robert out of the water, and she felt compelled to do it again. So she put her full effort into producing the most attractive, engaging, and exciting timeline and budget, which she would submit directly to headquarters.

About twenty-five minutes into her budgeting blitzkrieg, some- one knocked on her flimsy battleship-gray office door.

Jocelyn didn't recognize the fortysomethingish-looking man at first without his shower cap and complementary white scrub-room outfit, but he was one of the guys from the static-free-environment break room she had inadvertently stumbled upon while trying to locate her new office.

Once she figured out where she had seen him before, Jocelyn greeted her visitor with, "Hey! Welcome to my humble abode." She swiveled herself around in her chair with her arm outstretched and palm up, Vanna White style, as if showing off her gracious accommodations, and rolled away from her computer so that she could talk with him. "What brings you here?" Jocelyn asked, honestly curious.

He smiled. "We got a bunch of boxes delivered to us, and I'm pretty sure they are yours. They aren't ours."

"Mine personally?" queried Jocelyn.

"No, your company's."

"My company? What the heck are you talking about? Don't we work for the same company?" Jocelyn asked, more than a bit confused.

"No." Now it was Static-Free Guy's turn to look confused. "I don't think so, anyway. Our company rents the space from Adam's wife. Sorry. Ex-wife."

"Reeeeeaaaally ..." This explained why Jocelyn had never seen those two guys before, and why their break room was exquisitely maintained.

"Um, yeah. You didn't know that?" Static-Free asked.

"No." Jocelyn answered simply. "Hey, was it you who called me and left a message earlier?"

"Yeah," he replied with a sheepish grin. "All these boxes kept coming in, and I thought ..." He was starting to look embarrassed but continued, "Why don't you come over and check it out? We need them cleared out of our space."

Jocelyn agreed to go with him around the corner to his company's rented space to look at the boxes. And boxes there were. Lots of boxes of various sizes, some as large as refrigerators, were stacked up along the hallway.

"And look at this," Static-Free Guy said as he led her down the box-lined hallway and out through a door to their loading dock, which had also been hit with the box-delivery ugly stick.

"Why don't you call Vince? I'm really not the person who handles deliveries."

"I did. He said he didn't know anything about it, and that I'd have to call the warehouse. That's how I ended up getting your extension—which is still listed as the warehouse, by the way. I left that message." He rubbed the back of his neck as he looked around. "More boxes kept coming, and Ronnie and I decided that we might as well call it a day, because the delivery was so disruptive. I stayed until the couriers said that they had unloaded everything, but one of them said he would probably be back tomorrow."

"Couriers? You mean FedEx or UPS?" Jocelyn asked.

"No. It was a courier company with a moving truck."

Jocelyn looked at the shipping label on the box nearest her. There were US Customs stamps on it, and it clearly said, *Point of Origin: People's Republic of China.* The intended recipient was listed as DVIE.

"Well, who is DVIE? Why don't you call them?" Jocelyn said.

"I looked for their number, but it's not listed. I asked the courier who they were, and he said all he personally had was this address, which as you can see is ours. He said he'd check back at his office for a phone number and get back to me. But he did say someone at his office had called and confirmed the address before they sent the guys out to the airport to pick all this stuff up."

Both Jocelyn and Static-Free Guy stood and surveyed the situation.

He continued, "They gave all this stuff to us because our company is Davis/Veritas Electronics, Inc. They figured that the name on the delivery label must be an abbreviation of our company name, which would be DVEI, which is pretty darn close to DVIE. They wouldn't stop unloading their truck. They insisted that this was the right place."

"Well, did you sign for all this?" Jocelyn asked, unable to believe that someone would willingly accept a shipment this large if it wasn't theirs.

"Well, Ronnie did when they first showed up. But he didn't realize that it was more than just a couple of packages. Then when he tried to tell them that they had made a mistake, they wouldn't believe it and just kept unpacking the truck."

"Dude ... this is messed up. What are you gonna do?" Jocelyn commiserated.

"I'm not sure. I was hoping that you would know if

your company had a big order coming in, or if you knew what DVIE was."

Just then, the Davis/Veritas Electronics, Inc., phone rang. Static- Free Guy ran to pick it up at one of the nearby empty workstations.

Jocelyn turned to view the packages on the loading dock. It appeared all were addressed to DVIE and that all came from the People's Republic of China. Jocelyn didn't know what else she might offer as assistance, so she decided that after Static-Free Guy got off the phone, she would make her exit and get back to that budget/timeline document that headquarters was looking for.

"Well, that was the courier's," Static-Free said. "They gave me this phone number for DVIE. It looks like they may be in this build- ing. Look." He handed Jocelyn the phone number he had written down on one of those pink "While You Were Out" message pads.

Sure enough, Jocelyn recognized the first part of the phone number. Overtaken by curiosity, she decided to wait until he got an answer before she headed back to her battleship-gray confines. "Call them!" Jocelyn urged.

Without hesitation, he punched in the number. Jocelyn stood close enough to hear the phone ring two times, and then she heard the unmistakable vocal stylings of Mimi the receptionist, "Good afternoon, Darling Vintners Import Export, how might I direct your call?"

"Mimi! That's Mimi!" Jocelyn whispered excitedly.

"Uh, uh, yes. I am in receipt of a shipment intended for you. A large shipment. I would like it removed from my office suite immediately."

JOCELYN MADE HER WAY BACK to her office, but not before she and Static-Free Guy exchanged names and phone numbers. His name was Randall Veritas (but Jocelyn could call him Randy), and he was one of the owners of

Davis/Veritas Electronics, Inc., a small company of eight employees.

Randy said to Jocelyn as they parted, “Maybe we could go get some coffee sometime?”

Finding the statement mutually amusing, Jocelyn replied back with a cheeky, “Well, maybe if those large-caliber gems start showing up ...” They both grinned, and she made her exit.

As she sat down to continue her marketing work, she found herself completely useless while trying to complete the corporate- assigned task. She was preoccupied by the fact that Mimi had answered the phone for Darling Vintners Import Export.

Ahhh. That’s Adam’s fiancée’s company. Jocelyn stared at her phone. Her hands were placed on the keyboard as if she might actually type something. But she was quite distracted by this recent turn of events. *What is Adam’s girlfriend’s company doing shipping in this much stuff from China? What are they bringing in, buttloads of sake? No. No. Sake is from Japan ...* And before she could really throw herself into researching the best-selling alcoholic beverages in China, her mind wandered back to the scene at dinner with Dad and Adam as they hashed out their plans of making him a building consultant for the Indonesia contract.

“That doesn’t make any sense, though,” she thought out loud. “The RFP specifically stated that all delivered content is to be made in the United States.”

Forcing herself to forget about the mystery of Adam, his ridiculous fiancée, the ridiculous fiancée’s construction-magnate dad, the much-anticipated Indonesia-contract signing, the preposterous stash of boxes sitting in the Davis/Veritas Electronics, Inc., office next door, and China, Jocelyn completed the marketing report, but it wasn’t nearly as satisfying as she had initially anticipated. She was far more interested in figuring out if those boxes were meant for Indonesia than one-upping her boss. She sent her final product in to corporate with a click of her mouse and went home.

CHAPTER TWENTY-SEVEN

THE NEXT DAY, SHE CAME into the office at her regular time, eight in the morning. Several people had already been at work now, in this office, for an hour and a half. But her coworkers the world over had been working while she slept. There was never a time anywhere on the planet when someone from her company was not working to affect the stock price of the Conglomerate.

When she arrived at her battleship-gray, fluorescently illuminated, seven-foot-tall office door, she immediately sensed that some- one had been in her office. Everything looked okay. She couldn't put her finger on it. But she knew someone had been there.

Brushing this nagging feeling off, she turned on her computer, hung up her jacket, and headed to the break room to grab her first cup of coffee. On her way back, she swung over to see if the same temp from yesterday had shown up. *Nope.* There was a new temp today, whose name she promptly forgot. Temps were floating in and out on a regular basis, and she had given up trying to remember their names after that first one, Shelly. Shelly had been so quick on the uptake compared to the people the temp agency kept throwing her way. And it was rather heartbreaking when Shelly unexpectedly didn't show up for work one day and no one, not the temp agency, not even Mimi with her friends over at the police station, could track her down. It was like she never existed at all. Just showed up the day Nancy died and then just as suddenly disappeared without a trace.

Jocelyn began the arduous task of trying to explain, once again, how Nancy would format all the different parts of the proposals submitted by the various departments. The "cut and paste and rework within MS Word" thing was critical so that the final product would print out properly on the publication department's printers and, even more importantly, comply with corporate-branding protocol.

Jocelyn also took the time to instruct the new temp as to how to bind the various-sized proposals. It was over an hour later, while Jocelyn was attempting to explain the point of the proposal log, that she noticed it. The log was missing pages. Randomly.

Knowing that missing pages would not be of any significance to the temp, Jocelyn decided to seriously pare down the educational overview of the proposal log. She closed up the log's binder and placed it on top of the other two binders sitting on the desk.

"How 'bout I leave you to format the new covers, and I'll come back with the text for the first two sections in about twenty minutes and see how you did?"

The temp seemed agreeable to this, so Jocelyn excused herself, picked up the proposal log binders, and brought them back to her office. She plopped them down on the corner of her desk. Although she wanted to immediately study the logbooks, she knew she would have to wait until she got at least a modicum of work done on the two pending proposals before she would be able to really dig into the missing-pages mystery.

Jocelyn sat down in her chair and glanced over her e-mail inbox as she waited for Microsoft Word to load. "Oh, great. They want me down in Virginia the day after tomorrow. Great timing," Jocelyn mumbled as she instinctively, and without looking, opened her top right desk drawer so that she could consult her calendar. When she finally finished reading the summons from corporate, she glanced down at the drawer. What she saw was many times more baffling than the pages missing from the proposal log.

The out-of-place object was about the size of a quarter,

and it sat all by itself. She noticed it right away as it caught the fluorescent light drizzling down upon it. Someone must have rearranged the pens, paper clips, and random rubber bands in her drawer organizer so that it would sit resplendently and in its own singular glory until she discovered it. Jocelyn blinked and stared at it while realizing that her initial impression that someone had been in her office had been correct. A bit tentatively, she picked up the gold coin and studied it.

The coin featured the image of a hopping gazelle and the year 1984 on one side. It appeared to have English and some other language on it. *Krugerrand* was spelled out in capital letters above the frolicking gazelle, and below the animal were the words *Fyngoud 1 Oz Fine Gold.* On the reverse, there was a profile of a bearded man with the inscription *Sud-Afrika South Africa.*

Clearly intrigued by this turn of events, Jocelyn quickly went to Yahoo and typed in *Krugerrand*. In a matter of milliseconds, her computer's monitor was filled with links that brought her to plenty of images and information about this coin. Although Jocelyn had never seen a coin like this before in her life, according to the Internet it was fairly well recognized by collectors the world over and worth over $300.

"Whoa," she said quietly as she turned from the monitor to look at the coin. *Who the heck walks around with a gold coin in their pocket? And what is it doing in my desk? Who would put it there?* Jocelyn's mind was aflutter with questions as she continued in earnest to learn more about the mysterious coin. *Can you use it to buy things? Or is it more like a piece of jewelry?*

It dawned on Jocelyn that maybe someone was playing a joke on her. *This is a joke!* she thought while smirking but still clicking on the links, which revealed more in-depth information about the coin.

No one just puts real gold in someone's desk drawer. It's probably fake.

"Hey! Whoever left me a gold coin, thank you! But stay out of my office!" Jocelyn shouted over her executive cube's seven-foot wall. At this moment, Jocelyn would have preferred a traditional cube, like they had in accounting, so that she could see if anyone was reacting to her. But no one responded. Not even the typical snicker or "Shut up!"

Humph.

With the lack of response, Jocelyn grabbed a Sharpie marker and quickly wrote up a "Please *stay out of my office* if I'm not here. *Thank you!*" sign and taped it to her door.

Aside from finding a one-ounce gold coin in her desk drawer, the day was pretty uneventful. Jocelyn and the temp finished the two small proposals. However, Jocelyn didn't get the chance to go through the proposal logbooks as she had hoped. Instead, she decided to take all three of the binders home with her so that she could figure out exactly which pages and which proposals were missing. Naturally, if Nancy had been around, this would have been forbid- den, but seeing as she wasn't ...

THAT EVENING, WEARING HER YOYA pants and her alma mater's cozy MassArt Champion sweatshirt, she picked on some Chinese takeout while flipping through the proposal logs. *Why are only some of these pages missing?* Jocelyn had set up shop on the floor next to the coffee table. Her favorite show, *24*, was going to start in a little bit, and this proposal log thing was keeping her busy until then. It appeared that six pages were missing from Nancy's amended document—one from 2002, two from 2001, and one each from 1999, 1994, and 1984.

"1984 ... that's the date on the coin," Jocelyn said in surprise as she pulled the coin out of her purse, which was flopped down next to the takeout bags on the coffee table. Sure enough, the date on the Krugerrand and the year associated with one of the missing logbook pages was a match. *Hmmm ... Funny coincidence.*

CHAPTER TWENTY-EIGHT

THE NEXT DAY, JOCELYN ROLLED into work earlier than usual so that she could return the proposal logs to what was still referred to as Nancy's office. She put them back exactly as she had found them, and she was glad that the temp hadn't locked the door.

Now with the logbooks returned, Jocelyn was ready to move on with the day's real-life challenges. As she approached her own office, the "stay out of my office" sign she had scribbled the day before welcomed her. Once inside, she took the time to quickly check the desk drawer. Just in case. And although she hadn't really expected to find anything, she found herself feeling a smidge disappointed that nothing was in the empty little compartment for her.

She set to work completing the travel paperwork for her corporate-mandated trip to Virginia. She hadn't had time to do it yesterday, and she was supposed to leave the next day, bright and early on the red-eye flight. Ideally she would like to go tonight and sleep over so that she might look less disheveled for her meeting the next morning. But naturally, a hotel stay was out of the question—too expensive. She had given up on that a long time ago. But she still held out hope for a Reagan International flight, and just for giggles she filled the paperwork out as such. She knew that they would be sending her to BWI no matter what.

Jocelyn looked over her "things to do today" list from the day before and checked off the box she had drawn next to "travel paperwork." She tapped the papers purposefully on her desk and was about to head over to the accounting department to turn in the travel requisition when she noticed the time. *No way.* She looked around for her cell phone to double-check the time. Yes way. How did I just spend the whole day doing a travel requisition? And where is everyone else?

"Good God! What's that smell in here?" Martin Mays exclaimed as he entered the former warehouse now known as the new marketing area. "What are they trying to do to us now? Gas us?"

Jocelyn, seated in her wheeled desk chair, rolled over to her cube's doorway so that she could see Martin approaching. He was wearing a suit. He never wore a suit.

"Oh, for goodness' sake, Jocelyn, you're here, in this mess? You should get out. Can't you smell that?"

Jocelyn looked blankly up at suited Martin as she took the time to deliberately assess the air quality. "I guess I smell something—spray paint, right? I think they are doing something in the warehouse. I've been hearing things banging around all day. Anyway, you look nice."

"You must have been sitting here too long and you can't even smell it. Go get some fresh air, kiddo. You look like you need it."

"I don't need a cigarette. You know I don't smoke, Martin," Jocelyn said, knowing what "fresh air" meant to the smokers.

"No. I mean real fresh air. This place smells like a chemical dump, and you look a little loopy," Martin said.

"Oh, okay, if you insist. Why are you here then? And looking so nice?" Jocelyn asked as she reached for her coat.

"I just came from a job interview."

Jocelyn meekly smiled. "Oh, good for you."

Martin continued as Jocelyn buttoned her coat, "I figured I'd swing by the office and touch up some of the code I had been working on. But I'm not sitting in this noxious cloud!" He scrunched his nose and grimaced in disgust. "C'mon. I'll just grab my stuff and head out with you. Now I need some of that specialty 'fresh air' you were talking about."

After Martin picked up a notebook and a few of his trade magazines and locked the door to his closet-slash-office, the two of them headed outside. Once in the parking lot, Martin smoothly produced a cigarette from a pack of Newports conveniently located in his breast pocket while simultaneously flicking a Zippo lighter to life. His movements were so effortless and natural as he lit his cigarette, it was apparent that what he was doing was a part of his being. Jocelyn waited while he inhaled before she spoke.

"I'm heading to corporate tomorrow."

"I don't know whether to congratulate you or beg you to reconsider," Martin smugly grumbled in the signature way that Jocelyn had come to appreciate.

She smiled as she poked her hands into her coat pockets. "I'll be presenting my marketing budget, I think. I'm a little sketchy as to why they need me in person so immediately for this," Jocelyn said.

"They didn't ask Robert to go?" Martin asked as he took another drag off the cigarette.

"I don't think so. He didn't have anything to do with approving the travel."

"Uh-huh. Very well done, Jocelyn. Very well done."

"What the heck are you talking about, Martin?"

He shook his head as he flicked the ashes off his cigarette. "Someone likes you."

"Who?" Jocelyn asked.

"You got me. Otherwise I'd be beating a path to their office right now and not sharing the information with anyone," Martin said.

Jocelyn looked at him and grinned at his dramatics. "If this mystery person reveals himself to me, I'll be sure to share it with *you*, Martin." Then it dawned on her to ask him. "Speaking of mystery people liking me, would you happen to know who might have left a little gift in my desk recently?"

"*Inside* your desk?"

"Yeah."

"Nope." He took another puff and shook his head. "I can't imagine anyone who would dare venture so boldly," Martin replied in his deadpan fashion before he exhaled the majority of smoke he was holding in his lungs. "Good luck tomorrow with those jokers at corporate, Jocelyn. I think you'll be fine." He winked at her and offered up one of his rare smiles.

"Thanks, Martin. I'm not really looking forward to it. See you when I get back."

Martin turned toward the parking lot to find his car, and Jocelyn headed back into the building. Even before she reached the marketing area, she could smell what Martin had been talking about. It was pretty amazing that it hadn't really bothered her before. The smell must have been very slowly permeating the room, and being so focused on her pointless desk work, she just didn't notice.

Whoa. Okay, now I know what he was talking about. Jocelyn could feel a headache roaring her way. Like Martin, she decided it was time to leave. She grabbed her budgets and her purse, eager to get out of what could only be called a toxic olfactory disaster.

Instead of leaving directly, she decided to head down to maintenance and find Vince. She knew it would be a futile waste of breath, but at least it would make her feel proactive, like she was actually attempting to fix the situation when she knew it wouldn't be until tomorrow when someone even reported it.

Naturally, Vince wasn't in the maintenance office when Jocelyn arrived. He was in the nearby break room with some other guys, munching on some picked-over pastries, when Jocelyn finally located him.

"Vince! What the heck is going on? The new marketing area smells like someone squirted spray paint over a pile of burning plastic chairs. Why am I being forced to endure this?" Jocelyn implored.

All the guys around the table grinned as they sipped their coffee and looked at Vince, eager to hear his response.

"Oh, hi, Jocelyn, you've got a pretty good nose there. Warehouse figured that today would be a good day to do this, seeing as it looked like everyone was on travel or leaving early. I'm sorry. I guess no one realized that you were still here."

"My head is killing me, Vince. Obviously, ventilation is a problem in the new marketing area. Is there anything you can do to clear out that smell? No one is going to be able to work in there tomorrow," Jocelyn complained.

"It's not that bad."

"Oh, yes it is! Here, come down with me right now and check it out for yourself."

Vince took leave of his break-room compatriots and accompanied Jocelyn back to the new marketing area—but not before stopping at the maintenance closet and picking up a can of lemon-scented air freshener.

Jocelyn flicked on the slightly buzzing and tediously tremulous fluorescent lights as the two of them stepped into a room that could have easily been misconstrued as a basketball court had it not been for the battleship-gray indoor–outdoor carpeting and matching high- walled executive cubes.

"There. You smell that?" Jocelyn asked Vince while surveying the room as if she might spot where the smell was coming from.

Vince's expression made evident that of course he smelled it. He headed straight over to Jocelyn's executive cube and entered. He looked around and slowly began pushing her filing cabinet away from the rear wall that was a real floor-to-ceiling wall, not a portable cube wall. It was the wall that Vince had constructed to partition the warehouse in order to make space for the marketing area.

"Well, this must be where its coming from," Vince said as he folded his arms across his chest and studied the heating vent that had been buried behind the filing cabinet.

"But how in the hell ..." Vince was clearly confused by the situation.

"Vince, my head is pounding. How in the hell *what*? Isn't the warehouse right behind this wall? What were they doing in there?" Jocelyn asked.

"Oh, it's not them that I'm worried about. They were just un- packing and packaging up some boxes. Probably spray-painting some stuff. But the smell of burning plastic, that's coming from someplace else," Vince said, now fully engaged in technical problem-solving. "And I'm not sure how this might have happened, but ..."

He exited Jocelyn's cube and headed over to Martin's locked closet of an office. He took a set of keys off his belt and opened the door. Jocelyn, forever curious, followed him and watched as he climbed up on top of Martin's desk and inspected a heating return.

"I'm going to have to get the HVAC guy in here. This doesn't make any sense."

"Hey! Anyone home? Vince? You in here?"

Vince, still standing on the desk, and Jocelyn both turned around to see Randall Veritas, from the office suite next door, approaching. He was outfitted in his all-white garb, complete with booties and shower cap, complemented by a respirator hanging around his neck.

"Yup! I'm in here, Randy," Vince called out.

"Oh good, I found you," Randy said with relief. "Oh, hi, Jocelyn, fancy meeting you here," he said with a schoolboy's grin.

"You here to complain about the smell, Randy?" Vince asked.

"Was it the OSHA-approved combination respirator that gave me away?" Randy sardonically chided in a way that only a guy dressed in white booties and a shower cap can, while pointing to said piece of equipment. "Yeah. That's exactly why I'm looking for you, Vince. Is this going to end soon? We can't work like this next door."

Vince responded, "Honestly, I'm not sure what that smell is. I know the guys in the warehouse were spray-painting today. But the plastic smell is from somewhere else. I'll put a call in to the HVAC guys and have them come and check it out. Until they show up, I'm going to shut off the heat in this building." Vince hopped rather spryly (for a man getting ready to retire) off Martin Mays's desk. "I'll keep you posted. Here, take some of this with you in the meantime."

Vince produced the lemon-scented air freshener and offered it to Jocelyn, who looked at it as if he were joking. So Vince offered it to Randy, who also seemed less than enthused. Their responses prompted Vince to pop the lid off the can and shoot out some random spritzes of air freshener. "This stuff works great. Kills all sorts of odors."

"Jeez, Vince. My head is going to explode!" Jocelyn protested. "We don't need another chemical!"

"Nah ... its good for you," Vince said as he replaced the cap and headed toward the door. "Remember to bring a sweater tomorrow. The heat is going to be off."

Jocelyn and Randy looked at each other as if to say, *Oh, of course. No heat. Perfect.*

"We should get out of here. This place is toxic," Randy said as they both started toward the exit.

"Yeah. In more ways than one," Jocelyn said. "Seriously, though, this isn't cool."

"Oh, Vince will figure it out," Randy said reassuringly as he turned to look at her and smile.

With that warm smile, a little lightbulb went on in Jocelyn's head.

"Hey, you didn't happen to leave me something the other day, did you?" Jocelyn asked.

"I don't think so."

"Maybe it was something kind of *valuable*?"

"Ha! No. Of that, I can be sure!"

Perceiving her instant deflation, Randy quickly offered the consolation prize of going out for coffee. Jocelyn declined, saying that she had a headache and needed to get home to get some rest before she left for Virginia early the next morning. Together, but clearly apart, the two of them left the building. Meanwhile, work continued in the warehouse.

CHAPTER TWENTY-NINE

THE NEXT MORNING AT ZERO-DARK-THIRTY, Jocelyn was standing in line with the other red-eye passengers, clutching a Styrofoam coffee cup and waiting her turn to check in and pick up her ticket and boarding pass. It was just a day trip. Not a big deal. She'd be home cozy in her own bed by eight thirty that night, latest. The woman at the desk asked for her name and destination.

"Jocelyn McLaren. BWI."

"Hmm. I don't have a McLaren on the BWI flight. Spell it for me, please."

"M-c-l-a-r-e-n," Jocelyn said as she attempted to crane herself over the counter to see the computer monitor. An inordinate amount of time seemed to pass as the woman searched the computer's flight roster.

"I don't have ... Oh, wait, are you sure it's BWI?"

Now Jocelyn was getting nervous. "Yes. I'm sure." *How much is this going to suck if I don't make the meeting today?* She put her coffee cup on the counter and started searching through her pocketbook for the cell phone. She wondered if anyone was at work who could answer travel calls this early in the morning.

"I'm pretty confident it's BWI, but I didn't hear back from any- one yesterday. We were having kind of a ... a stinky day at the office," Jocelyn answered feebly while finally catching hold of the cell phone.

"Oh, I'm sorry. I think you have the wrong flight."

Jocelyn's heart sank. *Shit. I hate travel requisitions. What a convoluted process ...* Jocelyn began mentally berating the accounting department and all corporate accounting practices as she started dialing the office. She hadn't yet come to the part where she would begrudgingly admit that it was her own damn fault for handing in the documents so late when the woman said, "I have a McLaren on the Reagan International flight leaving in ten minutes. Is that you?"

"Seriously?" Jocelyn looked up from her phone in disbelief.

"Yes. It says Jocelyn McLaren right here," she said, pointing to the computer monitor. "I'm sorry. If you need BWI, I can book something for you, but I will need ..."

"Oh no! This will be more than fine! This is perfect!" Jocelyn enthused happily to the entire airport as the woman behind the counter stashed the tickets and boarding passes efficiently into a little folder.

"Well, Ms. McLaren, you just made my day," the woman said as she handed the tickets to Jocelyn. "I don't often get customers as excited as you this early in the morning. Enjoy your flight."

"Sweet!" Jocelyn couldn't believe it! How long had she been schlepping to BWI and complaining about it? *The squeaky wheel really does get the grease!* She was so proud of herself as she dashed to her gate and boarded the plane.

When Jocelyn arrived at Reagan, she followed the crowd toward the exit intending to hail a cab. Since she was much closer to her destination than she would have been at BWI, she actually had quite a bit of time to spare before her meeting.

"This is awesome!" Jocelyn congratulated herself when she realized how early she was. As she rounded the corner leading to the exit, she was surprised to see an older man wearing an ill-fitting suit holding a piece of paper with "J. McLaren" scribbled on it. He was surrounded by a bunch of other men of a similar ilk, holding hand- written signs signaling other travelers.

Just because she was feeling so wonderful that she had magically been afforded the flight to Reagan, and believing that nothing ventured nothing gained, Jocelyn flashed a smile at the man. When he seemed receptive to her smile, she approached him saying, "I'm wondering if *I* might be the person you're looking for?"

"I am looking for a woman. What's your first name?" the man asked, unmoved.

"Jocelyn," she answered.

"Yup. I'm here to take you to your meeting," the man said, folding up his sign. "My name is Frank," he said as they shook hands. "We should be there in about twenty-five minutes."

"That sounds great! Thanks, Frank," Jocelyn said and followed up by leaving "this seriously *rocks*!" unarticulated. But honestly, she couldn't believe her luck. Frank led her to a black Lincoln Town Car waiting at the curb and held the door open for her as she climbed in. She wondered if she was supposed to tip this guy and figured she'd ask him once they got moving.

What just happened that makes me eligible for this royal treatment?

Frank was a man of few words, so Jocelyn watched in silence as they left the airport and entered the highway traffic. It was about ten minutes into the drive when Jocelyn noticed that they were not following the signs pointing toward Alexandria, home of the Conglomerate's corporate branch office set up specifically to deal with the Pentagon. "Um, aren't we supposed to be going that way?" Jocelyn leaned forward and pointed behind them. Frank gave her a look in the rearview mirror.

"I certainly hope not," he said.

"But it looks like we are going away from Alexandria," Jocelyn said as she turned around to see what the opposing highway traffic signs said.

"I'm taking you to a breakfast meeting in DC," Frank

said.

"Really?" Jocelyn retorted, more than a bit taken aback by this information.

At first all of this had seemed enchanting, but now it was just confusing, and a full-on panic was beginning to settle in. It would have easily erupted into emergency self-defense mode if it had not been for Frank, right at that moment, saying, "Yeah. The congressman is going to meet you there."

Jocelyn could literally feel the pieces of the puzzle mentally slip into place. "Stan ... Stan the congressman. Wow. He's pretty smooth. I wonder if he knows I have to be at a meeting this morning in Alexandria?" Less than a millisecond elapsed before she allowed herself to reach the logical conclusion: *Of course he does!*

She sat in silence as she ruminated about how she had allowed herself to be willingly kidnapped yet again. *First the Project LISA thing and now this! What the hell? Girl, grow a pair for goodness' sake! Or at least think things through! You can't be led around like this. Do you think Stan would do this to Robert? No!* Jocelyn got pretty worked up convincing herself that she would stand up to the forces that manipulated her. That was until she arrived at the five-star Hay-Adams Hotel where the forces that were manipulating her were hidden in plain view almost everywhere she looked.

The black Lincoln Town Car slid up to the main entrance of the hotel, where a doorman with a well-chiseled jaw opened the car door for her.

"I'm sorry. Am I supposed to tip you?" Jocelyn asked Frank.

"I won't say no," was Frank's response.

Jocelyn dug around in her wallet and found a ten-dollar bill that she was just going to give to some random cab driver anyway. She passed it up to Frank while thanking him for the safe journey and made her way out of the car.

Okay, so now what?

The doorman stood at the ready to shut the car door as

soon as Jocelyn made her move, but she didn't, and that prompted the doorman to ask, "Might I help you?"

Thankful for this offer, Jocelyn said, "Yes, actually. I'm here to meet my congressman for breakfast."

"Just go through the main entrance and take a left. Go up the stairs. You can't miss it."

Jocelyn really wasn't sure if she should tip this guy either, so she gave him a ten-dollar bill as well. *What the heck? It's all going on the expense report. I would have spent it on taxis anyway.* She gave him the money and headed off to give Stan the congressman a piece of her mind.

The Hay-Adams Hotel was extraordinary. Just lovely. It clearly wasn't your typical Holiday Inn or Sheraton. Even the lobby's flower arrangement was outstanding and worthy of stopping to appreciate. Jocelyn followed the doorman's directions to the Lafayette Room, where breakfast was being served.

As soon as she crossed the threshold, she saw the familiar figure of Stan approaching. Only this time, he was much more demure in greeting her. He walked up in a deliberately casual manner and kissed her cheek while holding both her shoulders.

"Oh, Jocelyn, I am so happy that you could join me here today. Let's find a place to sit down and talk," Stan said as they made their way toward the windows.

Jocelyn followed him to a white-linen-covered table set with a bud vase containing a stunning stem of soft blush-colored orchids.

"Are you hungry? They have great food here," he said, holding the chair for her to take a seat. "Anything you want, they'll make it for you, and it's the best you've ever had." He sat down across from her.

"I'm sure it is, Stan. This place looks really nice. Super nice. Why are we here, Stan?" Jocelyn asked. "I have a meeting to go to in Alexandria, as I'm sure you're probably aware, and I can't ..."

Stan cut her off. "This place is the current hot spot to see and be seen. Just enjoy yourself," Stan said, taking hold of his napkin as his eyes darted around the room. A waiter approached offering coffee, which they both accepted.

"Well, that's great, Stan. We are seeing and being seen. I have to get to a meeting very soon. Was there something specific that you wanted to talk with me about? Or were you just trying to whisk me away so that people would think you were having an affair?" Jocelyn asked with more than a hint of aggravation in her voice.

Stan burst out laughing, "Oh, Jocelyn! That would make my day! It's all part of the scene around here. Don't you fret. Besides, the doorman already knows you didn't stay here, and he'll see you leave. I just wanted to grab some time with you before you headed to your meeting."

"Did you hook me up with the Reagan flight?" Jocelyn asked.

"Not directly," Stan answered honestly, but Jocelyn couldn't help but notice the mischievous twinkle in his eye as he said it. Before she could comment, a beautiful waitress emerged.

"Are you ready to place your order?" she asked.

She wasn't holding a pen or pad to jot down their breakfast selections. Jocelyn had learned a long time ago that this was a sign of a quality institution, when the waitstaff basically memorized what you wanted. She always wondered when she encountered this herculean mental feat of culinary final presentation that maybe, just maybe, the server had a little Dictaphone tape recorder in his or her pocket. She knew that when she worked at Pizzeria Uno during college for exactly twelve shifts before she tearfully walked off the job that she would have never been able to pull it off. But the tape recorder wouldn't be necessary today. Stan declined ordering anything, and Jocelyn ordered up a fruit salad and a croissant.

The pretty waitress walked away, and Jocelyn asked, "So Stan, really, why am I here?"

Stan didn't answer but proceeded to quickly unbuckle his pants, untuck his shirt, and reach down into his pocket.

Jocelyn sat with mouth agape. *What the ...*

The congressman fumbled around in his pocket and finally produced a syringe. He then unceremoniously stabbed himself in the stomach.

Obviously, Jocelyn had not been expecting that. After he had finished administering the injection, Jocelyn asked with trepidation, "What is that, Stan? What's going on? Are you okay?"

"Oh, I'll be fine. Diabetes. It's a bitch."

"Can I get you anything?" Jocelyn said as she hurriedly glanced around the room, looking to see if she might be able to get a waiter's attention.

"No. No. I'm fine." Stan licked his lips and took some deep breaths. Jocelyn waited for him to recover as she watched him in- tensely, making sure that he wasn't going to drop dead in front of her.

"Look, Jocelyn, things are changing. The country is changing. I doubt that I will win reelection, and ..."

"Oh, Stan, stop. How can you possibly know for sure? Maybe you'll get a big surprise on election day."

"Oh, you are such a darling. But my dear, I regret to say that my time has come. I'm ready to move on to greener pastures. I will be officially lobbying soon, and I would like for you to be in charge of my marketing." When Stan noticed that Jocelyn seemed honestly confused by what he was saying, he quickly followed up with, "Or maybe you could just do up my website."

"Seriously? That's why you brought me here? To see if I would create a website for you?" Despite the fact that Jocelyn might very well be out of a job soon, she wasn't convinced that this was the actual motivation for Stan surreptitiously putting her on a markedly more expensive flight and hiring a driver to bring her to this place. "Why am I not buying this, Stan?" she said as she glanced around the room. "And more importantly, why would you want to get into lobbying?" Jocelyn inquired as the fruit salad and croissant were silently slipped in front of her. "I thought lobbyists were the bane of your existence."

He grinned. "Oh, I've been at this for decades now, Jocelyn. Lobbyists make much more than I do. In reality, they have much more power than any congressman or any citizen," he said as he sat back to enjoy the view of her putting fruit into her mouth. Even though he had just staved off some sort of diabetic coma, he still maintained his trademark inappropriate lewdness. "The lobbyists literally push the edges of our existence here in this country—not to mention those poor souls living in other countries." He motioned vaguely to the poor souls. "It's lobbyist against lobbyist in there, Jocelyn. Congress and the American public are simply speed bumps for them. And who's better than me to capitalize on this? I mean, honestly, it takes at least two terms to even know where the bath- room is, let alone know who's scratching whose back. I'm at a point where I can legitimately charge for my expertise."

She put her fork down. "I'm sure you could, Stan. I'm also sure that I could hook you up with a decent website. But who will your customers be? I'd need to know who I'm marketing to. Have you got any market research, or anything like that, that I could work from?"

This inquiry about market research was received in much the same way as Stan's initial suggestion of making Jocelyn part of his lobbying firm. Both seemed to bounce off the intended recipient because of complete subject-matter ignorance.

"Like I said, Jocelyn, the world is changing. I'm sure you've read through the Uniting and Strengthening America by Providing Appropriate Tools Required to Intercept and Obstruct Terrorism Act."

"Huh?" she mumbled, not even bothering to hide her confusion. "The USAPATRIOT Act of 2001. I left it on your desk a while back."

She hadn't read it. She really couldn't care less.

He leaned in close and said almost excitedly, "That was it, Jocelyn. Say good-bye to the United States of America as you have known it. There's a whole new market wide open for lobbyists. Tons of government money is going to be spent in the name of security. Things like RFID and vaccinations and military equipment for the police, not to mention the justification for hunting down terrorists all over the world." He sat back in his chair. "Oh, the list goes on."

In reality, Jocelyn was only feigning interest as she munched on her perfectly prepared fruit salad while allowing herself to enjoy the warmth of the sunlight streaming through the window. But when she heard the term RFID, she recalled that after 9/11, like within weeks, requests for proposals (RFPs) were spilling into her office calling for a new type of technology. The Federal government wanted the ability to read radio frequency identification digital chips—digital chips that were to be implanted into first responders' bodies.

"Oh. I know RFID," she said. "Adam wanted me to make friendly with Oracle, because Theo Cullian and I finally figured out that they were really just looking for database work. I mean, Theo could have somehow wrapped Catastrophe! around the whole RFID requirement, but ..." She kind of winced and shook her head. "It wasn't really a good match for us, considering it was ultimately somehow supposed to be linked to a huge health records database."

She watched Stan's reaction, trying to figure out if he was aware of what she was talking about, because after numerous meetings and rereadings, she was still quite unsure of what the government had been calling for. So she continued, "It must have been because they were worried about rescuing people squished under buildings or something. You know, wanting to be able to locate them, identify them, and then know what their blood type or allergies were so that they could treat them."

Stan took a sip of his coffee and nodded.

Another waitress, not quite as pretty as the last but still nice-looking, silently poured more coffee into her cup. "Kinda wild that Gillette razors created that sort of RFID inventory-tracking technology and ended up including it in the handle of a razor. Who knew that theft of single razors between production and distribution would kick off that sort of development effort?"

Stan was chuckling. "Well, you've got to keep track of your pennies if you want to make a dollar."

She smiled, but it made her kind of queasy to think about some- one getting one of those things implanted into them. *Honestly, if they're that concerned, why don't they just make everyone carry one of those razors around with them and call it a day?*

She was quiet as she speared a banana slice and remembered the whole scene from 2001—Theo going off on Adam about there being no more research and development money left because he had already squeezed twenty-seven more of Adam's "must have" features into Catastrophe!. Then he went ballistic on Robert because marketing had yet to sell or even secure any sort of interest in the crisis-management software.

It was a weird combination of pride and dread that she'd felt when Adam had assigned her, instead of one of the *drosophila melanogaster* sales guys who might have delivered a more convincing overview of Catastrophe!, to be liaison to the database giant Oracle. The memory of that conflicting set of emotions reemerged, waved hi, and briefly presented itself via her fruit salad, coffee, and croissant-filled stomach. She put down her fork, dabbed the sides of her mouth with her napkin, and decided to focus in on what Stan was saying.

"... and it's not just within this country, Jocelyn. The money has moved. It's already moved out to places like Dubai and Kuala Lumpur. Honestly, Kuala Lumpur is like

Miami Beach for Europeans these days. And you know how things are going with the old Soviet Union states—not nearly as tidy, but with the potential to be equally as profitable for the right lobbyist."

Jocelyn was taken aback by how freely her congressman was speaking about financial gain ... but at the same time, she found herself not surprised at all. As he was discussing money and his prospective world travels, Jocelyn's mind wandered back to the little gold coin that she had found in her desk.

Could it have been Stan who put it there? She considered him a bit more critically, looking for clues.

When Stan finally concluded his spiel about "flights of capital," which Jocelyn was having a hard time following, she took the opportunity to ask what she thought was a well-crafted question.

"Stan? What's the deal with gold?"

The congressman looked at her with interest as he carefully placed his coffee cup down on its saucer. "I'm not aware of this deal. Which deal are you talking about? Has Adam gone and done something like that Argentinean vineyard again?" he asked with a bemused smirk.

"Oh. No. Nothing like that." Jocelyn smiled. "No. I mean, who uses gold? All those places you've just talked about, Kuala Lumpur and Dubai, what's the deal with gold there?"

"Oh, well, I guess it's the same as it is anywhere. It's gold."

Jocelyn wasn't getting any vibes like she had when she'd asked about the flight to Reagan International. So she put it a little differently.

"Stan, if someone were to give me some gold, could I use it as money? "

"Do you like gold, Jocelyn?"

"That's not the point, Stan." Jocelyn was getting frustrated. "I mean, who uses gold?"

"Someone who isn't worried about money" was Stan's quick reply as he signaled to the waitress that he was ready to settle up.

Realizing that this gold inquisition was going nowhere fast since Stan didn't seem to be the perpetrator, she dropped it and picked up where Stan had left off.

"I'll put together a draft of a homepage for you to look over. You obviously know where to find me, and we can take it from there," Jocelyn said, letting Stan know that she had been listening to him ... sort of.

Jocelyn watched as he signed the tab presented to him. He put the pen down with a certain finality and said, "Frank will be around shortly to pick you up."

"Thank you for taking care of that, Stan. And thanks for break- fast, but honestly, you shouldn't have."

"Oh, it was my exquisite pleasure to be here with you today, Jocelyn. Thank you for joining me."

"As if I had a choice, Stan! Please promise me that the next time you cook up something like this, you'll give me a heads-up before I get hustled into an unmarked ice-cream truck or an ambulance or something."

He grinned sheepishly and quickly twitched his eyebrows, letting her know that the hamster concealed in this congressman's head was still running on its wheel at full speed.

"I'm serious, Stan!" she said as they exited the Lafayette Room.

Jocelyn and Stan headed down the wide stairway leading to the lobby and stopped so as not to accidentally disrupt the photo a young couple was trying to take by the lobby flower arrangement. She gave them a weak smile.

"Oh, would you please take our picture for us?" the young man, who sounded as if he had been born and raised in Virginia, asked Jocelyn.

Jocelyn agreed, took the little camera, snapped a couple of shots of them, and handed it back.

"Oh, let's take a picture of the person who took our picture!" the female counterpart giddily exclaimed.

Jocelyn declined. "No. I've got to get going. No, thank you."

"Oh, it really won't take but a second. We do this everywhere we go. We've got a whole collection of pictures of people who have taken our picture."

Stan winked at Jocelyn.

"Fine."

"Smile!" The young woman gleefully called out and snapped off a few shots.

"Thank you kindly, ma'am," her partner said.

"No problem," Jocelyn replied, still blinking from the bright flash as Stan shook the young man's hand.

The couple headed up the stairs toward the Lafayette Room. When Jocelyn looked back at Stan, she noticed for the first time that his shirt was still untucked and hanging out of his pants untidily from the insulin-shot episode.

"Aw, man, Stan. For goodness' sake, people really are going to think something is going on," Jocelyn reproved Stan as she pointed to his shirt.

"Oh, let them talk. Gives them something to do," Stan said happily as he tucked his shirt back in as they walked outside.

"I have about forty minutes to get to Alexandria, Stan."

"Frank should be here any minute now to take you back. Alexandria is only about twenty minutes away, so you should be fine," Stan said as he motioned for the doorman, who responded with military correctness as he quickly moved to address the congress- man's signal. Upon closer inspection of the doorman, Jocelyn could easily imagine him to be an ex-marine. In fact, she was sure of it.

Probably makes a lot more money at a place like this. Jocelyn considered what the guy might look like in his Marine Corps dress uniform.

Not bad, she virtually hummed to herself.

Man, she was such a sucker for these military types. She had to admit, there was something about those well-trained killers who felt compelled to throw aside all personal dignity and self-respect to undergo what she would personally consider physical and psychological torture only to be molded into a nonentity who unquestioningly followed commands from a master unseen. It was all so foreign to her, and it seemed somehow, well, somehow kind of kinky. She suspected that behind the outwardly well-groomed, polite manners was some highly suppressed rage, creativity, sadomasochism, or Lord knows what, but some sort of issue just bursting to get out and express itself, and it caused Jocelyn to blush as she glanced up at the doorman again.

The doorman pulled away from the apparently gripping conversation Stan was having with him to open the door of the black Lincoln Town Car that had glided up to the curb. Stan nodded to Jocelyn and motioned that it was time for her to go. She turned to shake the congressman's hand. Stan smiled, shook it firmly, and then kissed her hand as the doorman stood in a "Tomb of the Unknown Soldier" stance next to the car waiting for her to get in.

"Oh, Stan, I almost forgot. I'll have some DVDs for you to pass around. They used some shots of our prediction models on *24* this week. The committee chair you've been working with might like to see it. I'm trying to get them to somehow get a screenshot of Catastrophe! on air."

"That's my girl!" he said as he helped her into the car.

"I love that show, Stan," she said as she crawled in. "I wish we could have a president as honest and awesome as that black guy they've got on there."

"Oh, they're working on it, honey," he said smiling.

Once she was settled, the door was closed, and with a wave and a smile, Jocelyn was on her way to meet with corporate.

CHAPTER THIRTY

FRANK WAS DRIVING AGAIN, AND again he only spoke when spoken to. Jocelyn thought briefly about the type of web page she would make for Stan but then refocused on the reason she was here in Virginia in the first place—the marketing meeting. She took the budget she had made copies of out of her corporate adaptation of a bicycle-courier bag and visually devoured it as if it were the answer key to some sort of standardized test. She wanted to know this budget inside and out should she have to defend any part of it.

Stan was right; the trip to headquarters went by quickly. Jocelyn searched around in her purse for another ten-dollar bill, and before she handed it to Frank, she asked if he might be available to take her back to the airport later. Frank said if he wasn't, he would put her in touch with someone who could. He gave Jocelyn his pager number, and they worked out the details before she hopped out of the car ten dollars lighter.

Standing on the sidewalk, Jocelyn looked up at the building. It was smaller than she had expected. And when she went inside, corporate was even smaller. After showing her driver's license and signing in with the armed guard apathetically fighting crime at the building's front entrance, she discovered that the Conglomerate only occupied one floor of the building.

She made her way up in the first available elevator and again showed her ID and signed in at the reception desk, which was much quieter than her division's reception area despite the visual dissonance of two fifty-one-inch flat-screen displays hung in the latest finger-on-the-pulse, completely pointless format of vertical instead of horizontal, slinging images of the Conglomerate's latest products back and forth. This ping-pong mélange of gyroscopes, radar equipment, and smart-bomb parts was interspersed with a healthy dose of the Conglomerate's logo and stock-ticker symbol and was automatically refreshed every fifteen seconds with the latest asking price of the stock for those obsessed enough to actually care.

The young lady expertly positioned in front of this silent bombardment of visual information offered Jocelyn some coffee, which Jocelyn for once declined. She wanted to appear as professional as possible at this meeting, and to saunter into an appointment at corporate with a coffee seemed junior varsity at best.

After enduring almost sixty stock-price updates during the silent video presentation, Jocelyn was finally ushered into a small, simply appointed conference room. It looked like something in the mid- range of a Staples office-furniture catalogue or a really high-end trade-show booth. Unlike in Jocelyn's division, the walls were pure white offsetting the corporate logo, which dominated the far wall rather nicely.

Jocelyn immediately recognized Donna, the Conglomerate's executive vice president of communications, whom she had finally met in person during the September 11 fire-drill meeting at the Sheraton. General Vaughn was also there, along with three other suited men and one woman about Jocelyn's age. Jocelyn recalled that Mimi had once told her to always address the highest-ranking military person in the room first. Jocelyn didn't know if that was true or not, but seeing as Mimi had been around these military types a lot longer than she had, and seeing as these other folks seemed really corporate-y, she went with it and walked directly up to General Vaughn and shook his hand. After reintroducing herself, she shook Donna's hand.

At that point, Donna took the lead and made

introductions around the table. Jocelyn met Leonard Shnelby, one of the corporate lawyers; shook hands with Arthur Browne, a supposedly famous stock analyst; and met Timothy Brucker, one of the board members who apparently spent a lot of time lobbying "under the radar." And finally, she was introduced to Sarah Vandermere, the corporate PR person based out of the Manhattan Worldwide Headquarters, which was just a block away from Wall Street. Notably absent was anyone bearing the title of vice president of sales and marketing. Jocelyn would later surmise that the Conglomerate's corporate echelon did not bother itself with the nitty-gritty details of sales and marketing. That was left to the divisions.

For whatever reason, the initial "breaking of the ice" conversation revolved around Sarah. It was Sarah who mostly handled the day-to-day press releases coming in from the divisions regarding new products, acquisitions, personnel changes—basically anything that could be spun to affect the stock price or at the very least get the name of the Conglomerate in front of everyone's face on a daily basis. These tidbits of division-generated intelligence were funneled through Sarah and then distributed out to the world of investment and finance media outlets. Once they hit their intended target, the Conglomerate's website would be updated to include a link to the published story. That was Sarah's job and why they paid her six figures.

Apparently, Sarah had just gotten married, and Jocelyn was forced to live through a rather passionate account of exactly how news of the nuptials ended up being featured in the *Wall Street Journal*, the *New York Times*, *Barron's*, and *Forbes*. Sarah dropped lots of names, as if the marriage itself were secondary. Everyone in the room seemed very impressed that she had pushed the story as far as she had with her well-cultivated list of press connections. Naturally, the stories all mentioned that she worked for the Conglomerate, and that would count as a press mention for the company.

What Sarah's husband did, Jocelyn didn't quite gather, but obviously that was neither important nor the point.

Finally, when all the wedding/PR talk was over with, Donna called the meeting to order. Jocelyn took the leather, logo-embossed legal-pad portfolio she had received before the fire drill at the September 11 marketing-director's meeting and put it on the table in front of her.

"Well, I'm glad to see that was money well spent," Donna said, eyeing the legal-pad portfolio.

"Oh, I love this thing! I bring it with me whenever I have to show up somewhere important." Jocelyn caressed the cover before she opened it up and flipped over the pages about the countries the US was going to be "involved with" and the stuff about LISA in anticipation of having to record important facts and figures. She realized that she hadn't really been anywhere important since then.

Donna proceeded to give a very brief overview of the Conglomerate's seven-year history and her role within the company as vice president of communications. She explained the vision for the Conglomerate and its divisions moving forward.

"Jocelyn, I would like to move you to where your skills and abilities would best be utilized," Donna said. "We've gotten good reports about you from a few different sources now. We'd like to get you off of proposal work and get you more involved with placing stories."

Jocelyn fought back the urge to say, *But I only have an art degree!* Then she remembered that she didn't have any idea about how to put together a proposal for a government contract when she had started either.

Donna continued, "Sarah is hoping to start a family soon, and she let us know that she will be leaving us in the not-so-distant future." Everyone looked at Sarah and smiled, nodding their approval while voicing how much she would be missed.

"Jocelyn, in the meantime, you are going to be

working closely with Sarah to learn all that you can."

Jocelyn nodded at Sarah and said to Donna, "Will I have to physically move?"

"No. Not at this time."

Wow, that's a relief.

"Divisions will be reconfigured," Donna continued. "Some of your coworkers will be offered jobs in Colorado, and some will move to Utah. This will, of course, be presented in the most positive light for the Conglomerate."

Jocelyn scribbled in her leather-bound legal pad.

Utah.
Colorado.
Positive press position.

"Sarah will be giving you access to her database of press contacts and will introduce you to them all personally before she leaves. General Vaughn will put you in touch with some of his retired colleagues who can be called upon as experts to help clarify or give quotes for the press releases," Donna said as she nodded to both Sarah and the general.

"Yes, ma'am," the general chimed in. "Jocelyn, I'll have Marie give you a list of guys you can count on. They seem to be pretty well accepted over at that up-and-coming news channel FOX."

Jocelyn had heard of FOX News, but honestly always deferred to CNN when she personally wanted to tune in to see what was happening and felt pretty well-informed because she listened to NPR during her drive in to work. She couldn't get past the idea that "Fox" was the name of one of her favorite characters in one of her all-time favorite TV shows, *The X-Files*. Even worse, she really had a hard time getting her head around a FOX channel being useful for anything other than TV shows about aliens, conspiracy theories, and lowest-common-denominator comedies like *Married with Children*.

But FOX does have 24! Love that show. And they do showcase our products ...

So Jocelyn scribbled:

Marie.
Experts.
FOX.

Sarah said, "You may want to start becoming familiar with your state's representatives and senators. And you should do the same for the elected officials in Utah and Colorado. These guys are always looking to get their faces in front of a camera and ..."

"Oh, I just had breakfast with my congressman this morning," Jocelyn offered as she continued scribbling on her legal pad. When she looked up from her writing, she could tell that the invisible pieces of the corporate chess game that she was typically so helplessly oblivious to had just moved. Jocelyn quickly added, "Yeah. We were over at the Hay-Adams Hotel. I had fruit salad."

Eyebrows went up as the suited group exchanged glances.

"So, you're already registered?" the board member/lobbyist, Timothy Brucker, asked.

"Registered? To vote? Of course," Jocelyn said.

Attorney Shnelby said, "No. If you're going to have any sort of contact with an elected official, you must be a currently registered lobbyist. Are you a registered lobbyist, Jocelyn?"

"No."

"Okay," Donna jumped in. "You're in Connecticut, right? Before you leave, I'll have you fill out the paperwork. There is a small fee associated with it. You'll be responsible for paying that every year. Remember to save the check carbon. You can write it off on your taxes," Donna said.

"Oh, yes. Make sure you let your accountant know

about it," Mr. Brucker helpfully added. "They'll be able to get creative with that."

"Sarah, do you know what would also be very helpful for Jocelyn?" Arthur Browne, the aging stock analyst, added. "That list of universities that she can call upon."

"Sure thing, Arthur. I'll get that to her," Sarah said.

Lobbyist paperwork.
Small fee.
Let accountant know.
List of universities.

Jocelyn jotted it all down, although she didn't know exactly why she needed any of it.

The meeting continued with overviews of the Conglomerate's new acquisition announcements. Jocelyn wondered if it was a smart move to bring up the marketing budget she had worked so hard on. And she began to wonder why they even had her do it up at all. Her budget was comparatively puny and weak compared to the numbers being slung around in the new acquisition announcements. She decided to only bring it up if someone mentioned it. No one did.

Things seemed to be wrapping up. The general looked around and asked if there was anything else on the agenda. When Donna indicated that she didn't have much else, the general took some red, hardbound books out of his attaché case and put them on the table.

"I wanted to share this with all of you. Some of our guys worked with this author and had this book put together about what we do as war-zone contractors." The general pushed a book to each person at the table, and each of them instantly picked it up and flipped through the pages. Jocelyn got hers and opened directly to the page featuring a black-and-white photo of a roadside sign near Camp Victory, Baghdad, Iraq, that read: "Professional, Polite, Prepared to

Kill."

"Looks good, Claude. How much did this cost?" Donna asked.

"Oh, it was cheap. The author is ex-Special Forces and knows one of our guys. We paid him five thousand and paid the publisher another few grand for the copies we needed. Classic win–win," General Vaughn said with his hands folded on the table in front of him. "Jocelyn, it's probably good for you to have at least a few of these around as marketing material. They're good handouts."

After everyone congratulated the general on the book, he promised that Marie would get his list of go-to guys over to Jocelyn and excused himself while dropping his card in Jocelyn's general vicinity. Attorney Shnelby left with him, but first he handed his card directly to Jocelyn and told her to call him if she needed any legal advice about anything.

Donna pushed a button on the conference-room phone, and a young well-dressed woman appeared and disappeared after depositing the critical lobbyist paperwork on the table in front of Jocelyn. Timothy Brucker helpfully pointed out where she should sign and indicated which boxes she should check off. She couldn't help but notice his gold cuff links and smooth hands.

Just like Robert.

"Well, it looks like Miriam Stein made a pretty good recommendation," Mr. Brucker said while smiling and shaking Jocelyn's hand. "Nice to have met you in person. I'm looking forward to working with you."

Jocelyn returned the smile and asked, "Miriam Stein? Where have I heard that name before?"

"She's a board member here. We came back from visiting your division, and I guess you made a good impression on her. That's why you're here."

Jocelyn immediately remembered the brief meeting in front of Robert's office, the one where Stan came by to tell them that the Malaysia deal was a go.

"Oh, for goodness' sake! I just shook her hand."

He shrugged his shoulders. "Well, whatever you did, it worked," he said as he took what looked like a hockey puck out of his pocket and grabbed for his coffee cup. "I'm sure we'll be seeing each other soon." And he was off.

This is crazy. Jocelyn shook her head and smiled as she collected the books and her belongings. *The world works in mysterious ways, I guess.*

CHAPTER THIRTY-ONE

THE NEXT MORNING, AFTER FILLING Mimi in on the Hay-Adams being the new place to see and be seen, the croissant, and the fruit salad, she followed her nose down the cold hallway to her battleship-gray office. The smell of burnt plastic and lemon air freshener hung ever so delicately in the unheated air and offered just enough of a reminder of the stench from two days previous to be seriously nauseating.

If Jocelyn hadn't been somewhat excited to start learning the ropes as the corporate-appointed "media-placement person," she probably would have turned around and tried to escape the odor as she attempted to find Vince to complain. But she was eager to start work that day and headed directly to her executive cube.

When Jocelyn reached her gray laminate desk, there was a FedEx package waiting for her. It was from corporate headquarters in New York City. Still in her coat, she opened the package. It contained a binder, a little yellow sticky note, a CD marked "For Your Eyes Only," and a letter from Sarah.

Dear Jocelyn,

Enclosed herein you will find a binder containing the legal documents you will need to be familiar with. Study this and have these documents easily available at all times. Inside the binder, in the front-cover pocket, you will find contact information for the universities, organizations, and vendors that we have worked with. The CD contains a copy of company proprietary press contacts saved as a Microsoft Access file.

The Post-it note has information supplied by Marie.

I will be officially leaving in two weeks. Call or e-mail with any questions.

Best, Sarah

Oh shit. Two weeks? As Jocelyn turned on her computer and hung up her coat, Robert came barreling into her office.

"I heard you were at corporate yesterday."

"Yeah," Jocelyn said, bracing herself for some sort of confrontation.

"Well, I'm glad you're back. We need to prepare."

Although pleasantly relieved that Robert didn't seem bothered by her trip to Virginia, Jocelyn recognized his usage of the word *we*, which typically signified that he was closing in on desperation. She sat down in preparation for whatever it was he was going to say and crossed her legs.

"The generals are heading to AUSA in a few days. They want to put together a hotel suite, and they want you there. We need to come up with some sort of display that really showcases the scope and features of Catastrophe!."

"What do you mean?" Jocelyn cut him off. "A hotel suite? AUSA is a trade show. It's on my calendar. Nobody at this division showed any interest in it, so the expense never got approval for funding. Because of that, we never secured a place in the multidivision booth."

Jocelyn knew AUSA was a big deal as a military trade show. It was the Association of the United States Army. All the big-name defense contractors were there. In fact, one of the Conglomerate's larger divisions had called and asked her if any of the product lines she was involved with wanted to pitch in to secure an even larger booth. Jocelyn didn't know why these guys in California would want a larger booth; the one they had was pretty darn big already. It included a waterfall, koi pond, and second-story conference room.

Robert grumbled, "Jocelyn, perhaps what you don't

realize is that AUSA is an important *lobbying* group."

She looked at him, confused. She had never considered why they kept going to trade shows like AUSA despite a seemingly negative return-on-investment.

"Look," he explained, "this isn't so much a trade show as an annual meeting. The association puts together pieces of legislation incorporating the latest that the vendors have to offer for the benefit of the army at this meeting."

"Oh, so you mean the price of the booth actually covers 'free' lobbying?" she said, using her fingers as little quotation marks.

"Well, if we can sell them on our products and services. AUSA lobbies Congress for millions and millions of dollars at a time," he said with one of his smooth, perfectly manicured hands in his trouser pocket. The other, she noticed, was adorned with a new watch. A Breitling. It was stainless and gold with diamonds. It was flashy and certifiably distracting.

"Okay, so we're lobbying the lobbyists to lobby for us?" Satisfied with her attempt at a joke, she leaned back in her chair.

"Right. Our division doesn't have a booth presence. But the generals have something better. A hotel suite." Jocelyn listened as Robert explained how the real deals happened not on the trade-show floor but in hotel rooms filled with hors-d'oeuvre platters and cigar smoke and ...

"Um ... I don't think I want to go, Robert. Doesn't sound like the place for me. Sounds like a frat party."

"Oh, they're not that bad. They can be fun, and the food and drinks are usually pretty good. The generals don't skimp," Robert said.

But Jocelyn persisted, "I have proposals I have to finish up before I start really dealing with the press. By the way, who is going to be dealing with proposals now?"

Robert's baffled look immediately let her know that he hadn't the faintest idea of what she was talking about. So she took the time to explain what had happened the day before. Robert listened with clenched jaw and replied, "Well, you can thank corporate for in- creasing your workload, Jocelyn. I'll see what I can do to help you. In the meantime, I need you to be at that hotel suite and just be your friendly, sunny self. Okay?"

"Look, Robert, I'm not a booth bunny, okay? I've got stuff that I have to get done around here," she said loud enough to incur a couple of way-too-nonchalant walk-bys past her open executive-cube door.

"Well, then, if you're not going, I need you to make that suite as attractive as possible. We need pictures of the Command and Control Center in South Carolina, and we need computers there to give demos of Catastrophe!." Almost as an afterthought, he added, "And we need beer. Good beer."

"We don't have pictures of the center in South Carolina."

"Why not?"

Jocelyn gave him a what-do-you-mean-why-not look. "The place is restricted. They don't allow cameras in."

"They are our trial group. They are running our software. Get a picture."

The only thing missing from his departure was a slamming of the cube door. Thankfully he didn't do that, because it probably would have caused at least two other connected executive cubes to crumble. Jocelyn begrudgingly looked at the proposal files she had lined up on her desk and at the binder and CD she had just gotten from Sarah. She was already feeling overwhelmed. The cold, stinky office was not helping either.

Well, at least I'm not going to that sausage party, she said to herself, trying to look at the bright side. She knew she had two proposals due within two days. She also knew that she could do the "old Adam trick" and photocopy a proposal that had already been sent out as a response to a different RFP. She'd just have to look through the proposal logbook to find the exact one she was thinking of and have the temp du jour print it out with new proposal numbers and covers. That would be easy. But this picture thing? How was she going to handle that? She knew that the center was not going to just take a picture and send it to her for marketing purposes. She'd been through that before.

It must have been out of complete desperation, but she got the bright idea to look at the "For Your Eyes Only" CD of propriety press contacts. She opened up the Access file and scrolled down to find South Carolina. There she found a name and a number followed by the letters AP. She decided to call.

"Hello?"

"Hi, this is Jocelyn McLaren. Sarah gave me this number. I'm going to be taking over her position in a couple of weeks, and I thought I would call and introduce myself." It turned out that the *AP* on her spreadsheet actually meant AP. She was speaking with an Associated Press reporter who had very kind words for Sarah and her new husband. Jocelyn indulged the reporter's conversation and then carefully cut to the chase.

"You wouldn't happen to know of any photographers who can get into the Emergency Command Center over there? Someone with a clearance?"

"Hmm. I've used William Eckert before. Try him. I think he has clearance. But you'd have to set it up with the center. He'd have to have permission from someone inside to be there. People just don't walk in waving cameras around."

"Of course." Jocelyn said her good-bye and hung up the phone. She looked up the Command Center's number and asked to speak to anyone associated with software trials.

Next thing she knew, after some friendly chatting about how much they both disliked Microsoft products and her letting the Command Center lieutenant know that she needed to get a picture of the place for the army immediately (AUSA was basically the army, right?), she received permission to send a security-clearance-approved photographer in for fifteen minutes that afternoon. The large screens would have to be empty of content, and not one employee could be photographed.

"They usually all take a coffee break around that time anyway. They'll probably get a kick out of it," the Command Center lieutenant said with a chuckle.

Jocelyn thanked the lieutenant profusely and promised to send him a copy of the final photo. Now she just had to get that photographer. After finally getting a hold of William the photographer, Jocelyn negotiated the terms of a panoramic shot of the Command and Control Center. She paid him three times his going rate, but Jocelyn would get the high-resolution photo file that night. *Perfect.*

Knowing that there wasn't much else she could do at the moment, she decided to go check at the publications office and look through the proposal logbook to see if she could figure out which proposals to copy and send out.

When Jocelyn finally reached Nancy's old office, the door was locked. She hung around a bit waiting for the temp to return. The now-near-pointless HR director, Elaine Gibson, ambled by looking as if she was deeply concerned about something.

"Hi, Jocelyn," Elaine said gloomily.

Jocelyn gave a little wave.

"You waiting for someone?"

"Yeah. I have two proposals that have to get done. Is anyone around?"

"I haven't seen anyone lately, but then again, maybe the temp took a long lunch."

Elaine sighed, and it prompted Jocelyn to ask, "Are you okay?" As soon as she had asked the question, she regretted it.

"Doctors don't know anything! They told her she was fine that whole time."

"Who are we talking about? Nancy?"

Elaine looked at Jocelyn as if she was joking. "Yes. Of

course. Nancy. Every time she would go to the doctor, they would just treat her like she was some crazy person! They would never believe her when she complained about anything. You know, women really don't get the respect they deserve!"

Jocelyn couldn't help but appreciate the irony at this point in Elaine's rant as she recalled advocating for their coworker from Singapore, Rachel, and the HR director's pathetic response.

"I swear, I visited Nancy's husband yesterday, and he still can't get over it. It was so sad. He was reviewing all of Nancy's test results. He had them spread all over the dining-room table, and he showed them to me," she said, rubbing her forehead.

"And?" Jocelyn asked.

"And nothing! She was fine! He's getting a lawyer. He wants to sue them. All of them. He's flat broke from all of her medical bills and has to declare bankruptcy. He's really, really mad. They never picked up on anything. Not one of those tests found anything wrong with her! And look where she is now! She's dead and they are going to take his house in foreclosure."

"Woah, that's heavy. Foreclosure? Is he really going to attempt to sue the doctors? It's been a few years now..." And as soon as Jocelyn said that, Elaine burst into tears. Jocelyn didn't know exactly what to do, so she just touched the woman's arm.

Elaine started searching her cardigan pockets for a beat-up Kleenex, and when she finally showed signs of calming down, Jocelyn said, "Are you going to be okay? I've got to go get Vince. I need to get into Nancy's office to look at the proposal logbooks."

"Oh!" Elaine perked up and dabbed her eyes. "I have a key right here in my office. Hold on, I'll let you in." She blew her nose and trotted over to her nearby office, from which she produced a key. "As director of human resources, I have a key to every office," she said with overly exaggerated importance.

"Wow, that's pretty impressive," Jocelyn said.

"Not really. Vince has one, Sharon has one, Janice has one, and Mimi has one at the front desk. And I'm not too pleased about that. I've had to ask Mimi more than once to keep that thing secure."

"Jeez, I'm surprised Stan doesn't have one," Jocelyn said, referring to their congressman. But she made a mental note of what Elaine had just said about a key being unsecure at the front desk.

Elaine gave a little laugh. "Are you going to vote next week, Jocelyn?"

"Yeah, of course. Because of my family and upbringing, I'm genetically incapable of not voting," Jocelyn said with a sideways grin. "I've voted in every election since I was eighteen. I like having an excuse for coming in late to work while wearing that little 'I voted' sticker." They both snickered at that comment as they headed over to unlock Nancy's office.

"I've been helping out at Stan's campaign headquarters, stuffing envelopes and making phone calls," Elaine said. "I really hope he wins. All of us at the campaign have put so much into this election. I'm going to be crushed if he loses."

"Did you place your bet in the office election pool?" Jocelyn asked.

"Oh sure! I put twenty bucks on Stan. Based on that office pool, I think Stan has a good chance of winning. Marty Mays and a few of the guys from the warehouse are the only people who put money on Stan's opponent. You know how Mays is. He's so contrary."

Elaine opened the office door for Jocelyn and snapped on the lights. "Here you go. Just lock it up when you're done."

"No problem. Thanks."

Once inside, Jocelyn went directly to the logbooks. She flipped through some pages trying to locate the number of the proposal she had in mind to lift and repurpose for the current RFPs. She quickly found it. But while she was there, she noticed that someone had re- placed the missing 1984 page.

"What the heck?" Jocelyn whispered. Again she reveled in the gold-coin mystery.

Now thoroughly curious, Jocelyn tried to remember what other years had been missing pages. She recalled that one of the missing pages was from 1994, ten years later. She flipped through the log- book. *Ta-da! Someone has been busy! I wonder who did this?*

Unable to remember the other missing years, Jocelyn started to finger through the rest of the document. It appeared that every page was now accounted for. She wondered if someone had put one of the many temps who had rolled through on the task of doing up the pages. She'd have to make it a point to ask. Jocelyn put the binders back, turned off the lights, and locked the door.

On her way back through the Gauntlet to her cold, stinky executive cube, Jocelyn passed General Walton's office and decided to ask him what type of beer would be acceptable for the AUSA hotel-suite boondoggle she was putting together. Of course, General Walton had his own personal secretary, Shawna, who sat right outside of his office. Jocelyn had to check in with her to speak with him.

"Hey, Shawna. Is the general available?" Jocelyn asked, although she could see right through the door leading into his office that he was.

"I'll check." Shawna picked up the phone and dialed the general's extension.

If she didn't like Shawna so much, Jocelyn would have laughed out loud at how silly this was—using the phone to call someone a few feet away who had his door open. But stuff like this was par for the course with these generals.

"Sir, Jocelyn is here to see you. Are you available?"

"Sure. Send her in," was the reply clearly heard through the open office door.

Jocelyn positioned herself in front of his desk. "Sir, I'm working on that AUSA suite. I have arranged for a photographer to take a panoramic interior shot of the Emergency Command and Control Center in South Carolina this afternoon. I plan to blow that up and mount it on a piece of eighteen-by-twenty-four-inch foam core so that people can see where Catastrophe! is installed."

"Foam core! What the hell kind of rinky-dink bullshit is that?" the general barked. "Look, Jocelyn," he jammed his index finger onto his desk. "This needs to be impressive. This has got to blow the socks off these people. Don't you have a trade-show booth that we can use? I want people to feel like they are really inside the Command Center. Like they are actually using Catastrophe! in real time."

"Up in the hotel suite?"

"Yes, goddamn it! Up in the hotel suite!"

"Sir, we weren't supposed to be at AUSA, so the booth is still in Florida and won't be back here until after your event."

"I don't want to hear the drama! Just get it done. Knock their socks off!"

"Okay. Do I have permission to use the company card?"

"Yes. Just make it really classy. This is probably the most important meeting this year. It's got to be top-notch."

Jocelyn nodded and turned to leave. "Oh, I almost forgot. Robert said that you were going to serve beer. What type of beer do you want me to order up?"

"Budweiser."

"Oh, of course. No problem."

Shawna gave departing Jocelyn the double thumbs-up. Jocelyn grimly smiled back and headed to the break room. She needed a coffee to think this through. When she got there, she met up with Ted, one of the shipping/receiving guys from the warehouse. Between the two of them, they hatched a plan. He knew where some leftover heavy-duty steel shelving was sitting around waiting to be recycled. He offered to weld it all together to make an armature for Jocelyn's display.

"Will you have time to do this, Ted? I don't want to take you away from something important," Jocelyn cautioned.

"What? Like pulling 'Made in China' stickers off of stuff for one day is going to jam everything up?" Ted said sarcastically.

Jocelyn suspected that Ted just wanted a chance to use the arc welding tools, but she didn't care, she was in a pinch. She would find out the dimensions of the enlarged picture and let him know in a few hours how big he should make the thing.

On the way back to her office, she checked in with the IT guy, Jerry Apario, to make sure he had desktop computers to use for the AUSA demonstration.

"We don't have anything just sitting around," he said, apparently completely bummed out by having to tell her this. "I can order some new ones up, but by time the paperwork goes through ... Oh! Wait. I have Ahmed's old computer back here!" Jerry said as he trudged through the bowels of what appeared to be a computer-science museum's recycle bin and scooped up the CPU. "It hasn't been used since Ahmed left."

Of course, Jocelyn remembered Ahmed and eyed it suspiciously. "You want me to send an old computer filled with kiddie porn to AUSA? You're high on crack, dude."

"No." He laughed. "I still have that hard drive. There's a new one in here now. It should work for PowerPoints and stuff." He gave the computer a loving pat.

"I don't know, Jerry. That thing looks a few years old now, and I know General Walton isn't gonna like it. I need to make Catastrophe! look slick. I'll just rent some desktops from the hotel. I'm sure they've got connections to some serious AV companies for AUSA."

"Um, I don't know if that will work, Joss."

She peeled her eyes from Ahmed's computer and looked Jerry in the eye. "Why?"

He kind of winced like some sort of abused dog and said, "Well, I've tried to install Catastrophe! a few times now, and ... uh ..."

"Yes ... go on," she prompted him.

"Well, I honestly think that the only place it works is the demo on Robert's and Ken Palmer's laptops."

"You're kidding me."

"No," he said sadly, shaking his head. "You should have seen me in Algeria trying to install it."

She rolled her eyes and sighed.

"Okay, fine. We'll have to run the program off of someone's lap- top and just have a few desktops placed around with JPGs of screen dumps for dramatic effect."

Not what she wanted, but whatever. It would look great. Now Jocelyn swung by to see if any of the temps had come in. Nope. That meant that Jocelyn was going to have to do both of the proposals herself, so she set to work doing that.

By the end of the day, Jocelyn was feeling very accomplished. Not only did she complete two government proposals, she had also ordered up, for delivery the next day, a fifteen-foot-long, six-foot- wide color photograph of a restricted facility in which she had Photoshopped high-resolution screen captures of Catastrophe!, making it appear as if the Emergency Response Center actually used the trial software.

Sweet! Jocelyn congratulated herself as she left work that night at ten. *All I have left to do tomorrow is package this thing up and place the food and beverage order. I'm gonna knock their socks off!*

CHAPTER THIRTY-TWO

FOUR DAYS LATER, AS JOCELYN was bundled up in her coat with an electric space heater chugging away under her desk reading through the legal documents Sarah had sent her, General Walton entered her office.

"Jocelyn, I just wanted to let you know that we missed you at AUSA. Everyone was asking for you. That display was great. Next time we need to have computers that actually work, though. But that's not your department. Robert tried to hook the laptop up to those computers sitting there, but it didn't work. He ended up doing the demos directly off the laptop. The photo was really good. I liked how it arched around the room for a total immersion effect."

Pleasantly surprised that the general had come to report back, Jocelyn said, "Thank you, sir. Ted over in the warehouse welded that together and helped me and Gary package it up. I could have never done that by myself."

"Well, keep up the good work, soldier." And he was off.

About twenty minutes later, Robert rolled into her office, and he was not quite as happy. "Jesus Christ, Jocelyn! Shipping down as an overnight? Do you know how much that thing weighs?" Robert bellowed.

Jocelyn didn't have a clue as to how much the thing weighed. Nor had she thought to even check how much it was going to cost to ship. Gary had handled the shipping paperwork. "I'm not sure ..."

"Well, I'll tell you. It's fucking heavy! I had to put that thing together! By myself! Then, to add insult to injury, I had to break it down and load it into an airport taxi shuttle bus. It wouldn't fit in a regular cab!"

"I thought General Walton was there. He didn't help you?"

"Oh, all the generals were there." His fists were clenched. "Sure. But do you think any of them would diminish their own importance in front of the others to help? They just stood around watching me struggle with that fucking bullshit thing! And then, Jocelyn, I personally unloaded it over at headquarters." He jerked his thumb over his shoulder. "And that's where it is now! In a storage closet!"

"Why is it at corporate?" she asked, thinking that they must have liked it so much that they wanted it for themselves.

"Because it was so goddamn heavy, Jocelyn! There was no way I was going to pay for shipping that pile of junk!"

"So they are storing it for us at corporate?"

"I don't give a fuck what they do with it! Shipping is not coming out of my budget!" He glared at her for a long time in silence. During this period of silence, Jocelyn, for the first time, was really able to study the rhythm of Robert's pulse by carefully watching the veins on his temples and in his neck as they throbbed.

"Now probably isn't a good time to tell you how much that photo cost, huh?" Jocelyn said.

"Jesus fucking Christ, Jocelyn!" Robert covered his face with his hands. She noticed he wasn't wearing one of his fancy watches, and his hands, typically soft as a baby's bottom, looked pretty beat up. There was a painful-looking blood blister under his left thumbnail. He quickly repositioned himself so that he could rub his temples.

"Look. Who did you think was going to pay for all of this?" Robert asked in a tightly controlled voice, as it was now apparent that absolutely everyone in the new marketing area was restlessly wandering outside her door to get a glimpse of the action. Jocelyn noticed that Martin Mays had wandered by twice already, pretending to read the *Wall Street*

Journal. She would have laughed at his pantomime if she wasn't so focused on defending herself from this verbal evisceration.

"Well, I talked to General Walton, and he gave me the company card."

Slowly and shakily, Robert asked, "Where do you think the accounting department is going to pull the money from to pay that bill, Jocelyn?"

"Look, Robert, I told you that I didn't have any plans, nor a budget, to go to AUSA. I turned down the opportunity for us to be included in one of the largest booths on the trade-show floor because no one seemed like they wanted to go when I asked. Next thing you know, three days—count 'em, three days!—before everything has to be up and running, I have you *and* General Walton all up in my grill telling me to produce the impossible and knock their socks off. Well, guess what? I did it! Walton came in this morning and told me so."

Both of them stared contemptuously at each other. Martin nonchalantly folded down a page from the entertainment section as he meandered by for a third time. Jocelyn wasn't budging.

"We're going to have to figure out how to settle this bill, Jocelyn," Robert said as if trying to recall at least one of the *7 Steps to Effective Workplace Conflict Resolution* mentioned in that paperback that was so prominently featured on his bookshelf.

"We don't even know what the bill is yet," said Jocelyn. "I'll go down and ask Gary how much it ended up costing us. Okay?"

"Fine," Robert said and left her office.

JOCELYN TRACKED DOWN GARY IN the shipping/receiving office. He was sitting at his desk doing up the various shipping forms, which included everything from FedEx to UPS to customs declarations.

Jocelyn walked over and peered down at the form he

was filling out. "Hey, Gary, Robert needs to know how much that thing Ted welded cost to ship."

"Oh, hey, Jocelyn. No problem. I have the paperwork right here. $980."

Jocelyn let out a low whistle. "Okay, now I know why he was freaking out. That's a lot of money." She didn't know what else to say and just stared at the shipping form for a while. "The marketing budget can't take that kind of hit for just shipping. I'm screwed," Jocelyn lamented. "What am I gonna do?"

"About what?"

"About that!" She quickly pointed to the $980 FedEx shipping document and in her haste accidentally knocked over a large roll of stickers. The sticker roll tumbled off Gary's desk and unfurled itself, revealing sticker after sticker marked *Made in USA*. She bent over to collect them.

"Oh, sorry," Jocelyn said as picked up the stickers, rolled them back up neatly, and put them on his desk. "Shit. I should have checked into this before I had you do anything. I'm sorry, Gary. It did turn out really nice though. Thank you," she said with a weak smile.

"Oh, don't mention it. I enjoyed it, and I know Ted did too. He hasn't stopped talking about it. And don't worry about the shipping. I charged it to Indonesia."

Now Jocelyn, despite her constant belittling of corporate accounting practices, knew that you could not "charge" something to a country account unless there was a contract in place. As far as she knew, the Indonesia contract to build six maritime schools outfitted with their top-of-the-line training simulators was still in limbo. No word had come down that it was actually happening.

"How did you do that?" Jocelyn asked.

"It's the only charge that I'm allowed to use, so I used it." Gary looked confused by Jocelyn's confusion. "We've been receiving stuff for the contract and sending stuff out to Indonesia for a while now. That's all we have been doing back here in the warehouse. Bringing stuff in and sending it right back out. Of course, for some reason, we have to make sure every single little thing is marked 'Made in USA.' That's the kick-in-the-pants part. Dealing with your picture stand was a joy!"

"So you didn't charge the shipping to marketing?" Jocelyn asked in disbelief. Gary shook his head in confirmation.

She was confused, because something as big as getting the Indonesia contract should have been plastered all over the news. And that should have been her job. So why hadn't she been told about this? Why hadn't the entire company been told? She couldn't believe that corporate hadn't been told yet. Or had they? She was very skeptical.

"I guess they wanted to announce it after the election," Gary said.

"What are you talking about? The congressional election? Stan's race? Why would we time the announcement of this contract around an election?" Jocelyn wanted to know.

"I haven't the foggiest. But that's not my department."

"Well, it's supposed to be mine! I'm not sure about this, Gary," Jocelyn said, feeling completely conflicted. She really hoped that the shipping could be charged off to Indonesia. That would make her life so much easier. "And even if what you say is true, won't you, or more importantly *I*, get in trouble for shipping this thing with the wrong charge?"

"To tell you the truth, Joss, I doubt it would ever show up," Gary said.

Jocelyn thanked him and headed back to her office. While walking back, she decided just to sit on this bit of shipping information. Robert would be more than aggravated with the price of the panoramic photo's rush-service invoice. He was going to eventually see that, because she had charged it to her marketing budget. Maybe Gary was right. Maybe they really did get the contract. If she didn't bring up the shipping, maybe no one would notice.

Yikes. $980. Too bad I couldn't use that gold coin to pay for it. Then no one would have to know. It would be totally off the radar. But then she realized that she would need like three of those gold coins to pay for it. And of course, she had the small problem of not knowing exactly how to perform a transaction with the darn thing. *Kind of a worthless gift, if you ask me.*

As it got colder and colder in the hallway, she knew she was getting closer to her office. The fact that the heat was still not on was starting to get her down. Vince had come by with space heaters for everyone a couple of days before while she was rushing around finishing the proposals and helping Ted with the design of the AUSA hotel-suite steel-frame display. The very fact that Janice had approved the purchase of a dozen electric space heaters did not bode well as an indicator that the heat would be fixed anytime soon.

"Hell is a cold, cold place," she had heard Martin Mays loudly grumble as Vince plugged in the space heater under his desk.

"Roger that!" someone else had shouted back. That, at least, had provided some temporary levity at the time, but now it wasn't funny. It was *cold*. Jocelyn cranked up her space heater to maximum and whipped a wool scarf around her neck in preparation for an extended study of the corporate binder on media relations.

There was lots of stuff that Jocelyn hadn't considered before. She could contract with a company that created real-looking news stories about a product or service. And for another fee, she could have that corporate-created news story, otherwise known as a video news release or a VNR, pimped out to the local news stations. FOX and NBC affiliates seemed to appreciate VNRs, and contact information was provided.

There was also a tear sheet about a company called NeuroFocus. She'd have to look the company up, but she didn't think it had any- thing to do with what she was doing because it looked very technical. They strapped electrodes onto children's heads in order to figure out what parts of the brain a commercial or news spot was tickling.

Wow. Who knew? she thought as she flipped through some of the pricing sheets.

Of course, the Conglomerate's division sales were contingent on the stuff that was sold to the Pentagon or foreign governments, not stuff you could easily create a paid infomercial about. At least that's what she figured as she flipped through the binder.

Jocelyn found it interesting that the binder from corporate was not so much focused on press relations as she imagined it would relate to the sales of the various divisions' products and services; instead, it was firmly built on managing the perception of the company in terms of its stock price. That made sense, seeing as corporate was really in the business of maintaining a brand that acted as an umbrella holding very diverse businesses together.

As far as Jocelyn could suss out, she now had two jobs. The first was to help her division sell products to the Pentagon (or any government that was willing to pay for their stuff). The other, and probably more important, job was to maintain the publicly traded stock's image as a good investment.

Jocelyn sat back and thought about this as she blew warm breath into her cupped hands. Didn't sales always make the stock price go up? Not necessarily. Perceived need for something could do the same thing. Also, the idea that the stock price would continue to climb and was a good investment could make the stock price go up too.

Jocelyn jotted these thoughts down. She circled the operative words in both of her sentences and noted that the corporate part of her job was based upon something conceptual—perceived need and an idea. Okay, so she was selling a *belief*. She had to make sure people believed that the

Conglomerate was going to preserve their hard-earned wealth better than any of the other 3,100 US-owned companies listed on the New York Stock Exchange.

As far as her duties regarding the divisions went, well, that was pure sales. And the ideal customer was the Pentagon. The Pentagon got its money to spend on purchasing her division's stuff from the US Congress. So it was no wonder that the Conglomerate, and all of the major defense contractors, had offices and/or production facilities in every state of the union. The larger the state was, the better it was for the Conglomerate to plunk down more factories. These states had more representatives in Congress who would be receptive to defending the jobs offered by the Conglomerate in their home state. These congressmen and congresswomen could be called upon to propose legislation that would power the defense-sector jobs in their state. And what congressperson wants to see hundreds, if not thousands, of members of the voting base losing jobs because the Pentagon lost part of its budget? Especially after 9/11?

As Jocelyn thought this through, she became aware that the better portion of her job was basically to help the Pentagon maintain its income, and that a really big part of that was lobbying. No wonder she had to register as an official lobbyist.

But Congress can't do anything unless the people decide it's necessary, right?

On her yellow legal pad, under the two sentences she had just written, Jocelyn wrote the word *Congress* with a double-headed arrow going back and forth to the phrase *the people*. The heater under her desk started to make a funny noise. She crawled under the desk and smacked it. It stopped.

"Cheap, Chinese-made piece of crap," she said.

It didn't come that day, but it wouldn't be long before the realization dawned on Jocelyn that her job for the Conglomerate was really to work on behalf of the Pentagon, and that the Pentagon's modus operandi was to make "the people" believe that funding for the Pentagon in order to buy the Conglomerate's products and services was a matter of life and death.

If she did her job right, it was a win–win situation for all involved. The divisions would realize a profit and not be liquidated. And, more importantly, Jocelyn figured, the Conglomerate's stock price would rise. Clearly, that was critical, because it was printed almost a million times in that binder that Sarah had sent her: "The primary objective of the Conglomerate is to enhance shareholder value." And, as an almost happy coincidence, Jocelyn's work would provide a job for a regular guy so that he could feed his family, pay his mortgage, and watch the game on Sunday. Win–win.

She spent the whole day studying Sarah's binder and the Access database of press contacts. She drove home that night trying to get her head around everything she had just read and wondering why she needed that list of universities.

CHAPTER THIRTY-THREE

DARK WINTER. AS JOCELYN SLOWLY slid back into consciousness around five thirty in the morning, those two words were the first thing she became cognizant of.

"Dark Winter," she mumbled. "Of course ..."

Although she still had to think it through, her dreaming self had already figured out why she needed the list of universities. She sleepily shut off the alarm before it sounded and allowed herself to enjoy the warm coziness of her merlot and chocolate down comforter for a few more minutes as she sleepily pieced together what exactly Operation Dark Winter was all about.

It was before September 11. She knew that. And she recalled that Adam's original business partner, Bradley Williams, had come back from Florida where he had been happily retired and occupying his time buying and selling racehorses. This Williams Racehorse Guy and Stan the congressman had both barged into Jocelyn's office and demanded that she get in touch with someone, anyone, at the Bloomberg School of Public Health over at Johns Hopkins University.

"Okay, of course. No problem," Jocelyn had responded, eager to make a good impression on the congressman because Robert had told her that he was "incredibly important." This was only the second time she had ever met Stan. "But what am I supposed to talk with them about?"

"We need them to use Catastrophe!," Racehorse Guy nearly shouted.

"I need an invitation. Please arrange that for me,

Jocelyn," Stan had said.

At this point, Robert had wandered up to shake the former partner's hand and say hello to Stan. But really, Robert knew that whatever it was that had called Mr. Williams out of seclusion in Florida and back into the office, with a congressman in tow no less, must be a serious sales lead. God forbid Robert missed out on grabbing at least a part of that commission, let alone the opportunity to let everyone know that Jocelyn worked for him and that anything that Jocelyn was tasked to do would have to go through him.

Once all the niceties of the reunion between Robert and Mr. Williams were over, Stan disclosed that he had heard through the grapevine that there was going to be a big biohazard exercise going on over at the Johns Hopkins Center for Civilian Biodefense Strategies, and that it would be perfect for Catastrophe!.

"It's like it was made for it! It's going to be a big deal. The Dark Winter exercise will be the perfect place to showcase the software," Stan said excitedly. He rambled on about who was going to be there and concluded with, "I need to be there."

"Okay, it's at the Bloomberg School of Public Health, you said?" Jocelyn asked, getting her handy yellow legal pad to take down as many clues as she might be able to glean off of the conversation the three men were having.

"Yeah, find the number for CSIS and the ANSER Institute for Homeland Security. Call them," Mr. Williams said.

"Wow. That sounds pretty heavy, 'Homeland Security.' Is the organization American?" Jocelyn asked, thinking it sounded like some sort of decrepit, time-forgotten bureau left over from World War II Germany.

Little did Jocelyn, or the rest of the country for that matter, realize that the *Washington Times*, owned by North Korean Reverend Sun Myung Moon, would play such an important role in normalizing the term "homeland security" for the American public. The term was not widely used in the press until 2002. However, after September 11, 2001, the *Washington Times*, along with the other journalistic assets owned by Reverend Moon—including UPI, *Insight* magazine, and an impressive array of foreign outfits—would be the first to use the term consistently and lead the charge for a paradigm shift by insisting that its journalists use the antiquated Nazi-esque term *homeland* in their writing.

The *Washington Times*, in those early days of public adaptation to the term, would often cite the ANSER Institute for Homeland Security website, which would lend credibility to the phrase as well as to the institute, which was closely associated via partnership agreements with the Center for Strategic and International Studies (CSIS) and the RAND Corporation. The Council on Foreign Relations gave the ANSER Institute for Homeland Security two thumbs up in its *Foreign Affairs* magazine in 2002, thus establishing some serious credibility for the first-ever federally funded research and development center (FFRDC), otherwise known as a "think tank," initiated in 1999 and formally established in April 2001. By the time the presidential executive order came down in February 2003 establishing a cabinet position for homeland security, the term was easily accepted, as it was by then part of the national lexicon.

"I know. Yes, it's American," Stan said, nodding his head. "It's a division of Analytic Systems, Inc. It's an FFRDC." Back on topic, Stan continued, "If that doesn't work, get in touch with CSIS or MIPT. The general over there knows me from the Oklahoma City bombing stuff he's into."

Jocelyn scribbled it all down: FFRDC, CSIS, MIPT. She really didn't want to look stupid or interrupt their conversation, but damn! Talk about alphabet soup! And what did Oklahoma City have to do with any of this? She continued to write down as much as she could and just let the guys talk.

"Get Palmer on showing them Catastrophe!. His wife

is some sort of professor over at Texas A&M. He's used to dealing with those academic types," Robert had said as Williams the Racehorse Guy shook his head in disdain. Clearly, Horseface would not be the best choice to present Catastrophe! to academia.

Jocelyn had felt lucky to be included in their brainstorming session. It sounded important. She was going to have to do some serious research for this, but of course, she was up for the task. Jocelyn had made the appointments for Ken and had sent the proposals addressing Catastrophe!'s relevance to Dark Winter's abstract, which had concluded with:

This exercise is intended to increase awareness of the scope and character of the threat posed by biological weapons among senior national security experts and to bring about actions that would improve prevention and response strategies. This exercise was made possible by a Grant from The McCormick Tribune Foundation and the Oklahoma City National Memorial Institute for the Prevention of Terrorism.

Now, as she stared at the angle of her bedroom's cocoa-colored cathedral ceiling, Jocelyn though about how Dark Winter had played out. It had been a certifiable "fail" on her part, and it made her a bit sick to her stomach to think about it. She could not get Stan an invitation. And Ken Palmer, despite being married to a professor at Texas A&M, was not able to convince anyone at John Hopkins University, the Bloomberg School of Public Health, the Center for Strategic and International Studies (CSIS), or the ANSER Institute for Homeland Security, that Catastrophe! was worth using for their senior-level exercise.

The only response Ken had received was that something was wrong with the model Catastrophe! was using to simulate a cataclysmic outbreak of smallpox in the United States.

Perhaps if Jocelyn, as she lay wrapped in her fluffy comforter, had known that the simulation model that had actually been used in Dark Winter to freak out eighty congressmen and another twenty foreign ambassadors and had quickly prompted the president of the United States to order up three hundred million doses of smallpox vaccine—a disease that the World Health Organization had officially claimed to have been eradicated in 1979—had been cranked up to three times the normal transmission rate for smallpox, thus rendering just about any response hopeless, she wouldn't have taken her inability to make inroads with the exercise planners so personally.

Maybe she would have even thought it was an excellent marketing ploy if she had known. Hard to tell, because it wouldn't be for many years, until Republican Senate leaders inserted language into the 2006 Defense Appropriations bill granting legal immunity to vaccine manufactures, even in cases of willful misconduct, that Jocelyn would become sorta-kinda-maybe concerned about any of this.

Jocelyn rolled over and looked at her alarm clock again. She might as well get up. Even though she was going to go vote before work and would have the excuse of the little "I voted" sticker for coming in late, she just wanted to get up and start the day. It would be about eighteen hours later that the world would know via an Associated Press feed that Stan the congressman had lost reelection.

"WELL, THE MYSTERY IS SOLVED!" Vince happily announced to the shivering residents of the new marketing area. Just about three weeks had now lapsed since they had officially been without heat, and most everyone had given up hope. Knitted hats with pompoms, scarves, and even gloves for those claiming to suffer from Raynaud's disease had become de rigueur. But now, at last, Vince proudly strode in to proclaim that he had turned on the heat.

“What was the problem?” Martin Mays asked as he wandered out of his closet wearing a hunting cap equipped with earflaps.

Everyone exited the executive cubes, looking as if a markdown sale had just occurred at Barney’s Discount Ski Shoppe, and gathered around Vince wanting to hear for themselves what the scoop was with the heat.

“Well, I don’t know why, but the ductwork had been hooked up in some sort of nonconventional way. The HVAC guys fixed it, and I am happy to announce that you can all take those hats off!” Vince proclaimed as if he might be imagining the marketing department wildly throwing their hats in the air in appreciation of him turning the heat back on.

“Well, what the hell does *nonconventional* mean in this instance, Vince?” Mays asked from under his earflapped hat.

All heads turned inquisitively toward Vince in anticipation of an answer.

“I guess the ductwork that was running into and out of this area had been joined somewhere along the way with the vent-fan exhaust over in the fabrication workshop, and ...”

“What the hell, Vince? You, or at least the HVAC guys, are going to get sued! By me!” Martin shouted as the snow bunnies looked on. “There is no way that would have passed any sort of code inspection! What the hell are you trying to do, kill us?” The crowd just looked on. Martin was on a tear, and no one felt compelled to stop him. “Vince, really! Is it easier for them to kill us than lay us off? This is nuts! Why would Adam think this was okay? Oh that’s right! Adam! *Aaaa-fucking-dumb*. Otherwise pronounced *Adam*. That asshole would cut off his nose to spite his face while pinching, no make that stealing, a goddamn penny!”

After a good ten minutes of Martin and then others jumping on the “We Won’t Be Mistreated!” bandwagon, people became disturbingly emboldened and began to spout off about all sorts of work-related issues. If the HR department had been any sort of relevant presence, it would have been really very interested in what was being said.

However, seeing as by all counts it was clear that the employees here were existing in some sort of anarchistic state of corporate freeform, the mob scene was not in any way productive. Jocelyn, although concerned about the health implications of the ductwork, had started to feel bad for Vince and angled to get him out of there.

It didn't work. Vince, not a candidate for the debate team, attempted to feebly hold his ground when he should have just pleaded the fifth and left the room.

Eventually, people started to get warmer as the heat kicked in, and the mood in the room got even more confrontational. They all began taking off their hats and scarves as the rants, no longer necessarily directed at Vince or the heating situation, started to get more impassioned. In fact, at one point, even Vince joined in with the raucous complaints being hurled around about the brand of coffee being served in the break room.

At this unfortunate low point of workplace dissatisfaction, Stan the congressman showed up to do the equivalent of an inverse victory lap and graciously, albeit dramatically, bid *adieu* to these workers who had for many years worked to keep him in office.

"What's going on in here?!" Stan yelled above the fray as he entered the new marketing area. Everybody turned around and instantly stopped talking.

"Jeez, I'm glad I don't have any foreign dignitaries with me! You guys sound like you're going to riot soon," Stan the Former Congressman said as he looked around at the perturbed faces and awkwardly started shaking people's hands as if he was the main at- traction at an impromptu receiving line at a wake. Absolutely no one in that room knew how to act—no one. Especially when someone brought up 1994, the election Stan had won by a whopping four votes out of the 186,000 votes cast, after seven nail-biting days of recount.

"Even the secretary of state said vote-counting is not an exact science," Stan said as he reminisced and moved on in the receiving line.

One of the sales guys, Chris Sherman, attempted to jog Stan's memory about how he had contributed to the congressional campaign by spending a month of weekends going door-to-door passing out flyers that touted Stan's most agreeable attributes. It was clear that Stan had no recollection of this guy. The obviously disappointed supporter sulked as Stan tried to engage with another unknown member of the irritated group.

"Thank you for your many years of support," Stan said as he shook the woman's hand and smiled warmly.

"I'm a Jehovah's Witness. I don't vote," the saleswoman said.

The room stared in silence at Stan and the Jehovah's Witness as everyone recalled Janice's decree that no religious material be allowed on the premises after printed material began silently showing up next to the Cremora and sugar in the break room. It had devolved into a company-wide debate that raged for several weeks about some sort of amendment right to express yourself. Thankfully, Stan decided to completely change the subject before it became any more uncomfortable.

"Here. Everyone put those hats back on. Come with me outside and see my new car! I wanted to show it to Adam, but he's not here. I'll happily show you guys instead."

The somewhat stunned group of thirteen complied and followed Stan, their soon-to-be-former congressman, down the Gauntlet.

"What kind of car did you get?" someone asked as they shuffled along while replacing their hats.

"Chrysler Prowler," Stan grinned.

Jocelyn, not knowing what a Chrysler Prowler looked like and wanting to contribute to the change of scene, asked the most important car question her womanly conversationalist mind could think of: "What color is it?"

"Yellow."

And yellow it was. To Jocelyn, the car looked like something an automotive designer tripping on LSD, who had the auspicious happenstance to meet the offspring of a banana and a praying mantis on his way to the local bar, would cook up.

"That's some $45,000 midlife-crisis-mobile, Stan," someone mumbled as they all stood around and beheld the retro-styled hot rod. Stan giddily said, "It sure is! I think I deserve it!" and he started to rattle off the particulars of the car's performance. Martin Mays and Vince seemed especially interested in these fun facts. Although Jocelyn was not very interested, she was impressed with how Stan, by establishing a neutral, common ground based upon a universal boyish fascination, had been able to get the marketing department back to work pitching smart-bomb parts, gyroscopes, imaging technology, mercenaries, and vaporware.

THE DAYS BECAME MORE COMFORTABLE in Jocelyn's heated battle-ship-gray executive cube. Robert seemed to bother her less, as he was completely consumed with securing himself a job in New York City. And of course, Stan the congressman was no longer around to provide unannounced breaks in the routine. It was when Stan's opponent, Ripley Summers, was officially sworn in that word came down for Jocelyn to prepare the sweepstakes-style check and the photo op for the local press. Her division had sealed the Indonesia deal!

"Wow. Surprise, surprise," Jocelyn muttered as she looked up the phone number of the local print shop. She found it and punched it into her phone.

"Hey, Ben! How's it going?" Jocelyn greeted the print-shop owner. "Yeah, well, we're going to need the four-footer this time. Adam said the picture of them released for the Egyptian Navy thing, yeah, with the three footer, uh-huh, that one made them all look a little too friendly." She let out a little snort of a laugh at Ben's reply. "They were all packed in there a bit too close for comfort so that they could all be in the picture holding the check." Jocelyn paused to listen to Ben. "I know. It's ridiculous. But people love it ... Great. Okay, thanks. And just remember that it's you, Ben, who brings this happiness to the people via your printing press!" They both laughed, and Jocelyn gave him her corporate credit-card number to pay for the rush order.

The check was delivered the next day to the front desk, and Mimi absolutely flipped out, gushing about the enormous check. It was actually kind of cute how childlike she was with it.

"Ooooh! Jocelyn! It's fantastic! Can I hold it?" she said as she scrambled out from behind the reception command and control center she called home eight hours a day to expertly model the gi- ant check. "Look! I'm like Vanna White or one of the *Price Is Right* girls!"

"Looks like you've done this before," Vince said as he strode through the reception area to get a look at the foam-core-mounted enlargement of a reasonable facsimile of a bank check. "Maybe you've got a future at the casino after all," he said, referring to Mimi's penchant for going to the casino with her longtime boyfriend after work to gamble. Vince always teased her about this. And she always told him that they went because of the food.

"Oh, Vince, leave me alone. It's great there. It's affordable, and I don't have to cook. No fuss, no muss. Plus it's nice to get out with my sweetie," Mimi retorted while providing Vince with an entertaining performance as she pranced around the reception area striking various poses with the four-footer.

Within a few minutes, the new congressman, who'd had no part whatsoever in getting this contract, arrived with his driver. He was all smiles, shaking everyone's hand, meeting everyone for the first time. Jocelyn noticed immediately that the new Republican congressman, Ripley Summers, was as adept, if not more so, at slinging the obligatory cocktail small talk as Stan was. And that he was very eager to follow Jocelyn's direction as the photographers came in from the various news outlets.

As Congressman Summers posed for pictures, Jocelyn grabbed Adam's arm and tipped him off to a critical catchphrase that she'd noticed being used a lot on the printed materials coming across her desk. Thinking that it sounded pretty cool, she encouraged him to use it when he spoke.

When it was time, Mimi called everyone into the large conference room where Jocelyn had properly hung a gold-fringed American flag vertically. She had wanted to hang an Indonesian flag next to the American one, but when she couldn't get her hands on one, she was forced to settle for the flag of Monaco.

Are you kidding me? They've only been working this contract for most of my adult life, and no one ever thought to get one of their flags and bring it back here?

The flags looked almost exactly the same: a red stripe on top and a white stripe on the bottom. Hanging on the wall to the right of Old Glory, the white stripe would be on the left. The only difference was that the real Indonesian flag was longer in its size ratio. The flag from Monaco, which must have been hanging around in the marketing storage closet from some event years ago that undoubtedly Stan had been involved with, was more of a stubby rectangle, almost a square.

She toyed with using the Polish flag, which they had, but it was too small. Deciding that the size difference was unacceptable—it would make the American flag look way too imposing—she settled upon Monaco. She'd just have to make sure she was on top of the photographers to make sure they framed the shot properly.

As she fussed with the flags and the staple gun, she couldn't get over the fact that someone was actually paying her to do this. But later, as the new congressman, Adam, a random guy from the ware- house, and last but not least the representative from the bank took their places around the podium, Jocelyn had to confess that the place looked great.

That's why they pay me the big bucks! Jocelyn congratulated herself, recalling Stan's dramatics. *Man, it's really too bad Stan isn't here for this. He really does deserve some sort of recognition.*

Adam started the speaking portion of the program by thanking everyone for their many years of hard work to achieve this monumental collaboration with the Indonesian Merchant Marines. He then blabbed on a bit about how great the simulators were that were included in the deal. They would facilitate the proper maritime training so that Indonesians could "set sail in the new global economy."

Good, he said it. Jocelyn smiled.

After the cameras popped off a couple of flashes and the polite applause petered out, the guy from the bank took the podium. John Kepler was not the snappiest speaker, and he droned on much longer than necessary about the features of the new online banking system that the bank had just installed. This speech elicited a response some- thing akin to a "golf clap" but with a little less enthusiasm.

Polishing off this whole production was the main event: Ripley Summers, the new congressman, who had no real knowledge of the deal that had been in the works for almost a decade. Congressman Summers thanked everyone for showing up and delivered commend- able lip service to his Democratic predecessor, Stan, appreciating the former congressman's more than twenty years of effort on behalf of the state and its local businesses.

"Although the former congressman and I differed on many issues, this was one point that we both agreed upon: the need to encourage business in this state," Congressman Summers said.

The crowd applauded as the photographers snapped

their photos.

"Guess AIPAC likes this guy better than Stan," someone muttered. Jocelyn quickly spun around and shot the culpable party a shut-up look, something akin to how an Irish mother would deal with her ten-year-old kid at Sunday Mass sans the smack on the back of the head.

Still, she couldn't help but consider the comment. *The American Israel Public Affairs Committee? Why would that matter? Especially since Stan is Jewish?*

She returned her full attention to the new congressman as he continued letting everyone know that the needs of local businesses were his "top priority," and that he hoped that his party, the Republicans, would "work across the aisle" to cut taxes and lure new businesses into the state while he "handled" the federal government so that the local people could get the real work done. Businesses like Adam's were the ones that drove the economy. This comment was followed by more polite applause.

It appeared that no one had clued this guy in about the Conglomerate and the impending layoffs. But that was improbable. He most likely knew exactly what was going on. This event was for the benefit of the press, and Jocelyn had to admit that the guy did a pretty decent job. It may have even bought Adam's division some time before the pink slips started their rounds.

The podium was rolled out of the way, and the photographers— who had been prepped by Jocelyn beforehand about how to frame the picture so that no one would appear uncomfortably homosexual or notice that the Indonesian flag was actually representing Monaco— began kneeling on the floor to get the "keeper" shot.

Jocelyn made sure to circulate and to chat with all of the reporters in attendance and to distribute press releases that included the proper spelling of each presenter's name, a little preapproved summary about each of them, and a general overview of the project that included the anticipated benefit this contract would bestow upon the state. Jocelyn fully expected that the press release would essentially be cut-and-pasted into the local stories that the press would run. Everyone applauded as the event drew to a close. The whole thing lasted roughly twenty minutes.

IT WAS ABOUT A YEAR later when the delivery of the Indonesia contract came to a grinding halt. Naturally, the Conglomerate, the World Bank, the IMF, and all the concerned parties had insurance for such an Act of God. Insurance based upon derivatives.*

__* de·riv·a·tive /diˊrivətiv/: an unregulated global casino for banks.

CHAPTER THIRTY-FOUR

December 27, 2004

GOLD: US$442.00
OIL: $41.26
NYSE: GLOM: $75.90 vol: 2955.80k

"PROBABLY HAARP," THEO GRUMBLED WHILE filling his nasty coffee-stained mug. Another person from engineering smirked and nodded as he walked out of the room with his steaming cup. The place was pretty empty, as it was the Monday after Christmas and most people had taken the whole week off. Jocelyn went to work because she really didn't have much of a life other than working at this point, and she liked when no one was around. There was no one to bother her or notice that she had taken a longer-than-usual lunch break.

Feeling like she was being left out of the joke, Jocelyn asked what a harp would have to do with anything as she filled up her coffee mug.

"Look it up Jocelyn. Seriously." Theo rolled his eyes. "I'm talking about Indonesia," he said glumly. But that wasn't unusual for Theo. Jocelyn had noticed that he always seemed to be under immense pressure lately.

"Just insert a little bit of the stock-market stuff if you can't get the predictive stuff going. It's not rocket surgery," Adam had been overheard telling Theo right before the Indonesia contract was officially signed.

"What's up with Indo?" Jocelyn asked. "It's gone."

"What do you mean it's gone?" Jocelyn asked, her eyebrows furrowing. She imagined that the whole project got scooped up by a competitor, sort of like how a couple of the Conglomerate's divisions had teamed up and angled to take an established contract away from Raytheon in Iraq. It happens.

"You didn't hear about that tsunami yet?"

"No," she responded flatly. "Tsunami? You mean like a tidal wave?"

"Yes, Jocelyn. Like a tidal wave."

"NO WAY, JOCELYN HUFFED as she clicked through the stories on her screen. Just when things were officially cranking on the delivery of this contract, boxes moving in and out of the warehouse on a daily basis, project managers running around with Excel spread- sheets waiting for approval by Dad the Overpriced Construction Consultant, who would have believed that a massive undersea earth-quake, tripping the Richter scale at 9.1, would lay doom all over the emerging financial sector of the planet?

The tsunami killed three and half times as many people as the atomic bomb at Hiroshima. Fifteen countries—including Indonesia, Sri Lanka, Thailand, Myanmar, and India—were drowning and beginning the process of rotting in their own excrement. The tsunami displaced 1.7 million people and ended 230,000 lives, not to mention the $14 million contract that Adam, and tangentially everyone within Post-it note delivery circumference, had worked so hard to win.

This sucks. It can't impact the stock price favorably to announce that $14 million just got washed away and is floating out to sea. Could it?

Jocelyn sat in silence in her fluorescently illumined gray cube. She was just thinking how messed up everything was when an e-mail popped into her inbox. And not just any e-mail—she knew what this was by the subject line and hungrily opened it. Never mind that it was spam.

Jocelyn had developed an almost unnatural affinity for the text spam e-mails that had been creeping in through the company website despite a cadre of spam filters. They were intriguing to her. She was sure it was the same person behind these e-mails. She was also sure it was a code. Every one of these e-mails contained either twenty-eight or thirty-two words. It didn't seem to matter the length of the words. Jocelyn counted every word in every e-mail every time one would flutter into the marketing inbox. She had tried counting characters and spaces and concluded that was just crazy. The total character count didn't seem to matter at all.

What kind of wacko sits around and fixates on this crap?

She tried to refocus her attention on something more important—namely, the task that Janice had recently assigned her: creating an appropriate seasonal backdrop for the stock-price display in the break room.

Jocelyn, however, couldn't help but notice that every one of these e-mails included a prominent international city. Every one of these e-mails included a direction like north, south, east, or west. Every single one of these e-mails included a month and a numeral spelled out. All of this splayed out as one big pile of gibberish that Jocelyn's mind perceived as a poem.

It had dawned on Jocelyn about eighteen months ago—right about the time their contract started in Iraq—that although the suspect e-mails (which she printed out and kept in a manila envelope in her bottom desk drawer) were written in English, they were obviously composed by someone who didn't speak English. Verbs were consistently in the wrong place.

These e-mails had taken on poetic dimensions for Jocelyn, and they were much more engaging than the task of contacting art-department guys to get her hands on the latest and greatest illustration of a wildly complex underground bunker in the hills of Afghanistan, or scanning the news outlets to see if there was any indication of a possible sales lead. These rogue spam e-mails had become the equivalent of little love notes to her latent creativity over the past year and a half.

As Jocelyn's eyes scanned the dubious e-mail's scrawling text, she remembered the feeling of trying to read the poems in a falling-apart little hardbound volume her mother kept displayed on the bookshelf by the TV.

She liked the smell of that book. When she was six years old, little Jocelyn would try unsuccessfully to read the verse. Even though she did not fully know how to decipher all the symbols yet, she knew that what was written was important and that the words meant a lot to her mother. The book, a collection of famous love poems from the 1800s, had belonged to her grandmother. It had an impressive handwritten signature on the first page. And because of that, Jocelyn was always very careful with the nearly decomposed canvas binding when she put it back on the shelf.

Jocelyn smiled as she read the spam she had printed out. The feeling was so similar.

What Jocelyn was holding was in no way high-tech. It was very simple. She imagined a solitary person cleverly crafting a desperate message, sending spam to the whole wide world hoping that another person with the right key would get the message in his or her spam box and unlock it.

Jocelyn thought that it was really ingenious, the whole "hiding absolutely everywhere" thing, and she was rooting for whomever it was. Jocelyn could tell all the e-mails were written by the same person (or computer program, she would remind herself in order to maintain an emotional distance). Everyone else she showed them to couldn't discern that—or more correctly, couldn't care less.

"It's *spam*, Jocelyn—s-p-a-m. Rubbish." Or, "Just hit delete. I'll update the spam filter later." That's what she would hear every time she tried to clue someone in on her hunch. It wasn't until people started to show up in the new marketing area complaining that they'd received about fifteen copies of this poem from the marketing e-mail account in their own Outlook inbox that anyone noticed what Jocelyn had been trying to tell Robert, the generals, and just about anyone who would listen: namely, that a defense contractor, i.e., their division, was disseminating some sort of secret message on behalf of someone else.

Maybe it was because of those spam e-mail poems she had discovered, or it could have been sometime within those paltry twenty minutes of a press conference announcing the Indonesia deal, that Jocelyn's e-mail address was exchanged and somehow included in the new congressman's invitation-only conversation group about open-source intelligence.

"What the heck?" Jocelyn muttered when she got the first e-mail, which she ignored. It wasn't her job to interface with stuff pertaining to intelligence-gathering—whatever that meant. Sounded like something for someone higher up on the food chain. Regardless, she soon began to receive weekly e-mails from the congressman's office indicating that she was supposed to be in a conference call at a certain time and log in with a special code not to be shared with anyone. She checked with Robert and General Walton, who told her to "just go for the ride" since they didn't know how she got on the list either.

So much for "open source," she said to herself as she punched in the secret code and listened in as people from various companies like the BBC and the Department of Defense chimed in about how to make way for open-source intelligence (OSINT).

Apparently, the new congressman was going to introduce a bill regarding OSINT. As far as Jocelyn could ascertain, OSINT had something to do with interoperability during collection and processing of intelligence data. The FBI was there. The army was there too. But as far as she could tell, the Central Intelligence Agency was not represented on this phone conference. She would later come to find out that the CIA was not one for abandoning the idea of keeping secrets, although she was pretty sure no secrets were being passed around and that's probably why they weren't there. This was more like an academic coffee klatch trying to come up with verbiage justifying the new congressman's bill.

"This isn't a meeting for me," Jocelyn griped to Robert after the first call she sat through. "Maybe Theo would like to attend instead?" she offered, thinking that it all sounded so technical. She hoped that maybe it was more of an engineering-department item if it wasn't Robert's. She resentfully figured that she had gotten picked for this because Robert didn't want to do it, and he had signed her up instead.

Jocelyn really struggled with these phone conferences. She hardly ever knew what all the acronyms were—but like most things in marketing, and life in general, if you acted like you knew what you were doing, someone was going to believe it and pretty soon you would too. Not even after being on the phone for a grand total of eight hours of this secret-pass-code-accessed open-source conversation did she have any more of an idea as to why she was included in on this weekly conference call. *What does this have to do with enhancing shareholder value?*

She took the information sent to her and studied it in anticipation of the next phone conference. As she reviewed it, it didn't seem to be relevant to the topic of open-source intelligence at all, at least in the way she was coming to understand it. The publication forwarded to her focused on filmmaking and, for some reason, the archiving of films. It looked like these films were supposed to be submitted by average citizens.

After listening in and not understanding what was going on, she felt irritated enough to speak up. She addressed the new congressman and thanked him for including her. He warmly welcomed her to the discussion and encouraged her to speak. She introduced herself and the company she worked for and, as politely as she could, asked if she was understanding what this open-source thing was all about.

"Sir, I understand that the call for transparency in all sorts of intelligence-gathering and sharing is the primary directive of this project. I had it in my head, please correct me if I'm wrong, that all this stuff being gathered would have to be available to the public. Everything, all the proprietary stuff that the taxpayer paid for, would be available for anyone to look at. That's a cool idea, but ..."

"Back up." Someone (not the friendly neighborhood congressman) interrupted. "Josh Morgan here. Before attempting to address knowledge management, it's probably a good idea to develop some perspective regarding this 'stuff' called knowledge."

"Okay. Yes, please help me out, Dr. Morgan," Jocelyn responded.

Dr. Morgan, whose voice she had come to recognize over the past month and nicknamed "the professor" because he sounded like someone who was used to pontificating while people sat unquestioningly and took notes, said, "A collection of data is not information. A collection of information is not knowledge. A collection of knowledge is not wisdom. A collection of wisdom is not truth. So what have we?"

Oh brother. Jocelyn had not anticipated walking headlong into a Zen koan. She thought for a moment, and before she could even utter a sound, the man continued on.

"When we deal with a situation, we do so based on all that we bring with us. All the experience, real—" he paused "—or imagined that makes us what we are. And to the extent to which the pattern of the situation connects to all that we are, well, that will govern our actions and the timing of those actions."

"Okay," Jocelyn started, but she still didn't know what the heck that had to do with open-source intelligence or with the item about film archiving that she was supposed to read for this meeting, let alone enhancing shareholder value. She sputtered out the first thing she thought of to counter the professor's riddle. "Are we talking about gathering intelligence from a single person? Or a collection of people? Who is defining what is going to be classified as intelligence? And how does time play into the collection and processing of this 'stuff'? Is that factored in? I mean, are we supposed to be collecting everything? Forever? Is that even possible? Does stuff get purged?"

Jocelyn thought that sounded pretty good. She got all her points in and was surprised that no one had bothered to stop her.

"Yes, there will be instances where a single person is worth keeping tabs on. However, the primary concern is how whole communities are dealing with this 'stuff.'" The professor continued, "How do communities pass on their knowledge? How quickly it moves is only a matter of the technology used to transmit it."

"I see," said Jocelyn as she recognized that she might have just mentally grabbed a hold on why the British Broadcasting Corporation was in on a call sponsored by an American congressman about opensource intelligence.

"Is that why the reading we were assigned was all about film archiving?" Jocelyn asked, not really believing that a community would take it upon themselves to make a film with the sole intent of sharing knowledge—let alone knowledge worthy of government concern. This seemed pretty far out there and really academic to the point of absurd to Jocelyn, considering that the films her classmates made back in art school were usually pretty horrible and all but impossible to get shown to anyone other than the occasional heroin- addict-in-training or the "marawize legalwanna" crowd in the basement of the film building. The idea that regular citizens would take it upon themselves to make a movie, for free no less, to share what they knew about the world around them seemed optimistic at best, in Jocelyn's estimation.

"This is a completely new effort," a new gruff voice barked, aggressively cutting off the professor. The new voice continued, "This is for every citizen in every country on the planet. We should name this group of first adopters 'The Intelligence Minutemen.'"

Right! With their new album, The Clandestine Musket. *What the heck am I doing here?* She looked at her watch.

Congressman Summers cut in and asked the man to introduce himself. The gruff voice apologized, hastily introduced himself as Bruce Remick, PhD, and continued.

"In the aftermath of September 11, attacks which were obviously carried out by an actor skilled in asymmetric warfare, it is critical that everyone on the planet have a clear-headed understanding of what's at stake. Everyone, I mean *everyone*, must know what needs to be done to keep not only America but all civilized cultures safe. What the US currently fails to understand is that it already *is* World War Three. We're steppin' in it! And no one seems to smell it over here! There are millions of refugees in sixty-seven countries, mass starvation in twenty-seven countries, plagues affecting fifty-nine countries, and deliberate genocide campaigns in eighteen countries. Seriously, this is the cold, hard shit that our media, our best schools, and even our piecemeal intelligence-gathering community has been unwilling or unable to convey coherently. It's against this goddamn self-imposed ignorance that terrorism germinates and procreates."

"I see," said Jocelyn. "So what I hear you saying is that open- source intelligence will raise awareness of the global state of affairs?" "Absolutely, but it's not as simple as that. It's simpler! Everyone around here is so stuck to their fucking systems of classification and hoarding of information that we are getting absolutely nowhere with this."

This might be good for the Conglomerate. Jocelyn was getting somewhat energized by the idea that she might finally be understanding what they were talking about and how it might relate to enhancing shareholder value. The more people are freaked out by global events, the more the general population might support Congress approving more money for Conglomerate products. That's got to be why I'm here!

"I'm sorry, but I want to clarify something. I'm still confused," she blurted. "Maybe because I've only sat in on few of these meetings, but are we including everything from schematics of nuclear power plants to the White House's layout? Are all those things sup- posed to be open source under the congressman's new bill?"

"In a perfect world, yes."

"But aren't there some things that need to be a secret? You know, for the safety of everyone involved?"

"You are not understanding this."

Okay, right there, that statement kind of ticked Jocelyn off, despite the fact that it was undeniably true.

"Sir, what I *am* understanding from what I've gathered over the past month of these phone calls is that the only logical defense Americans would have with this free and open-source approach would be a concerted effort to disseminate fake 'stuff' to confuse everyone. Maybe more than one version of a confusing story would have to be released. I can see intentional confusion being our only means of defense in this open-source world. Confusion creation would have to be raised to the level of a defense strategy," she paused, "or is it *tactic*? I always get the two confused."

Neither Jocelyn nor her phone was prepared for the explosion of simultaneously overlapping audio, buzzing static, and downright fighting that her statement unleashed. The only thing she could pick up from the aural fray were fragmented references to someone or something called "Jantsch" and the terms "100 percent confirmation" and "100 percent novelty" intermingled with arguments about how people learn. The whole thing had devolved into a giant mess within minutes. Jocelyn concluded that it was the technical difficulty of relaying the audio that had inadvertently ended the phone conference.

Jocelyn never heard from the new congressman or his OSINT conversation group again, which was fine by her. However, there were three things that all happened around the time of that last phone conference that left her with an uncomfortable buzz:

1. A new gold coin showed up in her desk.

Instead of finding this quirky and neat, she found it menacing. She had found the new coin in the exact same location as the last one in her desk drawer. This time it depicted a cute little panda bear munching on some bamboo. On the reverse it had a giant pagoda thing that she knew she knew the name of but couldn't remember, with the date 1994 under it. Everything was in Chinese, but Jocelyn had no problem recognizing what AU 1 oz .999 meant.

2. The video-sharing site YouTube was launched, and

3. Most distressingly for Jocelyn, the spam e-mail poetry stopped coming in.

CHAPTER THIRTY-FIVE

THE GOLD COIN APPEARING SO soon after the last OSINT meeting was what had really freaked her out. It meant that the first one was not a fluke, and it was still making her nervous. She wasn't sure what to do about it. Obviously she wasn't going to go talk to the HR director about it. And what was she going to do? Complain that someone was leaving her expensive gifts?

Even if she wanted to, Jocelyn really had no one to tell about this. It was too strange, and for some reason her gut reaction was to keep it a secret. It wasn't like someone was harming her. Obviously, someone liked her. But why like this? If someone wanted to ask her out on a date, he didn't need to ply her with gold coinage. This was bizarre.

Jocelyn wondered exactly what kind of person would do some- thing like this. She couldn't imagine that whoever it was would be very personable. At first, her curiosity was beyond intense. It was all-consuming.

Maybe it's like a bonus or something and they want to keep it off the books. Is this happening to other people around here and no one is talking about it? she would ask herself as she glanced around the marketing department suspiciously.

Her attempts to keep a video recorder on in her office overnight did not pan out. The battery always ran out, and finally, when the battery wouldn't recharge anymore, she was forced to shop for a new one. The accounting paperwork requesting funds for the new battery, for some reason, kept falling to the bottom of her to-do list, and eventually she gave up on it after a drawn-out conversation with Jerry Apario. She didn't tell him about the gold, of course. But Jerry insisted that a webcam was cheaper than a video camera for surveillance purposes, and he seemed really enthused as he installed not one but three in her office.

"See, Joss?" he proclaimed as he finished installing three eye- ball-like cameras in her corporate cell. "You can swivel the cameras to point wherever you want. And at nighttime, you can monitor the live feeds from the comfort of your own home."

"That's great, Jerry. Thanks," Jocelyn said, primarily to get him out of her office. She wasn't going to be sitting up at night at her house watching live feeds of her desk. What kind of loser does that? And more importantly, when was she going to sleep? This technology wouldn't really help solve her problem. But she listened politely as he explained how to remotely view what the cameras were seeing.

It was amongst this milieu of three fluorescently illuminated eyeball cameras hanging precariously off of a hulk of a monitor that Jocelyn took a call from a coworker at one of the Conglomerate's divisions out in California. She was honestly grateful for the call, because it created an excuse to bring an end to the exchange between Jerry and herself regarding webcams. For some reason, Jocelyn suspected that Jerry and webcams had an intimate relationship, and the thought of it was making her a little uncomfortable. She gave him the pursed-lips, raised-eyebrow expression and reached for the ringing phone. Jerry nodded and headed out.

"Jocelyn," Mimi declared, "it's Peter Schumer from the imaging division out in California."

"Thanks, Mimi, send him through."

"Oh, and Jocelyn? We are going to put something together in the death notices recognizing the six-year anniversary of Nancy's passing. Everyone thought that since you deal with the press ..."

"Wow. It's been six years already?" Jocelyn was honestly surprised. "Sure, how many words do you need me to do up?"

"I don't know. Janice or Sharon probably have something done up already and just need you to place it."

"Okay. Thanks for the heads-up. Please send Schumer through, Mimi." She jotted "death notice" on her yellow legal pad on her list of things to do as Mimi patched the call through.

Jocelyn had never met Peter Schumer, but she knew of his division and wondered why such a big-cheese-type player would be calling her tiny, soon-to-be-defunct place of business.

After the initial greetings, which included him erroneously thinking that he had met her at the Qatar Arms Show the year before and the customary comparisons of local weather, Peter, who was in sales and marketing on the other side of the country, went on to explain the purpose of his call.

"I was wondering, it looks like you have a pretty significant warehouse according to corporate. Do you know who I would talk to about possibly borrowing or renting some of that space?"

Holding the phone with one hand and adjusting one of the eye- balls on the top of her monitor so that it wasn't staring right at her, she replied, "I could find out. Why, what's up?"

"Oh, we've got a bunch of full-body scanners that we thought Israel was going to buy and now we need to put them somewhere. Doesn't look like they want them right now," Peter said.

"*Right now*. Spoken like a true salesman." Jocelyn smiled as she said it.

"Yeah. We were pretty sure they would gobble this up, but they basically told us to fuck off."

Jocelyn was not completely stunned by his choice of words. The generals slung that type of language around all the time, especially when they thought women weren't around. But usually the sales guys were a bit more finessed, at least until you got to know them.

"And you think they're going to take you back?" she asked.

"Probably not. But we've got to unload these. They took the concept hook, line, and sinker, so we produced a bunch of them. But then, when they saw it in action, they showed us the door."

Jocelyn knew that her division was notorious for creating vaporware and marching all over the world trying to sell it. But she honestly wouldn't have expected a report like this from this guy. His division was pretty freakin' important.

"Well, that sucks. Can you do more market research or something?"

"I doubt it. Not with them. They saw it. It's supposed to be used in place of a metal detector at the entry of a building. Someone steps inside and their naked body shows up as varying grades of gray and white on a black background on the monitor. A guard is supposed to be able to see if that person has a gun or a bomb hidden on them," Peter explained.

"Wow. Seriously? You're able to see the whole body? And Israel doesn't want that?" Jocelyn asked incredulously.

"They did," he sighed. "But it went like this: one of the commanders in attendance took my jacket off the back of my chair, put his gun inside my jacket pocket, and handed the coat to me." Peter paused.

"And ..." Jocelyn said.

"Well, he told me to step inside the scanner with the coat on and hold my arms out. And I did."

"Yeah, so?"

"So, everyone saw that it was almost impossible to make out a metal, which shows up as black, on a black background."

Just then, one of the eyeballs that Jerry had positioned on the side of Jocelyn's monitor fell off and rattled around on the desk. Jocelyn picked it up and examined the sticky black polymer that had been used to affix it while continuing her conversation with Peter.

“Well. What were they expecting? It’s an X-ray right?”

“No. It’s a different type of ray, and that’s why they went for it. They thought that the metal would show up as a significantly different tone than the background color. They argued that someone could sew a weapon into their clothes, and if the clothes were baggy enough, slip through unnoticed. They weren’t going to pay for it. They literally said, ‘Fuck you, stop wasting our time.’ I wasn’t kid- ding when I said that earlier,” Peter said downheartedly.

“Well, I wouldn’t want it either then, I don’t think,” was Jocelyn’s response as she tried unsuccessfully to remount the eyeball to her computer.

“Now I’ve got to do something with all these scanners until I can figure out how I can unload them. We hadn’t planned on them refusing this order.”

“Well, I’d love to help you out there, Peter, but our warehouse is actually half the size it was when we were acquired. Corporate may not have that info. They made half of the space into our new marketing and sales area. I’m sitting in it right now. How many do you have to put in storage?” Jocelyn asked.

“About a hundred.”

“Ouch. Nope. I can tell you right now, that is not going to fly over here. I’m sorry. I can put you through to our VP of operations, but honestly, we just don’t have the room to warehouse your stuff,” Jocelyn told the defeated salesman as she ended the conversation and focused on trying to delicately arrange little eyeballs.

THAT NIGHT, WHEN SHE GOT home, she followed Jerry’s directions and attempted to watch in real time what was happening in her office. Unfortunately, the only thing visible was a tiny, faint EXIT sign.

That must be the camera mounted on my desk, near the door, she figured while tilting her head sideways trying to ascertain if anything else might be visible in the mostly black picture. The two other cameras were relaying completely black images. “Well, it was worth a try,” Jocelyn said, deciding it was time for bed.

When she finally climbed into her wrought-iron sleigh bed, she made sure to check the contents of her bedside stand’s top drawer, as she did every night. There they were, two little circles of metal starring back up at her like unblinking eyes. “Why are you here?” she asked the coins as she tucked them in and turned off the light.

The next morning, Jocelyn removed the webcams from her computer. She simply did not like the idea of having surveillance gear surrounding her. It didn’t make her feel safer. Aesthetically, it looked horrible, not to mention that it was just creepy knowing that there was a camera pointing at her that someone like Jerry Apario could easily hack and see what she was up to.

These things are stupid. Besides, whoever this gold-giver is, they are obviously slow movers and are going to eventually want me to know who they are anyway.

CHAPTER THIRTY-SIX

BEIGE. BLAH. BORING. BANAL. SHE had nothing outside of work to look forward to. Nothing except for weird-ass mystery gold that only served to creep her out. She had n-o-t-h-i-n-g. Not even spam e-mail. She was the most unfulfilled woman in the world, in her unbiased evaluation.

She got up morning after morning and went through the same motions of strapping on her pantyhose and sensible heels, and headed smiling into her own private fluorescent-flicker hell. At this point, she had forgotten why she was even bothering. The bills would roll in, and she would press *send*, and automatic bill-pay would pay them. This job was holding her to a perfect bill-payment schedule. It was how she knew time was passing.

Just about two electric bills after pulling the webcams off her monitor, Jocelyn was walking past the front desk in a New England March funk.

"Turn that frown upside down!" Mimi called out from behind the reception desk, which was festooned with a little daffodil plant that someone must have bought at the grocery store. "You look so pretty when you smile."

"Thanks, Mimi. But I can't handle it. It's March, and you'd think I'd be happy that spring is here, but honestly, it's so gray outside and then I come in here and it's beige and gray ... I just wanna sleep until summer."

"Oh, stop. Then you'll be upset that you'll have to come in when it's so nice out!"

"Yeah. You're probably right."

"What you need is a nice night out, Jocelyn. Why don't you come to the casino with me tomorrow night? We'll have some delicious food and play some cards. You need to relax, sweetie," Mimi purred from behind her communications desk.

"Nah, that's really nice of you to offer, but I'm not much of a card player."

"There are some really nice-looking gentlemen there I could introduce you to," Mimi countered.

Jocelyn smiled and shook her head. "Thanks, Mimi, but it's not my scene."

And so it went. Jocelyn would come to work each morning, look at the legal pad with her checklist of things to do, and set to work enhancing shareholder value until everyone else had left the building.

Despite the fact that Nancy had been dead for over six years now, Jocelyn had to admit that she missed the interaction with her on some sort of social level. Elaine Gibson, the HR director, had not bothered to hire anyone after Nancy and relied upon the temp agency, which was, as Jocelyn had correctly estimated, a million times more expensive than just hiring a high-school dropout who could type.

"When are they finally going to shut this place down and let me collect my unemployment?" Jocelyn grumbled as she shuffled back to her desk from the publications area where she had unofficially become the MS Word format trainer for all the near-remedial temps who would file in and then quickly out of the place. She had begun to really appreciate that first temp, Shelly.

What I wouldn't give to have that woman back at publications again. She was so quick on the uptake compared to these people.

Jocelyn theorized that maybe this place had just freaked Shelly out too much and that maybe the temp had decided to disappear in order to avoid the callback. As she was pondering the loss of the only good temp who had ever set foot in the place, Jocelyn ran into General Walton, who was purposefully heading back from the reception area.

"Hello, sir," Jocelyn greeted the general as they approached each other in the hallway.

"Jocelyn," the general nodded as he acknowledged her greeting.

Just as they were about to cross paths, the general stopped in his tracks. "Jocelyn. Our man in Iraq, Ethan Lowe, is back. I was just speaking with Mimi, and she suggested that you take him out to the casino for some R and R. He would probably appreciate that, and you might as well get the full report about the clusterfuck of jackasses they've got running around over there."

Jocelyn's jaw dropped in disbelief. *Mimi!* she silently screamed.

Walton continued, "Mimi said that she has some meal-ticket coupons that she is going to forward to you. You and Lowe might as well use them and enjoy yourselves. I'll be expecting a full report on opportunities in Iraq sometime next week."

Before Jocelyn had time to make up some harebrained excuse about why she wouldn't be able to do this, General Walton gave a casual salute and continued on his way.

"What ... the ...?" Jocelyn said as she spun around and headed directly to the front desk.

Mimi was carefully brushing some crumbs off her chest and picking the lint off her sleeve when Jocelyn arrived.

"Mimi! What the heck are you doing to me?" Jocelyn hissed.

"Oh, hi, Jocelyn. Did General Walton already speak with you?"

"Yes, Mimi. That's why I'm here at the front desk wanting to jump over it and throttle you. You know I don't want to go to the casino."

"Then go someplace else." Mimi pushed the pathetic little daffodil plant a couple of inches to the left.

"Maybe I don't want to."

"Oh, don't be such a fuddy-duddy. Here, take these tickets," Mimi said as she produced an envelope and stood up. "Enjoy some free drinks. Go have a nice night out, for goodness' sake."

Jocelyn sighed. "Mimi, what if this guy is a dick? I mean, honestly, what kind of nut job volunteers to go to war as a mercenary? It's one thing if you're in the service. But c'mon!"

"He's very nice, Jocelyn," Mimi said, still holding the envelope. "He was a Navy SEAL, and he probably just wanted to make more money. I don't know."

"He was? I thought he was one of the computer guys. A programmer or something."

Mimi put her arm down and tapped the envelope on the reception desk. "He is. He's both."

"Both? Really? He must be smart." Jocelyn was impressed.

"And good-looking," Mimi said as she winked at Jocelyn.

"Oh, for goodness' sake, Mimi. Stop." Mimi stopped tapping the envelope.

"No, I'm serious. He'd be perfect company for a night out."

Taking a deep breath, Jocelyn asked, "Well, how old is he?"

"What does that matter? He's a dream, Jocelyn. Smart, in shape, will hold the door for you and ..."

"Mimi, I don't believe you." Jocelyn leaned against the desk to point to the Rolodex. "You have your own desk reference of the personal statistics of every employee here, and you don't know how old he is?"

"I think he's your age."

"Really?" Jocelyn said in surprise, because when she would scan his e-mails from Iraq, she would imagine someone much older than herself.

Mimi was still holding the envelope. "Here, take this,"

she said as she outstretched her arm.

"I really don't want to go out," Jocelyn protested.

"Now listen, Jocelyn, General Walton just spoke with me, and he is very concerned about what is going on in Iraq right now. I don't know what has him all in a pinch, but why don't you just go and get the particulars?" Mimi said as she thrust the envelope closer to Jocelyn's face.

Sensing that she was not going to win this fight, Jocelyn said, "Fine, Mimi. I'll take him out sometime next week."

"Next week! But Jocelyn, today is Friday! I've already told this fine young man that you were taking him out tonight."

"Tonight! Mimi! What if I have something important to do? Like go to a wedding or something?" Jocelyn looked almost frantically around for an excuse. "Why would you do this to me?"

"I made an educated guess that you wouldn't be doing anything. I saw an opportunity, and I took it," Mimi said confidently as she and Jocelyn engaged in a short but intense stare-down.

"I'm gonna kill you. You know that, right?" Jocelyn said as she snatched the envelope from Mimi's hand.

Mimi smiled as if she had just won some sort of personal victory. The phone on the reception desk summoned Mimi back to her usual position and dismissed Jocelyn from further engagement, but not before Jocelyn grudgingly asked, "Where's his office?"

"Would you hold, please?" Mimi told the person on the phone while punching the hold button to address Jocelyn's question. "He's down that corridor," Mimi said as she pointed with one of her salon-perfect fingernails down the hall. "Janice put him in the office next to Theo Cullian."

With her yellow legal pad and the envelope from Mimi in hand, Jocelyn turned curtly and headed to Iraq Guy's office.

"Oh, Jocelyn," Mimi called out before she picked up her phone, "those tickets are only good for tonight. That's why I gave them to you. I couldn't go tonight."

If Jocelyn was the type who chewed gum, she would have been chomping vigorously. She was really very irritated that Mimi would put her in this position. Going out that night was the last thing, *the very last thing*, she wanted to do. As she rounded the corner and headed into the engineering area, Vince the maintenance man walked past her and, not stopping, said, "Have fun tonight. You know, those were supposed to be *my* meal tickets."

Jocelyn stopped short and her shoulders fell. Her eyes narrowed as she stifled the urge to yell something profane. She was going to strangle Mimi. That's all there was to it. She allowed herself a moment to regain her composure and continued down the hall.

Soon she reached her destination. From the hallway window, she peeked into the office. It was very tidy. Some programming books with what looked like woodblock prints of different animals on the covers were arranged neatly alongside some Arabic and Farsi dictionaries in the bookshelf. Hanging on the wall behind the bookshelf was a framed print of *Blue II*, a painting by Joan Miró, which Jocelyn immediately recognized. This was not what she had expected to see. She inched closer to the door and knocked. No one was home. She stepped into the office and stood admiring the Miró print for the dash of color it brought to the dull beige environment. It was during this moment of silent contemplation and art appreciation that Ethan Lowe, holding his coffee cup, entered his office and startled her.

"Oh, hello," he said.

Jocelyn whirled around at the sound of his voice.

"Are you Jocelyn?"

Somewhat embarrassed that she was standing uninvited in the middle of this man's office, she stammered, "Yes. Yes. I'm Jocelyn. Jocelyn McLaren." She transferred the yellow legal pad and envelope from her right to her left hand and outstretched her arm.

He in turn quickly placed the coffee cup on his desk and shook her hand. “Ethan Lowe. Nice to finally meet you.”

Dear God, Mimi was right. Jocelyn was somewhat stunned. She hadn’t been expecting this. For some reason, she found herself at a loss for words.

“I ... I was just looking at your artwork. I love the color.”

“Me too,” Ethan said. “Blue is my favorite color, but I really like that one big red streak right there,” he said, pointing to the print. “It’s so powerful.”

Jocelyn smiled. *Red.*

“I used to have my office right down the hall, and I had the walls covered with red scraps of paper just to brighten the place up,” she told him. “It looked pretty cool.”

“They let you do that?” asked Ethan.

“What do you mean?” replied Jocelyn, honestly confused by the question.

“I’d like to do something like that. Get some color in here. Who do I ask?”

“Oh, I didn’t ask anyone. I just did it. But I’m pretty sure Vince would be in here in a heartbeat telling you to take it all down. I got him pretty upset when he had to pick all the taped paper off the wall and repaint it.”

“I should think so,” responded Ethan.

Jocelyn was so thrilled to talk about red and blue with this handsome newcomer that she had forgotten why she was there in the first place.

“Mimi told me about you,” Ethan said as he studied her face. “You’re not exactly how I imagined you.” He quickly added, “You know, when we would e-mail each other.”

“Mimi told you about me? What did she say?” Jocelyn asked, truly curious.

“She said you were gorgeous.”

Jocelyn blinked.

Ethan did not look away. She could feel her face blushing. The fact that she knew her flesh was changing color was even more embarrassing than hearing Ethan say what he just said.

"Oh, please," Jocelyn said as she rolled her eyes, trying to down- play the compliment. "Mimi can be so dramatic." But inwardly, she was very pleased by this. Remembering the envelope that Mimi had given her, she said, "Oh, speaking of Mimi, she gave me some meal tickets that we can use at the casino tonight. Want to go? General Walton wants me to hear about your interaction with the Department of State. We can discuss it over dinner."

"Oh," Ethan said, "I don't think I want to go to the casino tonight."

Did she just get turned down? Jocelyn was surprised to feel her heart sink. She was even more surprised that she now *wanted* to go to the casino.

Turning over the meal-ticket envelope in her hands, she said, "Mimi told me that these tickets were only good for tonight ..."

"We can go if you really want to, but I'm not really the casino type. I'd rather head over to Newport. Would you like to go there with me? We can talk about anything you want."

Almost dizzy with relief and a newfound admiration for this guy, Jocelyn accepted. They made plans to leave work at 4:45. He would drive, and she would leave her car at the office parking lot while they were having dinner. Perfect.

Jocelyn practically skipped out of Ethan's office and headed back to the new marketing area. On her way, she swung by Vince's office to leave the envelope with the meal tickets on his desk. She stuck a yellow Post-it note to the envelope that read: *You can have them. I don't need them. Enjoy!*

The day was remarkably long, and 4:45 could not come soon enough. Even the photocopy machine seemed to be running slower than usual. The more Jocelyn thought about going to Newport, the more self-conscious she got. This would be the first time she had been out on anything that remotely resembled a date in years.

Oh, for Christ's sake, Jocelyn! You're going to have dinner to discuss the State Department, of all things! Can you just relax? she scolded herself. But still, she was nervous.

CHAPTER THIRTY-SEVEN

AFTER SPREADING NOT QUITE FIFTEEN minutes in the bathroom in preparation for her big night out, Jocelyn emerged at 4:45 and headed to the parking lot. Ethan was standing right by the door waiting for her.

"Ready to go?" he asked.

"Uh-huh. Let's go. I haven't been to Newport in a while," she said, trying to seem cool as they walked through the parking lot to a brand-new enormous black pickup truck.

"Is this yours?" she asked.

"Yup. I just bought it a couple of days ago. I hope you like new- car smell. Here, hop in," he said as he held the passenger door open for her.

As much as she wanted to, she wasn't sure how to. Her skirt and sensible heels did not seem conducive to a ladylike entrance to this vehicle. So Ethan showed her where the little pegs were for her to step on to make the assent. And he gently grabbed her around the waist to support and guide her as she perched herself atop the leather-couch-like passenger seat. She hadn't ever seen a pickup truck this huge. Forget cupholders, it had a place to plug in a laptop. And a phone. It was like an office on wheels. Really big wheels.

"Is this what they call a monster truck?" she asked.

"No," Ethan said, obviously deflated by her question. "It's the new 2005 Dodge Ram 2500. I bought it with some of the money I got from being in Iraq. I wanted something really *American* after being over there. It was either this or a Mustang. I thought I would get more use out of a truck, and this one has a HEMI."

Of course, Jocelyn didn't know what a HEMI was, and because she sensed that she had somehow said the wrong thing by calling his new purchase a monster truck, she didn't ask.

"Well, it is very comfortable. I don't think I've ever ridden this high up off the road, though. Is it tough to drive?"

The small talk about the truck went on for most of the trip to Newport. Once there, they decided upon a little Irish pub that Jocelyn seemed to remember served decent food. They settled into a booth and both ordered up a Guinness as they perused the menu.

"Little different than the food in Iraq, huh?" Jocelyn said as her eyes scanned the menu.

"What are you talking about? MREs are delicious," Ethan said so drily that Jocelyn wasn't sure if he actually enjoyed those little prepackaged Meals Ready to Eat that the military relied upon to feed itself in a pinch. She took a sip of her beer while she eyed him.

"Just curious," he said, teasing it out of her, "did Walton send you out with me tonight because of NAMA and the 06?"

Of course she wanted to seem like she was on top of it, even though she had no clue that an "06" was the DOD-designated rank of colonel, let alone what a *neemah* was. So she responded back, "General Walton seems pretty annoyed by something going on with the Department of State, and you had sent me some e-mails there for little bit. What's the problem?"

"Oh, that." Ethan seemed visibly relieved. He grabbed his pint glass and took a gulp of Guinness before he answered her. He kept his eyes down, looking at the menu. "Oh, it's kind of a mess over there, Jocelyn. State has gone in and totally changed up the game." He looked up from the menu to meet her gaze and continued, "I guess it's just a change in philosophy, but something seemingly as intangible as philosophy might turn this into a nightmare for us."

This is lovely. Just lovely. Jocelyn took another sip of her Guinness and studied the man across the table from her. *I can't believe he's concerned about philosophy. I'm going to hug Mimi when I see her Monday. Mimi is the best!*

Ethan continued, "The DOD had it so that Saddam's army would be part of the reconstruction. The intelligentsia of Saddam's Ba'ath Party would be integrated back into the new government. The Department of Defense's plan was that coalition forces would welcome all these people who obviously knew everything about how to run their country, conduct a war, and gather intelligence around the region. You know, give them a job, make them part of the solution."

"Seems kind of optimistic, doesn't it? Considering we just bombed the living daylights out of them," Jocelyn said.

Ethan took another big gulp of his Guinness, and the pub waitress appeared and asked, "What can I get you guys tonight?"

Jocelyn ordered up some sort of salad topped with salmon, and Ethan got the largest steak available. He made sure to alert the waitress that another round of Guinness would be needed soon as he handed the menus back.

The two of them sat for a moment in silence as the waitress walked away with their order.

"Where were we?" Jocelyn asked.

"Where were we," said Ethan as he finished off his Guinness. "We were talking about State. They came sauntering in dressed in fine suits and nice shoes and started issuing all sorts of mandates, decrees, executive orders, or whatever they want to call them, telling the Iraqis how to cross the street." He let out a forced laugh. "The one that made me write to you was Executive Order 81."

Jocelyn looked at him blankly and shook her head, letting him know that she did not know what he was talking about.

"Remember I wrote to you that day and said that I didn't think Americans were really getting the full story?

Remember?"

Jocelyn smiled. "Oh yeah. I remember. You needed to know how much money weighed. What was that all about? Was that part of the executive order?"

"No. I don't know what that was. I think they were trying to see how well I could program. I was supposed to figure out how many bills would fit on a pallet. How much each pallet would be worth depending on the denomination of the bill. And how much the full pallet would weigh—exactly."

"A pallet?" All she could think of was an artist's pallet.

"Yeah. A pallet. A wooden pallet. You know, like in a warehouse. It was kind of ridiculous the amount of hemmin' and hawin' that went into *that* exercise. It was crazy. I was so tired and still feeling sick from the vaccines they gave me. The heat wasn't helping either. Thanks for the info from Treasury, though. That did help get the job done."

"Here we are, two more Guinness," the waitress said as she carefully removed the two pint glasses from her tray and placed them on the table.

"Just in time. Thank you," Ethan said. Jocelyn gave a little nod in recognition of the second glass now sitting in front of her.

"So why did that executive order freak you out?" Jocelyn wondered aloud as she picked up the pace of her beverage consumption.

"There were about one hundred of these orders made by the Coalition Provisional Authority," Ethan said flatly. "Executive Order 81 is forcing Iraqi farmers to destroy their crop seeds or face penalties."

"Seeds? So what's so upsetting about that?" Jocelyn asked, figuring that complaint was pretty tame compared to some of the stuff she had mentally categorized under *War Is Hell* in her mind.

"They have to use Monsanto seeds. Seeds that are only good for one season. A farmer has to keep buying them every year because they're designed not to last. Our guys are over there fighting a war on behalf of a seed company ... among other things," Ethan said.

"Humph," sighed Jocelyn. "Seriously? You mean a *seed* company got itself included as part of the reconstruction effort over in Iraq? That's weird. I wonder how Monsanto got that sort of product placement. They must have some awesome lobbyists."

"You can thank American politics," he said, looking irritated. "Last year the American Congress granted over $10 billion for the reconstruction of Iraq. Congress was told that expenditure would create 250,000 Iraqi jobs. People with jobs aren't likely to rise up and cause a scene, you know? But so far, just about $2 billion has been spent. Only 15,000 jobs have been created. So where do you think that money is going?"

He paused, watching her. When she had no answer, he continued, "There are literally hundreds of young Americans in their twenties, Republican political wannabes, running Iraq right now. They got appointed by the CPA, which was formerly led by decree by Paul Bremer, a State Department implant who told everyone that he was an Enron refugee making up for lost time. Who says things like that, like it's cool?" Ethan stared at her as he downed the rest of his Guinness.

"I don't get it," she said, taking a larger gulp of beer. Ethan gave a sideways grin.

Jocelyn tried to spout off as much as she knew about Iraq, which she was beginning to appreciate wasn't sounding like much from the way Ethan was responding.

"There's a lot going on over there," Ethan said as he surveyed the pub. Then, turning to look directly at her, he leaned over the table. "Jocelyn, it's not about liberating the people of Iraq to give them democracy. It's not even about oil. Well, not directly. Saddam wanted to accept gold for payment of Iraqi oil. That freaked out a lot of concerned parties. Especially with that pipeline connecting Turkmenistan, Afghanistan, Pakistan, and India being financed by the Asian Development Fund going on. If Iraq started accepting gold as payment for oil, guess what would happen to the price of gold? And more importantly, as far as the US and the entities it owes money to are concerned, what would happen to the US dollar? The only thing that gives the dollar credibility anymore is that other countries have to hold them to buy stuff like oil, which is sold pretty much exclusively in USD."

Jocelyn, starting to feel the effects of the alcohol, sat and considered this. But her head was getting confused by the ever-increasing volume of the Celtic-flavored music, and she couldn't do anything but smile and shrug her shoulders.

Their dinner arrived, and more drinks were ordered up. It seemed that people were spilling into the pub in large groups now and crowding the bar. Boisterous laughter was beginning to drown out Ethan's explanation of the importance of Saddam's Ba'ath Party. "The new Coalition Provisional Authority has gone and proclaimed that the Ba'ath Party is not welcome. Something like 97 percent of the people who worked for Saddam were in that party." He sawed off a chunk of beef with his steak knife and popped it in his mouth.

"Interesting," Jocelyn said, noticing that he held his silverware like a European, knife in right hand and fork upside down in left.

"Of course they were all the same religion as Saddam. These are the people that should probably still be involved in the new government. I mean, you can get rid of an army in a day, but it literally takes years to build one." He pushed his food around with the fork and began sawing again. "These Ba'ath Party members know the system. They know everyone. They know how to wage war. They control the bank."

He looked at her as if trying to figure out if she could hear him over the music. "Iraqis are not viewing this purging favorably. Even though they did not like Saddam ..." He put his silverware down and trailed off, clearly recalling something before he abruptly and excitedly changed gears and told her about the night Udai and Kusai, Saddam's sons, were killed.

"Oh man! We thought we were under attack! Gunshots were going off all over the place. From every direction, but no one was getting hit. We thought these guys were either the worst shots ever or that we were the luckiest guys ever. No one knew what the heck was going on. Turns out that it was just the Iraqis' way of celebrating. They were shooting into the air like cowboys in the Old West! It was like a giant fiesta. They were so happy those guys were dead." He was smiling as he reminisced.

She had stopped chewing. "Seriously? No way."

"When we opened the suitcases Saddam's kids had on them, it looked like they were trying to sneak out of the country with stacks and stacks of US dollars and lots of Viagra."

"Viagra?" Now she put her fork down.

Ethan laughed. "Yeah. I guess they wanted to ensure that they had a good time wherever they were going. Iraqis didn't like them. It was basically good riddance."

Jocelyn smirked and shook off the mental image of Ahmed, that summer intern back in 2001, as Ethan continued.

"But the Ba'ath Party and the government in general ..." He sucked down some more Guinness. "I think people thought that it was operating okay. You know, up to expectations and all. Removing Saddam and especially his asshole kids seemed sort of appreciated, at least by some of the people walking around. But the CPA's forced exodus of the Ba'ath Party, which was a combination of Marxist, Hegelian, and nationalist ideologies united under the banner of Arab unity to overcome artificial boundaries imposed in the Middle East by colonial powers ..."

He lost her at "colonial powers," and she started back

in on the salmon salad. She liked the pub, and being out having a real conversation was awesome. Just awesome. Even if she didn't even know what he was talking about now. She looked up to appreciate him, and they made eye contact. He continued on, "So yeah, the *idea* of the Ba'ath Party was pretty popular. CPA kicking them to the curb was almost like putting out a welcome mat for an insurgency. I mean really, this would pretty much be the equivalent of a foreign army taking over the US—you know, for the US's own good," he said with a twinge of sarcasm, "and proclaiming that anyone working for the US government that was Christian had to go. To add insult to injury, replacing them with, I don't know, pick something, Hindus, Muslims, Jews, whatever. You don't think that would put the people on high alert?"

"So you're saying this was religiously motivated?" Jocelyn asked, remembering one of those seemingly impromptu presidential press conferences next to Marine One, where the president referred to the American response to 9/11 as "a crusade."

"That's probably exactly how the Iraqis are taking it. I mean, wouldn't you?" He thought about that as he stabbed a chunk of steak. "But they pray like a million times a day over there. And religion is much more a part of their everyday lives than ours. Being the same religion means, at least to the US generals, that you are instantly in a network and have the opportunity to organize. So I guess someone made the command decision to just toss all of them."

Jocelyn watched Ethan. He ate and drank like this was his first and last meal, and he was so talkative. She wasn't used to that. She was actually learning something from this guy other than baseball statistics. "This is a place where Saddam, who has had a longstanding relationship with the CIA, would pretty regularly round up the Kurds. The Kurds are kind of the hillbillies of Iraq, a different religion than members of the Ba'ath Party. They have a reputation of being really into independence. The Kurds are not Arabs, and they of course live on top of some pretty serious oil reserves up in the northern part of Iraq. They don't call it 'herdin' the Kurds' for nothin'," he said as if telling a joke that Jocelyn was supposed recognize.

Jocelyn looked at him quizzically while running through her mental Rolodex of bullet points about what the specific difference was between an Arab, a Kurd, and a Muslim. And what the heck did *Hegelian* mean? She'd have to look that one up sometime. But she let him continue. Her salmon was pretty darn good.

"Okay, maybe that's not the best example. America is where we are supposed to have freedom of religion. That would be a direct affront to the Constitution, and I would hope that people would flip out well before our Constitution started getting hammered. People here in the US would be up in arms once it became apparent that a foreign power was trying to take over their government ..." He trailed off again as if considering something.

Jocelyn was only half hearing him as she chomped her salmon salad to the Celtic beat. She was starting to really like the music that was playing.

"Hey! You wanna play some darts?" she asked above the music.

Ethan looked at her, shook his head, and smiled as if giving up on making a case for anything. "Sure, why not?" he said. He had already finished his plate.

As the two of them chucked darts around for the rest of the night, Ethan relayed his experience of clearing Saddam's palace and setting it up for coalition forces—that is, the US Department of Defense. It sounded interesting. He had found some of Saddam's handwritten letters in the palace, which he kept for himself because everything was getting thrown into a giant bonfire anyway—everything except the fit-for-a-king, impressively carved desks that the incoming generals had personally claimed with yellow Post-it notes so they would have somewhere to sit worthy of their efforts plotting strategy and tactics.

"Spoils of war, eh?" Jocelyn said as she launched her dart into the 25 on the target.

"Yup. Been like that for centuries. Hasn't changed much," Ethan said as he tossed his dart. "That bonfire was nuts though. Everything. Filing cabinets. Answering machines. You name it." He grinned. "It was kind of toxic with all the burning plastic, but what the hell, kind of the least of our worries. Right? I mean, there were oil fields burning all around. What's an '80s-style ConAir hair dryer gonna do?" He rolled a dart between his fingers. "I was telling Jerry Apario about it yesterday, and he told me about how he and Dr. Lambert had to burn all the old backup computer tape and disks that she had brought in. I guess the doctor had been storing the backups in, get this, her kitchen cabinets."

Jocelyn stopped in midtoss. "She was storing the division's back- ups in her kitchen? I thought proprietary code was supposed to be stored in some sort of safe or something."

"Hee hee! I know. It's great, isn't it?"

"You know, that place is a disaster sometimes, I swear," Jocelyn said, completing her throw. "What? Like running a magnet over it or cutting it up wouldn't have done the job? He and Betty had to burn it? How medieval is that?"

"He said they took it all over to the workshop because there was an exhaust fan in there, but it still smelled like hell. He wants to sue the division because he's got breathing problems now."

"Jerry's full of it," Jocelyn said as she watched Ethan's dart hit the bull's-eye. "He said he was going to sue after he got back from an install in Algeria and the place he was staying at had the exterminators fume everything while he was sleeping. He thought they were trying to kill him. He ran around pissing and moaning about that for a while until Adam had to tell him to shut up."

When the bartender announced, "You can stay

anywhere you want tonight, but you can't stay here," Jocelyn and Ethan headed out. As she was walking beside him, it became apparent to both of them that Ethan probably shouldn't be driving, and she asked for his keys. He gave them to her.

"Anything you want, baby."

As they happily traipsed back to the parking spot talking about how the night had exceeded expectations on all fronts—food was good, drinks were good, company was good, heck, even the music was good—Jocelyn stopped in her tracks.

"What's wrong?" Ethan asked when he noticed that she had stopped walking.

"I have to go to the bathroom," Jocelyn said.

"Seriously?" he asked.

She nodded.

"Okay, I bet they haven't locked up yet. C'mon, let's jog back and see if they'll let you in."

So Jocelyn and Ethan trotted back as quickly as they could, only to find the staff contentedly counting their tips. So involved, it seemed, that they did not bother to even look up at the couple banging on the door.

"Do you need to pee? You could go behind that dumpster. I won't look," Ethan said.

"That's okay. I'll wait."

"All right, *I'll* go behind the dumpster." Once Ethan was done, the two of them headed back to the truck, where Jocelyn was filled with a renewed appreciation of the sheer size of the vehicle.

"Ummm. You're going to have to help me get into this thing again," Jocelyn said as she stood by the driver's-side door. "I'm sorry."

"Oh, don't you be sorry. It would be my pleasure." Ethan opened the door and, unlike last time when he gently guided her up, he used his considerable strength to quickly hoist her up and unceremoniously plop her into the driver's seat.

Oh, for goodness' sake. Jocelyn took her prescription glasses out of her purse, put them on, and tried to acclimate herself to the vehicle as Ethan jumped into the passenger seat.

"Oh, hey! You look cool with those glasses on. You gonna be all right to drive?" he asked her.

"Um, yeah. I think so. I've got my night-vision goggles on." She tapped her prescription lenses and smiled. "I need them for distance." But then she became serious. "I just don't know about driving this thing. It's pretty big."

"Oh, it's just like a regular car. Seriously. It's power everything. You're just not used to seeing the world from up here," Ethan said with a smile.

"Okay, if you say so," Jocelyn replied as she twisted the key in the ignition. "We'll stop at that gas station I noticed by the bridge so that I can use the ladies' room."

Ethan was right. The truck was easier to handle than she had expected, but Jocelyn still wouldn't compare it to driving a car. It was more like navigating a hovercraft as it floated high above the ground. She drove very slowly and deliberately around the dark, tiny, twisted streets of the port town. They found the gas station, and Jocelyn left the truck running with the radio on as she hopped out and ran to the bathroom.

"Yup. Okay. I knew it," Jocelyn sighed as she tried to create her own version of a maxi pad out of the available squares of one-ply toilet paper. "I knew I shouldn't have gone out tonight," she grumbled, frustrated with herself for leaving the now-necessary items on the counter in the ladies' room at work. Not entirely satisfied with the results of her impromptu feminine-protection item, she washed her hands, fixed her hair, and carefully applied some lipstick.

She jauntily approached the pickup and convinced herself that she could get into it by herself. Her skirt hitched itself up, and one of her sensible-heeled shoes fell off as she clambered into the driver's seat. Grateful that she had made it up by herself but irritated that her shoe had fallen off, she kept her eyes locked on the shoe as if it would walk away by itself if she took her eyes off it.

"Ethan, could you hop out and get that shoe for me? You're better at getting in and out than I am." Not hearing a response, she looked over to find him fast asleep in the passenger seat. She begrudgingly hopped out of the truck, picked up the shoe, threw it into the cab, and repeated the awkward climb back onto the driver's seat.

She had flown the hovercraft successfully for about three quarters of a mile when she noticed the flashing lights behind her. She continued at her current rate of speed and edged over to let the police car continue on its way as it fought crime. But of course, it didn't pass her.

"Oh shit," Jocelyn said out loud. This woke Ethan up.

"What? What's going on?" Ethan said in a more than frenzied way as he quickly studied his flashing environment.

"A cop is stopping me," Jocelyn said as she pulled up next to a telephone pole.

"Don't submit to a breathalyzer. Don't tell him ..."

"Okay. Just you never mind, go back to sleep." Somehow trying to calm him down made her feel less nervous. She hadn't considered that a guy just getting back from Iraq, being awakened from comfortable sleep by flashing lights, might be problematic. She had shoes to find. She looked for the shoe she had thrown in at the gas station but couldn't locate it. Ethan searched too.

"What's worse? No shoes or one shoe?" They debated that, and then Jocelyn made the command decision and hopped out of the truck without shoes.

"What are you doing?" Ethan hissed. "He's supposed to come over to your window. Just stay put."

"Well, I don't think it's cool that I climb back in," she whispered from the ground. "Don't worry, I'll handle this."

Ethan tried to get out of the truck to join her, but the telephone pole she had parked next to prevented him from opening his door wide enough to exit. Ethan was trapped as one of the two police officers positioned himself next to the passenger door in order to keep a watchful eye on the clearly agitated passenger.

Jocelyn noticed that a run was forming in her nylons as she walked toward the approaching police officer. *That's like the least of it, Jocelyn! Pick your head up and look him in the eye*, she coached herself.

"Nice night for a walk, eh?" the policeman said.

"Not really. I'd rather drive," Jocelyn said smiling.

"I don't know about that," Officer Friendly said. "We got a call from the guy at the gas station that you might be having some problems. Why don't you come over here?" He calmly grabbed her arm and led her to the side of the road. "See this yellow line?"

"Yes."

"Try to walk that line, one foot in front of the other. I want you to put your arms out like this as you walk." And he provided an exemplary display of perfect balance as if walking on a balance beam.

She stifled a giggle. "Okay. But I just want to let you know that I have MS, and that I don't have a very good sense of balance even on the best day," she said as she walked the line.

"Okay," Officer Friendly said. "Okay. Come back over here." Jocelyn complied and walked over to him.

"I want you to keep your head still and your eyes on this pencil's eraser," he said as he produced a pencil from his uniform chest pocket that was no doubt kept there for this very purpose. He held it up in front of her face and started to move it around v-e-r-y slowly.

"You mean you can tell how wasted a person is by how they watch a pencil eraser?" Jocelyn asked in disbelief. Still looking at the eraser, she said, "Look. I need to tell you something. I'm really not very good at math. I've never been good at reciting the alphabet backward. That guy in the truck, he just got back from Iraq. That's his truck. We're defense contractors. My boss wanted me to take him out tonight. I've never driven that thing before. It's huge and ..."

Officer Friendly cut her off. "Okay. Okay. I get it. Listen. I can't let you leave, what with a call in about you guys. I suggest you leave the truck parked here and get a cab. Do you have a phone?" he asked. She nodded, and he handed her a telephone number. "If I come back and the truck is gone, I have the plate, and he," the officer pointed to Ethan, "is going to get one hell of a ticket. Understand?"

"Yes, sir. Thank you, sir. We will leave the truck here. Understood," Jocelyn said as if speaking to General Walton back at the office after a Monday-morning meeting.

The two policemen hopped into their car shaking their heads and smiling darkly.

Jocelyn climbed, once again, back into the truck.

"I'm getting better at this," she said, smiling at Ethan as she hauled herself up into the driver's seat.

"You got off? That never happens! What did you say? It must be because you're a chick."

Jocelyn recounted what had just happened and told Ethan that they would have to leave the truck right where it was or else he was going to get a hefty ticket.

"I'm not leaving the truck right here!" Ethan exclaimed. "No way. Someone's gonna hit it. Look around."

He was right. It was a tight little spot that Jocelyn had wedged the truck into. Not really the most advantageous parking spot.

"Are you okay to drive? I don't care if I get a ticket. I'll pay it. Those guys were just trying to pull some sort of power trip on you," Ethan said angrily. "If you really weren't able to drive and they let you go, they'd be in some deep shit. Screw them."

Jocelyn countered with, "If I drive away and they pull me over again ... now that would suck. I don't think I should. He gave me the number of a cab company," she said as she produced the little piece of paper the officer had given her.

“Do you have any cash?” Ethan asked.

“No.”

“Neither do I. Plus, I’m not going to pay for a cab and then have to hitch a ride back here tomorrow to pick this thing up.”

They both sat in silence pondering the seemingly insurmountable obstacle of being free to go but not being able to drive the truck. After a while of Jocelyn watching Ethan nod off to sleep and getting very sleepy herself, Ethan awoke and said, “I’m exhausted. How are you holding up?”

“I’m pretty tired too,” Jocelyn said, rubbing her left eye and put- ting her night-vision goggles back on.

“Look, those guys are probably nowhere around here. Heck, they’re probably done with their shift. Let’s just drive to the motel I saw over by the bridge. I have my company card. I’ll charge it. We can get some sleep. This is nuts. If the cops give me crap, I’ll produce the receipt for the motel not even a mile away from where they stopped us.”

That sounded like a plan to Jocelyn, so she started up the hover- craft and slowly drove it over to the motel. Needless to say, with the combination of an inebriated mercenary just getting back from a war zone and Jocelyn, now flowing like a raging torrent of womanhood, things were bound to get messy.

CHAPTER THIRTY-EIGHT

SHE OPENED HER EYES SLOWLY. It was too bright. She closed them quickly. Her head had the faint feeling of fingers on chalkboard. Not a blazing "I'm never gonna drink again" headache, but enough to let her know that those cops really had done her a favor. She probably shouldn't have been driving the night before.

With her eyes closed, she smiled as she imagined what the gas-station attendant must have witnessed that prompted him to call the police. As she visualized that scene, a more pressing need presented itself. She needed some water. Determined to quench her thirst, she opened her eyes and ...

"Holy shit!" Jocelyn blurted out.

There, on the natty brownish-greenish carpet next to the bed, was a blood stain roughly the size of a small German shepherd. A path of tiny bloody stains led to the bathroom. Jocelyn, instantly awake, sat up. She noticed that she was naked. The bed was bloody too. The bedspread was on the floor on the other side of the room by the wall, which was covered with what appeared to be random bloody smears.

"Holy shit," Jocelyn whispered this time.

She looked over at Ethan. He was in bed with her, on his side, facing away from her. She stared at him wondering if he was still breathing. She was beginning to notice blood just about everywhere she looked. It was freaking her out.

Trying to contain a growing sense of panic, she chewed the inside of her cheek as she reached out and touched his naked back. He didn't move. If she stayed very still and watched very closely, she could swear he was still alive. She bravely touched him again. He was still warm.

Very warm. *That's a good sign*, she said to herself.

"Ethan," she said softly. "Ethan, honey. Are you all right?" Her fingers tapped his back as gentle as a butterfly. She didn't want to startle him or, God forbid, hurt him if he was injured. She couldn't be sure with all the blood everywhere. He didn't move.

"Ethan. Wake up," she said a bit more forcefully. When he still did not respond, she called out in not quite a scream, "Ethan! Wake up!" and tried to roll him over. He started to rouse and put his hand over his ear.

"What?" she heard him mumble. "What is it?"

"Are you okay?" Jocelyn, still touching his shoulder, asked, sincerely concerned.

"I think so. Are you?" As he responded, he rolled over to face her. She was struck by how remarkably blue his eyes appeared in contrast to the bloodstain that surrounded his mouth and covered his chin. He smiled at her and caressed her arm as he nestled his head back down into the pillow and shut his eyes.

In a brilliant moment of what could only be called hypercognition, Jocelyn arrived at the rather horrifying conclusion that all this blood all over the damn place was her own. As her gaze scanned around the well-past-its-prime Cozy Inn Motel room, piecing together the events of the night before and trying to find the bright side of this fiasco, she noted that at least she had helped the owners along with depreciation value.

Maybe their accountants can do something with that.

Oh, this far surpassed any of the scenarios of workplace awkward- ness that she had sketched up for herself as she fell asleep the night before. Little skits like the hallway encounter—"Oh, hi, Ethan ..."— or by the coffee machine—"Yeah. This coffee sucks ..."—or the random chance run-in at the parking lot—"Still enjoying that new truck smell?"

Oh no, this Cozy Inn Helter Skelter scene just took it to a whole new, until now undefined, level of personal humiliation. If her fears of sustaining embarrassment at work were originally assessed at the level of, oh, I don't know, let's say a tidy single pistol shot to her pride, the reality of the situation as she now perceived it was more on par with the final thrilling segment of the movie *War Games* starring Matthew Broderick, where the military's supercomputer, WOPR, starts frantically trying every conceivable combination of strikes in a geothermal nuclear war.

Yeah, her own private geothermal nuclear war scenario. That pretty much summed it up.

Damn, she was thirsty. She got out of bed completely naked. Her lily-white legs and bottom were smeared with an incredible color match to a mixed hue she had admired in a famous painting once, consisting of Alizarin Crimson and Burnt Umber with just the smallest trace of Mars Black thrown in for added dimensionality. But she wasn't even worried about it at this point. Seriously, if this wasn't the classic textbook definition of a *shit show*, she didn't know what was. She decided that servicing her thirst was more important than attempting to cover up and feign prudishness at this point, and she made her way to the bathroom to get a drink.

"Oh, would you look at that," she said as she noticed her skirt and panties hanging on the shower-curtain rod. She poured herself some water and drank it down as she congratulated herself for having the wherewithal to hand-wash her bloodstained clothes the night before. "They look dry already."

As she watched herself in the mirror filling up her second glass of water, she spotted Ethan ambling in. He was wearing his shorts and sleepily rubbing his head. She silently observed him as he noticed his bloodstained face. He didn't say anything, just raised his eyebrows and quickly made eye contact with her in the mirror.

"Yeah. It's everywhere," she said, giving a cursory gesture toward the wall, the rug, the bed—the whole panoply of exhibits—as she took a sip of water.

"Whoa," he said quietly.

"I'm sorry. Maybe ..."

"Sorry? Sorry for what?" Ethan questioned. "Don't be sorry." "Well, there's blood everywhere."

"You've never experienced blood everywhere," he said matter-of-factly.

She looked at him and considered what he had said before she replied with, "I guess you're right."

"This is just a ..." He paused as if composing his thought. "This is just a beautiful outpouring of your incredible sexiness."

Jocelyn burst out laughing. "Right!" she said sarcastically. "That's exactly how I've always thought about this monthly occurrence myself. Next you're going to tell me my farts smell like roses ..."

"No. Those would be my farts."

They both laughed. The release of anxious tension through their combined laughter felt so good. They were both in tear-streaked hysterics by time they finished surveying the damage that they had inflicted upon the room. They decided they would take the rest of the day to recuperate and enjoy all the amenities that the Cozy Inn Motel had to offer (which wasn't much). The plan was that after he got cleaned up, Ethan would head out to get some Resolve Carpet Cleaner and other supplies, specifically food and toiletries for Jocelyn.

"Hey, I have an idea," Ethan said as he turned on the tub's faucet. "Would you like to join me?" he asked expectantly.

"What? You mean join your Bath Party?" She smiled slyly. "It would be my pleasure."

CHAPTER THIRTY-NINE

ON MONDAY, JOCELYN WAS GREETED at the front desk by Mimi, who was visibly upset that Vince had ended up using her meal tickets at the casino. Because of Mimi's dejected, quasi-confrontational attitude, Jocelyn decided that she wasn't going to tell Mimi about going to Newport with Ethan. Besides, knowing Mimi, she probably knew someone at the police station over there and would undoubtedly end up hearing all about the scene with the truck. Jocelyn didn't say much more than, "Good morning, Mimi," and headed directly to her gray executive cube, where she purposefully set to work enhancing shareholder value.

She started in immediately on her Iraq report for General Walton. She recounted through bullet points that the Department of State had, in effect, relegated the trained and able-bodied middle class of Iraq to poverty by disallowing them to work in their former positions within the government and military. Opportunities for the Conglomerate included necessary training programs for the unskilled and formerly unemployed, seeing as that was the only group being allowed entry into the new government positions.

Jocelyn was quick to highlight General Vaughn's mercenary division, which not only sold military and police training but conveniently doubled as an excellent road show, showcasing many of the Conglomerate's war-gaming simulators as well as shooting simulators and truck-driving simulators and, and, and ... you name it. She could hook them up.

All sorts of stuff could be pushed through under the moniker of "training." The mercenary division was also able to provide democracy training, which basically schooled and transitioned national governments and/or communities not familiar with the concept of a constitution, voting, and lawmaking into legitimately recognized democracies.

Naturally, basic computer-skills training would be necessary for all involved as well. The other possible areas of reconstruction looked to be already locked up in noncompete awards by Vice President Dick Cheney's former employer, Halliburton, and the companies connected to the in-term provisional authority's director, Paul L. Bremer. However, there did appear to be a need for translators.

Damn. They need a lot of translators. We could jump on that.

She did a quick proofread and printed her report out in triplicate. She would deliver it to General Walton and Robert in person while on her afternoon break. Jocelyn was looking forward to maybe seeing Ethan over by the coffee machine.

HER COFFEE BREAK WAS tad longer than usual that afternoon. She just couldn't help but refresh that cup four or five times as she whiled away the minutes moseying back and forth between the stock-price display (which, for some reason, she was totally not interested in) and the kitchenette's simulated wood-grain table, where she'd sit and flip through an abandoned copy of *People* magazine.

Jerry Apario traipsed in with his mug, which proudly sported the Symantec logo, and greeted her with a warm smile. "Oh, hi, Joss. I wasn't expecting to see you here," he said as he grabbed the coffeepot.

"Hi, Jerry. What's up?" she said, glancing up from the magazine and taking a sip of coffee.

"Not much." He turned toward her and leaned against the counter as he poured his beverage. "Hey, you'd better remember to back everything up today. Not that you don't every day anyway ..."

Jocelyn giggled because she thought he was making a

joke. But he wasn't. He put the coffeepot back. "They're gonna be shutting down the power in this building, and I don't want you to lose anything."

"Oh, okay, thanks, Jerry. I will."

"Yeah, they're supposed to be doing it right after work. Not like how they did it to you in the middle of the day a couple of years ago."

"Huh? What are you talking about?" She stopped turning pages and looked at him.

"I was telling Mimi about the power being shut off and that she shouldn't be afraid if she's here and the fire alarms start sounding. That happens sometimes. They'll shut 'em off."

"Oh, that's good to know, Jerry. Thanks," she said as she flipped over to a story about Anna Nicole Smith and some sort of diet drink. "But what do you mean, 'like it happened to you'?"

"Oh. Mimi told me about that fire drill you were in over by the Pentagon back in '02." He motioned with his Symantec mug as if he were pointing though space and time to the Pentagon, then took a sip of his coffee.

"Oh, yeah. That was nuts." She shook her head. "Couldn't have been worse timing. The anniversary of September 11th and all. It really freaked me out."

"Yeah. Well. Maybe they wanted it like that."

"Who's 'they,' Jerry?" Now she was getting aggravated. "And what are you talking about?"

"That fire drill happened because someone had cut the under- ground cable for the entire street. Coincidence?"

"Well, I think the term you're actually looking for here is *accident*," Jocelyn said and went back to studying the colorful photographs surrounded by celebrity gossip.

"Well, it's pretty interesting that all the hotels on the street were occupied by one of the big-six defense contractors meeting with the Pentagon that day, don't you think?"

She looked blankly at him.

"It's called a *psy-op*, Joss. Look it up."

"Dude, we were right across the street from the Pentagon. That's why those hotels were built in the first place, for goodness' sake." She closed the magazine and stood up. "You know, so that people could go meet with Pentagon officials. How's that for a coincidence?"

They both smirked and sighed. But unlike Jocelyn, Jerry seemed very happy to have had this whole exchange. They were both leaving the break room when Ethan wandered in.

"Oh, hi, Ethan. I didn't expect to see you here." Jocelyn smiled and involuntarily batted her eyelashes.

"I'll see you later, Joss," Jerry said as he raised his mug and headed down the hall.

"See ya," she said, turning back toward the coffee machine. Ethan already had his cup full when she pulled up next to him.

"Need me to top that off for you?" he asked. His eyes took on an amazing color complemented by the robin's-egg blue of the sweater he was wearing.

"If you insist." She grinned. She didn't know if it was all the caffeine or if she was just nervous or excited to see him, but she found herself slightly trembling as he poured her coffee.

"Hey, there's a Flyers game this weekend. You wanna go with me?"

Yes! Yes! Yes! "I don't know. Who are they playing?"

"Bruins," he said simply.

Just as he said it, the fire alarms belted out a rousing cautionary chorus, and the two of them involuntarily jumped as if they were of one body.

Needless to say, for the rest of the week, Jocelyn spent the bulk of her free time studying the nuances of *icing* and *offsides*.

CHAPTER FORTY

SINCE SHE'D MET ETHAN, EACH new day afforded Jocelyn the opportunity to wake up and look forward to going in to work. Despite the fact that there was a little more spring in her step, she still wasn't too keen on her fluorescent flicker hell. But at least it was tolerable now. She'd upgraded from spam to real e-mails from a real person, and that was nice.

It was while Jocelyn was reading through Ethan's latest e-mail asking if she would like to get some pizza that Dr. Lambert came rolling into the new marketing area. She looked as if she had just finished an uncomfortable jog, with her pink sweat suit and Nike cross-trainers. The little snack-size packet of trail mix that she was picking on completed the look.

"Jerry Apario and I finally finished the final stages of the hookup to the corporate server last night!" she announced to the roomful of executive sensory-deprivation chambers. When no one responded to this news, she called out, "They have really up-to-the-minute virus protection and authentication protocols. So everything should be smooth sailing from now on!"

"That's good," Jocelyn called back over her seven-foot wall. But then something dawned on her. Jocelyn stood up from her desk and wandered out to catch Dr. Lambert before she left.

The fact that they had been some version of an official division or subdivision of the Conglomerate for years now and had not been interfaced completely or correctly to the corporate server initially was not a cause of concern for

Jocelyn. It wasn't her job. She could send and receive e-mails to get her tasks done.

What Dr. Lambert had just said made sense to Jocelyn. The division had been passed around like a trading card within the Conglomerate. Jocelyn knew that the legalities surrounding where they were supposed to be physically based and what they were technically supposed to be called had jammed her up on a bunch of proposals. And she couldn't imagine that it would be any different for the division's IT guys. They were always busy because they would get swooped into working on some on-the-fly product development related to one of Adam's frenzied idea bursts or sent out to some extremely hard-to-access location to install a demo. It actually wasn't surprising in the least when Dr. Lambert announced the accomplishment of hooking everything up the night before. But there was something on Jocelyn's mind.

"Hey! Dr. Lambert. Betty!" Jocelyn called out, waving as she closed in on the pink mass moving down the hall. "Did you happen to figure out what those weird e-mails were all about? You know, the ones I thought were a code?"

"Nah. It was probably just some sort of virus, Joss. You won't be bothered by that now."

Jocelyn was surprised by how disappointed she felt that the spam e-mails wouldn't be coming in anymore. Sure, one hadn't come through in a long time, but she still sort of liked the puzzle of it all and in a strange way considered the author something of a kindred spirit—even if it was just a virus. Deep down, she didn't like knowing she would never see those messages again.

"Oh. Well. I'm glad you got everything hooked up. That must be a relief," she said.

"Yeah. Now everything will be backed up on the corporate server too. And ..."

"Wait. You mean we've just been living off of that box in Jerry's office? Nothing was being archived by corporate this whole time?"

"I don't think so."

"You're kidding me."

"Corporate sent us a brand-new server. So we're good to go. It's like a fresh start," she said happily. "Have a great weekend, Joss." And she waddled off into the sunset.

It was getting darker outside, but inside was the same constant flicker-fest. Jocelyn was starting to feel queasy as she thought about that exchange with Betty. Her mind was trying to piece together a patchwork of little yellow stickies.

"Shred all documents," of course, was the first to flutter to the top of her mental list. Which was quickly followed by recollections of Cathy and the shredder. Images of faceless temps appearing to shred a warehouse full of paper copies of electronic correspondence were next to flash by. Of course, temps were in and out and all over the place when Nancy kicked the bucket. The only temp who Jocelyn could really remember was Shelly, because she was so darn good. And of course, no one could track that woman down. Not even the temp agency.

Jocelyn picked up the phone and called Jerry the IT guy, who picked up instantly.

"Hey, Jerry, quick question ..."

"Oh, hey, Joss! What's up?" he chirped, clearly happy to hear from her. "I'm just getting ready to head out, but I can swing over to your office if you need help with something."

"Oh, no. No. I spoke with Dr. Lambert, and she said that you guys just hooked us up to the corporate server."

"Yup. Last night. Your e-mails are coming through there now."

"Uh-huh. And before that? Was our correspondence being archived anywhere?"

"Well, according to our ISO flowchart, it was up to each department to decide what to archive."

"Okay. So who's in charge of the archive for sales and marketing?"

“Well, wouldn’t that be you?”

“Umm ... I don’t know. I don’t think so.”

Jocelyn heard Jerry rustling around for something, and then he said, “Okay. I just whipped out my handy-dandy ISO binder, and it says ...” She could almost hear him running his finger over the flowchart. “Uh ... umm ... okay. It says that *you* are the person in charge of archiving the marketing correspondence over there and that Nancy, well, she *was* in charge of archiving the finished proposals. Man, we haven’t updated this since then?”

Jocelyn sighed and rolled her eyes. “Well, that would have been nice to know. Who signed off on that?”

“Well, you, of course. Looks like you initialed it right here.” Jocelyn burst out laughing. “Oh, the irony!”

“Huh? What do you mean?” Jerry asked.

“I didn’t sign off on that,” she said

“You mean someone forged your initials?”

“Well, somehow it really wouldn’t surprise me.” Of course, she was thinking of what she put herself through with the Malaysia proposal. But then switching to critical corporate lifesaving skills— meaning, how does one cover one’s ass at a moment like this?—she recalled the proposal logbook that Nancy was always so fastidious about keeping in proper order. Which made her remember that there was, in fact, a marketing communications logbook. But since the switch to predominately e-mail, that thing had barely been cracked. It was a very sorry-looking list of snail-mail correspondence. The bulk of it *would* have been outgoing letters from Stan the congressman, but seeing as all his correspondence was sent on his personal stationery, even though Jocelyn was composing the letters and sending them out via the corporate FedEx account, none of his stuff got logged.

“Why? What’s the problem, Joss?” Jerry asked.

“Oh, I don’t know,” she said sarcastically. “This whole place could lose its International Organization for

Standardization certification if auditors come through. And that's sort of a prerequisite for even being able to respond to RFPs." Then more solemnly, she added, "I don't think marketing has archived anything lately. And, from what you just told me, I'm the one who's supposed to have been dealing with that."

"Oh ..." Jerry mumbled.

Then she sighed. "I guess it makes total sense. But I didn't know I was supposed to be in charge of keeping a log somewhere."

"Well, maybe we could re-create the marketing archive? I still have access to the old server. We didn't burn that! And there's got to be stuff on there we could pull out."

"Jeez, Jerry. I honestly can't get my head around this right now. I'm kinda screwed."

"Nah. It'll be easy. Don't worry."

Jocelyn was just about to end the conversation, thinking that it might actually be easier to amend the whole ISO process, when something Ethan had mentioned in Newport while they were slinging darts around seemed to click. "Hey ... wait! Are you talking about burning old computer tape?"

"Umm ... no," Jerry mumbled. "Forget I mentioned it."

"Yeah, but remember when the new marketing area had its heat shut off and—"

"Joss, please don't mention it to anyone. Seriously."

Jocelyn was almost bouncing in her chair as she spoke. "Dude! That stuff was toxic! You're lucky you didn't asphyxiate someone! Do yourself a favor; make sure Martin Mays doesn't find out, because he'll sue you." She was laughing, but Jerry seemed really depressed, so she turned it down a notch. "I won't mention it, Jerry. I promise. I guess it's ancient history now, but next time you get the bright idea to burn plastic, do it somewhere else."

"Well, it really wasn't my idea. Dr. Lambert was really nervous because she had gotten a Post-it note that said,

'Torch all tapes now.' So we did."

"Oh, on a Post-it?" Jocelyn smirked, thinking about how ingenious Adam was. "Figures. You really can't trace or log a Post-it note, now can you?"

"Don't worry about your e-mail correspondence archive, Joss. I'll hook you up. Please, I'm begging you, don't say anything about that sticky note."

CHAPTER FORTY-ONE

"OKAY, JOCELYN. YOU ARE GOING to Qatar," Robert announced at the Monday-morning meeting. Of course, most of the meeting was spent discussing the situation in Indonesia. *Again.* Nothing was needed from Jocelyn. Not yet, anyway. It was really a paperwork thing at this point. Insurance companies were getting called in. The whole Indonesia debacle would take at least another year to resolve itself. And because of that, everything was on hold. Everything but the layoffs.

Oh, please let me get laid off. Please, Jocelyn would silently beseech a higher power every Monday. But no. After this Monday meeting, Robert brought her into his office and explained, as he emphatically drew on his whiteboard, the new scheme of division mergers and chain of command. His efforts to deeply embed himself into the corporate hierarchy apparently had worked. And of course, since Jocelyn did so much of his grunt work, which he took credit for, she was moving with him.

Jocelyn couldn't tell if he was congratulating her or executing a masterful mental jujitsu on her as he outlined her new "powers"—all of which, of course, required his approval in order to be unleashed of their worldly confines and allowed to initiate ungodly amounts of control over the enhancement of shareholder value.

At least that's what she got out of the hour-long meeting. But she wasn't buying it. For some reason, "I'm awake! I'm alive! And I feel great!"—the mantra that she was forced to happily clap and chant before each Executive

Training for Women seminar that Robert had signed her up for—started to repeat itself over and over somewhere in the back of her skull, and she took that as a bad sign. Jocelyn did what she usually did in these cases when Robert, or one of the generals, started needlessly going on and on and on: she took extensive notes that included a hearty helping of abstract-shaped little doodles.

Her first assignment in this new position, which was just like the old position but with a lot more work, was to coordinate a plan of action with a bunch of the Conglomerate's divisions for the annual Qatar International Arms Show. She needed to put together the multimedia presentation and marketing collateral material for all of the Conglomerate's products that were to be represented. Each of the divisions had something to contribute, and each needed to have a generic proposal and a sales agreement ready just in case someone walked in and wanted to buy something right there on the spot and take it home, which wasn't unusual for Qatar.

The multiple-proposal part wasn't so hard. It was just a pain. The multimedia stuff was kind of fun to produce. She would be able to get out of the office and go to that ex-military production studio she had used for the website. They would know how to make the Conglomerate's products, like the gyroscope, look awesome. It would all be animated with computer graphics of the Unmanned Aerial Vehicle (UAV) that was using it zooming by.

They always used such impressive music too. It sounded like something you might hear on the radio. Almost like an exact copy of the song, but it would be in a different key, and it would easily loop back upon itself so that by time the trade show was over, everyone who had worked the booth wanted to just about slit their wrists when the real song made an appearance in real life.

Luckily, she didn't have to actually handle the trade-show booth. That was a light construction project, and you had to deal with lots of subcontractors. The big division in California would be handling that aspect. They wanted to use the waterfall and koi-fishpond setup for the booth again. Jocelyn had expressed concern during one of the phone conferences that she didn't really think that the koi pond helped express the overall theme of the Qatar Arms Show, which was something pretty darn close to "Preparing for Armageddon."

But Sheila from Arizona thought it was nice-looking. And when Brandon from Texas explained that every year people ended up throwing money into it for good luck, money that could easily pay for drinks after the show ... Well, that clinched the koi pond.

"*Qatar*, pronounced like *cutter* the *gutter*," as Robert was always quick to point out each and every time he spoke with Jocelyn about it (he must have thought that it was funny or something), was a teeny, tiny little country in the Middle East, not much larger than a landing strip for the US military. The arms show was a huge international affair featuring the latest state-of-the-art anti-bad-guy gear, from tanks to missiles to guns to computer programs. Anything that helped kill people faster and more efficiently, or at the very least intimidated the hell out an enemy, was showcased there and for sale. This was the trade show that all of the defense sector looked forward to each year. This was a big-money show.

After seeing pictures of past shows and noting the attire of those in attendance, she wondered what she should wear. Not so much in a "does this make my butt look fat?" type of way, but in a more pressing "am I going to offend someone really important by wearing a knee-length skirt?" or "is someone going to flip out if I'm not wearing some sort of head covering?" type of way. Robert, being the American man that he was, did not seem to fully comprehend her concern regarding cultural sensitivity.

"Oh, just call Texas. That division goes every year. They'll let you know what to wear from a woman's point of view."

So Jocelyn called Texas and was patched through to a lovely lady who listened to her detailed descriptions of what she had bought to wear.

"That all sounds perfect. Now tell me, hon, what color hair do you have?"

"What color hair?" Jocelyn asked, a bit confused by the question. "Blond. A sort of strawberry blond."

"L'Oreal 6RG?" the woman asked. "No. It's just the color of my hair."

"Oh, honey! Hold on for the ride of your life! You are going to be treated like royalty in Qatar. They really know how to throw a party over there. There is nothing like it here in the states. It's like a rite of passage for us. You're going to love it! Just make sure you have all your paperwork signed. Corporate takes no responsibility for anything that may happen to you while you are there."

With words of encouragement like that, Jocelyn wasn't sure whether she felt better about going to the show or not. She had been fighting off feelings of squeamishness about going. For some reason, probably because Qatar was conveniently located near the epicenter of an ongoing millennia-old war, she didn't want to go. But this woman had taken some of the edge off. Sort of. She would be fine. She just wanted to get some things taken care of before she headed out in a few weeks. Namely, doing up a will and going to the doctor. She hadn't been feeling like herself lately, and she figured if anything was wrong with her, she might as well get it taken care of now so that she wouldn't have to deal with it over there.

I probably just need some antibiotics or something, Jocelyn told herself as she dialed the doctor's office to make an appointment.

CHAPTER FORTY-TWO

"WELL, THAT CONFIRMS THE SAMPLE. It looks like there's two in there," the doctor said.

Jocelyn took a deep breath, trying to process what the doctor had just said. All she could think of was her deceased coworker Nancy, and how Nancy had always suspected that she had cancer before she dropped dead.

"Two tumors?" Jocelyn asked, bracing herself for the worst as she lay spread-eagled on the ob-gyn's examination table.

The doctor spun around from the monitor and faced her. "No," he said, seeming confused by her statement. "Your body is getting ready to have two babies."

What? Jocelyn thought as she felt a wave of supreme happiness intimately intermingled with the bitter after bite of *holy shit* wash over her consciousness.

The doctor whipped open her file with more than a look of concern. "Didn't they just give you a urine test?"

"Um-hum. Yeah. But I figured it had to be wrong," Jocelyn responded honestly. "How did this happen?"

"How old are you?" he asked, deadpan. "No one ever told you about the birds and the bees?"

"No. I mean, yeah. I know how babies are made," Jocelyn laughed. "I mean ... how did this happen?" Jocelyn was confused, seeing as after the Cozy Inn Motel experience, she and Ethan had been very careful. She knew relapse rates for MS usually kicked into high gear after childbirth, so she knew that she definitely didn't want to get pregnant. Jocelyn wasn't seeing anyone else. This didn't make any sense to her.

The doctor, still looking at the monitor, said, "You're pretty early along, aren't you?"

"I guess," Jocelyn said.

"Don't worry," the doctor said, thinking she was upset about hearing the news that she was going to have two mouths to feed. "One of these little grapelike items," he pointed to the monitor, "might just dissolve, or get absorbed by the uterine lining, or get flushed out. It happens all the time." He turned to look at her. "You are very early along. There is still plenty of time to do something if you don't want to go through with it."

Still spread-eagled in the examination stirrups, she asked, "What do you mean, 'do something'? You mean an abortion?"

"Why don't you hop down and get changed. We'll have a nurse go through your options."

Two babies! Oh my God. Not one, but two babies! I have two babies in me! Jocelyn was smiling as she got dressed. She walked in stunned silence over to the nurse's desk, where she sat down and waited. As she sat there, it dawned on her that she should probably let Ethan know.

She dialed his direct extension at work.

"This is Ethan," he answered.

"Hey, it's me."

"Hey! I wasn't expecting to hear your voice," he said, obviously happy to hear from her. "Did you get some medicine to take with you? You never know what the heck they're gonna give you somewhere else. Seriously."

Now Jocelyn got a little nervous. Maybe she should wait to tell him. Maybe it wasn't fair to spring this on him at work.

"Well, um-hum, yeah. I'm at the doctor's now."

"What? You're at the doctor's? I don't think we have a very good connection. Hold on."

She waited while he did something. When he got back on the line, she blurted out, "I have two in there."

"What does that mean?" he asked.

"The doctor says I'm getting ready to have twins."

There was a moment of silence, and then she heard what sounded like the phone bouncing off of something.

"Ethan?" she called into the phone.

"Sorry. I just dropped the phone. What did you just say?"

"Twins. It looks like I have twins in my belly. That's what has been making me feel so strange."

"Whose twins?" he asked.

"Yours and mine, silly. What do you want to do? I'm waiting to hear from the nurse about options."

"Are you sure they're mine?"

"Yes," she answered, a bit put off by this question but fully understanding why he would be skeptical. Heck, she didn't even believe it herself.

She waited in silence until he finally responded with, "Well, I think you should do whatever you think is best. It's your body."

That was a decent answer but really didn't inform her about his thoughts on the topic.

He probably wants me to get an abortion but just doesn't want to say it.

"All right," she said with a knot of emotion growing in her throat. "The nurse is coming in right now. We'll talk later?"

"Call me later," Ethan said, and they hung up.

"Okay," the nurse said as she fiddled with the medical file and sat down at her desk. "Jocelyn, the doctor told me that you want to discuss your options."

"Yes. Please. I really have no idea how I got pregnant, and now I have two in there. This isn't really the best time to have kids, and I have MS, and I don't know ..."

The nurse smiled. "Does your partner know you're pregnant?"

"Yes. I just called him and told him."

"And does he want children?"

"He said it's up to me."

"I see. How long have you two been together?"

"Oh, not that long at all. I work with him, and he's like my only friend. You know, at work. He makes me laugh, and sometimes we just talk about things. But I wouldn't even call us a real couple at this point."

"I understand. So you think you might want to terminate this pregnancy?"

"Well, I've never been pregnant before, and I've never imagined that I would ever want to get pregnant. I've never been the type to daydream about having kids. Never. I mean, I've made it through thirty-four years of life and have managed to avoid this. I honestly don't know what it entails to get an abortion. But I honestly don't know what it takes to be pregnant and have a kid. Let alone two kids."

She paused to take a breath. She knew she was rambling. She looked the nurse in the eye hoping to gain some clarity or at least a glimmer of the nurse's opinion. "Is it like an operation? You know, one where they put you to sleep?" Jocelyn asked, starting to get really nervous.

"Well, it looks like you are early enough to take something called RU486. You take this pill here today at the office," the nurse placed an oblong white pill on the desk in front of Jocelyn, "and then you'll come back and take this." She held up an amber-colored pill bottle. "This will cause you to get your period, and you will no longer be pregnant."

"Wow. That sounds easier than I thought."

"Is this what you want to do?"

"I guess so. I don't know why, maybe it was those people out front with the signs, but I thought it was going to be much more gruesome than that."

"Well, you are very lucky you came in today. Sometime, like the day after tomorrow," the nurse said, looking at Jocelyn's file, "you would be too far along for us to offer RU486. I will have to watch you take the pill. Hold on. I'll get some water," the nurse said as she got up to fetch a Dixie cup of tap water for Jocelyn.

While the nurse was away from the desk, Jocelyn picked up the pill and considered it. She noticed her hand starting to tremble. She wasn't quite sure she wanted to do this. She wanted someone else's opinion. This nurse wasn't giving her any vibe as to what to do, which Jocelyn had to give her credit for. Jocelyn imagined that it wasn't in this woman's job description to tell people what to do. And Ethan, well, he was leaving it up to her. *That's not fair*, she thought. But really, what could he say that she would think was fair at this point? She put the pill back down on the desk and waited for the nurse.

The nurse came back in holding a tiny cup of water. "You ready?" she asked.

"Umm ... What is it going to feel like?" Jocelyn asked the nurse. "Well, you are going to get a very heavy period after you take the second pill, and you will get some good cramps. You'll want to call in sick the day after tomorrow and possibly the next few days and just relax. It's not uncommon for women to have their period the whole month. But don't worry, it won't be as heavy."

Jocelyn's heart was racing now. "Can I take the pills home and just think about it?"

"No. I'm afraid not. These pills are strictly controlled. You will need to be in front of one of us here at the office when you swallow them and stay for a few hours while we observe you to make sure your body is handling the drug in a normal fashion. One today and the same deal for the one tomorrow."

"Okay," Jocelyn said as she slowly picked the pill up and studied it for the second time.

Not just one, but two. There's got to be some bad juju associated with getting rid of not just one, but two.

The nurse extended her arm to pass her the water. Jocelyn took a deep breath, trying to brace herself for what she was about to do. Just as she was about to accept the cup from the nurse, her phone rang.

"Oh, hold on. Let me take this," Jocelyn said as she placed the pill back on the desk and looked for her phone. Of course she knew the nurse knew she was stalling. But whatever.

Jocelyn answered the call as the nurse looked on. "Hello?"

"You didn't do anything yet, did you?"

As Jocelyn held the phone to her ear, Ethan's anxious voice clearly rang through the silence of the nurse's little office.

"Well, I'm just about to take a pill, and I have to ..."

"Wait! Can we talk about it? You know, tonight? I mean, you don't have to do it just this minute, do you?"

Jocelyn got that glimmer of opinion she had hoped for earlier as she watched the nurse purse her lips, close her eyes, and let her face relax into a gentle smile.

"Oh. Sure. I'd love to talk about it with you tonight."

"I'll come over to your place directly after work. I'll bring a pizza or something."

"Sounds like a plan."

As Jocelyn closed her phone, she looked over at the nurse. "I'm sorry for putting you through that."

"Oh, no." The nurse smiled. "I only wish half the women who came in here would get a phone call like that. That was beautiful. Go home and talk with him. You'll both figure it out."

Jocelyn thanked the nurse for her time and told her that she would call her first thing in the morning to let her know if she needed to come in and take the pills. The nurse reminded Jocelyn that she only had a very small window of time to be eligible to take the RU486. After the forty-nine-day mark, it would have to be a different procedure.

Still stunned and almost vibrating with anticipation for the upcoming conversation with Ethan, she hopped into her car. She sat holding her steering wheel thinking that she might start crying, but instead, and surprising even to her, she started laughing. “Not just one, but two!” What a mess this was. One beautiful mess.

CHAPTER FORTY-THREE

"JESUS CHRIST, JOCELYN. I'M SO sorry," Robert said while shaking his head. "That was supposed to be your flight."

Jocelyn sat stony-faced at her desk as she processed the news for the twentieth time that day. She tried to ignore Robert as he, for some reason, felt the need to continually pop into her executive cube and apologize to her. Sure he had been an ass when she'd announced three weeks ago that she wasn't going to Qatar, but she had kind of expected him to act that way seeing as the tickets had already been purchased and luggage tags had already been sent to her with the Conglomerate's logo and her name and address engraved on them. She knew it was uncool to just cancel her trip. But she figured that the company was so big they'd have no problem finding a replacement for her at the "Preparing for Armageddon Koi Pond" booth.

"Did you know anyone on board? You must have," Robert asked.

"Not really," she said as she absentmindedly fiddled with her new brass luggage tag. "Just some folks I've had to deal with on phone conferences. I think Brandon from Texas was supposed to be on that flight."

"They still haven't found anyone yet? Just the luggage?" Robert asked.

"I guess. I don't really know."

"I'm so sorry, Jocelyn. Really, I am."

She looked down and made something resembling a smirk as he made his exit for the umpteenth time. No one knew for sure what exactly happened to the little jet after it left Germany and headed over to Qatar. But it had been confirmed earlier that day that the US Navy had found some pieces of an Embraer 175 and some luggage floating around the Mediterranean. Luggage proudly sporting Conglomerate baggage tags.

That in itself would have been enough to freak anyone out, but coupled with the fact that Jocelyn was supposed to be on the flight with Brandon and the folks that she had been phone conferencing with ... well, that was blowing her mind. And what was blowing her mind even more were the two tiny little reasons why she wasn't on board her scheduled flight.

She and Ethan had discussed it weeks ago and decided that she should just stay in the US while she was pregnant. There was no need to be flying through war zones to sell drones and weapon-training simulators with two babies in her belly. Especially *his* babies.

They had talked about it at great length over pizza the night she found out that she was pregnant and decided that they were both grown adults with decent incomes and could do it. They would both be committed to their children. They could definitely do it. They would figure it out.

The initial plan was that Jocelyn would stay at her job as long as she could in order to keep her medical insurance for the birth of the kids. But over the past couple of weeks, Jocelyn's job had become more and more of a mind-fuck as she approved orders of printed material touting the attributes of military-grade killing machinery with two new lives growing exponentially faster inside of her each day.

Naturally, at this point, it goes without saying that Jocelyn really didn't like her job. But her job did provide security for her and her soon-to-be family. She had somehow thought, because of the economics of the situation, that she would be able to stick it out until she gave birth. But every day it got harder and harder for her to get her head around the "why?" and the "what for?" of sitting at her desk promoting implements of doom.

As she sat in her battleship-gray office holding her Conglomerate luggage tag, she absentmindedly poked through the stack of magazines that she had piled up on her desk: *Jane's Defence Weekly*, *Jane's Intelligence Review, DefenseSystems, The Economist, Surface Warfare.* The list went on.

"How pathetic," she sighed. Not able to stomach the selection of magazines, she swiveled around in her chair, and her gaze fell upon one of the only shreds of color in the place. She had been officially admonished for taping scraps of paper to her wall when she moved into this executive cube, so this solitary splash of color was contained within a large poster of a bar graph. She couldn't remember if it had come tucked in a copy of *Defense Magazine* or maybe it had been *Terrorism and Insurgency Monitor*, but she had liked how it looked and taped it to her wall not so much because it was useful information but because it was colorful.

The graph outlined the various known terrorist groups. Number one on the planet at the time of print was the well-known IRA, which religiously wreaked havoc over in Ireland. Its red bar on the graph was very tall, almost off the page, depicting the amount of money moving through the organization and the number of deadly attacks claimed by the group. The other organizations listed on the page paled in comparison.

She noticed that al-Qaeda, which she was continually mentioning in her press releases, was listed very near the bottom of the graph, although it had moved up from the year before where it previously held the very last position. Not very important, according to this chart, in terms of financing and global reach.

Humph. That's interesting. Jocelyn seemed to be looking at the three-year-old graph for the very first time, although it had been stuck to her wall every day. *Why? Why do I have a graph of terrorist organizations decorating my wall? This is not normal! I should be thinking about what kind of wallpaper my kids' room is going to have and reading parenting magazines!*

Truth be told, Jocelyn had absolutely no interest in picking out nursery wallpaper. She just didn't want to be doing what she was doing, and the pregnancy seemed to heighten her aversion to it. She could feel it. Literally *feel* it. It was almost like her body was telling her, "Run! Run right now!" She knew that she didn't belong there.

She had always felt as if she was acting—putting on a costume and playing the part of a character in some ridiculous TV series. Jocelyn didn't know exactly what she wanted, but she knew she didn't want this. Her thoughts were interrupted by the sound of a feeble knock on her executive-cube door.

"Anybody home?"

Startled by the voice, she pivoted her chair. "Oh, Jerry, you scared me. I was kinda thinking about something."

"Yeah. I heard," he said. "You okay? Mimi told me about it. Were you really supposed to be on that flight?"

She nodded.

"Do they know who did it?" he asked.

"Did what?"

"Shot down the plane."

"Jerry! Do accidents ever just happen in your world? Or is everything some sort of vast conspiracy?" She was more than a little annoyed by him suggesting foul play because she had successfully talked herself out of the idea about a half hour ago. "I really don't want to talk about it. Okay?"

"Okay," he mumbled and looked down at his new Adidas foot- wear. "Um ... I started working on your ISO communications logbook."

"Oh, that's really nice of you, Jerry, but seriously, you don't have to do that."

"No. I sorta want to."

"You're crazy." Jocelyn rolled her chair back over to the computer. "Thanks for the offer, though." Then she placed her hands on the keyboard as if she might start typing and was hoping he'd get the clue and leave.

But instead, he came over and knelt down next to her chair and whispered, "Who is Lisa?"

With her head still stuck in downed-jet mode and Jerry positioned as if he was going to propose to her, naturally Jocelyn didn't have a clue who Lisa was. "Huh? What?"

"Your boss, Robert, was e-mailing back and forth to someone named Lisa back in 2001 and 2002."

"And this is a problem?"

"Well, he was e-mailing this person from a couple of different machines here in-house."

In exasperation, Jocelyn took a deep breath and said, "As opposed to ...?"

"It was the middle of the night, Joss."

"Well, Lisa might have been in another country or something. You know, time zones and stuff." Then, looking down in disgust, she said, "Jerry, get off the floor."

Jerry promptly got up off his knee, but instead of backing away, he literally got in her face and whispered, "The subject line was 'Playdate.' There were twenty-seven e-mails with that subject line, Joss."

This got Jocelyn's attention, and she paused to consider this in- formation. "I guess he was having an affair or something." She really had a minimal amount of respect for Robert and wouldn't doubt that he was screwing around. Although she had no idea what type of woman would actually be attracted to him, he was so fake. *Must be some sort of gold digger. I mean, look at his watch collection. Talk about a gold-digger magnet.*

"Or something, Joss. I think she was setting him up with kids."

"Shut up!"

Jerry backed up but stood his ground. "No. This woman was some sort of, you know, madam or something. She was sending him photos of the kids she had available. And guess where he was saving them?"

"Jerry, this is none of our business," she said, becoming quite uncomfortable about nosing around in someone else's e-mail even though she was horrified by what Jerry was telling her.

"It looks like he saved a bunch of these pictures on Ahmed's computer back in 2001. Remember him? The kid from Egypt? He'd go into that big comfortable office in the middle of the night and look at the pictures there, I guess." Jocelyn looked around the room as if seeking some sort of emergency escape hatch and took a deep breath. "And, well, yeah, it kinda is my business. It's my job," he said with a newfound sense of assuredness. "I'm basically the IT guy here, because Dr. Lambert has no friggin' idea about anything, and these e-mails were coming off of Robert's corporate account here in-house."

"Well, see, you said it yourself—Dr. Lambert is in charge of this stuff, not you. You're in the clear." Jocelyn's reaction was surprising not only Jerry but herself. She was amazed that the Executive Training for Women seminar that Robert had approved for her was paying off like this.

Jerry looked at her as if she were melting. He was totally confused by her reaction. "Jocelyn, they were discussing in their last e-mail about switching to some other means of communication because Robert must have realized that all his e-mails were probably getting saved somewhere." He stopped to drill his eyes into her and added extra emphasis to his voice. "You know, like in an ISO logbook or something."

Instantly she took on all the attributes of a woman who meant business. "Okay, forget about that archive, Jerry. Let it slide. Dr. Lambert mentioned a new server. This place is going to get shut down at some point in the very near future anyway. Let the next division deal with the fact that we have no records and the hassle of an ISO audit of a defunct division, if that audit ever takes place. That marketing logbook is not important in the grand scheme of things." As she said it, she recalled that Nancy, the harried woman from the publications department who had been rolled out on a stretcher to meet death, had said basically the same thing once.

"Yeah, well, what *is* important, Joss?" This last statement left both of them speechless. Jerry studied her, waiting for an answer, and Jocelyn bit her lip as she put her hand on her stomach. She felt like she was going to throw up.

FULLY CONVINCED OF HER RESOLVE, she met with Robert the next day. With her typed resignation letter in hand, she told him she was pregnant and that she would give the company three and a half months. She asked that he not tell anyone about her pregnancy. Especially Mimi.

CHAPTER FORTY-FOUR

Early October 2005

HALLELUJAH! IT'S HERE! IT'S HERE! My last day at the Conglomerate! She could almost hear the resounding heavenly chorus as she pulled into the parking lot, and she could just about see the Smurfs and rainbows complete with comets of sparkly stars above the reception desk as she entered the building. She was just so elated that this day had finally arrived!

Hours. I've only got hours left at this place. I can't believe it! She giddily started her last day of work.

After Jocelyn had put the finishing touches on an impressive binder outlining the procedures related to enhancing shareholder value and had helped train her replacement, Robert called her into the big conference room. Apparently one of the generals needed something, and Robert didn't know what the general was talking about.

Oh man. Now what? I've literally got—she glanced at her watch— *two hours left at this place and ... oh, figures*, Jocelyn mumbled to herself as she grabbed her yellow legal pad and summoned the last smile she would ever have to fake. She was now over five months pregnant, and it was beginning to show. But she hid it very well under lightweight sweaters and stylish capes. No one thought her outfits were out of place, seeing that the new marketing area, as people continued to call it, still had the stigma of being very cold.

At least she thought she hid it very well. To Robert's credit, he never did tell Mimi, but he did tell Janice, and so it went like dominoes with the information eventually falling to

Mimi.

When Jocelyn got to the big conference room, the lights were off. She reached over and flipped the master light switch. "*Surprise!*" All her coworkers were in there smiling, excited to *not* be sitting at their desks.

Mimi came in holding the requisite sheet cake that had been ordered up for the "going-away party" and placed it ceremoniously on the conference table next to a blue envelope and a little jewelry box. For a brief moment, Jocelyn actually felt a warm feeling for all of these people (everyone except Robert, of course). This was their life. This is what they did. But she didn't belong there. It was time for her to go.

Jocelyn smiled and blushed and thanked everyone for the party. "I ... I wasn't expecting this," she said.

Someone hidden in the back of the room who was clearly vested in at least one of the top-secret betting pools operating around the outcome of her pregnancy—"Due Date," "X vs. Y: it takes a Y to make a guy! Which will it be?" and "Who's Your Daddy?"—shouted out, "But you're probably expecting something else!"

Jocelyn, with mouth agape, sought out Robert in the crowd. "Robert! You didn't!"

"No. I didn't," Robert answered truthfully. So Jocelyn turned her sight on Mimi.

"Mimi! How did you find out?" The partygoers in the conference room were clearly enjoying this sideshow as the cake was being cut and distributed by the women from accounting.

"Vince told me," Mimi said, smiling as she passed a piece of cake. "When's the due date?" someone else shouted.

"F e b r u a r y."

"Ohhh!" The room exclaimed in unison.

"Do you plan on coming back after the baby?"

"I'm not sure yet," she said as she scanned the crowd looking for Ethan. He wasn't there. They had talked the night before, and he said he was leaving on travel. But still, she had sort of hoped that he would be around.

More cake and coffee passed by, and people started fiddling with bags of plastic silverware.

"Do you know if it's a boy or a girl?" someone eagerly questioned. "It's both." The room went instantly silent. "I'm having twins." Uproarious laughter and applause ensued while a few of the guys from the break room shook their heads, kicking themselves for not including that in the odds for the "X vs. Y" betting pool.

Jocelyn never got confronted with questions about who the father was. But later, she found out that bets had been placed on everyone from "the guy who rents the office suite down the hall" to Stan the congressman. Only months later would one person emerge victorious in the "Who's Your Daddy?" pool. And that would be Ethan, who had anonymously bet on himself.

Martin Mays came up to her, digging into his sheet cake with a disposable plastic fork. "Congratulations, kiddo. Looks like you're outta here."

Jocelyn smiled while accepting a passed piece of cake for herself. "Not really the way I planned it, Martin, but yeah."

Before he jammed a chunk of bon-voyage sheet cake into his mouth, he asked, "So, is the dad of these twins going to support you? Or are you doing this solo?"

Jocelyn appreciated his concern and let him know that everything would be okay. The father and she were on the same page. "Plus, I ordered up a course by this guy Carlton Sheets so that I could learn how to invest in real estate. You know, be a landlady. Make a little income while I stay at home with the kids."

Martin's eyes grew wide. "I don't know if I would do that if I were you," Martin said with father-like concern. "You know that real estate is a big bubble right now. Housing starts are down and ..." And he explained every good reason why Jocelyn should not start buying up real estate. Of course, Jocelyn was not going to be dissuaded. She had a plan. She didn't trust herself with the stock market. She wasn't impressed with savings accounts. She had a great credit score, so she could easily get a mortgage (or two). Why not? It looked like the only safe place to put money for someone like her. She cited how well her parents had done with their purchases of houses over the years.

"I don't know, Jocelyn. Be careful with that," Martin said and then rattled off a bunch of his stock picks, which she promptly forgot. After opening her card, which was signed by all in attendance, and the little gift box that contained a god-awful piece of what could only be described as costume jewelry, which Jocelyn theorized probably came from Filene's Basement or Mimi's very own personal collection, she went back to her executive cube to do the final bits of packing.

She carefully positioned the few remaining outstanding proposals in chronological order on her desk. After making sure that every- thing in her filing cabinet was clearly marked and correctly alphabetized for the final time, she grabbed the white cardboard storage box that she had been preparing for the past week. Jocelyn figured the stuff in the box would be like a portfolio that she could show to her next employer.

The storage box contained the following items: samples of the printed material she had designed, a letter of recognition personally signed by General Vaughn, a few of her choice press releases, a file holding snips of newspaper and magazine mentions placed by her, a CD/DVD containing several minutes of television news stories she had helped craft, and another CD/DVD with clips of product placement within television series.

The box was topped off with the more important "keepers" like her leather legal-pad portfolio (the one with the Conglomerate logo embossed on the cover that she hadn't opened since her meeting with corporate, but she liked the way it looked, so that was coming with her), one copy of the red book that General Vaughn had given her when she got promoted, and of course the beige floppy disk she had created as a safeguard should any funny business arise about that Malaysia proposal.

Jocelyn took one more look inside the desk drawer she had found the gold coins in—just for old times' sake, of course. She didn't really believe that a coin would be in there today. But you never knew. Nope. Nothing. She looked around the office, shut off the lights, and headed out.

Six and a half years. More than six years since she had come to this place, and every step toward the exit was like a dream manifesting itself in real time for her. She was smiling broadly as she arrived in the lobby on her way out to the parking lot.

Mimi ran up to her and hugged her. "I forgive you about not wanting to tell me, honey. Good luck. If you need anything, any advice, you feel free to call me. Okay?"

Jocelyn assured her that she would, but really she didn't mean it.

"Oh, and don't forget this!" Mimi said as she hurriedly handed Jocelyn the gaudy, oversized butterfly pin that she had somehow forgotten and left on the conference-room table during the going-away party.

Jocelyn smiled and said, "Thanks, Mimi," and gave her one last hug. She held the pin in her right hand with the white storage box tucked under her left arm.

"This is what freedom smells like!" she said loud enough for Mimi to hear as she stepped out of the building and took a deep breath of the fresh October air. Her brain was happily reciting key parts of a Martin Luther King Jr. speech as she headed to the parking lot. Once there, while trying to juggle the storage box, the pin, her purse, and the keys, she looked at the pin and frowned, knowing that she would never ever, not in a million years, wear it.

"Not exactly to your taste?" someone asked. Startled,

she looked up at a dark-haired man holding a white Styrofoam cup. Since the man was standing at a distance and she didn't have her glasses on, she couldn't see his features. And his voice didn't sound like anyone she typically dealt with. So she kind of smiled as she unlocked her silver C280 Sport and put her stuff in the front seat without answering.

"Not as nice as a gold coin, huh?" he said. Jocelyn felt a rush of adrenaline hit her system. She popped out of the car and looked back at the man, who was now walking away. She ducked back in, grabbed her purse, and began reaching around for her glasses. She needed to see who this guy was.

"Hey! Hold on! I need to talk to you!" she called. Forgetting the car door, she started walking toward him while still bumbling around with her purse. *Goddamn it! When I need my glasses ...*

He looked back over his shoulder and said, "I'd take a closer look at that pin if I were you. That piece of jewelry can make or break a person," before he rounded the corner of the building.

"Wait!" she called and ran after him, but when she got to the corner, she saw no trace of the man. *Who was that guy?* she asked herself as she finally got her glasses where they needed to be and surveyed the area. *I've got to get contacts or something. This sucks.*

Jocelyn wandered around the building for what seemed like a long time as red-hued leaves silently dropped, swirled, and upon reaching their destination, decorated the pavement in front of her. She decided to check the locked emergency exits along the side of the building to see if that was how the man escaped the scene. When that proved fruitless, she headed back to her Mercedes.

The car's door was still wide open, like some sort of mechanical hug waiting to embrace her. She hoisted the white storage box over to the passenger side and hopped in, thinking through who that guy might have been and where he possibly could have gone. She eyed the white box. Slowly she took the lid off and began poking around at the contents, making sure that everything, specifically that beige floppy-disk insurance policy, was still intact. Everything was still there, right where it was supposed to be. Everything except the butterfly pin that she had left on the dashboard. It was gone.

END OF BOOK 1

Sneak peek at
Security Through Absurdity
BOOK TWO: BUBBLES WILL POP

October 2005
Switzerland

ETHAN LOWE BLINKED WHILE STARING at his reflection in the bus window. His image was merging with the drizzly weather outside, and it kind of fit his mood—if *moods* were what you could call them these days. Everything had sort of mushed into one long-standing malaise. It was only recently that he had started to recognize that maybe this might be a problem. His gray state of mind had originally been an asset for his line of work. But since finding out that he was going to be a father ... a father to twins ...

He shook his head, broke off another chunk of chocolate, and popped it into his mouth. As he sat munching, the bus stopped, and two winter-camouflage-outfitted military men boarded the bus, SG-550s slung over their shoulders. He imagined how people would react to the automatic rifles back in the states. *They'd probably grab the kids and push their way off the bus, totally freaked out.* He smirked and watched as the army guys settled down in the seats between an unfazed teenager and an elderly woman.

He liked it here. He had gotten to admire the mountains while on the train ride to the bus and was now sitting comfortably by the window, watching the watery smear of a farm-speckled landscape roll by.

The doors of the bus slid open at exactly 2:15. Like everything in Switzerland, his arrival was a testament to the predictable order of things, as was just about everything having to do with the care and maintenance of the Swiss citizenry. The place was organized and worked like a fine timepiece.

As soon as Ethan's feet hit the ground, the doors closed and the bus hissed away. A herd of sheep was staring right at him from behind an antique but well-maintained fence. He looked around and noticed a couple happily holding hands as they walked up the cobblestone path to his left. The drizzle was in full effect, and the leafless trees made it seem much colder than it really was. He pulled up his hood, zipped his black Arc'teryx jacket all the way up, and jammed his hands into his pockets.

Ethan discovered that the cobblestones led directly up a hill to a castle, and he figured that was where he was supposed to go. The message he had received about this meeting had been very vague. Cheese shops, restaurants, bakeries, and cafés lined both sides of the street on his ascent. When he was almost at the top, he noticed it: the polished stainless-steel statue. It was just like the one in Jonas Ledergerber's office (if that was his real name). No, not the castle— this old stone building was definitely where he was supposed to go.

Château St. Germain
1663 Gruyères
Museum HR Giger

He paid his entry at the front desk and headed in. The place, unlike most museums he had been in, was dimly lit, with pin lights illuminating the artwork. Wandering somewhat aimlessly and uneasily around the building, he was surprised to encounter an enormous cast-bronze statue depicting the creature from the movie *Alien*. And it wasn't until he was upstairs and through some arched stone passageways that he took the time to really look at the artwork—large-scale, five-by-five-foot, black-and-white, surreal-meets-technical drawings of pentagrams impaling and/or otherwise violating drawn and quartered naked women. There were goat heads and mysterious symbols and lots of mechanical stuff married with the feminine form. The drawings were clearly expertly done.

As Ethan studied one of the more titillating pieces, a tall salt-and- pepper-haired man in a perfectly fitted dark charcoal overcoat and a scented cloud of Clive Christian "V" for Men silently slipped up next to him. "Good day, Mr. Lowe," Ethan heard in a Swiss-German accent. "Thank you for agreeing to meet."

Startled, Ethan turned to the man and replied, "As if I had a choice." And he quickly took the wad of a handkerchief out of his pocket and attempted to pass it over, because after all, that was why he was here—to deliver roughly a million dirty dollars, all of which had been cleverly transferred and fashioned into a very flashy jewel-encrusted butterfly brooch.

Arms folded across his chest and not looking at Ethan, eyes still fixed on the woman being defiled by the top corner of the pentagram, Mr. Jonas Ledergerber answered, "Now, now, it was you who needed me. The neema incident with the colonel," he said, shaking his head, "I regret to say was ridiculous, but you were intelligent enough to accept my help."

Ethan looked at him with restrained distain as he absently fiddled with the clump he was still left holding. He knew that Jonas Ledergerber was exerting his dominance by making him stand there like a confused child cradling a small fortune. But he also knew he had no right to say anything. He had, in fact, gotten out of hand while working at the "no blood, no foul" operation beneath the Baghdad International Airport, otherwise called NAMA. He thought back on his role as a "translator," the currently accepted euphemism for *torturer*. The Huachuca-trained CIA and Fort Bragg Special Forces had all been professional enough. But it had been during a relatively mild session when the guy everyone called "colonel," with whom he had been partnered for the case, started describing how he had slowly mangled and killed a young Serbian prostitute back in the day.

At first Ethan had figured this was for the benefit of the terrified SOB strapped in the chair. But when the story started to sound a bi too familiar, Ethan lost it. He just lost it and killed, not the guy in the chair, but the "colonel" from Fort Bragg.

Mr. Ledergerber turned to face Ethan. "Now that the regrettable incident is behind us," he made a gesture as if brushing flour off his hands, "it is time that you help me." Without a smile, he patted Ethan's shoulder and said, "Come. Let us enjoy the local fondue before I send you on your way home." Ethan thrust the bundle he was holding into Mr. Ledergerber's hands. Ledergerber took it and, without even looking at it, put it in his pocket. "You will take some time off now, yes? I will call upon you when necessary."

Ethan's head was now officially in the dark gray zone as he made his way downhill to the anything-but-delightful fondue Jonas Ledergerber was promising. He had no clear idea how he was going to manage any of this. Especially now with Jocelyn expecting.

AVAILABLE NOW

About the Author

RACHAEL L. McINTOSH'S FIRST SERIES, *Security Through Absurdity*, was inspired by her real-life experiences working for a major US defense contractor, her dealings with national news outlets, and her involvement in a US presidential campaign. She currently lives in Rhode Island, where she invests her time in writing and homeschooling her two children.

http://www.rachaellmcintosh.com

www.ingramcontent.com/pod-product-compliance
Lightning Source LLC
Chambersburg PA
CBHW060555310726
48982CB00008B/1128/J

* 9 7 8 0 6 9 2 4 8 9 1 8 5 *